FORGE OF EVIL

Raising the hammer, Joram hit the clay box, shattering it at one blow. The firelight gleamed orange on his skin as he crouched over the dark object lying in the midst of broken clay and splintered wood.

"It isn't hot," whispered Joram in awe, holding his hand above the object. "Come nearer, Saryon! See what we have created!"

What had he expected? They had failed. Recoiling, Saryon jerked his arm from Joram's grasp. This thing that lay upon the stone floor was not beautiful. It was ugly. A tool of darkness, an instrument of Death, not a bright shining blade of light. Joram was a beginner, untrained, without skill, without knowledge, with no one to teach him. The sword he had fashioned might have been wielded a thousand years before by some savage, barbaric ancestor.

But there was something more horrifying about the sword, something devilish — the rounded knob on the hilt combined with the long neck of the hilt itself, the handle's short, blunt arms, and the narrow body of the blade would turn the weapon into a grim parody of a human being.

Lying like a corpse at his feet, the sword was the personification of Saryon's sin.

"Destroy it!" Saryon gasped hoarsely. "Destroy it, Joram, or it will destroy you!"

THE DARKSWORD TRILOGY

VOLUME ONE

Forging The Darksword

MARGARET WEIS & TRACY HICKMAN

BANTAM BOOKS
TORONTO · NEW YORK · LONDON · SYDNEY · AUCKLAND

FORGING THE DARKSWORD
A BANTAM BOOK 0 553 17586 6

First publication in Great Britain

PRINTING HISTORY
Bantam Books edition published 1988
Bantam Books edition reprinted 1989 and 1990

Bantam Books are published by Transworld Publishers
Ltd., 61–63 Uxbridge Road, Ealing, London W5 5SA, in
Australia by Transworld Publishers (Australia) Pty. Ltd.,
15–23 Helles Avenue, Moorebank, NSW 2170, and in New
Zealand by Transworld Publishers (N.Z.) Ltd., Cnr. Moselle
and Waipareira Avenues, Henderson, Auckland.

Printed and bound in Great Britain by
Cox & Wyman Ltd., Reading, Berks.

Prologue

The black, greasy column of smoke wafted away on the chill air as the ashes of the victim drifted down to fall upon those who complacently believed they had just saved a soul. Here and there, amid the smoldering ruins, tongues of flame licked out, greedy for more. Finding nothing but charred remains, the fire crackled and died. Smoke rolled into the sky, casting a shroud over the wretched village, drawing a pall over the sun.

The crowd dispersed, many making the sign of the cross, combining this with gestures to ward off the evil eye or any other curses that might be lingering in the tainted air. Muttered remarks of "foul witch" were a dark accompaniment to the priest's sanctimonious pleadings with someone—it may have been God, though the priest didn't sound at all certain about it—to forgive the sins of this tortured being and provide it with eternal rest.

Two figures huddled together in a rat-infested alleyway. Both were dressed exactly alike, in black robes with hoods pulled low over their heads. One leaned upon a carved wooden staff, highly polished and decorated with nine strange symbols. This was obviously the older of the two, for he was stooped and the hand upon the staff was gnarled and wrinkled, though its grip was firm.

His companion was obviously much younger; he stood tall and straight, though his shoulders slumped and he seemed bowed down with grief. He held a cloth across his nose and mouth, ostensibly to keep away the sweet stench of burning flesh, but in reality to hide from the old man the fact that he wept.

The two had remained unobserved by the crowd because they had chosen to remain unobserved. Silently they stood, silently they watched. Now, as the last ashes of one they had loved blew down the cracked stone streets, the old man let out a slow breath.

"Is that all you can do?" cried the other, nearly choked with grief. "Sigh? You should have let me —" He made violent, intricate patterns with his hand in the air. "You should have let me —"

The old man laid a restraining hand upon his arm.

"No. That would have only made matters worse for us. She was strong. She could have saved herself but she kept our secret, though they broke and burned her body. Would you take that triumph away from her?"

"Why have they done this? Why are they doing this to us?" the young man cried wretchedly, his long, fine-boned hands endeavoring to wipe away the tracks of his sorrow. "We have done no evil! We have only tried to help . . ."

The old man's face grew stern, his voice crackled like the flames as he spoke. "What they do not understand, they fear. What they fear, they destroy. So it has ever been with their kind." Sighing again, he shook his hooded head. "But I see it growing worse. A new age is coming, an age in which there will be no place for us. One by one, they will seek us out and drag us from our homes and feed us to their envious fires. They will hunt down and destroy our creations, slaughter our familiars —"

"So we stand here and sigh about it and go to our deaths in silence," the young man interrupted bitterly.

"No!"

The old man's grip tightened on his arm. "No!" he repeated in a voice that sent a thrill of hope and a shiver of fear through the younger man, who turned to stare at him. "No, we do not! I have been thinking long on this, weighing the dangers, the alternatives. Now I am satisfied. Now I see that we have no choice. We must leave."

"Leave?" repeated the younger man in soft, dazed tones. "But, where will we go? There is no place that is safe, for our brethren tell us that this persecution exists wherever the sun rises . . ."

As if his words had conjured it up, the sun appeared from behind the gray clouds. But the charred remains of the corpse gave more warmth than did the shriveled orb that shone pale and bleak in the winter sky.

Staring at it, the old man smiled grimly.

"Wherever the sun rises? Yes, that is true."

"Then —"

"There are other suns, my boy," said the old man thoughtfully, staring into the heavens and caressing the carven symbols upon his staff. "Other suns. . . ."

BOOK ONE

The Prophecy

When a Bishop of the Realm of Thimhallan receives in solemn ceremony the miter that marks his standing as spiritual head and heart of the world, his first official act as Bishop is one that is secret, private, unseen by the eyes even of those he calls Ruler.

Acting upon orders from the *Duuk-tsarith*, the Bishop retires to his chambers and activates the enchantments that seal him off from the world. Then he admits one person — a warlock, Head of the dread Order of *Duuk-tsarith*, who brings His Holiness a box, of the purest gold, made by the alchemists. This box is surrounded by such spells of warding and protection that only the warlock himself may open it and remove that which the box contains. This is nothing more than a single sheet of old parchment covered with handwriting. Carefully, reverently, the warlock places this bit of paper before the mystified Bishop.

Lifting the sheet of parchment, the Bishop examines the document carefully. It is old, dating back centuries. There are spots on the paper, as though tears have stained it, and the handwriting, though obviously that of a trained scribe, is practically unreadable.

As the Bishop endeavors to decipher this missive, his expression changes from one of mystification to a look of shock and horror. Invariably, he looks up at the Head of the Order of *Duuk-tsarith*, as if asking the man whether he knows what the letter contains and if it is true. The Head of the Order simply nods, since these people rarely speak. Ascertaining that the Bishop has absorbed the document's contents, the warlock makes a motion and the parchment leaves the Bishop's hand and returns to the box. The *Duuk-tsarith* then withdraws from the Bishop's presence, leaving behind a man shaken and distraught, the words on the parchment burning in his mind.

Forgive me, those of you who are reading this at some future date. My hand is unsteady — the Almin help me! I wonder if I will ever cease to tremble! No, I know I will not, while I still picture so clearly that tragic event it is my duty to record and while I still hear those words ring in my ears.

Be it known then that in the dark days following the Iron Wars, when the land is in chaos and many predict the end of our world, the Bishop of the Realm undertook to see into the future, that we might calm the people. For one year, he prepared himself to endure the casting of this spell. Our beloved Bishop prayed daily to the Almin. He listened to the proper music recommended by the Theldara, music that would attune the spiritual with the physical. He ate the proper foods, abstaining from all strong spirits. His eyes saw only those colors soothing to the mind, he breathed the prescribed incense and perfumes. The month prior to the Prophecy, he fasted, drinking only water, purging his body of all unwelcome influences. During that time, he spent his days and nights in a small cell, never speaking to anyone, never spoken to.

The day of the Prophecy came. Ah! How my hand shakes! I cannot contin- [A blot upon the paper, the writing trails off the edge.]

There, forgive me. I am master of myself once more. Our beloved Bishop descended to the holy Well in the heart of the Font. He knelt upon the marble rim of the Well that is, so we are taught, the source of the magic within our world. The highest ranking catalysts in the land had returned to this holy ground, to assist the theurgist in the casting of this spell. They stood around the Well, their hands linked so that Life flowed through them.

Standing beside our Bishop was the old theurgist — one of the last in this world, we fear, since their kind sacrificed themselves in their attempts to put an end to the terrible war. Drawing Life from the catalysts around him, the Spirit Shaper worked his powerful magic, calling upon the Almin to give our Bishop knowledge of the future. To this spell, our Bishop added his prayers, and though his body was weak from fasting, his voice was strong and earnest.

And the Almin appeared.

We, all of us, felt His presence, and we fell to our knees in fear and awe, unable to look at His terrible beauty. Staring into the Well, his face rapt and spellbound and under powerful enchantment, our Bishop began to speak in a voice not his own. What he said was not what we had expected. These are his words. I pray that I have the strength to write them.

"There will be born to the Royal House one who is dead yet will live, who will die again and live again. And when he returns, he will hold in his hand the destruction of the world —"

More there might have been, but at that moment our beloved Bishop suddenly gave a great and terrible cry — a cry that will echo in my heart as his words sound in my ears — and, clasping his chest, he fell forward and lay on the lip of the Well, dead. The theurgist collapsed at his side as if struck by lightning, his limbs paralyzed, his mouth moving but making no sensible sound.

And we knew that we were alone. The Almin had left us.

When will this Prophecy come about? What does it mean? We do not know, though our best minds are studying it word for word, even letter by letter. The new Bishop thinks to undertake another Vision, but that seems unlikely, as the theurgist lies at the point of death and he is surely the last of his kind left alive in this world.

It has been decreed, therefore, that I write these words to you who may perchance see a future many of us do not believe will come to pass. This parchment will be given into the *hands of the Duuk-tsarith to keep. It will be known only to them, who know everything, and to the Bishop of the Realm, revealed to him the day of his coronation.*

Let it then be kept secret, lest the people rise up in panic to destroy the Royal Households and a reign of terror descend upon our land like that which drove us from our ancient home.

May the Almin be with you . . . and with us all.

The name penned below is illegible and not important.

Since that time, all Bishops of the Realm — and there have been many — have read the Prophecy. All have wondered fearfully if it would come to pass within their lifetime. All have prayed that it would not . . .

. . . and secretly planned what they would do if it did.

Catalyst of Merilon

The child was Dead.
In regard to that, everyone was in agreement.

All of the wizards, magi, and archmagi who floated in a shimmering circle above the marble floor, the shade of which had been changed hastily the previous night from radiant white to a proper shade of mourning blue, were in agreement. All of the black-robed warlocks, who maintained their attitude of cool aloofness and strict attention to duty as they hovered at their assigned posts appeared, by the even more rigid posture of their stance, to be in agreement. All of the thaumaturgists — catalysts — who stood humbly upon the blue floor, were, by the somber hues of their robes, in agreement.

A gentle rain, whose tears slid down the vaulting glass of the crystal walls of the magnificent Cathedral of Merilon, wept in agreement. The very air that stirred in the cathedral, tinged with the soft aura of moonlight conjured up by the wizards to glow upon this solemn occasion, agreed. Even the golden and white trees of the Cathedral's park, whose graceful branches glistened in the pale, misty light, agreed — or seemed to Saryon to agree. He fancied he could hear their leaves rustling in low, mournful whispers . . . the Prince is Dead . . . the Prince is Dead.

The Emperor agreed. (For which agreement, Saryon thought caustically, Bishop Vanya had undoubtedly spent most of last night upon his knees, exhorting the Almin to grant him the smoothness of tongue of the serpent.) Hovering in the air in the nave of the cathedral, the Emperor floated beside the ornate rosewood crib that stood in the center of a marble dais, staring at the baby, his arms folded across his chest to signify rejection. His face stern and set in rigid lines, the only outward sign of his grief was the gradual change of his *Golden Sun* robes to a shade of *Weeping Blue* — the same color as the marble floor. The Emperor himself maintained the stately dignity expected of him even at this time, when his last chance for an heir to the throne had died with this tiny baby; for Bishop Vanya had undertaken the Vision and had foreseen that there would be no more issue for the Empress, whose health was fragile and precarious.

Bishop Vanya stood upon the marble dais near the rosewood crib. He did not float above it, as did the Emperor. Standing himself, Saryon could not help but wonder if Vanya felt the envy that gnawed at the catalyst; envy of the magi, who, even on this solemn occasion, seemed to flaunt their power over the weak thaumaturgists, hovering over them in the air.

It is only the magi of Thimhallan who possess the gift of Life in such abundance that they are able to travel the world on the wings of the air. The catalyst's Life force is so low that he must conserve every spark. Because he is forced to walk through this world and this life, the symbol of the catalyst's order is the shoe.

The shoe: a symbol of our pious self-sacrifice, a symbol of our humility, reflected Saryon bitterly, wrenching his gaze from the magi and forcing his thoughts back to the ceremony. He saw Bishop Vanya bow his mitered head in prayer to the Almin, and he saw, too, the Emperor keeping close watch on Bishop Vanya, watching for his cues, awaiting instruction. At a subtle sign from Vanya, the Emperor bowed his head as well, as did everyone in the court.

Saryon glanced again at the magi hovering around and above him out of the corner of his eye as he absently murmured the prayer. But this time the glance was a thoughtful one. Yes, a humble symbol the shoe —

Bishop Vanya raised his head briskly. So did the Emperor. Saryon noticed that Vanya's relief showed markedly in his face. The fact that the Emperor had agreed with him that the Prince was Dead made matters much easier. Saryon's gaze strayed to the Empress. There would be trouble here. The Bishop knew it, all the catalysts knew it, everyone in court knew it. In a hastily convened meeting among the catalysts last night, they had all been warned how to react. Saryon saw Vanya tense. Ostensibly, he was going over the formalities with the Emperor in the ritual proscribed by law.

". . . this Lifeless body will be taken to the Font where the Deathwatch will be performed . . ."

But, in reality, Vanya was keeping a sharp eye on the Empress, and Saryon saw the Bishop frown slightly. The color of the Empress's robe, which should have been the most vivid, most beautiful shade of *Weeping Blue* among all present, was slightly off — a sort of dull *Ash Gray*. But Vanya refrained from tactfully reminding her, as he would have at any other time, to change it. He was thankful — everyone present was thankful — that the woman was apparently in control of herself once more. A powerful wizardess, one of the *Albanara,* her initial reaction of outrage and grief upon hearing the news that her child was Dead had caused all the catalysts to withdraw their conduits to her for fear she would use the Life force they granted to wreak terrible destruction upon the Palace.

But the Emperor had talked to his beloved wife, and now even she, too, appeared to be in agreement. Her baby was Dead.

In fact, the only one present who was *not* in agreement that the baby was Dead appeared to be the baby himself, who was screaming frenziedly. But his cries were lost, ascending as they did into the vast, vaulting crystal heaven above him.

Bishop Vanya, his gaze now fully on the Empress, launched into the next part of the ceremony rather more hurriedly than was absolutely proper. Saryon knew why. The Bishop feared the Empress might pick up the baby, whose body had been washed and purified. Only Bishop Vanya himself was now permitted to touch him.

But the Empress, exhausted by the difficult birth and by her recent outburst, apparently had no energy left to defy Vanya's orders. She lacked even the energy to float above the crib, but sat on the floor beside it, shedding crystal tears that shattered upon the blue marble. These sparkling tears were her sign of agreement.

A muscle in Vanya's face twitched when those tears began to fall with a musical sound upon the floor. Saryon even thought he saw the Bishop start to smile in relief, but the man recollected himself in time and carefully arranged his face to a more suitable expression of sorrow.

When the Bishop came smoothly to the end of the ritual, the Emperor nodded once with grave dignity, repeating the ancient, prescribed words, whose meaning no one remembered, with only the slightest hint of a tremor in his voice.

"The Prince is Dead. *Dies ireae, dies illa. Solvet saeclum in favilla. Toeste David cum Sibylla.*

Then Vanya, who was growing more relaxed as every passing moment brought the ceremony nearer completion, turned to look around at the court to make certain that each was in his proper place, that each had his or her robes changed to the proper shade of blue to match his or her station.

His gaze went from the Cardinal to the two Priests present to the three Deacons. And there his gaze stopped. Bishop Vanya frowned.

Saryon trembled. The Bishop's stern eye was on him! What had he done? He had no idea what was wrong. Frantically he looked around, hoping to catch some hint from those standing near him.

"Too damn much green!" muttered Deacon Dulchase out of the corner of his mouth. Hastily Saryon glanced down at his robes. Dulchase was right! Saryon was *Turbulent Water* in the midst of *Weeping Skies!*

Feeling his face flush until it was a wonder he wasn't dripping blood upon the floor as the Empress was dripping tears, the young Deacon endeavored to change the color of his robe to match those of his brethren standing in the Illustrious Circle of the Court. Since changing the color of one's raiment requires only the smallest use of the Life force, it is magic even the weak catalysts can perform. Saryon was thankful for that. It would have been embarrassing past endurance if he had been forced to ask one of the magi to assist him. As it was, he was so flustered that he barely had it in him to cast this simple spell. His robe went from *Turbulent Water* to *Still Pond*, hovered there an agonizing moment, then finally — with a wrench — the young Deacon achieved *Weeping Skies*.

Vanya's eye remained on him until he got it right. The eyes of everyone were on the poor young man by now, even the Emperor. It was probably just as well that I was *not* born a magus, Saryon thought in agony. I would have vanished on the spot. As it was, he could only stand there, wilting beneath the Bishop's glare, until, still frowning, Vanya completed his inspection, his gaze continuing on around the semicircle to the nobles of the court.

Satisfied, Vanya turned back to face the Emperor and embarked upon the final portion of the ceremony for the Dead Prince. Saryon, absorbed in his own shame, did not attend to what was being said. He knew he would be reprimanded. What would he say in his own defense? That the baby's wailing distressed him?

That, at least, was true enough. The child, only ten days old, was lying in his crib, crying lustily — he was a strong, well-formed child — for the love and attention and nourishment he had once received but would now receive no more. Saryon could offer this as his excuse, but he knew from past experience that Bishop Vanya's face would simply attain a look of vast patience.

"We cannot hear the cries of the Dead, only their echoes," Saryon heard him say, as he had said last night.

Perhaps that was true. But Saryon was well aware that those echoes would haunt his sleep for a long time to come.

He could tell the Bishop this, which was the truth but only part of the truth, or he could tell him the rest — I was distressed because the death of this child has ruined *my* life.

It may or may not be to the Bishop's credit, Saryon thought gloomily, but he had a feeling that Vanya would be more apt to sympathize with the second excuse for his failure in the matter of the robe better than the first.

Feeling a swift jab in the ribs — Dulchase's elbow — Saryon quickly lowered his head again, forcing the ritual words out from between clenched teeth. Desperately he sought to pull himself together, but it was difficult. The child's wailing pierced his heart. He longed to rush from the hall, and wished devoutly that the ceremony would come to an end.

Vanya's chanting voice fell silent. Raising his head, Saryon saw the Bishop look questioningly at the Emperor, who had to give his permission to begin the Deathwatch. The men stared at each other for an eternity, as far as Saryon was concerned. Then, with a nod, the Emperor turned his back upon the child and stood, his head bowed, in the ritual mourning posture. Saryon heaved such an audible sigh of relief that Deacon Dulchase, looking shocked, jabbed him in the ribs again.

Saryon didn't care. The ceremony was almost over.

His arms outstretched, Bishop Vanya took a step forward toward the cradle. Hearing his robes rustle, the Empress looked up for the first time since the court had assembled. Glancing around dazedly, she saw Vanya approaching the crib. Frantically her gaze went to her husband, and saw only the Emperor's back.

"No!" With a heartbroken moan, she threw her arms over the cradle, clutching it to her breast. It was a pitiful gesture. Even in her grief, she dared not defy the catalysts enough to touch her baby.

"No! No!" she sobbed over and over.

Bishop Vanya glanced at the Emperor and cleared his throat significantly. The Emperor, who was watching Vanya out of the corner of his eye, did not have to turn. Slowly, he nodded his head again. Vanya stepped forward resolutely. Then, greatly daring, he opened a conduit to the Empress, trying to use the flow of Life to ease her unreasoning sorrow. It seemed to Saryon a foolish thing to do, giving additional power to this already powerful wizardess. But then perhaps Vanya knew what he was about. After all, he had known the Empress for thirty years, ever since she was a child.

"Dear Evenue," Vanya said, abandoning her formal title. "The waiting time may be long and painful. You need rest to recover your health. Think of the loving husband, whose grief is equal to your own and yet must endure in addition your suffering as well. Grant me that I may take the child and perform the Deathwatch for all Thimhallan —"

Raising her tear-streaked face, the Empress stared at Vanya with brown eyes that now glittered as black as her hair. Suddenly she drew upon the power, sucking Life from the catalyst. The conduit of magic, normally not visible to the eye, flared brilliantly between the two of them, arcing with a blinding white light as, with a motion of her hand, the Empress sent the Bishop flying backward five feet in the air. No one in the court dared move, each staring in awe at the tremendous flow of power as Vanya landed heavily upon the weeping-blue marble floor.

Drawing the Life force flowing through the Bishop's conduit, the weakened Empress gained strength from him that she herself did not possess. Springing into the air, the wizardess hovered above her child's cradle. Words of magic crackled. Spreading her hands wide, she caused a flaming globe to appear, encasing herself and the child safely within its fiery walls.

"Never! Get out!" she shrieked, her voice searing like the heat of the fire. "Get out, you bastard! I don't believe you, any of you! Get out! You lied! My baby did not fail your Tests! He is not Dead! You fear him! You fear he'll usurp your own precious power!"

A murmur and a rustle spread through the Illustrious Circle, no one knowing where to look. It was unseemly to stare at the Bishop in his undignified position. His miter on the floor, his tonsured head gleaming in the moonlight, the Bishop had become entangled in his ceremonial robes and was struggling to stand up. A few people glanced at the Empress, but it was painful to look upon her, and more painful still to hear her sacrilegious words.

Saryon took refuge in staring at his shoes, wishing most desperately that he were a hundred miles from this pathetic scene. It was obvious that most of those in the court shared his feeling. The colors of *Weeping Blue*, so carefully gradated to reflect rank and status, shifted with each wearer's nervousness so that the overall effect was one of ripples passing over a calm and placid lake.

With the Cardinal's help, the Bishop at last managed to stand up. Seeing his livid face, everyone in the court shrank back, many of the magi sinking weakly nearer the floor. Even the Emperor, who had turned around, paled visibly at the sight of the Bishop's anger. As the Cardinal replaced the miter upon his head, Vanya twitched his robes into place — the man had such control that they had not changed color in the slightest degree — and, gathering what strength he had remaining, abruptly closed off the conduit to the Empress.

The fiery globe vanished. The Empress had gained enough Life from the Bishop, however, that she continued to float above the child, her crystal tears falling upon the baby. As the tears hit the tiny, naked chest, they shattered, causing the child to shriek louder, screaming in a hysterical paroxysm of terror and pain. Everyone in the court could see blood running down the baby's skin.

Vanya's lips tightened. This had gone too far. The child would have to be washed and purified all over again. The Bishop cast another look at the Emperor. This time, Vanya's look was not questioning. He was commanding, and everyone in the court knew it.

The Emperor's stern expression softened. Floating through the air, he came to rest beside his wife and, reaching out his hand, gently stroked her lovely, glistening hair. It was said among the members of the Royal Household that he doted on this woman and would have given anything in his vast power to please her. But the one thing she wanted, apparently, he could not give her — a living child.

"Bishop Vanya," the Emperor said to the catalyst, though he did not look at him directly, "take the child. Send us the sign when it is ended."

Relief flooded through the court. Saryon could hear it sigh upon the air. Glancing around, he saw that the color of nearly everyone's robes had shifted slightly again. Where there had once been a perfect blue spectrum of mourning, now the shades and hues wobbled and wandered among sickly greens and woeful grays.

Relief mingled with anger was obvious on the Bishop's face, as well. Even he was too weakened to conceal it any longer. A trickle of sweat rolled down his shaved head from beneath the miter. Wiping it away, he exhaled deeply, then bowed to the Emperor.

Moving much more hurriedly than was proper for such a solemn occasion, all the while keeping his eyes on the Empress, who was still hovering above him, the Bishop reached out and lifted the frantic baby in his arms. Turning to a warlock, a Marshal of the Enforcers, Vanya said in a low, husky voice, "Through your talent, take me to the Font." Then he added, speaking to the Emperor. "I shall send the sign, Your Majesty. Be waiting."

The Emperor, his eyes still on his frail wife, did not appear to hear. But the Bishop wasted no more time. Beckoning to the Cardinal, the next highest ranking of the Order beneath himself, Vanya whispered several words. The Cardinal bowed and, turning to the Marshal, opened a conduit to the warlock full force, granting him more than sufficient Life to make the journey through the Corridors back to the mountain fastness of the Font, the center of the Church in Thimhallan.

Even in his distraught state of mind, Saryon found himself routinely making the tricky mathematical calculations for a journey of such distance. Within moments, he had it completed, and he realized that the Cardinal had wasted his energy — a grievous sin among catalysts, for it leaves them weak and vulnerable and grants the magi extra energy that they can store and use again at will. But, Saryon supposed, it didn't matter this time. Though a skilled mathematician, it would take the Cardinal long moments of study to arrive at the same answer that Saryon had reached in seconds. Both Saryon and the Cardinal knew that those were long moments he didn't dare waste.

Acting quickly upon Vanya's order, the warlock entered the Corridor that opened up, a gaping blue disk, before him. The Bishop, carrying his tiny burden, followed. When all three were inside, the disk elongated, compressed, and vanished.

It was over. The Bishop and the baby were gone.

The court began to function again. Members of the Royal Household floated up to the Emperor to offer their condolences and their sympathy and to remind him of their presence. The Cardinal, who had given his all to the Marshal, dropped over like a rock, sending most of the brethren of his Order running to his aid.

One catalyst, however, did not move. Saryon remained standing in place in the now-broken Circle, his plans and hopes and dreams falling around him, shattering like the Empress's tears upon the weeping-blue floor. Lost in his own grief, Saryon fancied he could still hear, lingering upon the air, the faint wail of the baby, and the mournful whispering of the trees.

"The Prince is Dead."

2

The Gift of Life

The wizard stood in the doorway of his manor house. A plain, serviceable dwelling, it was neither opulent nor ostentatious, for this wizard, though of noble birth, was yet of low rank. Though he could have afforded a glittering crystal palace, this would have been considered unseemly for one of his station. He was content with his life, however, and now stood looking out over his lands in the early morning with an air of calm satisfaction.

At a sound behind him in the hall, he turned. "Hurry, Saryon," he said with a smile for his little boy, who was sprawled on the floor, struggling to put on his shoes. "Hurry, if you want to see the Ariels deliver the disks."

With a final, desperate wrench, the child tugged his shoe over his heel; then, leaping to his feet, he ran to his father. Catching the child up in his arms, the wizard spoke the words that summoned the air to do his bidding. Stepping into the wind, he was lifted from the ground and floated over the land, his silken robes fluttering about him like the wings of a bright butterfly.

The child, one hand clinging to his father's neck, opened the other to greet the dawn.

"Teach me to do this, Father!" Saryon cried, delighting in the rushing of the spring air past his face. "Tell me the words that summon the wind."

Saryon's father smiled and, shaking his head, solemnly tweaked one of the little boy's feet encased in its leather prison. "No word of yours will ever summon the wind, my son," he said, fondly brushing back the child's flaxen hair from the disappointed face. "Such is not your gift."

"Maybe not now," Saryon said stubbornly as they drifted above the long rows of newly plowed ground, smelling the rich, dark fragrance of wet earth. "But when I am older, like Janji—"

But his father was shaking his head again. "No, child, not even when you are older."

"But that's not fair!" Saryon cried. "Janji is only a servant, like his father, yet he can tell the air to take him on its back. Why—"

He stopped, catching his father's gaze. "It's because of these, isn't it!" he said suddenly. "Janji doesn't wear shoes. You don't either. Only me and Mother. Well, I'll get rid of them!" Kicking his feet, he sent one of the shoes flying, to tumble down onto the plowed ground where it would lie until a Field Magus, happening to come across it in her work, picked it up and took it home as a curiosity. Saryon kicked at his other shoe, but his father's hand closed over the little boy's feet.

"My son, you are not strong enough in Life—"

"I am, too, Father," Saryon insisted, interrupting. "Look! Look at this!" With a wave of his small hand, he caused his own knee-length robe to change from green to a vivid orange. He was about to add blotches of blue in order to create a costume of which he was quite fond, but one that his mother never allowed him to wear at home. His father didn't mind, however, and so he was generally permitted to wear it when they were alone together, traveling about the estate. But today the child saw his father's usually kind face grow stern, so, with a sigh, he held his tongue and checked his impulse.

"Saryon," said the wizard, "you are five years old. Within a year, you will begin your studies as a catalyst. It is time you listened and tried to understand what I am about to tell you. You have the Gift of Life. Thank the Almin! Some are born without it. Therefore, be grateful for this gift and use it wisely, never wishing for more than you have been blessedly allotted. That is a path of dark and bitter despair, my son. To walk that path leads to madness or worse."

"But if I have the gift, why can't I do with it what I want?" Saryon asked, his lower lip trembling at both his father's unaccustomed seriousness and the knowledge deep within the child that he knew the answer already but refused to accept it.

"My son," his father replied with a sigh, "I am *Albanara*, learned in the arts of ruling those under my care, of running and maintaining my house, of seeing to it that my land brings forth its fruit and that my animals give their gifts as they were born to do. That is my talent, given to me by the Almin, and I use it to find favor in his eyes."

Dropping down from the sky, the wizard came to rest in a wooded glade at the edge of the plowed land, shivering slightly as his bare feet touched the dew-damp grass.

"Why are we stopping?" the child asked. "We're not there yet."

"Because I want to walk," the wizard answered. "There is a stiffness in my muscles this morning that I need to work out." Setting his son down, he started off, his robes trailing in the grass.

Head bowed, Saryon trudged through the grass after his father, one shoe off and one shoe on, forced to walk with an awkward, waddling gait. Glancing back, the wizard saw his son lagging behind and, with a wave of his hand, caused the child's remaining shoe to disappear.

Looking down at his bare foot in momentary astonishment, Saryon laughed, enjoying the tickling sensation of the new grass.

"Race me, Father!" he called and dashed ahead.

Mindful of his dignity, the wizard hesitated, then shrugged and grinned. The wizard, was, after all, only a young man himself, being in his late twenties. Gathering up his long robes in his hand, he ran after his son. Across the glade they raced, the child screeching in excitement as his father pretended to be always on the verge of (but never quite) catching up with him. Unaccustomed to such strenuous exercise, the wizard was soon out of breath, however, and was forced to bring the race to a halt.

A jagged-edged boulder jutted up out of the earth near them. Panting slightly, the wizard walked over to the boulder and, touching it gently with his hand, caused it to grow smooth and polished. Then, sinking down upon the newly shaped rock in relief, he motioned his son to come to him. After catching his breath, he opened up the subject of their previous conversation.

"Do you see what I have done, Saryon?" the wizard asked, patting the rock with his hand. "Do you see how I have shaped the stone that, before, was useless to us but is now a bench that we may sit upon?"

Saryon nodded, his eyes fixed intently upon his father's face.

"That much I can do with the power of my magic. But, wouldn't it be wonderful, I ask myself sometimes, to be able to raise this boulder up out of the earth and shape it into . . . into . . ." he paused, then waved his hand, "into a house, for us to live in . . . just you and I . . ."

A shadow darkened the wizard's face as he glanced back in the direction of the house he had just left, the house where his wife was already up and busily attending to her ritual of morning prayer.

"Why don't you, Father?" his child asked eagerly.

The wizard's attention returned to his surroundings, and he smiled again, though there was a bitterness in the smile that Saryon saw but did not understand.

"What was I saying?" the wizard murmured, frowning. "Oh, yes." His face cleared. "I cannot shape a house from rock, my son. Only the *Pron-alban*, the craft magi, possess that gift of the Almin's. Nor can I change lead to gold as can the *Mon-alban*. I must use what the Almin has given me . . ."

"I don't think much of the Almin, then," said the child petulantly, poking at the grass with a toe, "if all he gave me was these old shoes!"

Saryon glanced up at his father out of the corner of his eye after he spoke to see the effect of such a daring, blasphemous remark. It would have had his mother quivering in white-faced anger. But the wizard put his hand upon his lips as though to keep them from smiling against his will. Clasping his arm around his son, he drew the child close.

"The Almin has given you the greatest gift of all," said the wizard. "The gift of Life-transference. It is in your power, and yours alone, to absorb the Life, the magic, that is in the ground and the air and all around us into your body and focus it and give it to me or someone like me so that I may use its power to enhance my own. This is the gift of the Almin to the catalyst. It is his gift to you."

"I don't think it's a very good gift." Saryon pouted, squirming in his father's embrace.

Lifting him up, the wizard set the little boy upon his lap. Better to explain things to the boy now and let him get the bitterness out of his system when they were alone together than to upset his pious mother.

"It is a good enough gift that it has survived through the centuries," the wizard answered severely, "and it has helped *us* survive the centuries, even the times in the old Dark World where the ancients lived, so we are told."

"I know," said the little boy. Nestling his head against his father's chest, he recited the lesson glibly, speaking unconsciously in the clipped, cold, precise voice of his mother. "Then we were called 'familiars' and the ancients used us as a repos — reposi — repository" — he stumbled over the hard word, but eventually brought it out, his face flushed with effort and triumph — "of their energy. This was done so that the fire of the magic did not destroy their bodies and so that their enemies would not discover them. To protect us, they shaped us into the likeness of small animals, and thus we worked together to keep magic in the world."

"Just so," said the wizard, stroking the child approvingly on the head. "You recite the catechism well, but do you understand it?"

"Yes," said Saryon with a sigh. "I understand, I guess." But he frowned as he said it.

Putting his finger beneath the boy's chin, the wizard turned the solemn little face up to look into his.

"You understand and you will be thankful to the Almin and work to please him . . . and to please me?" the wizard asked softly. He hesitated, then continued. "For you will please me, if you try to be happy in your work, even though

. . . even though I may not be around much to let you know that I am watching you and interested in you."

"Yes, Father," said the child, sensing a deep sorrow in his father's voice that he longed to ease. "I will be happy, I promise. But why won't you be here? Where are you going?"

"I am not going anywhere, at least not for a little while," his father said, smiling again and ruffling the fair hair. "In fact, it will be you that leaves me. But, that will not be for a time yet, so do not worry. Look —" He pointed suddenly at four winged men, who could be seen flying over the treetops, bearing two large, golden disks between them. The wizard stood up, setting the little boy down again upon the boulder. "Now, stay here, Saryon. I must cast the enchantment upon the seeds —"

"I know what you're going to do!" Saryon cried, standing up upon the rock so that he see better. The winged men flew closer, their golden disks shining like youthful suns bringing another dawn to earth. "Let me help!" the boy pleaded eagerly, reaching out his hand to his father. "Let me transfer the magic to you as Mother does."

Again the shadow darkened the wizard's face but it vanished almost instantly as he looked down upon his small catalyst. "Very well," he said, though he knew the boy was too young to perform the complicated task of sensing for the magic and opening a conduit to him. It would take the child many years of study to attain the art. Years in which his father would no longer have a part of his own son's life. Seeing the small face looking up at him eagerly, the wizard checked a sigh. Reaching out his hand, he took hold of his son's hand in his and solemnly pretended to accept the Gift of Life.

A person born in Thimhallan is born to his or her place and station in life, something not uncommon in a feudal society. A duke is generally born a duke, for example, just as a peasant is generally born a peasant.

Thimhallan had its noble families, who had ruled for generations. It had its peasants. What made Thimhallan unique was that certain of its people had their place and station determined for them — not by society — but by the inborn knowledge of one of the Mysteries of Life.

There are Nine Mysteries. Eight of them deal with Life or Magic, for, in the world of Thimhallan, Life *is* Magic. Everything that exists in this land exists either by the will of the Almin, who placed it here before even the ancients arrived, or has since been either "shaped, formed, summoned, or conjured," these being the four Laws of Nature. These Laws are controlled through at least one of eight of the Mysteries: Time, Spirit, Air, Fire, Earth, Water, Shadow, and Life. Of these Mysteries, only the first five currently survive in the land. Two — the Mysteries of Time and of Spirit — were lost during the Iron Wars. With them vanished forever the knowledge possessed by the ancients — the ability to divine the future, the ability to build the Corridors, and the ability to communicate with those who had passed from this life into the Beyond.

As for the last Mystery, the Ninth Mystery, it is practiced, but only by those who walk in darkness. Believed by most to have been the cause of the destructive Iron Wars, the Mystery was banished from the land. Its Sorcerers were sent Beyond, their tools and deadly engines destroyed. The Ninth Mystery is the forbidden mystery. Known as Death, its other name is Technology.

When a child is born in Thimhallan, he or she is given a series of tests to discover the particular mystery in which that child is most skilled. This determines the child's future role in Life.

The tests might indicate, for example, that the child is skilled in the Mystery of Air. If he is from the lower castes, he will become one of the *Kan-Hanar,* whose duties include the maintenance of the Corridors that provide the swiftest means of travel within Thimhallan, and the supervision of all commerce within and among the cities of the land. The child of a noble family with this skill will almost certainly ascend to the rank of archmagus and will be made *Sif-Hanar,* whose vast responsibilities include controlling the weather. It is the *Sif-Hanar* who make the air in the cities balmy and sweet one day or whiten the rooftops with a decorative snow the next. In the farmlands, it is the duty of the *Sif-Hanar* to see that the rain falls and the sun shines when needed and that they neither fall nor shine when not needed.

Those born with the Mystery of Fire are the warriors of Thimhallan. Witches and warlocks, they become *DKarn-Duuk*, with the power to call up the destructive forces of war. They are also the guardians of the people. The black-robed *Duuk-tsarith*, the Enforcers, are among this class.

The Mystery of Earth is the most common of the Mysteries, accounting for the majority of people residing in Thimhallan. Among these are the lowest caste in the land — the Field Magi, those who tend the crops. Above these are the craftsmen, divided into Guilds depending on their varying skills — the *Quin-alban*, the conjurers; the *Pron-alban*, magicians; the *Mon-alban*, the alchemists. The highest of this class, wizards and wizardesses, or the *Albanara*, have a general knowledge of all these skills and are those responsible for governing the populace.

A child born to the Mystery of Water is a Druid. Sensitive to nature, these magi use their talents to nurture and protect all living things. The *Fibanish*, or Field Druids, deal mainly with the growth and prospering of plant and animal life. The Druids most revered however are the Healers. The art of healing is a complex skill, utilizing the magus's own magic combined with the magic of the patient to help the body heal itself. The *Mannanish* treat minor illnesses and injuries, as well as practice midwifery. The highest rank, that which takes most power and study, is attained by the *Theldari*, who treat serious illnesses. Though it is believed that anciently they had the power of resurrection, the *Theldari* can no longer restore life to the dead.

Those who practice the Mystery of Shadow are the Illusionists, the artists of Thimhallan. These are the people who create charming phantasms and paint pictures in the air with palettes of rain and stardust.

Finally, a child may be born to the rarest of the Mysteries, the Mystery of Life. The thaumaturgist, or catalyst, is the dealer in magic, though he does not possess it in great measure himself. It is the catalyst, as his name implies, who takes the Life from the earth and the air, from fire and water, and, by assimilating it within his own body, is able to enhance it and transfer it to the magi who can use it.

And, of course, a child is sometimes born Dead.

3

Saryon

Saryon was born a catalyst. He had no choice in the matter. He came from a small province located outside the walls of the city of Merilon. His father was a wizard of third-rank nobility. His mother, a cousin of the Empress, was a catalyst of some consequence. She left the Church only when told that the Vision had been performed and that it was foreseen that marriage to this nobleman would produce issue. The catalyst trait would be passed on to an heir.

Saryon's mother obeyed without question, though the marriage was beneath her. His father obeyed without question as well. A nobleman of his standing might or might not obey an order from the Emperor. But no one, regardless of rank, refused a request of the catalysts.

Saryon's mother performed her marriage as she performed all her religious duties. When the proper time came, she and her husband traveled to the Groves of Healing where his seed was taken from him by the *Mannanish*, the minor healers, and given to his wife. In due time, their child was born as the Vision had foreseen.

Saryon was typical in that he began his training at the age of six. He was not typical in that he was allowed to train under the tutelage of his mother, due to her high ranking within the Church. On the sixth anniversary of his birth, the boy was brought into his mother's presence. From that moment on, for the next fourteen years, he spent every day with her in study and in prayer. When Saryon was twenty, he left his mother's house forever, traveling through the Corridors to the most holy, most sacred place in Thimhallan — the Font.

The history of the Font is the history of Thimhallan. Many, many centuries before, in a time whose memories were crushed and scattered amid the chaos of the Iron Wars, a persecuted people fled to this world, voluntary exiles from their own. The magical journey had been a terrible one. The great energies needed to perform such a feat drained the last vestige of life from many of their number, who gave up their lives willingly so that their kind might survive and prosper in a land they themselves would never see.

They came to this place because the magic in this world was strong; so strong it drew them to it — a lodestone leading them safely through time and space. They stayed in this place because the world was empty and alone.

There were drawbacks. Terrible storms raged over the new, raw land. Its mountains spewed fire, its waters ran savage, its vegetation was thick and untamed. But, as their feet touched the ground, the people felt the magic stirring and beating beneath them, like a living heart. They could feel it, sense it; and they searched for its source enduring countless hardship and untold suffering on the way.

At last they found it, the source of the magic — a mountain whose fire had burned out, leaving the magic behind to glow like a diamond beneath the bright, unfamiliar sun.

They called this mountain the Font and here it was, at the Well of Life, that the catalysts established their home and the center of their world. At first there had been only a few catacombs, hurriedly shaped and hewn by those eager to escape the perils of the world outside. During the centuries, these few, crude tunnels had grown into a maze of corridors and halls, of chambers and rooms, of kitchens and courtyards and terraced parks. A university, built on the side of the mountain, taught the young *Albanara* the skills they would need to rule their lands and their people. Young *Theldari* came to advance their healing arts, the young *Sif-Hanar* to study the ways of controlling wind and clouds, all assisted by young novitiates among the catalysts. The craft guilds had their centers of learning here as well. In order to provide for the students and their teachers, a small city sprang up at the foot of the mountain.

At the very top of the mountain was a grand cathedral, the summit of the mountain peak itself forming the vaulting ceiling, the view from the windows so magnificent many wept for the sheer awe and beauty of the sight.

Few there were on Thimhallan who saw the view from the summit, however. Once, the Font had been open to all, from Emperor to housemagus. Following the Iron Wars, that policy had changed. Now only the catalysts themselves, plus those privileged few who worked for them, were permitted within its holy walls, and only the highest officials of the Church allowed to enter the sacred chamber of the Well. There was a city within the mountain as well as without, the catalysts having everything they needed to live and continue their work within the Font. Many novitiates walked through its doors as young men and women and, if they left at all, it was only in whatever form the dead take as they journey Beyond.

Saryon was one of these novitiates, and he might have lived his life out peacefully here as had countless others before him.

But Saryon was different. In fact, he came to think of himself as cursed. . . .

The *Theldara*, one of those few outsiders chosen to live in the Font, was working outdoors in his herb garden when a venerable old raven hopped gravely down the pathway between the neat rows of young seedlings and, with a croak, informed his master that the patient had arrived. With a word of gracious thanks to the bird — who, being so old that he was losing the feathers on top of his head, looked not unlike a catalyst himself — the Druid left his sunny garden, returning to the cool, darkened, peaceful confines of the infirmary.

"Sun arise, Brother," the *Theldara* said, entering the Waiting Chamber quietly, his brown robes brushing the stone floor with a soft, whispering sound.

"S-sun arise, Healer," stammered the young man, starting. He had been staring moodily out a window and had not heard the entry of the druid.

"If you will walk this way with me," continued the *Theldara*, his sharp, penetrating gaze taking in every aspect of the young catalyst from the unnatural pallor of his complexion to the chewed fingernails to the nervous preoccupation, "we will go to my private quarters, which are more comfortable, for our little talk."

The young man nodded and answered politely, but it was obvious to the Druid that he might have invited the catalyst to walk off a cliff and received the same vague response. They passed through the infirmary with its long rows of beds, the wood lovingly shaped into the image of cupped hands holding mattresses of sweet-smelling leaves and herbs, whose fragrant combination promoted sleep and relaxation. Here and there, a few patients rested, listening to prescribed music and concentrating their bodies' energies on the healing process. The *Theldara* had a word for each as he passed, but he did not stop, leading his charge out of this area into another chamber, more closed off and private. In a sunny room whose walls were made of glass, a room filled with growing, living things, the Druid sat down upon a cushion of soft pine needles and invited his patient to do the same.

The catalyst did so, plopping down upon it awkwardly. He was a tall young man, stoop-shouldered, with hands and feet that seemed too big for his body. He was carelessly dressed, his robes too short for his height. There were gray smudges of fatigue beneath the dull eyes. The Druid noticed all this without seeming to take any unusual interest in his patient, chatting all the time about the weather and inquiring if the catalyst would partake of a soothing tea.

Having received a muttered acquiescence, the *Theldara* gestured and a sphere of steaming liquid obediently floated from the fire, filled two cups, and returned to its proper place. The Druid took one cautious sip of his tea, then casually caused the cup to float down to the table. The herbal concoction was intended to relax inhibitions and encourage free talking. He watched carefully as the young man gulped his down thirstily, seemingly unmindful of the liquid's heat and probably never even tasting it. Putting his cup down, the young man stared out one of the large glass windows.

"I am very pleased we have this chance to visit, Brother Saryon," said the Druid, motioning to the sphere to fill the young man's cup again. "So often I see you young people only when you are sick. You are feeling well, are you not, Brother?"

"I am fine, Healer," said the young man, still staring out the window. "I came here only at the request of my Master."

"Yes, you seem well enough in body," the *Theldara* said mildly, "but our bodies are merely shells for our minds. If the mind suffers, it harms the body."

"I am fine," Saryon repeated somewhat impatiently. "A touch of insomnia . . ."

"But I'm told you have been missing Evening Prayer, that you do not take your daily exercise, and you have been skipping meals." The Druid was silent a moment, watching with expert eyes the tea begin to take effect. The stooped shoulders slumped, the eyelids drooped, the nervous hands slowly settled into the catalyst's lap. "How old are you, Brother? Twenty-seven, twenty-eight?"

"Twenty-five."

The Druid raised an eyebrow. Saryon nodded. "I was admitted to the Font at the age of twenty," he said by way of explanation, most young men and women entering when they are twenty-one.

"And what was the reason for this?" the *Theldara* asked.

"I'm a mathematical genius," Saryon answered in the same nonchalant tone he might have used in saying "I am tall," or "I am male."

"Indeed?" The Druid stroked his long, gray beard. That would easily account for the young man's early admittance to the Font. The transference of Life from the elements to the magi who will use it is a fine science, relying almost completely upon the principles of mathematics. Because the force of magic thus drawn from the surrounding world is concentrated within the catalyst, who will then focus that concentration of Life upon his chosen subject, the mathematical calculations for the amount of energy transferred must be precise indeed, since the transference of magic weakens the catalyst. Only in the most dire emergencies, or in times of war, is a catalyst permitted to suffuse a magus with Life.

"Yes," said Saryon, relaxing under the influence of the tea, his tall, awkward body sinking back into the cushion. "I learned all the routine calculations as a child. At the age of twelve, I could give you the figures that would lift a building from its foundations and send it flying through the air and, in the same breath, provide calculations that would conjure up a royal gown for the Empress."

"This is remarkable," murmured the Druid, staring at Saryon intently through half-closed lids.

The catalyst shrugged. "So my mother thought. To me, it wasn't anything special. It was like a game, the only real enjoyment I ever had as a child," he added, beginning to pick at the fabric of the cushion.

"You studied with your mother? You didn't go to the schools?"

"No. She is a Priestess. In line for Cardinal, but then she married my father."

"Political arrangement?"

Saryon shook his head with a wry smile. "No. Because of me."

"Ah, yes. I see." The Druid took another small sip of tea. Marriages are always arranged in Thimhallan and are, in general, controlled by the catalysts. This is due to the gift of the Vision. The only remnant left of the once flourishing art of divination, the Vision allows the catalysts to foresee if a union will produce issue and will therefore be a wise match. If no issue is foreseen as forthcoming, the marriage is forbidden.

Since catalysts can only breed catalysts, their marriages are even more strictly governed than those of the magi and are arranged by the Church itself. Catalysts being so rare, having one in the household is considered a privilege. In addition, the expense of a catalyst's education and training is borne by the Church. His place in the world is established, insuring both the catalyst and his family of a better-than-average livelihood.

"Your mother is high in the Order. Your father must be a powerful noble — "

"No." Saryon shook his head. "The marriage was beneath my mother, a fact she never let my father forget. She is a cousin of the Empress of Merilon and he was only a duke."

"Your father? You speak of him in the past . . ."

"He's dead," Saryon answered without emotion. "Died about ten years ago, when I was fifteen. A wasting illness. My mother did what she could. She called in the Healers, but she didn't try very hard to save him and he didn't try very hard to live."

"Did this upset you?"

"Not that much," Saryon muttered, poking his finger through a hole he had worked in the cushion. He shrugged. "I hadn't seen him for a long time. When I was six, I began my studies with my mother and . . . my father began spending more and more time away from home. He enjoyed the court life of Merilon. Besides"—frowning, Saryon concentrated on widening the hole in the cushion, his fingers working busily—"I . . . had other things . . . to think about."

"At fifteen, one generally does," the *Theldara* said gently. "Tell me these thoughts. They must be dark ones, they lie like a cloud over the sun of your being."

"I—I can't," Saryon mumbled, his face growing alternately flushed and pale.

"Very well," the Druid said complacently, "We will—"

"I didn't want to be a catalyst!" Saryon blurted. "I wanted the magic. It—it's the first clear thought I remember having, even when I was little."

"That is nothing to be ashamed of," the *Theldara* remarked. "Many of your Order experience the same jealousy of the magi."

"Yes?" Saryon glanced up, looking hopeful at first. Then his face darkened. He began to pluck pine needles from the cushion, pinching them between his fingers. "Well, that isn't the worst." He fell silent, scowling.

"What type of magus would you be?" asked the Druid, knowing where this was leading but preferring that it unfold naturally. He beckoned to the sphere to fill the catalyst's teacup again. "*Albanara* . . ."

"Oh, no!" Saryon smiled bitterly. "Nothing that ambitious." He looked up again, staring out the window. "I think I'd be *Pron-alban*—a shaper of wood. I love the feel of wood, its smoothness, its smell, the twists and whorls of the grain." He sighed. "My mother said it is because I sense the Life within the wood and reverence it."

"Very proper and correct," remarked the Druid.

"Ah, but that's not it, you see!" Saryon said, his gaze going to the *Theldara*, his smile twisting. "I wanted to change the wood, Healer! Change it with my bare hands! I wanted to join one piece of wood with another and make something new of it!" Sitting back, he regarded the Druid smugly, expecting a shocked, horrified reaction.

In a world where the joining together of anything — lifeless or living — is considered to be the most unforgivable of sins, this admission of Saryon's was a dreadful one, bordering on the Dark Arts. It is only the Sorcerers, those who practice the Ninth Mystery, who would think of such a thing. The *Pron-alban*, for example, does not build a chair, he shapes it. Taking the wood — a solid, living tree trunk — he uses his magic to lovingly shape that wood into the beautiful image he sees in his mind. Thus the chair is just another stage of Life for the wood. Were the magi to cut and mutilate the wood, bend it with his bare hands, and force those mutilated, misshapen pieces together into the semblance of a chair — the very wood itself would cry out in agony and it must certainly soon die. Yet Saryon had confessed he wanted to perform this heinous act. The young man expected the Druid to turn pale with horror, perhaps even order him out of his home.

The *Theldara*, however, simply regarded the catalyst placidly, as if Saryon had stated he had a fondness for eating apples. "We all have a very natural curiosity about such things," he said calmly. "What else did you dream about in your youth? Joining wood? Is that all?"

Saryon swallowed. Looking down at the cushion, he jammed his finger through the fabric. "No." Sweating, he put his hands over his face. "The Almin help me!" he cried brokenly.

"My dear young man, the Almin is trying to help, but first you must help yourself," the Druid said earnestly. "You dreamed of joining with women, did you not?"

Saryon raised his head, his face feverish. "How — how did you know? Did you see my mind —"

"No, no." The *Theldara* raised his hands, smiling. "I do not have the mind-draining skills of the Enforcers. These dreams are quite natural, Brother. Left over from the dark days of our existence, they serve to remind us of our animal natures and how we are bound up in the world. Didn't anyone ever discuss this with you?"

The look on Saryon's face was so comical, being one of mingled relief, shock, and naïveté, that the Druid was hard-pressed to keep a serious aspect, even as he inwardly cursed the cold, sterile, loveless environment that must have fostered such guilt within the young man. In a very few words, the *Theldara* set about explaining the matter.

"It is speculated that in the dark, shadowy land of our past, we magi were forced to join the flesh together to produce issue as do animals. This gave us no control over the reproduction of our kind, and caused our blood to mingle with that of the Dead. Even years after we came to this world, so it is believed, we still mated that way. But then we learned that we had the power to take the seed of the man and transfer it — using the Life force — to woman. Through this, we could control the numbers of our population as well as raising the people above the bestial desires of the flesh. But that is not as easy as it sounds, the flesh being weak. I take it you outgrew these dreams," the *Theldara* continued, "or perhaps you are still bothered —"

"No," said Saryon hurriedly, in some confusion. "No, not bothered by them — I didn't outgrow, I don't think. That is . . . Mathematics," he said finally. "I — I discovered that what had once been . . . a game was my . . . salvation!" Sitting up, he looked at the Druid, his face brightening. "When I am in the world of my studies, I forget all about everything! Don't you see, Healer? *That* is why I miss Evening Prayers. I forget all about eating, the exercise period; it's all a waste of time! Knowledge! To study and learn and create — new theories, new calculations. I've cut the magical force needed to form glass from rock in half! And this is nothing — *nothing* — to compare to some of the things I've been planning! Why, I've even discovered —" Saryon broke off abruptly.

"Discovered what?" asked the Druid casually.

"Nothing you'd be interested in," the catalyst said shortly. Staring down at the cushion, he suddenly noticed the hole he had made in it. Flushing, he began trying, without much success, to repair the damage he had done.

"I may not understand the mathematics," the *Theldara* said, "but I'd be very interested to listen to you talk about it."

"No. It's not anything, really." Saryon stood up, somewhat unsteadily. "I'm sorry about the cushion . . ."

"Easily repaired," the Druid said, rising to his feet and smiling, though he was once more studying the young catalyst intently. "Perhaps you will come back and we can discuss this new discovery of yours?"

"Possibly. I . . . I don't know. Like I said, it isn't really important. What is important in my life is the mathematics. It's more important to me than anything else! Don't you see? The gaining of knowledge . . . *any* type of knowledge! Even that which is —" Saryon broke off abruptly. "May I go now?" he asked. "Are you finished with me?"

"I'm not 'finished' with you, because I never 'started' with you in the first place," the *Theldara* reproved gently. "You were advised to come here because your Master was concerned for your health. So am I. You are obviously overworking yourself, Brother Saryon. That fine mind of yours depends upon its body. As I said before, if you neglect one, the other will suffer as well."

"Yes," Saryon murmured, ashamed of his outburst. "I am sorry, Healer. Perhaps you are right."

"I will see you at meals . . . and out in the exercise yard?"

"Yes," the catalyst answered, checking an exasperated sigh; and turning, he started for the door.

"And quit spending *all* your hours in the Library," the Druid continued, following. "There are other —"

"The Library?" Saryon whirled about, his face deathly pale. "What did you mean, the Library?"

The *Theldara* blinked, startled. "Why, nothing, Brother Saryon. You mentioned studying. Naturally, I assumed you must spend much of your time in the Library . . ."

"Well, you assumed wrong! I haven't been there in a month!" Saryon snapped vehemently. "A month, do you hear me?"

"Why, yes . . ."

"May the Almin be with you," the catalyst muttered. "No need to show me out. I know the way." Bowing awkwardly, he hurried through the door of the Druid's quarters, his too-short robes flapped about his bony ankles as he walked rapidly through the infirmary and out the far door.

The Druid stared after the young man thoughtfully for long moments after he had gone, absently stroking the feathers of the raven, who had flown in the window and perched on his shoulder.

"What was that?" he asked the bird. "Did you say something?"

The bird croaked a response, cleaning its bill with its foot, as it, too, stared after the catalyst with its glittering black eyes.

"Yes," answered the *Theldara*, "you are right, my friend. That soul flies on very dark wings indeed."

4

The Chamber
of the Ninth Mystery

The Master Librarian was not on duty when the incident occurred. It was late at night, long past the hour of Rest. The only person on duty was an elderly deacon known as the Undermaster.

Actually, the term Undermaster was a misnomer, since he wasn't really master of anything, either Under or Over. He was, in reality, nothing more than a caretaker, his main responsibility in the Inner Library being to discourage the rats who, not caring for scholarly pursuits, had taken to digesting the books rather than the knowledge imprinted therein.

The Undermaster was one of the few in the Font permitted to stay up during the Resting Time. This mattered little to him since he had the habit of nodding off at no particular time whatsoever anyway. His yellow-skinned bald head was, in fact, just beginning to droop a bit closer to the pages of the tome he told himself he was perusing when he heard a rustling, shuffling noise at the far end of the Library.

The sound made him start and gave his heart an uncomfortable jolt. Coughing nervously, he peered across the vast distance of the Library into the shadows in the hope (or fear) of seeing what caused the sound. At that point he remembered the rats, and it struck the Undermaster rather forcibly that a rat large enough to make a sound heard from that distance must be an uncommonly large specimen of the species. It also struck him that he would have to cross a very dark section of the Library in order to deal with the miscreant. Putting these two thoughts together in his head, he decided, after a moment's profound consideration, that he had heard no sound at all, but had only imagined it.

Vastly comforted, he returned to his reading, beginning with the same paragraph he had been beginning to read for a week and which never failed to put him to sleep about halfway through.

This time was no exception. His nose was actually touching the page when there came the rustling, shuffling sound again.

This Deacon had seen marvelous things in his youth, having witnessed a skirmish between the kingdoms of Merilon and Zith-el. He had seen the skies rain fire, the trees sprout spears. He had seen the Masters of War transform men into centaurs, cats into lions, lizards into dragons, rats into slavering monsters. The rat having now grown in his mind proportionate with his memories, the Deacon rose, trembling, from his chair and hastened for the door.

Leaning his head out of the library, but not venturing out himself (let it never be said that he abandoned his post!) the Deacon started to call to the *Duuk-tsarith* for help. But the sight of the tall black-robed and black-hooded figure standing still and motionless, its hands clasped before it, gave him pause, filling him with a fear almost equal to that of the mysterious noise. Perhaps it was nothing. Perhaps only a *small* rat . . .

There it was again! And this time, a sound of a door shutting!

"Enforcer!" hissed the Deacon, gesturing with a palsied hand. "Enforcer!"

The hooded head turned his direction. The Deacon was aware of two glittering eyes and then, within the drawing of a breath and without seeming to move at all, the black-robed figure stood silently before him.

Though the warlock did not speak, the Deacon heard, quite clearly, a question in his mind. "I — I'm not cer-certain," stammered the Deacon in answer. "I — I heard a noise."

The *Duuk-tsarith* inclined his head, as the Deacon could see by the tip of the black, pointed hood shivering slightly. "It — it sounded rather large, not the noise, that is. I mean, as if it were made by something rather large and — and I *thought* I heard a door shut."

A breath of warm, moist air whispered from the black hood.

"Of course not!" The Deacon appeared shocked. "It is Resting Time. No one is allowed in here. I have dispen — dispensation," he added, fumbling over the word in his nervousness.

The hooded head turned to look into the shadowy corridors formed by the crystalline shelves and their valuable contents.

"Th-there," quavered the Deacon, pointing toward the very back of the Library. "I didn't see anything. I only heard a sound, sort of a rustle, and then — then the door —"

He paused, at another whisper of breath. "What's back there? Just a moment. Let me think." His entire bald head wrinkled as he laboriously traversed the Inner Library in his mind. Eventually his halting mental footsteps evidently led him to a startling realization, for his eyes grew wide, and he stared at the *Duuk-tsarith* in alarm. "The Ninth Mystery!"

The Enforcer's black hood snapped around.

"The Chamber of the Ninth Mystery!" The Deacon wrung his hands. "The forbidden books! But the door is always sealed. How — What —"

But he was talking to empty air. The warlock had vanished from his sight.

It took a moment for the Deacon, in his rattled state, to assimilate this occurrence. Thinking at first that the *Duuk-tsarith* might have fled in terror, the Deacon was about to join him when more rational thought took over. Of course. The Enforcer had gone to investigate.

Visions of the giant rat loomed into the Deacon's view. Perhaps he should stay here and keep watch on the doorway. Then a vision of the Master Librarian replaced the giant rat. With a sigh, the Deacon grasped the skirts of his white flow-

ing robes in his hands, to keep them out of the dust, and
hastened through the Library toward the forbidden room.

Momentarily losing himself in a maze of crystal shelving,
he heard the sound of voices to his right and somewhat
ahead. This showed him the way, and he scurried on, arriving at the door to the forbidden chamber just as another silent, black-robed, black-hooded *Duuk-tsarith* materialized
out of the air. The first Enforcer having removed the seal
from the door, the second entered immediately. The Deacon
started to follow, but the Enforcer's unexpected appearance
had so unnerved him that he was forced to lean against the
doorway for a few moments, his hand pressed over his pal-
pitating heart.

Then, feeling more himself and not wanting to miss the
sight of two *Duuk-tsarith* battling a giant rat, the Deacon cautiously peered into the chamber. Although its ancient shadows had been driven back into their corners by the light of a
candle, they seemed to be waiting for any chance at all to leap
out and once more take possession of their sealed home. As
he stared into the room, the giant rat wafted away into the
thin air of the Deacon's imagination, replaced by a horror
more real and profound. He knew now that he had to deal
with something much darker, much more terrible.

Someone had entered the forbidden room. Someone was
studying its dark and arcane secrets. Someone had been se-
duced by the dread power of the Ninth Mystery.

Blinking, trying to accustom his eyes to the bright beam
of candlelight, the Deacon could not recognize, at first, the
figure that cowered in the grasp of the two dark warlocks.
He could see only a white robe with gray trim like his own. A
Deacon of the Font, then. But who—

A gaunt and miserable face looked up at him.

"Brother Saryon!"

5

The Chamber
of the Bishop

Rising ponderously to his feet from performing the Ritual of Dawn, Bishop Vanya smoothed his red robes and, walking to his window, stared out at the rising sun, his lips pursed, his brow frowning. As if aware of this severe scrutiny, the sun peeped timidly over the ranges of the distant Vannheim Mountains. It even appeared to hesitate for a few seconds, teetering on the sharp edges of the snow-capped peaks, seemingly ready to set again in an instant if Bishop Vanya but spoke the word.

The Bishop turned from the window, however, thoughtfully lifting and placing around his neck the gold and silver chain that was the mark of his office and matched the gold and silver trim upon his robe. As if it had been waiting for this moment, the sun sprang into the sky, flooding the Bishop's room with light. His frown deepening in annoyance, Bishop Vanya stalked back over to the window and closed the heavy velvet curtains.

A soft, self-deprecating knock interrupted Vanya as he was sitting down at his desk, preparatory to beginning the day's business.

"Enter with the Almin's blessing," he said in a mild, pleasant voice, though he heaved a sigh immediately after, scowling to himself irritably at the interruption as his glance went to the stack of missives, newly delivered by the Ariels, that sat upon the polished wood.

The scowl was gone by the time the visitor had appeared in the doorway. A rebellious ray of sunlight, managing to sneak through a chink in the curtains, flashed off a bit of silver trim on the man's white robes. Creeping into the room, his shoes making no noise at all on the thick carpet, the Cardinal bowed in greeting from the open door then, shutting it carefully behind him, ventured to cross the floor.

"Holiness," he began, licking his lips nervously, "a most regrettable incident —"

"Sun arise, Cardinal," the Bishop said from where he had seated himself behind his massive desk.

The Cardinal flushed. "I beg your pardon, Holiness," he murmured, bowing again. "Sun arise. May the Almin's blessing be with you this day."

"And with you, Cardinal," said the Bishop placidly, studying the missives the messengers had delivered into his hands last night.

"Holiness, a most regrettable incident —"

"We should never allow ourselves to become so involved in the affairs of the world that we forget to invoke the Almin's blessing," Vanya observed, apparently absorbed in reading one of the letters, enveloped in the Emperor's golden aura, with an abstracted air. In point of fact, he wasn't reading the letter at all. Another "regrettable incident"! Damn! He'd just been through one — a poor fool of a House Catalyst who'd gotten himself involved with the daughter of a minor noble to the point where they had committed the heinous sin of joining. The Order had decreed execution by means of the Turning. A most wise decision. Still, it had not been pleasant and had disrupted life at the Font for a week. "You will remember that, won't you, Cardinal?"

"Yes, of course, Holiness," faltered the Cardinal, his flush ascending from his face to his bald scalp. He paused.

"Well?" The Bishop looked up. "A most regrettable incident?"

"Yes, Holiness." The Cardinal rushed into the breach. "One of the young Deacons was discovered in the Great Library last night after Resting Time —"

Vanya frowned irritably and waved his pudgy hand. "Let his punishment be determined by one of the Undermasters, Cardinal. I do not have time to fool with every transgression —"

"I again beg your pardon, Holiness," interrupted the Cardinal, taking a step forward in his earnestness, "but this is not an ordinary transgression."

Vanya stared intently at the man's face and noticed, for the first time, its almost frighteningly serious and solemn intensity. His expression grave, the Bishop laid the Emperor's missive down on the desk and gave his minister his full attention. "Proceed, then."

"Holiness, the young man was found in the Inner Library" — the Cardinal hesitated, not because he was being intentionally dramatic, but in order to brace himself for the reaction of his superior — "in the Chamber of the Ninth Mystery."

Bishop Vanya regarded the Cardinal in silence, displeasure darkening his face.

"Who?" His voice grated.

"Deacon Saryon."

The frown deepened. "Saryon . . . Saryon," he muttered, absently tapping the fingers of one pudgy hand upon the desk in a crawling motion, a habit he had. The Cardinal, having seen it before, was always vividly reminded of a spider making its slow, steady way across the black wood. Involuntarily, he edged a step backward as he prodded his superior's memory.

"Saryon. The mathematical prodigy, Holiness."

"Ah, yes!" The bristling brows eased slightly, the displeasure receded somewhat. "Saryon." He was thoughtful a moment, then frowned again. "How long was he there?"

"Not long, Holiness," the Cardinal hastened to assure him. "The *Duuk-tsarith* were alerted almost immediately by the Undermaster, who heard a sound in the far section of the Library. Consequently, they were able to apprehend the young man within minutes of his entry."

The Bishop's face cleared, he almost smiled. Noticing, however, that the Cardinal was observing this relaxation with a growing look of shocked disapproval, Vanya immediately assumed a stern, severe air. "This must not go unpunished."

"No, of course not, Holiness."

"This Saryon must be made an example, lest others give way to temptation."

"My thoughts exactly, Holiness."

"Still," Vanya mused, sighing heavily and rising to his feet, "I cannot but think that this is partially our fault, Cardinal."

The Cardinal's eyes widened. "I assure you, Holiness," he protested stiffly, "that neither I nor any of our Masters ever so much as —"

"Oh, I don't mean that!" Vanya said, waving his hand negatingly. "I recall hearing some reports that this young man was neglecting his health and his prayers for his books. We have obviously let this Saryon get so wrapped up in his studies that he has been lost to the world. He very nearly lost his soul, as well," the Bishop added solemnly, shaking his head. "Ah, Cardinal, we might have been held accountable for that soul, but, thanks be to the Almin's mercy, we are given a chance to save the young man."

Receiving a reproachful look from the Bishop, the Cardinal muttered, "All praise to the Almin," but it was obvious that he did not consider this one of the great blessings of his life.

Turning his back upon his sulking minister, the Bishop walked over to the window and, drawing the curtain aside with one hand, looked outside as if to meditate upon the fineness of the day. But the day was far from his mind as evidenced by the fact that when the Cardinal did not speak further, Vanya — his hand still upon the curtain — glanced at him out of the corner of his eye.

"This young man's soul is of paramount importance, wouldn't you agree, Cardinal?"

"Certainly, Holiness," said the Cardinal, blinking as he stared into the bright light, seeing it glint in the Bishop's eye.

The Bishop returned to contemplating the morning.

"It seems to me, therefore, that we share some blame for this young man's downfall through negligence on our part in permitting him to wander alone, without guidance or supervision." Hearing no response, Vanya heaved a sigh and tapped himself on the chest with a heavy hand. "I include myself in this blame, Cardinal."

"Your Holiness is too good—"

"Therefore, doesn't it follow that his punishment should fall upon our shoulders? That we should be the example, not this young man, for it was we who failed him?"

"I suppose . . ."

Letting the curtain fall suddenly, plunging the room into cool shadows once more, Vanya turned from the window to face his minister, who was once again blinking, endeavoring to adjust his eyes to the dimness as he was endeavoring to adjust his mind to his Bishop's way of thinking.

"Publicly humiliating ourselves over this incident would, however, do the Church a disservice, wouldn't you agree, Cardinal?"

"Certainly, Holiness!" The Cardinal's shock increased. So did his confusion. "Such a thing is unimaginable . . ."

With a thoughtful, pensive air, the Bishop clasped his hands behind his back. "Does it not go against all our precepts, however, that we should allow another to suffer for our own transgressions?"

The Cardinal, now completely lost, could only murmur something noncommittal.

"Therefore," continued the Bishop in a soft voice, "I think it would be best for the Church itself and for the soul of this young man if this incident were . . . forgotten."

The Bishop kept his gaze upon his minister. The Cardinal's expression was irresolute, then it hardened stubbornly. Vanya's brows came together again. The fingers of his hands curled around each other in irritation, hidden, as they were, behind his back. The Cardinal was generally a mild, unassuming man whose best quality, as far as Vanya was concerned, was his slowness of thought. But this very slowness had its drawback on occasions. The Cardinal's own life was measured out in equal portions of black and white; consequently, he could never see beyond those stark stripes to the subtle shades of gray. If his minister had his way, Vanya reflected bitterly, young Saryon would probably be sentenced to the Turning!

Keeping his voice calm, Vanya murmured in low tones, emphasizing the last four words, "I would hate to give even the slightest moment of grief to Saryon's mother, especially at a time when she is deeply concerned, as are we all, with the health of *her cousin, the Empress.* . . ."

A muscle in the Cardinal's face twitched. He may have been slow of thought, but he was no fool — another of his valuable qualities.

"I understand," he said, bowing.

"I thought you would," Bishop Vanya said dryly. "Now" — crossing once more to his desk and continuing briskly — "who knows of this unfortunate young man's transgression?"

The Cardinal considered. "The Undermaster and the Headmaster — we had to inform him as a matter of course."

"I suppose," Vanya muttered, his hand crawling across the desk once more. "The Enforcers. Anyone else?"

"No, Holiness." The Cardinal shook his head. "Fortunately, it was Resting Time — "

"Yes." Vanya rubbed his brow. "Very well. The *Duuk-tsarith* will not be a problem. I can rely upon their discretion. Send the other two to me, along with that wretched young man."

"What will you do with him?"

"I don't know," Vanya said softly, lifting the Emperor's letter and staring at it with unseeing eyes. "I don't know."

But, an hour later, when the Priest who acted as the Bishop's secretary entered the office to say that Deacon Saryon was here to see him as requested, Vanya had made up his mind.

Having only an imperfect recollection of Saryon, the Bishop had been endeavoring all morning to call the young man's face to memory. This should not reflect unfavorably upon the Bishop's power of observation, for it was very acute. It is rather to his credit, in fact, that he was finally able to extract the gaunt and serious face of the young mathe-

matical genuis from the faces of the many hundred young
men and women who came and went from the Font.

Having fixed the face firmly in his mind, Vanya continued
his work for another half hour after the young man's arrival
had been announced. Let the poor fellow suffer a bit, Vanya
told himself coolly, well knowing that the most exquisite form
of torture is self-inflicted. Glancing at the timeglass upon his
desk, he noted, from the position of the tiny, magical sun that
was rotating above the sundial encased in its crystal prison,
that the allotted time had elapsed. Lifting his hand, he caused
a small silver chime to vibrate, sounding a tone. Then, rising
leisurely to his feet, the Bishop placed the miter upon his
head and smoothed out his robes. Moving to the center of the
sumptuously appointed room, he stood waiting in awful majesty.

The door opened. The secretary appeared for an instant,
but his form was swallowed in blackness as the robed and
hooded, silent *Duuk-tsarith* flowed past him, surrounding the
stumbling figure of the young man they held between
them, — surrounding him like his own private night.

"You may leave us," the Bishop said to the Enforcers,
who bowed and vanished. The door shut noiselessly. The
Bishop and his young transgressor were alone.

Keeping his expression carefully cold and stern, Vanya
eyed the young man curiously. He noted to himself with satisfaction that his recollection of Saryon's features had been
precise, though it took a few moments' study to ascertain
this, so changed was the face that presented itself to his view.
Gaunt it had been, from hours of study, but now it was ca-
daverous and touched with a corpselike pallor. The eyes
burned feverishly, and had sunken into the high cheekbones.
The tall spare frame trembled, the overlarge hands shook.
Suffering and remorse and fear were visible in every line of
the quivering body, in the red-rimmed eyes and the streaks
that tracked down the face.

Vanya permitted himself an inner smile.

"Deacon Saryon," he began in a deep, sonorous voice.
But before he could say anything further, the wretched
young man hurled himself across the room, and, falling to his
knees before the startled Bishop, grasped the hem of his robe

and pressed it to his lips. Then, wailing something incoherent, Saryon burst into tears.

Slightly discomfited, and seeing a large stain spreading over the hem of his costly silken robe, the Bishop frowned and snatched the fabric out of the young man's grasp. Saryon did not move, but knelt there still, crouched over, his face in his hands, sobbing in misery.

"Pull yourself together, Deacon!" Vanya snapped, then added more kindly, "Come now, my boy. You have made a mistake. It isn't the end of the world. You are young. Youth is a time of exploration." Reaching down, he took hold of Saryon's arm. "It is a time our feet carry us down untrodden paths," he continued, almost dragging the young man up off the floor, "where, sometimes, we encounter darkness." Steering his unsteady footsteps, the Bishop guided Saryon to a chair, talking soothingly the while. "We have only to look to the Almin for help in finding our way back. Here, that's it. Now, sit down. You've had nothing to eat or drink all night or this morning, I presume? I thought not. Try this sherry. Really quite fine, from the vineyards of Duke Algor."

Bishop Vanya poured Saryon a glass of sherry which the young man, appalled at having his Bishop serve him, shrank away from accepting as though it were poison.

Noting the young man's confusion with well-concealed pleasure, Vanya increased his kindness to him, placing the sherry in his reluctant hand. Then, removing the miter, the Bishop sat down in a soft, comfortable yet elegant chair opposite the young man. Pouring a glass of sherry for himself, he suspended it in the air near his mouth and smoothed out his robes, making himself comfortable.

Completely taken aback, Saryon could do nothing but stare at this great man, who now looked more like someone's overweight uncle than one of the mightiest powers in the land.

"The Almin be praised," said the Bishop, causing his glass to brush up against his lips, sipping a tiny bit of the excellent sherry.

"The Almin be praised," mumbled Saryon reflexively, attempting to drink and nervously sloshing most of the sherry onto his robes.

`"Now, Brother Saryon," said Bishop Vanya, assuming the air of a father about to punish a beloved child, "let us drop formalities. I want to hear from your lips exactly what occurred."

The young man blinked; the glass hovering before him wavered as his concentration on it slipped. Grabbing it hastily, he set it down upon a nearby table with a trembling hand. "Holiness," murmured the wretched Saryon distractedly, "my crime . . . is wicked . . . unforgivable. . . ."

"My son," said Vanya in a tone of such infinite patience and kindness that Saryon's eyes filled with tears again, "the Almin in his wisdom knows of your crime and, in his mercy, he forgives you. Compared to our Father, I am but a poor mortal. But I, too, would share his knowledge of the crime that I may share in its forgiveness. Explain to me what led you down this dark path."

Poor Saryon was so completely overcome that for several moments he could not speak. Vanya waited, sipping his sherry with that outward look of fatherly benevolence upon his face and the inner, unseen smile of satisfaction. Finally, the young Deacon began to talk. His words came haltingly, limping at first, as his eyes sought the floor. Then, as he glanced up now and then to see the effect of what he believed were confessions of a soul so blackened and corrupt as to be lost forever and saw only compassion and understanding, he became more relaxed. His sins gushed forth in a torrent.

"I don't know what made me do it, Holiness!" he cried out helplessly. "I used to be so happy, so content here."

"I think you know. Now you must admit it to yourself," Vanya said placidly.

Saryon hesitated. "Yes, perhaps I do know. Forgive me, Holiness, but lately, I've felt—" He faltered, as though unwilling to speak.

"Bored?" suggested Vanya.

The young man flushed, shaking his head. "No. Yes. Perhaps. The duties are so simple . . ." He made an impatient move with his hand. "I have learned all the skills to be a catalyst to any type of magi. Yes"—this in response to Vanya's skeptical look—"I'm not boasting. Not only that, but I have developed new mathematical formulas to take the place of centuries-old, traditional, clumsy calculations. I suppose that should have satisfied me, but it didn't. It left me hungrier." Forgetting himself in his words, Saryon talked faster and faster, finally standing up and pacing about the room, gesturing with his hands. "I started working on formulas that could pave the way for new marvels, magics never before dreamed of by man! In my research, I delved deeper and deeper into the libraries of the Font. Finally, in a remote part of the Library, I came across the Chamber of the Ninth Mystery.

"Can you imagine what I felt? No" — Saryon glanced at the Bishop in embarrassment — "how could you, who are goodness personified? I stared at the runes carved above the doorway and a feeling crept over me much akin to the feeling of the Enchantment that we feel every morning on sensing the magic. Only this feeling was not one of light and fulfillment. It was as if the darkness in my soul deepened until it was sucking me inside. I hungered and thirsted and literally shook with desire."

"What did you do?" asked Vanya, fascinated in spite of himself. "Did you enter it then?"

"No. I was too scared. I stood before the chamber, staring at it for I don't know how long." Saryon sighed wearily. "It must have been hours, because I was suddenly aware of an aching in my legs and a feeling of dizziness. I sank into a chair then, terrified, and looked around. What if I had been seen? Surely the forbidden thoughts I was thinking must be plain upon my face! But I was alone."

Unconsciously suiting his actions to his words, Saryon sank back into his chair. "Sitting there, in the Study Room near that forbidden chamber, I knew what it was to be tempted by Evil." His head lowered into his hands. "You see, Holiness, I knew, as surely as I sat in that wooden chair, that I could enter those forbidden doors! Oh, they are guarded and shielded by wards and runes" — he shrugged impatiently — "but they are such simple spells of sealing that anyone with any Life in him at all can easily undo them. It's as if they are guarded in this way as a mere formality, it being simply assumed that no one in his right mind would even want to be near the forbidden texts, let alone read them."

The young man was silent then. His voice dropping, he spoke almost to himself. "Perhaps I'm not in my right mind.

It seems lately that everything I look at is distorted and foggy, as though I'm seeing it through a gauze curtain." Glancing up at Vanya, he shook his head and continued, his voice tinged with bitterness.

"I realized something else in that instant, Holiness. I had not discovered those books by accident." His fist clenched. "No, I had been searching for them, deliberately hunting for them without admitting it to myself. Entire passages of other books I had read came clearly to my mind as I sat there, passages that made reference to books that I was never able to find and assumed must have been destroyed after the Iron Wars. But, when I found that room, I knew differently. They were in there. They had to be. I'd known it all along.

"What did I do?" He laughed hysterically, a laugh that cracked into a sob. "I fled the Library as though pursued by phantoms! Running back to my cell, I cast myself upon the bed and shivered in fear."

"My son, you should have talked to someone," Vanya remonstrated gently. "Do you have so little faith in us?"

Saryon shook his head, impatiently wiping away his tears. "I almost did. The *Theldara* sent for me. But I was afraid." He sighed. "I thought I could manage by myself. I tried to drown this thirst for forbidden knowledge in my work. I sought to cleanse my soul in prayer and obedience to my duties. I never once missed Evening Ritual, after that. I took to exercising with the others in the courtyard, letting myself get so exhausted that I couldn't think.

"Above all, I avoided the Library. Yet not a moment passed — waking or sleeping — but that I did not think of that room and the treasure which lay within.

"I should have known then that I was fast losing my soul." Saryon's words swept him on. "But the ache of my desires was too much. I gave in. Last night, when everyone else had retired to their cells for Resting Time, I slipped out and crept through the corridors until I came to the Library. I didn't know the old Deacon had been posted there to scare off rodents. I don't suppose it would have stopped me had I known, so completely consumed was I by my torment.

"As I had foreseen, undoing the spells of sealing was simple. I could have cast such magic as a child. For a breathless moment I paused on the threshold, savoring the sweet ache of anticipation. Then I entered that forbidden room, my heart beating so that it came near bursting, my body drenched in sweat.

"Have you ever been in there?" Saryon looked at the Bishop, who raised his eyebrows so alarmingly that the young man shrank back. "No, no, I — I suppose not. The books are not assembled neatly or in any sort of order. They're just piled up in stacks as though they had been hurriedly tossed inside by hands eager to cleanse themselves of the contamination. I picked one up, the first one I came to." Saryon's hands twitched. "The elation and fulfillment I felt when I touched the small book made me lose all sense of sight or sound or where I was or what I was doing. I remember only holding it and thinking what wonderful mysteries were about to be revealed, and that my burning pain would burst forth at last and free me from its torment."

"And what was it like?" Bishop Vanya asked very softly.

Saryon smiled wanly. "Dull. Boring. Turning the pages, I grew more and more confused. I understood nothing of it, absolutely nothing! It was filled with crude drawings of strange and senseless devices, containing oblique references to such things as 'wheels' and 'gears' and 'pulleys.'" Sighing, Saryon's head drooped and he whispered in the voice of a disappointed child, "It didn't mention one thing about mathematics."

Vanya's inner smile slipped out upon his lips, but it didn't matter. Saryon wasn't looking at him, the young man was staring at his shoes.

In a lifeless voice, Saryon concluded. "At that moment, the Enforcers came in and . . . everything went black. I — I don't remember anything more until . . . until I found myself in my cell." Exhausted, he sank back into the soft cushions of his chair, his head in his hands.

"What did you do then?"

"Took a bath." Looking up, Saryon saw Vanya's smile and, assuming it was at this statement, added by way of explanation. "I felt so filthy and dirty, I must have bathed twenty times last night."

Bishop Vanya nodded in understanding. "And, no doubt, you spent the night imagining what your punishment might be."

Saryon's head dropped again. "Yes, Holiness, of course," he murmured.

"Undoubtedly you saw yourself sentenced to become one of the Watchers — turned to stone to stand forever on the Border of the land."

"Yes, Holiness," Saryon spoke in a low tone, barely audible. "It is nothing more than I deserve."

"Ah, Brother Saryon, if we were all punished so drastically for seeking knowledge, this would be a land of stone statues — and deservedly so. The search for knowledge is not evil. You sought in the wrong place, that is all. This dreadful knowledge was banished for a reason. It very nearly destroyed our land. But you are not alone. All of us are tempted by Evil at one time or another in our lives. We understand. We do not condemn. You must trust us. You should have come to me or one of the Masters for guidance."

"Yes, Holiness. I am sorry."

"As for your punishment, it has already been inflicted."

Astonished, Saryon raised his head.

Vanya smiled gently, his voice pleasant. "My son, you have suffered far more this night than your mild crime merited. I would not add to it for the world. No, in fact, I am going to offer you something to try in some small way to make up for what I fear is my share in your crime."

"Holiness!" Saryon's face flushed, then went white. "Your share? No! I am the one —"

Vanya waved a deprecating hand. "No, no. I have not been open with you young people. It is obvious that you consider me unapproachable. The same is true, I begin to see, with the other members of the hierarchy. We will try to remedy that. But, for now, you need a change of scenery to brush these dusty cobwebs from your mind. Therefore, Deacon Saryon," said Bishop Vanya, "I would like to take you with me to Merilon, to assist in the Testing of the Royal Child, whose birth is expected to take place any day now. What do you say to that?"

The young man could not respond, being literally struck dumb. This was an honor for which the members of the Order had been politically vying and shuffling for months — ever since it was announced that the Empress was finally with child. Being absorbed in his studies and consumed by his lust for forbidden knowledge, Saryon had paid little attention to the talk. He was outside the circle of the popular young men and women in the seminary anyway and figured he would not have been asked to go, even if he had wanted it.

Seeing the young man's befuddlement, and realizing that it would take him some moments to work this out in his mind, Vanya talked of the beauties of the royal city and discussed the political ramifications of the birth until Saryon eventually was able to at least mutter an intelligible remark or two. The Bishop understood what the young man was thinking. Having expected to be cast out in darkness and disgrace, he was suddenly to be taken to the city of beauty and delight and presented to the Royal Court. His fortune would be made — not a doubt of it.

A Royal Child had not been born in years, the Empress having assumed the throne following the death of her brother, who himself was childless. The celebrations the city of Merilon was planning were to be spectacular beyond belief. As an honored and revered member of Bishop Vanya's staff, as well as related — if distantly — to the Empress on his mother's side, Saryon would be feted and entertained by the wealthiest nobles in the land. Undoubtedly, he would be invited by some noble family to be House Catalyst — there were several vacancies that needed filling. He would be set for life.

And, best of all, said Bishop Vanya to himself as he graciously walked the still-dazed Saryon to the door, the young man would be living in Merilon. He would not be returning to the Font for a long, long time — if ever.

6

Merilon

Enchanted city of dreams . . . Merilon. Named for the great wizard who led his people to this distant world. He looked upon it with eyes that had seen centuries pass, chose this place for his tomb, and now lies bound by the Last Enchantment in the glade he loved.

Merilon. Its crystal cathedral and palaces sparkle like tears frozen on the face of the blue sky.

Merilon. Two cities; one built on marble platforms constrained by magic to float in the air like heavy clouds that have been tamed and molded by the hands of man. Known as City Above, it casts perpetual, rosy-hued twilight upon City Below.

Merilon. Surrounded by a sphere of magic, its decorative snow falls beneath a hot summer sun, its balmy breezes perfume chill and brittle winter air.

Merilon. Can any visitor, riding upward in the gilded carriages drawn by steeds of fur and feather created out of wonder and delight, look upon this enchanted city without feeling his heart swell until its overflow of pride and love must trickle down his own face?

Certainly not Saryon. Sitting in the carriage created to resemble half a walnut shell made of gold and silver and drawn by a fanciful, winged squirrel, he looked at the wonders around him and could barely see them for his tears. This was nothing for him to be ashamed of, however. Most of the other catalysts in Bishop Vanya's retinue were affected in a similar manner, the exception being the cynical Dulchase. Having been born and raised in Merilon, he had seen it all before and now he sat in the carriage gazing upon the wonders with a bored air much envied by his fellows.

For Saryon, the tears he shed were both a relief and a blessing. The last few days in the Font had not been easy for him. Bishop Vanya had succeeded in keeping the matter of the young man's transgression quiet, and he had impressed upon Saryon that it was in the Church's best interest for him to keep silent upon the subject as well. Saryon was a very poor dissembler however. His guilt made him feel as though the words *Ninth Mystery* were blazing above his head in letters of fire for everyone to see. So wretched was he, despite Vanya's kind words, that he must sooner or later have blurted out his guilt to the first person who mentioned "Library" to him. The only thing that saved him and kept him too occupied to think of his crime was the flurry of activity into which he was plunged getting ready for this journey.

Precisely what Vanya had foreseen.

The Bishop himself, riding ahead of his retinue in the Cathedral's carriage that was formed of leaves of burnished gold and drawn by two birds of bright red plumage, was reflecting on this and wondering idly how his young sinner was getting along as he gazed about the city. Vanya, too, was unimpressed by the beauties of Merilon. He had seen it all many, many times.

The Bishop's bored gaze darted over the crystal walls of the three Guild Houses that could been seen, standing each upon its matching marble platform that together were known as the Three Sisters. He glanced once at the Inn of the Silken Dragon, so called because its crystal walls were decorated with a series of over five hundred fabulous tapestries, one for each room, which, when lowered simultaneously in the evening, formed the picture of a dragon whose colors flamed against the sky like a rainbow. He yawned when driven past the houses of the nobility, whose crystal walls shone with curtains of roses, or silks, or swirling fogs. Upon glancing up into the sky at the Royal Palace that shown above the city like a star, however, Bishop Vanya sighed. It was not a sigh of wonder and awe, such as his retinue was sighing behind him. It was a sigh of worry and of care, or perhaps exasperation.

The only building in all of the upper levels of Merilon that captured the Bishop's attention completely was the building to which the carriages were heading — the Cathedral of Merilon. Thirty years in the shaping, its crystal spires and buttresses burned like flame in the light of the sun, whose ordinary natural yellowish color had been changed to brilliant red and fiery gold this day by the practitioners of the Shadow Mystery, the illusionists, for the enjoyment of the populace. Vanya's attention was caught, not by the shimmering beauty of the Cathedral — the sight of which filled his followers with reverence — but by a flaw he noticed in the building.

One of the living gargoyles had shifted slightly in its attitude and was now facing the wrong direction. The Bishop mentioned this to the Cardinal sitting beside him, who appeared properly shocked. The secretary, sitting opposite the Bishop, made a mental note and mentioned it to the Regional Cardinal, who directed the affairs of the Church in Merilon and its surrounding environs and who now stood, resplendent in his green robes with their gold and silver trim, upon the crystal stairs waiting to greet his Bishop. Glancing upward, the Regional Cardinal paled. Two novitiates were immediately sent to deal with the offending gargoyle.

The infraction corrected, the Bishop and his retinue entered the Cathedral, accompanied by the cheers of people lining the bridges that connected the marble platforms of Merilon with cobweb strands of silver and gold. The Bishop paused to invoke a blessing upon the crowd, who hushed in reverence. Then Vanya and his retinue disappeared inside the Cathedral and the crowd dispersed to continue their merriment.

The city of Merilon, both Above and Below, was jammed with people. Merilon had not known such excitement since the coronation. Nobles from outlying districts who had relations in the city honored them with their presence. Nobles not so fortunate stayed in the Inn. From the tip of its nose to the end of its tail, the Silken Dragon was filled to capacity. The *Pron-alban* and the *Quin-alban*, craftsmen and conjurers, had been working overtime to add on guest rooms to the wealthy dwellings of Merilon's best families. Thus the Guild Houses were alive with unusual activity, many of their members having journeyed from far-distant places to assist with the extra work.

Day-to-day life in Merilon had practically come to a standstill as everyone prepared for the grandest holiday and celebration to be held in the city's history. The air was filled with the sounds of music being practiced in the gardens and courtyards, or with the sounds of poetry being rehearsed by the players in the theaters, or with the cries of the merchants selling their wares, or with the mysterious shrouds of smoke that hid the artists' work until it could be unveiled upon the grand occasion.

But no matter how busy, the eyes of every person in Merilon looked constantly upward, gazing at the Royal Castle that glittered so serenely in the burning sun. It would become a perfect rainbow of colored silks when the great event was at hand, when the Royal Child was born.

When that event occurred, the holiday would be declared and the city of Merilon would, for two weeks, dance and sing and glitter and revel and drink and eat itself into a state of bliss.

Within the Cathedral itself, all was quiet and cool and dark as the sun sank down behind the mountains and night covered Merilon with its velvet wings. For an instant, an evening star gleaming above the tip of a spire was the only light. But it faded almost immediately when the rest of the city burst into a blaze of flame and color. Only the Cathedral remained serenely dark; and, oddly enough, thought Saryon, staring up through the transparent crystal ceiling to where the castle floated in the sky above, there were no lights in the Royal Palace either.

But perhaps it was not so odd that the castle was dark. Saryon recalled hearing his mother mention that the Empress was expected to have a difficult time with this birth, her health being delicate and fragile at the best of times. Undoubtedly the normal routine of gay, glittering palace life had been curtailed.

Saryon's gaze returned to the city that was more beautiful than anything he had ever imagined, and he was momentarily sorry he hadn't gone out with Dulchase and the others to see the sights. On reflection, however, he felt content to stay where he was, surrounded by a comfortable darkness, listening to the sweet music of the novitiates practicing a celebratory *Te Deum*. He would go out tomorrow night, he decided, as he made his way to the guest quarters in the Abbey.

Neither Saryon nor any of the others in the Cathedral went out the next night, however. They had just finished the evening meal when Bishop Vanya received an urgent summons to the Palace, along with several of the *Sharak-Li*, the catalysts who work with the Healers. The Bishop left immediately, his round face stern and cold.

No one in the Cathedral slept that night. Everyone from the youngest novitiate to the Cardinal of the Realm remained awake to offer their prayers to the Almin. Above them, the Royal Palace was now ablaze with lights, their warmth a striking contrast to the cold stars. By dawn, no word had been received. As the starlight faded, dwindling with the rising of the sun, the catalysts were allowed to leave their prayers to attend to their duties, though the Cardinal exhorted them to be constantly praying to the Almin in their hearts.

Saryon, who had no duties to perform since he was a visitor, spent most of his time wandering the great halls of the Cathedral, looking through the crystal walls with untiring curiosity at the wonders of the city around him. He watched the people float past, their thin robes rippling around their bodies as they went about their daily business. He watched the carriages and their wondrous steeds; he even smiled at the antics of the University students who, knowing a holiday was imminent, were in high spirits.

Could I live here? he asked himself. Could I leave my quiet, studious life and enter into this world of splendor and gaiety? A month ago, I would have said no. I was content. But not now. I could never go into the Inner Library again, not without seeing that sealed chamber with the runes above the door. No, this is much better, he decided. The Bishop was right. I have let myself get too involved with my studies. I have forgotten the world. Now I must be a part of it again and let it be a part of me. I will attend the parties. I will put myself forward. I will do my best to be invited into one of the noble houses.

Pleased with his change of circumstance, Saryon's only misgivings came from being totally unaware of the duties of a House Catalyst in Merilon, and he resolved to discuss this with Deacon Dulchase at his earliest opportunity.

The opportunity did not come soon, however. During the Highhour, both Cardinals were summoned to the Palace and left, looking grave. The rest of the catalysts were called once again to prayer. By now, rumors had reached the street, and soon everyone in Merilon knew that the Empress was in labor and having a difficult time of it. The sounds of music ceased. The atmosphere of merriment was smothered in gloom. People gathered together upon the glittering spans of silver or gold, talking in hushed voices and looking up at the Palace with serious faces. Even the Silken Dragon did not flaunt his colors that day but lurked about in shadows as the weather magi, the *Sif-Hanar*, hid the sun's harsh brilliance beneath a blanket of pearl-gray clouds, more restful to the eye and conducive to prayer and meditation.

Night fell. The lights in the Palace shone with an ominous intensity. The catalysts, once more called to prayer after the evening meal, gathered in the great Cathedral. Kneeling on the marble floor, Saryon nodded as sleep overcame him and, looking up through the crystal ceiling, endeavored to concentrate on those lights to stay awake.

Then, near morning, the bells on the Royal Palace pealed out in triumph. The magical sphere surrounding the city exploded with dazzling flags of fire and of silk. The people of Merilon danced in the streets as word came from the Palace that the Empress had been safely delivered of a son and that both she and the baby were doing well. Saryon rose from the hard floor thankfully and joined the other catalysts in the courtyard of the Cathedral to watch the spectacle but not to join in the merriment. Not yet.

Though the Tests for Life were only a formality, the catalysts would not celebrate the child's birth until it was proven that the child was Alive.

∘   ∘   ∘

It was not the Tests, however, that were occupying Saryon's mind when, ten days after the child's birth, he and Deacon Dulchase descended the marble stairs leading down into one of the subterranean levels of the Cathedral. "So just what are the duties of a Father in one of the noble houses?" Saryon asked.

Dulchase started to answer but, just at that moment, they arrived in an unfamiliar hallway that branched off in three directions. The two Deacons paused, staring about them uncertainly. Finally, Dulchase hailed a passing novitiate.

"Pardon me, Sister," he said, "but we are searching for the room where the Royal Child will be tested. Can you give us direction?"

"I will be honored to escort you, Deacons of the Font," murmured the novitiate, a charming young woman, who, when her eyes went to the tall figure of Saryon, smiled at him shyly and led the way, occasionally glancing behind her at the young Deacon out of the corner of her eye.

Conscious of this, and conscious also of Dulchase's amused grin, Saryon flushed and repeated his earlier question.

"House Catalyst," Dulchase reflected. "So that's what old Vanya's got in mind for you. Didn't think you'd be interested in that sort of life," he added with a sidelong glance of his own at the young Deacon. "I thought all you cared about was mathematics."

Saryon's flush deepened, and he mumbled something confused about the Bishop having decided that he needed to broaden his horizons, realize his potential, that sort of thing.

Dulchase raised an eyebrow as they descended still another staircase, but, though he obviously suspected deeper waters here than were visible on the surface, he did not question the young man further, much to Saryon's relief.

"Be warned, Brother," he said in solemn tones. "The duties of a catalyst in one of the noble houses are strenuous in the extreme. Let's see, how to break this to you gently. You will be awakened some time around midmorning by servants bearing your breakfast on a tray of gold—"

"What about the Ritual of the Dawn?" Saryon interrupted, eyeing Dulchase uncertainly, as though suspecting he were being made the brunt of some joke.

Dulchase's lip curled in a sneer, a habitual expression for the older Deacon who, because of his sharp tongue and irreverent attitude, would probably be a Deacon the rest of his life. He had been brought along in Vanya's retinue only because he knew everyone and everything that lived or occurred in Merilon. "Dawn? Bosh! Dawn comes to Merilon whenever you open your eyes. You'd have the house in an uproar if you rose with the sun. Come to think of it, the sun itself isn't even permitted to rise at dawn. The *Sif-Hanar* see to that. Now, where was I? Oh, yes. Your first order of business is to grant the housemagi their gifts of Life for the day. Then, after resting from that fatiguing chore, which takes you all of five minutes, you are occasionally requested to do the same for the Master or Mistress, should they have any important work to do, such as feeding the peacocks or changing the color of milady's eyes to match her gown. Then, if they have children, you have to educate the little buggers in their catechism and give them sufficient Life so that they may tumble about the house, delighting their parents by wrecking the furniture. After that you may rest until evening when you will escort milord and milady to the Royal Palace, standing by in order to assist milord in creating his usual phantasms that leave the Emperor yawning or to grant Life to milady so that she may win at Swan's Doom or tarok."

"Are you serious?" asked Saryon, rather anxiously.

Looking at him, Dulchase burst out laughing and received a reproving glance from the serious-minded novitiate.

"My dear Saryon, how naive you are! Perhaps old Vanya is right. You do need to get out in the world. I'm exaggerating, but only slightly. Still, it's an ideal life, especially as far as you're concerned."

"It is?"

"Of course. You have all the resources of magic at your fingertips. You can spend the afternoon in the Library at the University here in Merilon, which, by the way, has one of the finest collections in the world on the lost magic, containing some volumes not even available at the Font. Step onto the silver bridge and you're there. Want to pursue some studies with the Guilds or show them your newest equation to cut the time in conjuring up a fainting couch? Step into milord's carriage and have it take you to the Three Sisters. Perhaps you want to see for yourself how milord's crops are doing. The Corridor whisks you to the fields where you can watch the little seeds sprout or whatever those poor wretches of Field Catalysts do. You'll be set for life. Why, you could even marry."

This was so obviously aimed at the novitiate that the girl tossed her head disapprovingly, but she could not refrain from casting another glance at the young Deacon.

"I think I might like it at that," said Saryon after a moment's reflection, "from an academic standpoint, of course," he added hastily.

"Of course," Dulchase replied dryly. "I say, my dear"— this to the novitiate—"you haven't gotten us lost, have you? Or are you leading us into some remote part of the Cathedral to rob us?"

"Deacon!" murmured the novitiate, blushing up to the roots of her curly hair. "It—it's down this corridor, the first room to your right."

Turning, with a last, doe-eyed glance at Saryon, the girl almost ran down the hallway.

"Was that necessary?" muttered Saryon irritably, his eyes following the novitiate.

"Oh, lighten up, boy," returned Dulchase crisply, rubbing his hands. "Lighten up. You'll see what kind of life Merilon offers tonight. At last! We can escape this moldy old tomb! We'll get this little twerp through his Tests, declare to the world that it has a Living Prince, and it's time for us to mingle with the rich and the beautiful. You do know what you're supposed to do, don't you?"

"With the Tests?" Saryon asked, thinking for a moment Dulchase might have been referring to the rich and beautiful. "I hope so," he answered with a sigh. "I've read the ritual until I can say it backwards. You've done this before, haven't you?"

"Hundreds of times, my boy, hundreds. You're responsible for holding the kid, aren't you? Most important thing to remember is to hold him with his little—mmmm . . . you know—pointing toward you, away from the Bishop. That way, if the little bastard urinates, it's on you and not His Holiness."

Fortunately for the shocked Saryon they had arrived outside the room now. Dulchase was forced to silence his cynical tongue and Saryon was spared responding to this last bit of advice that he had found just a bit too irreverent, even for Dulchase.

Entering on the heels of the others of Vanya's staff, the two performed the oblations of cleaning and purifying themselves, then were led by a Deacon of the Cathedral to the chamber where all children born in Merilon are brought for the Tests. Generally, only two catalysts are present. This day, however, there was an illustrious group gathered. So many, in fact, that there was barely enough room left for the two Deacons to squeeze inside the small chamber. In addition to Bishop Vanya, dressed in his finest robes, there were the two Cardinals — Cardinal of the Realm and Cardinal of the Region — and six members of Vanya's staff: four Priests, who would act as witnesses, and Saryon and Dulchase, the two Deacons, who would do the work. In addition, there was the Royal House Catalyst, a Lord, who held the baby in his arms, and the baby himself, who — having just been nursed — was sound asleep.

"Let us pray to the Almin," said Bishop Vanya, bowing his head.

Saryon bowed his head in prayer, but the words fell from his lips unthinkingly. In his mind he was reviewing, once more, the ceremony of the Tests for Life.

Centuries old, said to have been brought from the Dark World, the Tests are quite simple. When the child is ten days old and judged strong enough to withstand the Testing, his parents bring him to the Cathedral — or to whatever place of worship is near them — and give him to the catalysts. The baby is taken into a small chamber sealed off from any outside influences, and the Tests are performed.

First, the child is stripped of his clothes, then placed upon his back in water that has been warmed to his body temperature. The Deacon holding the child releases the babe. A Living child remains afloat upon his back, neither sinking nor rolling over in the water nor kicking — just floating peacefully, calmly — the magical Life within him reacting to preserve his tiny body.

Following this first test, a Deacon brings forward a shining bauble of shimmering, ever-changing colors. He holds it above the child, who is still floating in the water. Though the baby's eyes cannot yet focus, he is aware of the bauble and stretches out his hands toward it. When the Deacon drops the bauble, it drifts gently to the baby as, once again, the magical Life force within the child reacts to the stimulus without and draws the bauble toward him.

Finally, the Deacon lifts the baby out of the water. Holding the babe in his arms, the catalyst cuddles and caresses the baby until the child feels safe and at ease. Then, the other Deacon brings forward a flaming torch. Nearer and nearer the flame comes to the child's skin until — through no action of the catalyst — the torch is brought to a halt as the child's Life force instinctively envelops him in a magical protective shell.

These are the Tests — easily done, quickly ended. It was, as Dulchase had assured Saryon, a mere matter of formality.

"I don't know why they're still performed," Dulchase had grumbled only the night before, "except that it's a convenient way for some poor Field Catalyst to earn a few chickens and a bushel of corn from the peasants. Plus it gives the nobility an excuse to throw another party. Other than that, it's meaningless."

So it was, up until that time.

"Deacon Dulchase, Deacon Saryon, begin the Tests," said Bishop Vanya solemnly.

Stepping forward, Saryon took the baby from the Lord Catalyst of the Royal House. The child was wrapped tightly in a costly blanket made of lamb's wool. Saryon, unaccustomed to handling anything this small and delicate, fumbled as he attempted to divest the baby of his cocoon without waking him. At length, feeling every eye in the chamber watching him impatiently, Saryon held the naked child in his arms and returned the blanket to the Lord Catalyst.

Turning to place the babe in the water, Saryon looked down at the little boy sleeping peacefully in his arms and immediately forgot the eyes watching him. The young catalyst had never held a baby before, and he was captivated by this one. Even Saryon could see that the child was unusually beautiful. Strong and healthy with a mop of fuzzy dark hair, the Prince's skin was alabaster, with a bluish tint around the closed eyes. The tiny fists were curled shut. Touching one gently, Saryon was charmed to notice the perfect little fingernails and toenails. How marvelous, he thought, that the Almin should have taken time to attend to such mundane details in creating this small person.

An impatient cough from Dulchase recalled Saryon to his duties. The older Deacon had removed the seal from the basin containing the warm water. A pleasant, fragrant scent filled the air. One of the novitiates had scattered rose petals on the surface.

Murmuring the ritual prayer that he had been up half the night memorizing, Saryon gently placed the baby in the water. The child's eyes opened at the touch of the liquid upon his skin, but he did not cry.

"That's a brave one," murmured Saryon, smiling at the baby, who was looking around with the thoughtful, slightly puzzled expression of the newborn.

"Release the child," instructed Bishop Vanya formally.

Gently, Saryon removed his hands from the baby's body. The Prince sank like a stone.

Starting slightly, Dulchase stepped forward, but Saryon was there ahead of him. Reaching into the water, he snatched up the baby and hauled him out. Awkwardly holding the dripping-wet child, who was coughing and sputtering and attempting to cry at this rude treatment, Saryon looked around uncertainly.

"Perhaps it was my fault, Holiness," he said hurriedly just as the baby managed to draw a breath and let it out in a shrill scream. "I let go of him too soon . . ."

"Nonsense, Deacon," Vanya said crisply. "Proceed."

It wasn't unusual for a child to fail one of the Tests, particularly if he were unusually strong in one of the Mysteries. A warlock strong in the Fire Mystery, for example, might easily fail the Test of Water.

Recalling this from his reading, Saryon relaxed and held the baby as Deacon Dulchase brought forward the bauble and held it above the child's head. At the sight of the bright toy, the Prince ceased to cry and stretched out his tiny hands in delight. Deacon Dulchase, at a word from Bishop Vanya, dropped the bauble.

The toy struck the Prince on the nose and bounced to the floor amidst a dreadful silence that was immediately shattered by the baby's howl of pain and outrage. A spot of blood appeared on the child's fair skin.

Saryon glanced up fearfully at Dulchase, hoping to see some sign of reassurance. But Dulchase's normally sneering lips were now pressed tightly together, the cynical glint was gone from his eye, and he carefully avoided Saryon's gaze. The young Deacon looked around frantically, only to see his fellows staring at each other in confusion and alarm.

Bishop Vanya whispered something to the Lord Catalyst, who, his face pale and strained, nodded emphatically.

"Repeat the first Test," Vanya ordered.

His hands shaking, Saryon placed the screaming child in the water, then released him. As soon as it was obvious the baby was sinking, Saryon — at a hurried gesture from the Bishop — grabbed him out.

"The Almin help us!" breathed the Lord Catalyst in a trembling voice.

"I think it's too late for that," Vanya replied coldly. "Bring the child here, Saryon," he said, his nervousness apparent in that he forgot to include the formal title "Deacon" in his command. Clumsily attempting to soothe the baby, Saryon hurried to obey and came to stand before the Bishop.

"Give me the torch," Vanya ordered Deacon Dulchase, who, having reluctantly taken it up, was only too happy to release it to his superior.

Grasping the flaming torch, Bishop Vanya thrust it directly into the baby's face. The child shrieked in pain, and Saryon, forgetting himself, caught hold of the Bishop's arm, pushing him away with an angry cry.

No one said a word. Everyone in the chamber could smell singed hair. Everyone could see the red burn mark upon the baby's temple.

Trembling, clutching the injured child to his chest, Saryon turned away from the pale faces and the horror-filled, staring eyes. Patting the child, who was now screaming in a hysterical frenzy, Saryon's first incoherent thought was that he had committed another sin. He had dared touch the body of his superior without permission — and, worse, he had actually shoved him in anger. The young Deacon cringed, expecting a sharp reprimand. But it did not come. Glancing over his shoulder at Bishop Vanya's face, Saryon saw why.

The Bishop probably never even knew Saryon had touched him. He was staring at the baby, his heavy face ashen, his eyes wide. The Lord Catalyst wrung his hands and trembled visibly while the Cardinals stood by, looking at each other helplessly.

The Prince, meanwhile, was screaming with the pain of the burn so violently that he was near strangling. Not knowing what else to do and realizing that the baby's crying was shredding the taut nerves of everyone in the room, Saryon tried desperately to hush the child. At length he succeeded, more because the baby cried himself into a state of exhaustion than because the young catalyst possessed any skill in nursing. Silence settled upon the room like a dank fog, broken only now and then by the baby's hiccup.

Then Bishop Vanya spoke. "Such a thing," he whispered, "has never happened in all the years of history, even back before the Iron Wars."

The awe in his voice was plain, something Saryon could understand. It matched his own. But there was another note in Vanya's voice that made Saryon shudder — a note he had never heard in the Bishop's voice before — a note of fear.

Sighing and removing the heavy miter, Vanya passed a trembling hand over his tonsured head. With the removal of the miter, he seemed to remove all the aura of mystique and majesty that surrounded him and Saryon, patting the baby's back, saw a paunchy, middle-aged man who looked extremely fatigued and scared. This frightened Saryon more than anything and, from the looks on the faces of the others, he wasn't the only one who received this impression.

"What I am about to tell you to do, you must do without question," Vanya said in a thick voice, his eyes on the miter that he held in his hands. Absently he stroked the gold trim with shaking fingers. "I could give you the reason — No." Vanya looked up, his gaze stern and cold. "No, I vowed to keep silent. I cannot break my vow. You will obey me. You will not question. Understand that I take upon myself full responsibility for what I require you to do."

He paused a moment then, with a quavering breath, began to pray silently.

Holding the hiccuping child in his arms, Saryon glanced at the others to see if they understood. He didn't. He'd never heard of a child failing the Testing. What was coming? What terrible thing was the Bishop going to ask them to do? His gaze went back to Vanya. Everyone in the room was staring at the Bishop, waiting for him to use his magic to save them. It was as if each of them had opened a conduit to Vanya, not to give him Life, but to take Life from him.

Perhaps this very dependence gave him strength, for the Bishop straightened and raised his head. His lips pursed. His eyes grew abstract and he frowned, still considering. Then, apparently reaching a decision, his brow cleared, his face resumed its normal cool composure. He replaced the miter, and the Bishop of the Realm stood before his people once again.

Bishop Vanya turned to Saryon. "Take the child to the nursery directly," he ordered. "Do not take him to his mother. I will speak to the Empress myself and prepare her. It will be easier for her in the long run if we make this separation clean and swift."

The Lord Catalyst made a kind of sound here, a sort of choked wail. But Bishop Vanya, his paunchy face freezing as if the chill silence in the room had seeped into his blood, ignored him. Speaking in an emotionless voice, he continued, "From this hour on, the child is to be given no food, no water. He is not to be held. He is Dead."

The Bishop went on to say something else, but Saryon did not hear. The baby was hiccuping against his shoulder; his best ceremonial robes were wet with the child's tears. Having managed to capture one fist, the Prince was sucking on it noisily, staring at Saryon with wide, unfocused eyes. The Deacon could feel the tiny body quiver as, now and then, a soft sob shook it.

Saryon stared down at the child, his thoughts confused, his heart aching. He'd heard somewhere that all babies are born with blue eyes, but this child's eyes were a dark, cloudy blue. Did he look like his mother, who was reputed to be extraordinarily beautiful? The Empress had brown eyes, Saryon recalled hearing. And she had long blue-black hair, so luxuriant that she needed no magic to make it glisten like a raven's wing. Thinking of this and looking at the fuzzy head of dark hair, Saryon saw that the skin of the baby's temple was beginning to blister. Reflexively he reached to touch it, his lips forming the words of the healing prayer that would enhance the healing Life of the baby's own body. Then Saryon stopped, remembering. This child had no healing Life within his body. No Life stirred there at all.

The young Deacon held a corpse in his arms.

The Prince drew a deep, sudden, shaking breath. He seemed about to cry, but he continued sucking on his fist and this appeared to satisfy him. Snuggling against Saryon, he stared at him with those large, black-lashed eyes.

From this moment on, Saryon thought, his heart constricting in pain, I will be the last person to hold him, to pat his back, to run fingers over the tiny, silky-haired head. Swift tears stung his eyes, and he looked around helplessly, silently pleading with one of the others to take this burden from him. No one did. No one even met his gaze except Bishop Vanya, who frowned, seeing his orders not being obeyed.

Saryon opened his lips to speak, to question this cruel decision, but his voice caught in his throat. Vanya had said they must obey without knowing why. The Bishop would take upon himself the responsibility. Would the pleas of a Deacon move him? A Deacon already in disgrace? Not likely. There was nothing for Saryon to do but bow and leave the room, still awkwardly patting the Prince's back in a manner that seemed to soothe him. Once in the corridor, however, the young Deacon had no idea where he was going in the immense Cathedral. All he knew was that, somehow, he had to get to the Royal Palace. At the end of the hall, Saryon caught a glimpse of a dark shadow, an Enforcer. Saryon hesitated. The warlock could direct him to the Palace. He could send him there, in fact, using his magic.

Looking at the black-robed figure, Saryon shuddered and, turning, walked hurriedly in the opposite direction. I will find my own way to the Royal Palace, he thought with swift, frustrated anger. At least, if I walk, I can offer this poor child what comfort I can before . . . before . . .

The last thing Saryon heard as he left the corridor was Bishop Vanya's voice.

"Tomorrow morning, the Emperor and the Empress will make public their agreement that the child is Dead. I will take the baby to the Font. There, tomorrow afternoon, the Deathwatch will begin. I hope, for the sake of us all, that it passes swiftly."

For the sake of us all.

The next day, Deacon Saryon stood in the lovely Cathedral of Merilon, listening to the wailing of the dead child and the whispering of his plans and hopes and visions and dreams as they bade him good-bye.

There would be no celebrations in Merilon now, no introductions to noble houses. The people were in a daze. Gala parties ceased abruptly as the news spread. The *Sif-Hanar* shrouded the city in a gray fog. The players and artisans left town and the students were herded back into the University. The nobles flitted through the ghostly atmosphere, going from house to house, talking in hushed tones and endeavoring to find someone who remembered the proper form for observing the somber Hours of the Deathwatch. Few knew how such things should be conducted. It had been years since a Royal Child had even been born; no one could recall having heard of one dying.

Bishop Vanya, of course, had all the information at his fingertips, and eventually the word went forth. By the time Saryon was standing in the Cathedral, robed in his *Weeping Blue*, the entire city had undergone a change — the *Pron-alban*, the craftsmen, and the *Quin-alban*, the conjurers, having worked feverishly all night.

The gray fog remained over the city and deepened until the sun's rays could not penetrate the magical shroud that covered the deathly silent streets and drifted up among the rose-hued marble platforms. The gay colors that had decorated the glittering crystal walls of the dwellings vanished, replaced by tapestries of mournful gray, making it look as though the fog had been given shape and form and substance. Even the great Silken Dragon fled, creeping into his

lair — so parents told their children — to mourn the Dead
Prince.

The streets were silent and empty. Those not in attendance upon the grieving Royal Family were confined to their
homes, ostensibly adding their prayers to those of their
neighbors that the Deathwatch be swiftly ended. But, in
many of these homes, the prayers of the young mothers fell
from pale, trembling lips as they held their own children
close, while those expecting children placed their hands upon
their swollen bodies and could not make their lips form the
words of the prayers at all.

When the ceremony had been completed, the baby was
taken away. The Deathwatch began.

Within five days, word came back that all was ended.

After that time, more children of the noble houses of
Merilon failed their Testing, though none so drastically as the
Prince. Most of these babies were taken to the Font, where
the Deathwatch was performed.

Most, but not all.

Saryon, at Vanya's request, stayed in Merilon to work in
the Cathedral there. Part of his responsibilities included the
Testing of these children. At first he so hated it that he
thought he might rebel and demand a new assignment. Anything seemed better — even becoming a Field Catalyst. But it
was not in Saryon's nature to openly rebel and, after a time,
he grew resigned to his work, if not hardened.

Saryon could see the reasoning behind the destruction of
these children. It was expounded by the Bishop, in fact,
when the Test failures began to occur more and more frequently. People were confused and frightened and starting to
mutter darkly against the catalysts, who, meanwhile, were
delving into every conceivable source — even ancient ones —
searching for answers to their perplexing questions.

Why was this happening? How could it be stopped? And
why, in particular, was it happening only to the nobility? For,
it was soon discovered, the common city dwellers as well as
the peasants in the fields and villages were bearing healthy,
living children. The people of Merilon demanded answers,

forcing Bishop Vanya to deliver a sermon in the Cathedral, designed to calm the populace.

"These unfortunate children are not children at all," the Bishop cried earnestly, his hands clenched in his passionate intensity, his words echoing from the vaulting crystal ceiling. "They are weeds in the garden of our Life! We must uproot them and wither them, as the Field Magi wither the weeds in field, or they will soon choke out the magic within the world."

This dire prediction has its intended effect. After that, most parents accepted the will of the Almin and consigned their Dead into the hands of the catalysts. But some parents rebelled. In secret, they tested the children themselves and, if the baby failed, they hid the child until it could be smuggled out of the city. The catalysts knew of this, but there was nothing they could do except keep these occurrences quiet, so that they did not unduly alarm the populace.

And so, in increasing numbers, the Dead walked the land, Saryon recorded one night in his journal. *And our fears grew.*

7

Anja

The overseer hovered above the ground at the edge of the field, keeping his eyes upon the dozen or so magi flitting among the crops like drab butterflies. Up and down among the rows of beans they fluttered, their plain brown clothing standing out against the bright green of the bean plants. Dipping down, they withered weeds with a touch of their hands or gave a renewed burst of Life to a straggling plant or gently removed some predatory bug and sent it upon its way.

Nodding in satisfaction, the overseer transferred his gaze to the next field, where other magi were trudging through freshly turned soil. A crop had been harvested from that field last week and these magi were gleaning the last vestiges of grain. Then the field would be allowed to rest before the magi returned and, using the magic force within them, parted the soil in neat rows with a gesture of their hands, preparing the soil for planting.

Everything was proceeding well. The overseer would have been surprised if it hadn't. Walren was a small Field

Magi settlement, as most went. Part of the Duke of Nord-shire's holdings, it was a relatively new settlement, having been established about one hundred years ago when a terri-ble thunderstorm (caused by two warring groups of *Sif-Hanar*) started a fire that effectively cleared the land and left dead wood enough for homes. The Duke immediately took advantage of the situation, ordering a hundred or so of his peasants to remove to the settlement that was on the border of the Outlands, finish clearing, and then plant the land. They were far from the walls of the city, far from other settle-ments. Most of the magi working here had been born here and would undoubtedly die here. There was no grumbling or talk of rebellion, as there had been in some villages the over-seer had heard about.

Movement caught the overseer's eye. He immediately quit lounging and assumed a stern, businesslike air when he saw the Field Catalyst slogging through the bean field, com-ing toward him.

In Field Magi settlements, the catalyst works as hard or harder than the magi themselves. Field Magi are allowed only enough of the catalyst's transference of magical Life force to work efficiently, the reason for this being that magi have the ability to store this Life force within them and use it whenever they need. Because of certain signs of discontent and restlessness among the Field Magi from time to time, it is considered best to leave them as weak as possible. Therefore, the Field Catalyst is forced to move among the magi and restore their magical energies almost hourly — one reason why the job is abhorred among the catalysts and generally assigned to those of low standing or to those who had com-mitted some infraction of the rules of the Order.

Even as the catalyst walked through the field, his shoes — the sign of his calling — covered with mud, a magus dipped down to the earth and did not rise up again. Seeing the woman's hand lift into the air, the overseer caught the cata-lyst's attention, jerking his thumb in the direction of the spent magus.

"Call a rest," groaned the catalyst, plopping himself down upon the ground. Yanking off his mud-caked shoes, he began to rub his feet, not without first casting a bitter, envious glance at the bare feet of the overseer. Although brown from the sun, the man's feet were still smooth, the toes straight and widely separated — the sign of those who travel the world on the wings of magic.

"Rest!" bellowed the overseer, and the magi dropped from the air like dead moths to lie among the shade of the bean plants or drifted prone upon the air currents, closing their eyes against the bright sun.

"Now, what have we here?" the overseer muttered, his attention being drawn away from the field to a figure that had appeared on the roadway leading through the woods to the flat farmland. The catalyst, noting with dismay that he had a blister, lifted his head wearily to follow the overseer's gaze.

The figure approaching them was a woman. She was obviously a magus, by her clothing, yet she was walking, which meant that she had spent nearly all her magical Life force. Upon her back, she carried a burden — a bundle of some sort, probably clothing, the overseer judged, examining the woman attentively. This was another sign her Life force was weak, for magi rarely carried anything.

The overseer might have assumed the woman was a Field Magus, except that her clothes were a strange, vibrant color of green, not the brown, drab colors of those who tilled the soil.

"A noble lady," murmured the catalyst, hastily dragging on his shoes again.

"Aye," grumbled the overseer, scowling. This was out of the ordinary and the overseer hated anything out of the ordinary. It almost certainly meant trouble.

The woman was closer to them now, so close she heard their voices. Raising her head, she looked straight at them and quite suddenly, stopped walking. The overseer saw her sunburned face twist in haughty pride, then — with what must have been a supreme effort — the woman slowly rose up off the ground and floated toward the men in genteel fashion. The overseer glanced at the catalyst, who raised his eyebrows as the woman drifted, rather unsteadily, over the fields until she came to rest before them. Then, with a negligent air, making it appear as if she did this through choice, not because she lacked strength to continue on, the woman settled gently to the ground and stood gazing at them proudly.

"Milady," said the overseer, bobbing his head in a kind of bow, but not doffing his hat as was proper. Now that she was closer, he could see that the woman's dress, though rich and made of fine quality fabric, was worn and tattered. The hem had been dragged through the mud and muck of the roadside, there was a torn place on the skirt. Her bare feet were cut and bleeding.

"Is Your Ladyship lost or in need of aid . . . ?" faltered the catalyst, somewhat confused by the woman's shabby appearance and the fierce, defiant expression on her dirt-streaked face.

"I am neither," the woman answered in a low, tight voice. Her gaze darting from one to the other of them; she lifted her chin. "I am in need of work."

The catalyst opened his mouth to refuse, but at that moment the overseer coughed and made a slight gesture with his hand, pointing to the bundle on the woman's back. Looking where indicated, the catalyst swallowed his words. The bundle had moved. Two dark brown eyes stared out at him from above the woman's shoulder.

A baby.

The catalyst and the overseer exchanged glances.

"Where do you come from, milady?" asked the overseer, feeling it was up to him to take charge.

But the catalyst struck in. "And where is the babe's father?" This asked in a severe tone, as befitted a member of the clergy.

The woman appeared undaunted by either question. Her lip curled with a sneer, and, when she spoke, it was to the overseer, not to the catalyst. "I come from yonder." She indicated the direction of Merilon by a nod of her head. "As for the babe's father — my husband" — she said this with emphasis — "is dead. He defied the Emperor and was sent Beyond."

Both men exchanged glances again. They knew she was lying — no one had been sent Beyond in a year — but there was such a strange, wild glint in the woman's eyes that each man was wary of challenging her.

"Well?" she said abruptly, shifting the position of the baby that was swaddled in the bundle on her back. "Do I get work or not?"

"Have you sought aid of the Church, milady?" the catalyst asked. "I am certain —"

To his astonishment, the woman spit on the ground at his feet.

"My babe and I would starve, *will* starve, before I accept a crust from the hands of such as you." With a scathing glance at the catalyst, she turned her back upon him and faced the overseer. "Do you need another field hand?" she asked in her low, husky voice. "I am strong. I will work hard."

The overseer cleared his throat uncomfortably. He could see the baby peering out from the bundle, staring at him with wide, dark eyes. What should he do? Certainly nothing like this had ever come up before — a noblewoman seeking work as an ordinary field hand!

The overseer flicked a glance at the catalyst, though he knew he could expect no help from that quarter. Technically, the overseer, as Master Magus, was in charge of the settlement, and though the Church might question his decisions, it would never question his authority to make them. But now the overseer was in a tough spot. He had no liking for this woman. Indeed, he felt a certain revulsion as he looked at her and her baby. At best, it was probably an illegal mating — there were certain unscrupulous catalysts who would perform such a thing if paid enough. At worst, it was a rutting, the result of the abhorrent joining of male and female bodies. Or perhaps the child was Dead, he had heard rumors that such babies were being smuggled out of Merilon. His inclination was to send this woman and her child away.

But to do so, he knew, was to send them to certain death.

Seeing the overseer hesitate, the catalyst frowned and trudged over to stand beneath where the overseer floated in the air. Irritably motioning the overseer to come down to his level, the catalyst muttered, "I can't believe you're really considering this! She's obviously a . . . well . . . you know. . . ." The catalyst flushed in embarrassment, seeing the overseer leer, and hurried on. "Tell her to be on her way. Or, better still, send for the Enforcers —"

The overseer scowled. "I don't need the *Duuk-tsarith* to tell me how to manage my settlement. And what would you have me do, send her and the babe into the Outland? This is the last settlement this side of the river. You want to try to sleep nights, thinking about what'll happen to 'em out there?" He glanced back at the woman. She was young, probably not more than twenty. Once she might have been pretty, but now her proud face was marked with lines of anger and hatred. Her body was far too thin — the dress hung on her spare frame.

The catalyst indicated, from his sour expression, that he would take his chances on missing a few nights' sleep to be rid of this female. This helped make up the overseer's mind.

"Very well, milady," the overseer said grudgingly, affecting to ignore the catalyst's look of shocked disapproval. "I can use another hand. You'll be given a dwelling place — expense of His Lordship — a bit of ground to do with as you please, and a share in the crops. Be in the fields at dawn, leave at dark. Rest midday. Marm Huspeth'll watch the babe —"

"The baby stays with me," the woman informed him coldly, hitching up the straps of the bundle on her back. "I'll carry him in this while I work, to leave my hands free."

The overseer shook his head. "I expect a full day's work from you —"

"You'll get it," the woman interrupted, drawing herself up to her full height. "Do I start now?

Looking at her wan, pale face, the overseer shifted uncomfortably. "Naw," he said gruffly. "Get yourself and the babe settled. The cottage there at the end, near the trees, is vacant. At least go to Marm. She'll fix you some food —"

"I don't take handouts," the woman said and started to leave.

"Hey, what's yer name?" asked the overseer.

Stopping, the woman glanced back over her shoulder. "Anja."

"And the babe?"

"Joram."

"Has he been Tested and blessed in accordance with the laws of the Church?" asked the catalyst sternly, determined to try to salvage some of his lost dignity. But the attempt failed. Spinning around, the woman faced him directly for the first time, and the look in her glittering eyes was so strange, so mocking, and so wild that the catalyst involuntarily fell back a step before her.

"Oh, yes," Anja whispered. "He has been through the ceremony of the Testing and he has received the Church's blessing, you may be sure!"

With that, she began to laugh such eerie, shrill laughter that the catalyst flashed the overseer a look of smug satisfaction. If it hadn't been for that look, the overseer might have rescinded his decision and sent the woman on her way. He, too, heard the tinge of madness in that laughter. But he'd be damned before he'd back down in front of this weak-eyed, bald little man who'd been an irritant ever since he'd arrived a month ago.

"What are you all staring at," he shouted to the Field Magi, who had been watching the proceedings with interest, eager for anything that relieved the daily boredom and drudgery of their lives. "Rest is over. Back to work. Father Tolban, grant them Life," he said to the catalyst, who, with the self-conscious air of one who has been proven right, sniffed and began to chant the ritual.

Flashing a triumphant grin at the overseer, as if they shared some joke known only to the two of them, the woman turned and trudged off toward the wretched little shack that stood far apart from the others of the settlement, her fine green gown dragging in the dirt, catching on brambles, snagging in bushes.

The overseer was to come to know that dress well. Six years later, Anja still wore its tattered remnants.

8

The Borderlands

Joram knew he was different from the others in the settlement. It was something it seemed he had always known, just as he knew his name or his mother's name or her touch. But the reason for this difference puzzled the six-year-old.

"Why won't you let me play with the children?" Joram would ask during the evenings when he was allowed outside their dwelling to exercise by himself under Anja's strict supervision.

"Because you are different," Anja would reply coldly.

Or, "Why must I learn to read?" Joram would ask. "The other children don't have to."

"Because you are different from the other children," Anja would answer him.

Different. Different. Different. The word loomed large in Joram's mind, like the words Anja made him copy laboriously on his slate. It was because of The Difference that he was kept sealed inside the shack where they lived whenever Anja went to the fields. It was because of The Difference that he and Anja kept apart from the other Field Magi, never joining in their small holidays or the brief eventide talks before the early bedtime.

"Why am I different?" Joram asked petulantly one day, watching the other children playing in the dirt street. "I don't want to be different."

"May the Almin forgive you your foolish tongue," Anja snapped, casting the children outside a look of scorn. "You are as far above those as the moon is above this wretched ground we trod."

Joram glanced up above into the evening sky where the pale moon hung in the darkness, aloof from the world and the dim, twilight stars around it.

"But the moon is cold and alone, Anja," Joram observed.

"All the better for it, child. There is nothing that can hurt it!" Anja responded. Kneeling down beside her son, she took him in her arms and hugged him fiercely. "Be alone like the moon and there is nothing that can hurt you!"

Well, that was a reason, certainly, but it wasn't a very good reason, Joram thought. He had a great deal of time to think, being by himself all day. So he kept his eyes and ears open, spying on his mother, searching for The Difference. Once, he thought he might have found it.

"What do *you* want, Catalyst?" Anja demanded ungraciously, flinging open the door at the sound of a knock one morning before work began.

Father Tolban attempted to keep a smile upon his lips, but it was a strained, tight-lipped smile. "Sun arise, Anja. May the Almin's blessing be with you this day."

"If it is, it will be without your help," Anja retorted. "I ask again, Catalyst, what do you want? Be quick. I must get to the fields."

"I came to discuss—" the catalyst began formally but, starting to wilt beneath Anja's icy gaze, he lost his carefully planned statement and stammered in a rush. "How old is your— is Joram?"

Still asleep in the half-light of dawn, the boy lay huddled in patched blankets on a cot in the corner. "He is six," Anja answered defiantly, as though daring Father Tolban to challenge her.

The catalyst nodded and tried to regain his composure. "Just so," he said with an attempt at pleasantry. "That is the age he should begin his education. I meet with the children during Highhour, you know. Let me . . . That is . . ."

His voice trailed off, his smile and his words both slowly withering in the chill of Anja's sardonic sneer.

"I'll see to his education, not you, Catalyst! He is of noble blood, after all," she added angrily, as Father Tolban seemed about to protest. "He will be educated as befits one of noble blood, not as one of your ham-fisted peasants!"

With that, she brushed past him, sealing shut the door to the shack. Made of tree branches, the door, like all the doors in the village, was originally designed in the shape of welcoming hands. But the unkempt, untrimmed branches of Anja's door made it look more like grasping, skeletal claws. Giving the catalyst a final, suspicious glance, Anja surrounded the shack with the magical aura of protection that left her so drained of energy each morning she was forced to walk to the fields instead of float, as did the other magi.

Inside, Joram raised his head from the blankets cautiously. The catalyst had not left yet. He could hear the man shuffling about outside, then other footsteps approaching.

"You heard?" Father Tolban asked bitterly.

"Best leave her be," advised the overseer. "And the kid, too."

"But he should be educated . . ."

"Bah!" The overseer snorted. "So the brat doesn't know his catechism? As long as he's ready for the fields when he's eight, it doesn't matter to me whether or not he can recite the Nine Mysteries."

"If you could speak to her . . ."

"Her? I'd sooner speak to a centaur. You want the kid, you snatch him from her claws."

"Perhaps you're right," Father Tolban muttered hastily. "I don't suppose it matters much after all . . ."

The two walked away.

So that was part of The Difference, Joram thought. I am of noble blood, whatever that means.

But there was something else. There had to be. For, as Joram grew older, he began to realize that this Difference kept him apart from everyone — including his mother. He could see it sometimes in the way she looked at him when he performed some ordinary task, such as lifting an object in his hands or walking across the floor. He saw a fear in her eyes — a fear that made him afraid, too, though he didn't know why. And whenever he started to ask, she looked away and was suddenly very busy.

One difference between Joram and the other children was obvious — the fact that he walked. Though he had his assigned tasks and studies to perform during the long day of isolation in the shack, he often spent much of that day at the window, staring enviously at the play of the other children in the village. Every noon, under the watchful eye of Father Tolban, they floated and tumbled about in the air, playing with any object their fancy imagined and their limited skills as growing magi allowed them to create. Joram longed most desperately to be able to float, not to be forced to walk upon the ground like the lowest rank of the Field Magi or that most stupid of creatures according to his mother — a catalyst.

"How do I know I can't?" it occurred to the six-year-old to ask himself one day. "I've never really tried."

Leaving the window, the boy looked around the shack. Formed from a dead tree that had been magically shaped and hollowed out, the tree's branches had been skillfully laced and twined to form a crude roof. High above Joram, a single branch of the natural tree extended the length of the ceiling. Working industriously, Joram dragged the crude worktable, formed of a stump, beneath the beam. Then he lifted up a chair onto the table and, climbing on it, looked up. Not high enough. Frustrated, he glanced about and spotted the potato bin in the corner. Clambering down, he dumped out the potatoes, hoisted the huge, hollowed-out gourd, and, after a great deal of effort, managed to position it on top of the chair.

Now he could reach the beam, just barely. The gourd wobbling beneath his feet, Joram touched the beam with his fingertips and, with a jump that sent the gourd tumbling off the table, caught hold of the branch and pulled himself up onto it. Looking down, he saw that the floor was a long way beneath him.

"But that doesn't matter," he said confidently. "I'm going to float like the others," Drawing in a breath, Joram was just about to leap out into the air when suddenly the magical seal was broken, the door flew open, and his mother entered.

Anja's startled gaze traveled from the table to the chair to the gourd on the floor and, finally, to Joram, perched on the beam of the ceiling, staring at her with his dark eyes, his pale face a cold, blank mask. Instantly, Anja sprang into the air. Flying to the ceiling, she snatched up the child in her arms.

"What do you think you are doing, my little love?" Anja asked feverishly, clutching Joram to her as they drifted down to the floor.

"I want to float, like them," Joram replied, pointing outside and squirming to escape his mother's pinching grasp.

Setting her son down, Anja glanced over her shoulder at the peasant children and her lip curled.

"Never again disgrace me or yourself with such thoughts!" she said, attempting to sound stern. But her voice wavered, her eyes went to the crude device Joram had put together to gain his object. Shuddering, she put her hand over her mouth; then, with a look of revulsion, she hurriedly grabbed down the chair, flinging it into the corner. She turned to face Joram, her face deathly pale, words of reprimand on her lips.

But she couldn't say them. In Joram's eyes, she saw the question, framed and ready to ask.

And she was not prepared to answer it.

Without a word, Anja turned on her heel and left the shack.

Joram did, of course, attempt the leap from the roof, daring it during harvest time when he was certain his mother would be too busy to return to lunch, as she had taken to doing now more often. Balancing on the very edge of the beam, the child jumped, willing with all the strength of his small being that he hang suspended in the cool fall air like the griffins, and then drift to the ground, lightly as a windblown leaf. . . .

He landed, not like a windblown leaf, but like a rock hurled down the face of a mountain. The fall hurt the boy severely. Picking himself up, he felt a sharp pain in his side when he drew a breath.

"What is the matter with my pet?" Anja asked him playfully that evening. "You are very quiet."

"I jumped off the roof," Joram answered, looking at her steadily. "I was trying to float like the others."

Anja scowled, and again opened her mouth to reprimand the boy. But she saw, once again, the question in the boy's eyes.

"And what happened?" she asked gruffly, her hands plucking at the tattered remnants of her green dress.

"I fell," Joram answered his mother, who wasn't looking at him. "I hurt myself, right here." He pressed his hand against his side.

Anja shrugged. "I hope you have learned your lesson," she remarked coldly. "You are not like the others. You are different. And everytime you try to be like the others, you will hurt yourself or they will hurt you."

She is right. I'm not like the others. Joram knew that, now. But why? What was the reason?

That winter, the winter when he was six, Joram thought again that he might have discovered the answer.

Joram was a beautiful child. Even the hardbitten overseer could not help but pause in his daily grind to turn and stare on those occasions when the boy was allowed outside the shack. From being kept constantly indoors during the day, Joram's skin was smooth and white and as translucent as marble. His eyes were large and expressive, surrounded by thick black eyelashes so long that they brushed his cheeks. His eyebrows were black and set low on his head, giving him a brooding, serious adult air that accorded oddly with his childish face.

But Joram's most outstanding feature was his hair. Thick and luxuriant, black as the glistening plumage of the raven, it sprang from a sharp peak in the center of his forehead to fall down around his shoulders in a mass of tangled curls.

Unfortunately, this lovely hair was the bane of Joram's childhood. Anja refused to cut it, and it was now so thick and long that only hours of painful combing and tugging on Anja's part could remove the snarls and tangles. She tried braiding it, but the hair was so unruly that it sprang out of the braid almost within minutes, curling around the child's face and bouncing on his shoulders as if possessed of a life of its own.

Anja was extremely proud of her son's beauty. Keeping his hair clean and well-groomed was her great pleasure — her only pleasure, in fact, since she haughtily held herself apart from her neighbors. The combing of Joram's hair developed into a nightly ritual — a dismal ritual for Joram. Every evening, after their meager supper and his brief exercise period, the boy sat on a stool at the crudely shaped wooden table while Anja, with her magic and her fingers, lovingly combed out the child's wild, shining hair.

One night, Joram rebelled.

Sitting home alone that day as usual, he had watched from his window as the other little boys played together, floating and tumbling through the air, chasing after a shimmering ball of crystal their leader, a bright-eyed young lad named Mosiah, had conjured up. The rough game came to a halt with the return of several parents from the fields. The children crowded around their parents, clinging to them and hugging them in a way that made Joram feel dark and empty inside. Though Anja constantly fussed over him and hugged him, it was with a fierce kind of intensity that was more frightening than affectionate. Joram sometimes felt as if she wanted to crush him into her body and make them one.

"Mosiah," called out the boy's father, catching hold of his son who, after a quick greeting, was heading back to his play. "Y'er lookin' like a young lion," the father said, ruffling his son's hair that fell in long blond lanks over the boy's eyes. Drawing the child's hair between his fingers, the father gently sheared it off with a quick, deft motion of his hand.

That night, when Anja called Joram to the stool and began to take down what remained of the braids in his hair, Joram jerked away from his mother and turned to face her, his dark eyes wide and solemn.

"If I had a father like other boys," he said quietly, "he would cut my hair. If I had a father, I wouldn't be different. He wouldn't let you make me different!"

Without saying a word, Anja struck Joram across the face.

The blow knocked the child to the floor and left a bruised mark upon his cheek for days thereafter. What followed left a bruised mark on Joram's heart that never truly healed.

Hurt, angry, and alarmed by the look on his mother's face — for Anja had gone deathly white and her eyes burned with an inner fever — Joram began to cry.

"Stop it!" Anja dragged her son to his feet, her thin-fingered hand digging painfully into his arm. "Stop it!" she whispered fiercely. "Why do you cry?"

"Because you hurt me!" Joram muttered accusingly. His hand holding his stinging cheek, he stared at her in sullen defiance.

"I hurt you!" Anja sneered. "The slap of a hand and the child cries. Come" — she hauled the boy through the door of the shack and out into the mean little village, whose people were settling down to rest after their hard day's labors — "come, Joram, I will teach you what it is to hurt!"

Walking so fast that she literally dragged the stumbling child through the muddy street behind her (Anja always walked when she was with Joram — an odd circumstance that the other magi noted and wondered at), Anja came to the catalyst's dwelling at the far end of the village. Using her magic stored from the day's work, Anja caused the door to burst wide open. She and her child burst through after, propelled by the heat of her fury.

"Anja? What's the matter?" cried Father Tolban, springing up in alarm from where he had been resting before a cheery fire. Marm Hudspeth bent over the flames, cooking his dinner, this task taking more Life than a catalyst has. The sausages hung suspended over the fire, spitting and cackling very much like the old woman herself, who was preparing gruel in a sphere of magic bubbling on the hearth.

"Get out!" Anja ordered the old woman, never taking her eyes from the astonished catalyst.

"You — you had better go along, Marm," Father Tolban said gently. He would have liked to add, "and bring the overseer at once!" but the sight of Anja's glittering eyes and mottled face made him bite his tongue. Clucking and muttering, Marm sent the sausages from the flame to the table, then — staring at Anja and the boy with narrowed eyes — she flew out the door, making the sign against evil with her hand.

Her lip curled in derision, Anja slammed the door shut and stood facing the catalyst. He had not been to visit her since she had stopped him from educating Joram. She never spoke to him in the fields, if she could help it. So he was astounded to find her in his house, and even more astonished to see her child with her. "What is the matter, Anja?" he repeated. "Are you or the child ill?"

"Open the Corridors to us, Catalyst," Anja demanded with the superior air she used when speaking to underlings, an air that contrasted oddly with her shabby, patched dress and her dirt-smeared face. "The boy and I must make a journey."

"Now? But . . . but . . ." Father Tolban stammered, completely at a loss. This was unheard of! It could not be allowed. The woman had gone mad! And that brought another thought to the catalyst. He was alone and unprotected in the presence of a wizardess, an *Albanara* if one believed her story, whose Life force he could feel radiating from her like the heat of her anger.

She had probably saved up energy from the day's work. She wouldn't have much, but it might be enough to mutate him or wreck his small house. What should he do? Stall for time. Perhaps Old Marm would have brains enough to go fetch the overseer. Trying to remain calm, the catalyst's gaze went from the mother to the child, who stood beside her silently, half-hidden by the folds of Anja's rich, tattered dress.

Even in the midst of his fear and mental turmoil, Father Tolban stopped and stared. He had never seen the child up close, Anja always keeping them separated. And, though he had heard rumors of the child's beauty, the catalyst was certainly not prepared for anything like this. Blue-black hair framed a pale face with large dark eyes. But what was remarkable, besides the child's extraordinary beauty, was the fact that there was no fear in those wide, shimmering eyes. There was the shadow of pain—the catalyst could see the marks of Anja's hand upon the child's cheek. There were traces of tears. But there was no fear, only a look of calm triumph, as if this had all been carefully planned and arranged.

"Immediately, Catalyst," Anja hissed, stamping her bare foot upon the floor. "I am not accustomed to being kept waiting by the likes of you!"

"P-payment," stuttered Father Tolban. Tearing his gaze from the strange child, he turned to face the wild-eyed mother, feeling relief flood over him as he ducked into the safe refuge of the rules of his Order. "Th-there must be payment, you know," he continued more severely, gaining confidence as the rules loaned him the strength of centuries. "A portion of your Life, Mistress Anja, and also a portion of the boy's, if you travel with him . . ."

The catalyst had expected this to stop the woman — what Field Magus, after all, had enough magic left at the end of the day to grant the necessary portion demanded by the catalysts for the use of their Corridors?

And it did stop Anja, but only for a time, and then not in quite the manner Tolban had intended.

At the mention of the boy, she glanced down at the child in some perplexity, as if she had forgotten his existence. Then, scowling, she turned back to the catalyst, who was folding his arms across his chest and preparing to consider the matter closed.

"I will pay you parasites what you need to live!" she snapped. "But take nothing from the boy. I will pay you his portion from my Life as well. Come. I have sufficient! Take my hand!"

Anja stretched out her hand to the catalyst, whose confidence was oozing from him like sap from a wounded tree. Blankly, he stared at her and, for an instant, he did not see her dirty face or half-mad eyes, he did not see the ragged dress or the sun-browned skin of a Field Magus. He saw a tall and lovely woman, regally dressed, who had been born to command and to have her orders obeyed. Without really knowing what he was doing, the catalyst took hold of the woman's hand and felt Life surge into him with such force it nearly knocked him down.

"Wh-where would you go?" he asked weakly.

"The Borderlands."

"The Borderlands?" His mouth gaped in astonishment.

Anja's brows came together in alarming fashion.

Father Tolban gulped. Then he frowned, trying to recover some of his dignity. "I must leave the Corridor open, to guarantee your return," he said sourly.

Anja snorted. "Leave the Corridor open, then," she snapped. "It matters little to me. We will be gone only moments. Now get on with it!"

"Very well," the catalyst muttered.

Using Anja's Life, the catalyst opened the window in time and space to her, one of the many Corridors created originally by the Diviners, the Time Magi. The Diviners had long since vanished, and with them had died the knowledge of how to build the Corridors. But the catalysts, who had controlled them for centuries, knew still how to operate and maintain them, taking the Life needed to keep them active from those who used them.

Stepping into the window that appeared as a dark void within Father Tolban's cozy living quarters, Anja and the child vanished. Glancing at the open Corridor apprehensively, the catalyst discovered himself toying briefly with the idea of closing it and leaving them stranded on the other side. He came to himself with a start, shocked at what he had been contemplating.

The Borderland, he thought, shaking his head. How strange. Why go there, to that desolate, life-forsaken region?

There are no guards at the Borderlands. None are needed. To pass from the world into those drifting, floating mists is to step Beyond. To step Beyond is to die.

As for guarding the realm from what lies Beyond, there is no reason to do so. For nothing lies Beyond, nothing except the realm of Death. And from that realm, no one has ever returned.

The first line of the catechism states, "We fled the world where Death reigned, taking with us the magic and those creatures of magic we had created. We chose this world because it is empty. Here the magic will live, since there is nothing and no one to threaten us ever again. Here, on this world, is Life."

There are no guards, but there are the Watchers.

Stepping hesitantly into the Corridor, his hand clutching his mother's, Joram experienced an instant's sensation of being squeezed, very tightly. Lovely, sparkling stars burst in his vision. But before his mind could quite truly register what was transpiring, the sensation ended, the sparkling light faded, and he looked around him, expecting to see the catalyst's small room. But he wasn't in the catalyst's house. He was standing on a long, barren stretch of white beach.

The child had never seen anything like this before and was pleased by the feeling of the sun-warmed sand beneath his feet. Reaching down, he started to pick up a handful, but Anja jerked him roughly forward, striding across the beach with long steps, pulling the child after her.

At first, Joram enjoyed walking in the sand. That ended very soon, however, as the sand grew deeper and walking became more difficult. He began to sink in the shifting dunes, and when he tried to move ahead, they slid away beneath his feet, causing him to flounder and stumble.

"Where are we?" he asked, panting for breath.

"We stand on the edge of the world," Anja replied, stopping to wipe the sweat from her face and gain her bearings.

Glad to rest, Joram looked around.

Anja was right. Behind him was the world — the white sand yielding to sparse green grasses that in turn yielded to the lush green fields. Tall, darker green forests carried the life of the world upward into the purple of the mountains, whose snow-capped peaks lifted it into the clear blue sky. And the sky seemed, to Joram's gaze, to leap from the mountains, soaring in a vast, serene expanse above him. Following its curve, he turned and looked ahead of him to where the sky fell at last into the misty void beyond the white sand.

And then he saw the Watchers.

Startled, he clutched at Anja's hand and pointed.

"Yes," was all she said. But the pain and anger in her answer made the child shiver in the waning sunlight, though the heat of midday radiated still from the sand beneath his feet.

Gripping Joram's hand firmly, Anja tugged him forward, her tattered gown dragging behind, leaving a snakelike trail through the dunes.

Thirty feet tall, the stone statues of the Watchers line the Borderlands, staring eternally out into the mists of Beyond. Spaced at twenty-foot intervals, the stone statues stand on the edge of the white sand for as far as the eye can see.

Joram gaped in wonder as he approached them. He had never seen anything so tall! Even the trees in the forest did not tower above him like these giant statues. Coming up on them from behind, Joram at first thought they were all alike. The statues were all figures of humans dressed in robes. Though some appeared to be male and others female, there seemed no other difference. Each stood in the same position, arms hanging straight down from his or her side, feet together, heads facing forward.

Then, as Joram drew nearer, he noticed that one statue was different. On one statue, the left hand, which should have been open like the others, was closed, clenched into a fist.

Joram turned to Anja, bursting with questions about these wonderful statues. But when he saw her face, he stopped the words upon his lips so swiftly that he bit his tongue. Swallowing his questions, he tasted blood.

Anja's face was whiter, her eyes hotter than the hot sand upon which they walked. Her wild, fevered gaze fixed upon one of the statues — the one whose hand was clenched. Toward that statue, she moved resolutely, floundering and falling in the shifting sand.

Then Joram knew. With the sudden, uncanny clairvoyance of childhood, Joram understood, though he could not have framed his knowledge in words. A sickening fear swept over him, making him weak and dizzy. Terrified, he tried to pull away from Anja, but she only held his hand more tightly. Desperately, shrieking words that Anja — from the lost, preoccupied look on her face — never heard, Joram dug his heels into the sand.

"Please! Anja! Take me home! No, I don't want to see —"

He fell down, dragging Anja off-balance. Stumbling, she landed on her hands and knees, and was forced to let loose of Joram to catch herself. Scrambling to his feet, the child tried to run, but Anja lunged forward and caught hold of him by the hair, yanking him backward.

"No!" Joram shrieked frantically, sobbing in pain and fear.

Grasping him around the waist with a strength her work in the fields had given her, Anja lifted the child and carried him across the sand, falling more than once, but never deterring from her fixed purpose.

Coming to stand before the statue, Anja stopped. Her breath came in ragged gasps. For a moment, she stared up at the statue towering above them.

Its left hand clenched, its fixed gaze looking over their heads into the mists Beyond, it had — to all appearances — less Life than the trees in the forests. Yet it was aware of their presence. Joram felt its awareness, as he felt its terrible, tortured pain.

Exhausted, he ceased to cry out or struggle. Anja dumped him at the statue's stone feet, where he crouched, quivering, his head in his hands.

"Joram," Anja said, "this is your father."

The boy squeezed his eyes tightly shut, unable to move or speak or do anything except lie upon the warm sand beneath the giant stone statue.

But a splash of water upon his neck made Joram start. Raising his head from where it had been pressed into the sand, the child looked up slowly. Far above him, he could see the statue's stone eyes staring straight ahead into the realm of Death whose sweet peace must ever elude him. Another splash of water struck the boy. With a heartbroken sob, Joram buried his face in his small hands.

While far above him, the statue, too, wept.

9

The Ritual

"I was the daughter of one of the noblest houses in Merilon. He — your father — was House Catalyst."

Sitting at the table, once more in their shack, Joram heard Anja's voice coming to him from somewhere above him, trickling down through a haze of fear and horror like the tears of the statue.

"I was the daughter of one of the noblest houses in Merilon," she repeated, combing out Joram's hair. "Your father was House Catalyst. He, too, came of noble blood. My father refused to have a catalyst living with us like Father Tolban — little better than a Field Magus himself. I was sixteen, Your father was just turned thirty."

She sighed, and the fingers that tugged and pulled at the tangles in Joram's hair grew lingering and caressing. Glancing at her face reflected in the glass of the windows opposite where he sat at the wooden table, Joram saw his mother smile a half-smile and sway a little to some unheard music. Raising her hand, she patted her filthy, matted hair. "What beautiful things we created, he and I," she said softly, smiling dreamily. "I was gifted with Life, Mama used to tell me. Of an evening, to please and entertain my family, your father and I would fill the twilight with rainbows and phantasms of wonder that brought tears to the eyes of those who beheld them. It was only natural, your father said, that we, who could create such beauty, should fall in love."

The fingers in his hair tightened, the sharp nails dug into his flesh, and Joram felt the sticky liquid of his own blood trickle down his neck.

"We went to the catalysts for permission to marry. They performed a Vision. The answer was no. They said we would not produce living issue!"

Tearing at the tangled mass of black hair, she ripped at the knots with her talonlike nails. Clutching at the table, Joram welcomed the pain of his flesh that masked the pain of his soul.

"Living issue! Hah! They lied! You see!" Grasping Joram around the neck, Anja hugged him in fierce, greedy passion. "You are with me, my sweet one. You are my proof that they are liars!"

Pressing his head against her breast, she rocked him back and forth, crooning "liars" to herself and to him as she smoothed out the silken curls of his hair.

"Yes, heart's delight, I have you," Anja murmured, stopping in her combing for a moment to stare fixedly into the fire. Her hands dropped to her lap. "I have you. They could not stop us. No, even though they ordered your father to leave our house and return to the Cathedral, they could not keep us apart. He came back to me that night, the night after their foul Vision. We met in secret, in the garden where we had given life to such beautiful creations.

"He had a plan. We would produce a living child and prove to the world that the catalysts were lying. They would be forced to let us marry then, don't you see?

"We needed a catalyst to perform the ceremony that would create a child in my womb. But we could find none. Cowards! Those he ventured to approach refused, fearing the wrath of the Bishop if they were discovered.

"And then came word, he was being sent to the fields, a Field Catalyst!" Anja snorted. "Him! Whose soul was beauty and fineness, to be sent to a life of drudgery and toil. Little

better than the peasants who are born to it. And it meant we
would never see each other again, for once you have trudged
in the mud of the fields, you may never walk the enchanted
streets of Merilon.

"We were desperate. Then, one night, he told me that he
knew of a way — an ancient, forbidden way — that we could
use to produce a child."

Anja's hands twisted. She sank down upon a stool, her
eyes still staring into the fire. Joram could not look at her, his
stomach clenched with anger and a strange, almost pleasur-
able sensation of pain he did not understand. Instead, he
stared out the window at the calm, lonely moon.

"He described the ancient way to me," she said softly. "I
was sickened. It was . . . bestial. How could I do it? How
could he? Yet, how could we not? For if he left me, I would
die. We sneaked off . . ."

Anja'a voice dropped to where Joram could just barely
hear her.

"I remember little of the night you were conceived. He
. . . your father . . . gave me a drink made of some bright red
flower. . . . It seems to me that my soul left my body, leaving
the body for him to do with it as he would. As if in a dream
. . . I remember his hands touching me . . . I remember an
awful, searing pain. I remember . . . a sweetness. . . .

"But we were betrayed. The catalysts had been trailing
us, watching us. I heard him cry out, then I awoke with a
scream to find them standing over us, staring down at us in
our shame. They took him away, to the Font for his trial. I
was taken to the Font, too. They have a place there, where
they keep 'women like me' so they said." Anja smiled bitterly
at the fire. "There are more of us than you might suppose, my
pet. I looked for him, but the Font is a huge place, huge and
terrible. The next time I saw him was at the Punishment.

"You, my sweet, were heavy in my womb when they
dragged me to the Borderlands and forced me to stand in the
sand, the white, burning sand. Forced me to stand there and
watch them perform their heinous act!"

Snarling, Anja twisted to her feet. Coming to stand before Joram, she dug her nails into his shoulder. "Magi who
have broken the law are sent Beyond!" she whispered
fiercely. "That is their punishment for wrongdoing in this

world. 'The Living shall not be put to Death,' thus the catechism says. A magus walks out into mist, into nothingness,
and so perishes! Pah!" She spit into the fire. "What punishment is that compared to being turned to living stone? Wearing out the ageless days of your existence, gnawed at always
by wind and water and the memories of what it was to be alive!"

Anja stared into the night with eyes that might have been
stone, for all they saw. Joram stared at the moon.

"They stood him in the place they had marked upon the
sand. He wore the robes of shame, and two Enforcers held
him fast with their dark enchantment, so that he could not
move. Most catalysts, I have heard, accept their fate quietly.
Some even welcome it, having been convinced of the enormity
of their sins. But not your father. We had done nothing wrong."
Her nails dug deeper into Joram's flesh. "We had only loved!"

Breathing heavily, she could not speak for long minutes,
forcing herself to witness that terrible moment once again,
reveling — for an instant — in her pain and reveling in the
knowledge that she was sharing this pain with the boy.

"To the last," she continued in a low, husky voice, "your
father shouted his defiance. They tried to ignore him, but I
saw their faces. His words hit home. Furious, Bishop
Vanya — may the ground upon which he walks writhe with
scorpions — ordered the transmutation to begin.

"Twenty-five catalysts are needed to perform such a
change. Vanya had brought them from all parts of Thimhallan, to witness the punishment for our great crime — the
sin of loving!

"They formed a circle around your father and, into that
circle, walked the catalyst's own *Duuk-tsarith*, a warlock who
works for them and who, in return, is granted as much Life
as he needs to perform his foul duties. At his coming, the two
lower-rank Enforcers bowed and left, leaving your father
alone in the circle with the one known as the Executioner.
The warlock made a sign. The catalysts clasped hold of
hands. Each opened a conduit to the Executioner, giving him
unbelievable power.

"He took his time. The punishment is slow and painful.

"Moving his hand, the Executioner pointed at your father's feet. I could not see his limbs beneath his long robes,
but I knew from the expression on your father's face when he

first felt the transmutation begin. His feet turned to stone. Slowly, the icy coldness moved up his legs, then his loins, his stomach, chest and arms. Still he yelled at them until his stomach froze. Even when his voice ceased, I could see his lips move. At the last moment, with his last effort, he clenched his fist just as it turned to stone. They could have altered it, of course. But they chose to let that sign of his last bitter defiance remain as a warning to others."

Yes, thought Joram, reaching up and clasping his mother's hands in his own, they left the look upon his face as well — a monument to hatred, bitterness, and anger.

Anja's voice dropped. "I watched him draw his final breath. Then he could breathe no more — as normal man. But the breath of life is within him still. That is the most excruciating part of this punishment that these fiends have devised. Think of him when anything hurts you, my sweet one. Think of him when you are tempted to cry, and you will know your tears to be petty and shameful compared to his. Think of him, who is dead but alive."

Joram thought of him.

He thought of his father every night, as Anja told the story while she combed his hair, and every night when he went to bed, the words "Dead but alive" reached out to him from the darkness. He thought of him every night from then on, because Anja told him the story again and again, night after night, as she combed the tangles from his hair with her fingers.

As some use wine to ease the pains of living, so Anja's words were the bitter wine that she and Joram drank. Only this wine did not ease pain. Born of madness, it gave birth to pain itself. For at last Joram understood The Difference, or thought he did. Now at last he could understand his mother's pain and hatred and share in it.

During the day, he still watched the other children at their play, but now his look was not envious. Like his mother's, it was contemptuous. Joram began to play a game of his own, sitting day after day in the silent hovel. He was the moon, hanging in the dark heavens, staring down at the buglike mortals below, who sometimes looked up at him in his cold and shining majesty, but who could not touch him.

Thus he spent his days. And every night, as she combed his hair, Anja recited her tale.

From that time on, if Joram cried, no one ever saw his tears.

10

The Game

oram was seven when the dark and secret part of his education began.

One evening after dinner, Anja reached out her hands and ran her fingers through Joram's thick, tangled hair. Joram tensed; this was always the beginning of the stories, a time that he confusedly both longed for and dreaded every hour of his lonely day. But she did not begin to comb out his hair as usual. Puzzled, the boy looked up at her.

Anja was staring at him, fondling his hair absently. She studied his face, moving her hand to caress his cheek. All the while he could see that she was turning something over in her mind, fingering an idea as one of the *Pron-alban* fingers a gem to see if it is flawed. Finally, her lips tightened in resolution.

Gripping Joram by the arm, she pulled him down to sit beside her on the floor.

"What is it, Anja?" he asked uneasily. "What are we doing? Aren't you going to tell me about my father?"

"Later," said Anja firmly. "Now, we are going to play a game."

Joram looked at his mother in wary amazement. Never in her life had Anja played at anything, and he had a feeling she was not going to begin now. Anja tried to smile at the boy reassuringly, but Anja's strange, wild-eyed grins only increased Joram's nervousness. Yet he watched her with a kind of hungry eagerness. Whatever she did seemed to hurt him, but — like a man who cannot help running his tongue over an aching tooth — Joram could not seem to help touching his aching heart, feeling a certain grim satisfaction in knowing that the pain was still there.

Anja reached into a pouch that hung from a strip of leather she wore round her waist and drew out a small, smooth stone. Tossing the stone into the air, she used her magic to cause the air to swallow it up. As the stone disappeared, Anja looked at Joram with an expression of triumph that the boy found quite perplexing. There was nothing marvelous in the stone's disappearance. Such feats were commonplace, even in the lowly world of the Field Magus. Now, if she would only show him some of the marvels she had described that were created in Merilon . . .

"Very well, little pet," said Anja, reaching into the air and producing the stone, "since you are so unimpressed, you try it."

Joram scowled, his dark, feathery eyebrows drawing a grim line across the childish face. There it was. There was the hurt. He touched the dull ache.

"You know I can't," he said sullenly.

"Take the stone, my sweet one," Anja said playfully, holding it out to him.

But Joram saw no playful laughter in his mother's eyes, only purpose, resolution, and a strange, eerie glint. Reaching out, Joram took the stone.

"Make the air swallow it," Anja commanded.

Still scowling, the boy tossed the stone into the air with an exasperated sigh. It clattered to the floor at his feet.

In the silence that followed, Joram could hear the stone rolling around and around on the wooden floor. When it stopped, Joram glanced at his mother out of the corner of his eye. "Why can't I make it vanish?" he demanded in a low voice. "Why am I different? Even a catalyst can do such a simple thing . . ."

"Bah! And it will be a simple thing for you, too, some-day." Anja fondled the crisp, black curls that twined around Joram's face. "Do not fret. Those of the nobility are some-times slow to develop the magic."

But Joram was not satisfied. She did not look at him when she spoke, her gaze was on his hair. Angrily, he jerked his head back, away from her touch.

"When?" he demanded stubbornly.

The boy saw his mother's lips tighten, and he braced him-self to face her anger. But then Anja's hand fell limply into her lap. Her gaze grew unfocused.

"Someday soon," she replied, smiling vaguely. "No, don't bother me with questions. Give me your hand."

Joram hesitated, staring at his mother, as if determined to argue. Then, seeing it would do no good, he held out his hand. Anja took hold of it, studying it intently.

"The fingers are long and delicate," she said, speaking to herself. "Their movement quick, supple. Yes, good. Very good."

Causing the stone to rise up from the floor into the air, Anja deposited it in the child's open palm.

"Joram," she said softly, "I am going to teach you to make the stone disappear. This is magic that I am going to show you, but it is secret magic. You must never show anyone else or allow anyone else to see you use it or they will send both of us Beyond. Do you understand, my heart's delight?"

"Yes," Joram replied, wide-eyed and incredulous, his fear and suspicion replaced by a sudden, hungry desire to learn.

"The first time that I threw the stone into the air, I didn't really make the air swallow it. I only seemed to, just as I only seemed to pull the stone back out. No, I mean it. Watch. Look, I've thrown it up into the air. It has vanished. Right? Wasn't that what you saw? Ah, but look. The stone is still here! In my hand!"

"I don't understand," said Joram, once more suspicious.

"I fooled your eyes. Watch, I seem to throw the stone up in the air and your eyes follow the motion I make with my hand. But while your eyes are looking at that, my hands are doing this. And there goes the stone. This is what you must do from now on, Joram—learn to fool people's eyes. No, sweet one. Do not frown. It is not difficult. People see what they want to see. Now, you try. . . ."

Thus, Joram began his lessons in sleight-of-hand.

Day after day he practiced, safe in the protective magical aura that surrounded the hovel. Joram enjoyed the lessons. It gave him something to do and it was also something he discovered he was quite good at doing. Child that he was, he never wondered how Anja came to know this secret art or, if he did, he passed it off as just another of the strange things about her, like her ragged dress. Only one thing bothered him. Once more, The Difference bobbed to the surface of his mind.

"Why must I do this, Anja?" Joram asked casually, about six months later. He was practicing moving a round, smooth pebble along his knuckles, making it skitter rapidly across the back of his hand.

"You will need this skill when you go out into the fields to earn your keep next year," Anja replied absently.

Joram's head jerked up, quick as a cat pouncing on a mouse. Catching the boy's swift, dark-eyed glance, Anja hastily added, "If you haven't developed the magic yourself yet, of course."

Frowning, Joram opened his mouth, but Anja turned away. Looking down at her tattered, filthy dress, she smoothed the fabric with her brown, callused hands. "There is another reason, too. When we go to Merilon, my son, you will be able to impress the members of the Royal House with your talents."

"Are we going to Merilon?" Joram cried, forgetting his lessons, forgetting The Difference. Jumping to his feet, he dropped the pebble and clasped hold of his mother's hands. "When, Anja, when?"

"Soon," Anja answered calmly, plucking at Joram's curls. "Soon. I must find my jewels." She glanced vaguely about the hovel. "I've lost the jewel box. I cannot appear in the court without—"

But Joram was not interested in jewels or in Anja's incoherent ramblings that were growing more and more frequent. Clutching at the shredded remnants of his mother's skirt, he begged, "Please, Anja, tell me when. When will I see the wonders of Merilon? When will I see the Silken Dragon and the Three Sisters, and Spires of Rainbow Crystal, and the Garden of the Swan and the —"

"Ah, my sweet one, my pretty one," Anja said fondly, reaching out to stroke the black curls that tumbled about his face. "Soon we will go to Merilon. Soon you will see the beauty and the wonder that is Merilon. And they will see *you*, my butterfly. They will see a true *Albanara*, a wizard of a noble house. For this I am educating you, for this I am working. Soon I will take you back to Merilon, and then we will claim what is rightfully ours."

"But when?" Joram persisted stubbornly.

"Soon, my beauty, soon," was all Anja would say.

And, with that, Joram had to be content.

At eight, Joram took his place in the fields with the other children of the Field Magi. The tasks the children performed were not difficult, though the days were long and tiresome, the children working the same time span as the adults. They were assigned such mundane jobs as clearing a field of rocks or carefully gathering worms and other insects that fulfilled their small destinies by working in harmony with man to raise the food that nourished his body.

The catalyst did not grant the children Life; this would have been an uncalled-for waste of energy. So the children walked, not floated, among the fields. But most had enough natural Life force within them to be able to send the rocks to the air or cause the wingless worms to fly above the plants. Often they enlivened their work — when the overseer and the catalyst weren't watching — by holding impromptu contests in magic. On those rare occasions when Joram was cajoled or goaded into exhibiting his skill, he easily matched their feats using the sleight-of-hand techniques at which he had become adept. And so they took no particular notice of him.

Most of the time, in fact, the other children did not invite Joram to join in their play. Few liked him. He was sullen and aloof, instantly suspicious of friendly overtures.

"Don't let anyone get close to you, my son," Anja told him. "They will not understand you, and what they do not understand they fear. And what they fear, they destroy."

One by one, after each had been coldly rebuffed by the strange, dark-haired child, the other children let Joram severely alone. But there was one among them who persisted in his attempts to be friendly. This was Mosiah. The son of a high-ranking Field Magus, intelligent and outgoing, Mosiah was unusually gifted in magic — so much so that the catalyst, Father Tolban, had been overheard talking of sending him to one of the Guilds to earn his living when he was older.

Charming, outgoing, and popular, Mosiah himself couldn't explain why he was attracted to Joram, except perhaps that it was in the same way the lodestone is attracted to iron. Whatever the reason, Mosiah refused to be rebuffed.

He took every opportunity to work near Joram in the fields. He often sat with him during lunch break, talking away about this and that, never expecting or demanding a response from the silent, withdrawn boy at his side. The friendship might have seemed one-sided and thankless — certainly Joram did nothing to encourage it and was often curt in his infrequent responses. But Mosiah sensed that his presence was welcome, and so he kept on, chipping away at the stone facade Joram had built, a facade as hard and tall as the one that encased his father.

The years passed the village of Walren and its residents uneventfully, the seasons blending into one another, only occasionally assisted by the *Sif-Hanar* if nature didn't act in accordance with their designs.

As the seasons blended together, so the lives of the Field Magi flowed into the seasons. In the spring, they planted. In the summer, they tended. In the autumn, they harvested. In the winter, they fought to survive until spring, when the cycle would start again. But though their lives were lives of drudgery and hardship and poverty, the Field Magi of Walren counted themselves fortunate. All knew it could be worse. The overseer was a fair and just man who saw to it that everyone had his or her share in the harvest, and didn't demand a portion of anyone's share for himself. Bandits, reputedly raiding villages to the north, had neither been seen nor heard of here. The winters, the worst time of the year, were long and cold, but were not as bad as in the lands to the north.

Even Walren, far from civilization, heard word of uprising and rebellion. Discreet inquiries were made among the villagers, in fact, to determine if they didn't want to assert their independence. But Mosiah's father, a man content with his lot, knew from past experience that freedom was fine but someone had to pay for it. Thus he was quick to make it clear to any outsider that he and his people wanted simply to be left alone.

The overseer of Walren counted himself a fortunate man as well. He never once failed to bring in a bountiful harvest, never had to worry about the uprisings and disturbances rumored to be occurring elsewhere. He knew about the discreet contacts made by troublemakers and rabble-rousers from the outside. But he had an excellent working arrangement with his people, he trusted Mosiah's father, and therefore could, with equanimity, turn a blind eye.

The catalyst, Father Tolban, did not consider himself so fortunate. Every spare moment, and there were few enough in his bleak life, found him hard at work on his studies with the fond view in his mind of once more being accepted back into the fold. His crime — the crime that had made him a Field Catalyst — had been a minor offense, committed in the enthusiasm of youth. A treatise, nothing more, written on the *Benefits of the Natural Cycles of Weather, as Opposed to Magical Intervention, with Regard to Raising Crops.* It was a fine piece of work, and he was honored by the fact that it had been placed in the Inner Library in the Font. At least, that was what they told him when they gave him this assignment and shipped him out. He couldn't say for certain if it was actually in the Inner Library, never having been allowed back to the Font to find out.

As the seasons blended into years, and the overseer brought in his harvest and the catalyst pursued his fading dream, life changed little for Joram except, perhaps, to grow darker.

Fifteen years after she'd arrived at the settlement, Anja still wore the same dress, the fabric so worn and threadbare it was held together only by the spells she wove around it. The nightly stories continued, enhanced by tales of the wonders of Merilon. But, as the years passed, Anja's tales grew more confused and incoherent. She often slipped into delusions of being in Merilon itself and, from her wild descriptions, the city might have been a garden of delight or a pit of horrors, depending on where her madness led her.

As for returning to Merilon, Joram had come to realize as he'd grown older that Anja's dream was as tattered and frayed as the dress she wore. He would have thought her tales all make-believe, but there seemed to be fragments of her story that had substance to them, clinging to her like the fragments of her once rich clothing.

Joram's life was bleak and harsh, every day a struggle to survive. He watched his mother's increasingly rapid descent into madness with eyes that could have been his father's — eyes of stone that stared continually far away into some shadowy realm of darkness. He accepted her insanity in silence, as he had accepted all the other pain.

But there was one pain he could not make himself accept — he had never acquired the magic. Day by day he grew more adept at sleight-of-hand. His illusions fooled the eyes of even the watchful overseer. But the magic that he longed for and sought every morning to feel burning in his soul never came to him.

When he was fifteen, he stopped asking Anja when he would gain the magic.

Deep inside of him, he already knew the answer.

As the children grew older and stronger, the tasks they performed grew more difficult. Older boys and young men were given hard, physical labor — labor that kept them exhausted and their minds occupied. It was these boys and young men who, it was rumored, were stirring up trouble among the Field Magi, and though the overseer had no cause for complaint among his people, he didn't intend to play the blind fool, either, as the saying went. Therefore, when it was decided to extend the settlement's cropland, he assigned the young men the task of clearing the land. The work was strenuous. They had to haul or burn away the underbrush, lift large stones, kill the choking weeds, and there were a hundred other back-breaking tasks. Then the higher-ranking, more privileged Field Magi would come and, with the aid of the *Fibanish*, the Druids, use their magic to persuade the giant trees to release their roots from the ground and plant themselves elsewhere. After this, the young men had to haul those trees that were dead back to the village where, several times yearly, the *Pron-alban* sent the winged Ariel to transport the wood back to the city.

All of the physical labors had to be performed by hand. The young men were never given Life by the catalyst to help them in any of these tasks. Even Mosiah, with his natural gift for magic, was generally too worn out to call upon it. This was done purposefully, to break the spirits of the young men and mold them into proper, drab Field Magi, like their parents.

As for tools . . . Once Joram, tired of pushing a huge boulder across the ground, suddenly conceived the idea of taking a stick, placing it under the boulder, and using the leverage of the stick to make the boulder move. He was just thrusting the stick beneath the boulder when Mosiah, with a shocked look, grabbed hold of his arm.

"Joram, what are you doing?"

"Well, what *am* I doing?" Joram snapped impatiently, flinching away. He did not like people touching him. "I'm moving this rock!"

"You are moving it by giving Life to that stick!" Mosiah said. "You are giving Life to that which has none of its own."

Joram stared at the stick, frowning. "So?"

"Joram," whispered Mosiah in awe, "that is what the Sorcerers do! Those who practice the Dark Arts!"

Joram snorted. "You mean the Dark Arts are nothing more than using sticks to move stones? From the way everybody fears them, I thought they must at least sacrifice babies—"

"Don't talk like that, Joram," Mosiah remonstrated in hushed tones, glancing about nervously. "They deny the magic. They deny Life. By their Dark Arts, they would destroy it. They almost did destroy it, during the Iron Wars!"

"That's crazy," muttered Joram. "Why would they destroy themselves?"

"If they are Dead inside, as some say, then they lose nothing."

"What do you mean, 'Dead inside'?" Joram asked in a low voice, not looking at Mosiah, but staring at the boulder through the tangled mass of his black hair that had fallen down over his face.

"Sometimes there are children born without Life," Mosiah said, glancing at Joram in some surprise. "Didn't you ever hear about them? I would have thought your mother would have told you —" Mosiah stopped in embarrassment.

"No," Joram answered in the same low, expressionless voice, though his face went white and his hand clenched around the stick.

Mentally kicking himself for bringing Anja into the conversation, Mosiah continued to talk as he usually did around the silent, unresponsive Joram. "We're given Tests when we're born, and sometimes babies fail these Tests, which means they don't have any Life in them."

"What happens . . . to these babies?" Joram asked in such subdued and quiet tones that Mosiah barely heard him.

"The catalysts take them away to the Font," Mosiah answered, rather startled. Never before had Joram asked a question about anything. "They perform the Deathwatch. Some say that occasionally these children are hidden by their parents so that the catalysts can't take them. It seems kinder to me, though, to let them die quickly. Can you imagine what it would be like? Living like that? Without Life?"

"No," Joram answered in a tight, strained voice. Taking the stick, he hurled it far away from him. Then, staring at the boulder, his eyes dark and brooding, he repeated, "No. Not at all."

Watching his friend, wondering uneasily at his unusual interest in such an unpleasant subject, Mosiah saw a shadow envelop Joram with a darkness so intense that the young man almost glanced up to see if a cloud had covered the sun. Strange, black moods descended on his friend sometimes. During these times, Joram remained shut in the shack, while Anja reported defiantly to the overseer that he was sick.

Once, curious and worried about his friend, Mosiah had sneaked back to Joram's shack one day and looked in a window. There, he saw Joram stretched prone upon the cot, lying without moving, staring up at the ceiling. Mosiah tapped on the windowpane, but Joram neither stirred nor acted as if he heard him. He was lying in exactly the same position when Mosiah crept back to look that night. The sickness lasted a day or two, at the end of which time Joram returned to his work, maintaining his customary sullen aloofness.

But Mosiah had noticed something else, something no one else, perhaps not even Anja, had seen. These fits of black lethargy were almost always followed with fits of the most intense activity. For days on end, Joram would do the work of three men, driving himself to the verge of exhaustion so that he literally walked home in his sleep.

Now Joram stood wrapped in some dark, brooding thought and Mosiah, with the sensitivity and intuitive knowledge that had deepened through the years in regard to Joram, remained with him, knowing that he was — somehow — wanted and needed.

As he stood there, scarcely daring to breathe while Joram wrestled with whatever current demon possessed him, Mosiah studied his friend intently, trying as always to see inside that heavily guarded fortress.

As a result of his hard labor in the fields, Joram was, by the age of sixteen, strong and hard-muscled. His beauty, so striking as a child, had been roughly hewn and chiseled. Like the stone statue of his father, the marks of his inner torment had been carved into his face.

His alabaster skin was tanned a deep, smooth brown from working in the sun. The black eyebrows had thickened, slashing straight across his face in a dark line that dipped down slightly at the bridge of his nose, giving him a look of perpetual fierceness. The smooth, childish roundness of his cheeks had sunken into sharp, angular planes with high cheekbones and a strong jawline. His eyes were large and might have been considered beautiful, with their rich, clear brown color and long, thick eyelashes. But there was such anger, sullenness, and suspicion in those eyes that any who stood too long in their penetrating gaze soon grew nervous and uncomfortable.

Joram's hair was still the one true beauty left from his childhood. His mother had never allowed it to be cut. Those who sometimes dared to peep through the window of the shack at night, and watch as Anja combed his hair out, whispered in awe that it came down to the middle of his back, falling in long tendrils of black around his shoulders.

Though Joram did not admit it, his hair had become his one vanity. He wore it braided when he worked — a long, thick coil that hung down his back. This in sharp contrast to the other young men, who wore their hair blunt-cut and chin-length. The image of Joram, seated in a chair while Anja combed his hair, caused a story to spring up among the other peasants, who told that a spider with a comb spun a black web of hair around the young man.

This image was in Mosiah's mind, seeing the black web Joram was spinning around himself, when suddenly Joram lifted his head and turned to his friend.

"Come with me," he said.

Mosiah started, a thrill tingling through his veins. Joram's face was clear, the shadow lifted, the web broken.

"Sure," Mosiah had sense enough to answer easily, falling into step beside the taller young man. "Where to?"

But Joram didn't answer. Walking swiftly, he pushed ahead with a strange, eager expression of excitement and activity on his face that contrasted so vividly with the previous dark, brooding look that it seemed as if the sun had broken through a storm cloud.

On and on they walked, through the forested land the magi were gradually reclaiming from the wilderness, and soon left the ground where they had been working behind. The trees grew thicker as they moved deeper into the woods; the forest floor was choked with brush, almost impassable. Forced more than once to use his magic to clear a path, Mosiah felt his already low energy begin to drain. Having a good sense of direction, he knew fairly well where they were and this was confirmed by an ominous sound — the sound of rushing water.

Slowing his pace, Mosiah looked around uneasily.

"Joram," he said, touching his friend on the shoulder, noticing as he did so that Joram, in his strange excitement, did not flinch away as usual. "Joram, we're close to the river."

Joram did not reply, he simply kept walking.

"Joram," Mosiah said, feeling his throat tighten, "Joram, what are you doing? Where are you going?"

He managed to stop the young man, tightening his grip on his shoulder, expecting every second to be coldly rebuffed. But Joram only turned at his touch to look at him intently.

"Come with me," he said, his dark eyes glowing. "Let's see the river. Let's see what's across it."

Mosiah licked his lips, dry with walking in the bright sunlight of late afternoon. Of all the wild schemes! Just when he had been able, so he thought, to see the beginnings of a crack in the stone fortress where some light might penetrate, he must now close it up with his very own hand.

"We can't, Joram," Mosiah said quietly and calmly, though he felt sick with despair inside. "That's the border. The Outland lies beyond. No one goes there."

"But *you've* talked to people there. I know you have," Joram said with the wild eagerness that was so strange.

Mosiah flushed. "How did you know that? No, never mind," he muttered. "I didn't talk to them. They talked to me. And . . . I didn't like . . . what they said." Clutching Joram's shoulder, he tugged on him gently. "Come back home, Joram. Why do you want to go there? . . ."

"I *have* to get away!" Joram answered in a voice suddenly fierce and passionate. "I have to get away!"

"Joram," said Mosiah desperately, trying to think what might stop him, wondering what put this crazy notion into his head. "You *can't* leave. Stop and think calmly a minute! Your mother—"

At the mention of the word, Joram's face went blank. There was no shadow upon it, yet there was no light either. His face was as blank and cold as stone.

With a shrug, Joram jerked away from Mosiah's grasp. Turning, he plunged back into the brush, seeming to care little if his friend followed or not.

Mosiah followed, with pain in his heart. The crack in the fortress was gone, the fortress made stronger and more durable than before. And he had no idea why.

II

Spring's Bitter Harvest

Spring planting time came. Everyone worked together during spring planting. Each person, from the youngest to the eldest, toiled in the fields from before dawn to late evening—sowing the seed, or setting young seedlings which had been carefully nurtured through the winter, in the warm, freshly plowed ground. The work had to be done swiftly, for soon the *Sif-Hanar* would arrive to seed the clouds as the Field Magi seeded the earth, sending the gentle rains that would make the fields lush and green.

Of all the seasons of the year, Joram hated spring planting time most. Though now, at the age of sixteen, he was such a skilled sleight-of-hand artist that his tricks were almost impossible to detect, the seeds were so tiny that even with all his practiced dexterity, he appeared clumsy and slow in sowing them. His hands and shoulders ached at night from the hard work and the stress of maintaining the illusion that he possessed the magic.

This year it was particularly difficult, for they had a new overseer, the old one having passed away during the winter.

This new overseer had been brought from the northern part of Thimhallan, where rebellion among the Field Magi and the lower classes had been brewing and bubbling for years. He was alert to the danger signs of rebellion therefore; in fact, he was actively watching for it. And he found it immediately — in Joram. Early on, he determined to stomp out those smoldering coals of sullen anger he could see in the young man's eyes.

The magi were out in the fields early one morning, practically before sunrise. Gathering together in a group, they stood before the overseer, patiently awaiting their assigned duties.

Joram did not stand patiently, however. He shifted nervously from one foot to another, flexing his shapely hands to ease the morning stiffness. He knew the overseer was watching him. The man had singled him out for special attention, though for what reason he could not guess. More than once, he had looked up from his work to find the man's sharp-eyed gaze on him.

"Of course he watches you, my own proud beauty," Anja said fondly when Joram mentioned his suspicions. "He is jealous, as are all who see you. He knows one of the nobility. Likely he fears your wrath when you come into your own."

Joram had long ago ceased to listen to this kind of talk from his mother. "Whatever his reason," he snapped impatiently, "he is watching me — and not with jealousy, mark my words."

Though she made light of his fears, Anja was more frightened by Joram's worry than she admitted. She, too, noticed the overseer taking an unusual and apparently hostile interest in her son and she began hovering near Joram, working in the fields beside him when she could, trying to cover for his slowness. In her overeager protectiveness, however, Anja more often than not drew the overseer's attention rather than distracted it. Joram grew increasingly more nervous and upset, and the anger that always smoldered deep inside began to burn hotter, now that it had a target.

"You," called the overseer, motioning to Joram, "over there. Start seeding."

Sullenly, Joram moved off with the other young men and women, slinging the sack of seed over his shoulder. Though she hadn't been told to do so, Anja followed after Joram quickly, fearful the overseer might send her to some other part of the field.

"Catalyst," rang out the overseer's voice, "we're behind schedule. I want you to grant all these people Life. They're to hover, not walk, today. I figure they can cover one third more ground that way."

This was an unusual request, one that caused even Father Tolban to glance at the overseer questioningly. They weren't behind schedule. There was no need for this. But, though Father Tolban didn't like the overseer, he did not question him. The Field Catalyst had become immured in his life of tedious drudgery. He'd even, finally, given up his studies. Every day, he took his place in the fields with the magi, every day he trudged up and down the long rows of plowed earth. The winter winds froze him. The summer sun thawed him. He had turned as brown and dried and withered as a stalk of last year's corn.

As the catalyst began chanting the ritual, Joram froze. No matter how much Life he was granted, he was bound to the earth. Deep inside him, the old pain stabbed. The Difference. He almost stopped walking, but Anja, behind him, shoved him on, digging her sharp fingernails into the flesh of his arm. "Keep moving!" she whispered. "He won't notice."

"He'll notice," Joram retorted, angrily snatching his arm out of his mother's grasp.

Undeterred, Anja clutched at him. "Then we'll tell him what you always told the other," she hissed. "You are not well. You need to conserve your Life force."

One by one, the Field Magi, suffused with Life from the catalyst, used their magic to lift gracefully into the air. Like small brown birds, they began to skim over the surface of the ground, rapidly sowing the seeds in the freshly plowed soil.

Joram and Anja kept walking.

"Here! Stop! Wait a minute, you two. Turn around."

Joram halted, but he kept his back to the overseer. Anja stopped and half-turned, glancing through the matted mass of her filthy hair, her chin raised.

"Were you talking to us?" she asked coldly.

Ignoring them for a moment, the overseer stalked over to Father Tolban. "Catalyst," said the overseer, pointing at Joram's back, "open a conduit to this young man."

"I have done so, Overseer," replied Father Tolban, in injured tones. "I am quite capable of handling my duties—"

"You've done so?" interrupted the overseer, glaring at Joram. "And now he stands there, absorbing Life force, storing it up for his own personal use! Refusing to obey me!"

"I don't think that's true," returned the catalyst, staring at Joram as though seeing him for the first time. "It's very odd. I don't get the feeling that the young man is drawing Life from me at all—"

But the overseer, with a growl, left the catalyst still expounding and walked across the new-plowed earth toward Joram.

Joram heard him coming, but he did not turn around to face him. Staring straight ahead, unseeing, he clenched his fists. Why didn't the man just leave him alone?

Mosiah, watching nervously, felt the truth slip under his skin like a splinter. Quickly he motioned for Joram to turn and talk to the overseer. Joram could hide it! He had all these years. There were countless things he might offer as excuses.

But, if Joram even saw his friend, he ignored him. He didn't know how to talk to this man, let alone how to reason with him. He could only stand there dumbly, acutely aware that all the other magi had come to a halt and were staring at him. Blood rushed to his head; anger and embarrassment throbbed in his temples. Why couldn't they all just leave him alone?

Coming up behind Joram, the overseer reached out to grasp hold of the young man's shoulder, intending to physically impose his will on the sullen boy. But before he could touch him, Anja slipped between the overseer and her son.

"He is not well," she said quickly. "He must conserve his Life force . . ."

"Not well!" The overseer snorted, his gaze flicking over Joram's strong, young body. "He's well enough to be a damned rebel." Shoving Anja aside, the overseer put his hand on Joram's shoulder. At the man's touch, Joram spun around to face him, even as he involuntarily moved several steps backward, out of the man's reach.

Drifting in the air nearby, Mosiah started to float forward with some idea of intervening, but his father stopped him with a look.

"I'm not a rebel," said Joram, breathing heavily. He seemed to be suffocating. "Just let me get on with my work. And let me do it the way I do best . . ."

"You'll do it the way y'er told, you young dog!" the overseer snarled and started to take another step forward when Father Tolban, who had been staring at Joram with a pale face and wide eyes, suddenly gave a shrill cry. Stumbling forward, falling over his plain green robes, he grabbed hold of the overseer's arm.

"He's Dead!" the catalyst gasped. "By the Nine Mysteries, overseer, the boy's Dead!"

"What?" Startled, the overseer turned to the catalyst, who was shaking him frantically.

"Dead!" Father Tolban babbled. "I wondered . . . But I never tried giving Life to him! His mother always— He's Dead! There's no Life in him! I can't get any response—"

Dead! Joram stared at the catalyst. At last the words had been spoken. At last the truth he had known in his own heart entered his brain and his soul. Memories of Anja's story came to him. The Vision. No living issue. Memories of Mosiah's words. Dead children smuggled out of the cities. Dead children smuggled out of Merilon.

Alarmed and terrified, Joram looked at Anja . . .

. . . and he saw the truth.

"No," he said, letting the sack of seeds fall unheeded to the ground and backing up another step. "No." He shook his head.

Anja held out her arms to him. Her face was deathly pale beneath the dirt, her eyes were wide and fearful.

"Joram! My sweet! My own! Please, listen—"

"Joram," broke in Mosiah. Moving closer, ignoring his father's disapproving gaze, the young man had no idea what he might do, only that he could offer comfort.

But Joram did not see or even hear his friend. Staring at his mother in horror, the young man shrank back before her, shaking his head violently. His black hair sprang loose from its bonds. Dark curls fell down across his pale face, a mockery of the tears she had taught him not to cry.

"Dead!" repeated the overseer, having apparently just absorbed this information. His eyes glittered. "There's a reward for the living Dead. Grant me Life, Catalyst," he commanded. "Then open a Corridor! I'll keep him prisoner until the Enforcers arrive —"

It happened and was over in the beat of a heart, the blink of an eye, the drawing of a breath.

With the image of Joram's pale face before her eyes, Anja turned away from him to face the overseer. Her son, her beautiful son, knew the truth now. He would hate her forever, she could see the hatred in his eyes. It cut through her like the cold, conjured blades of an enemy. And sounding amid this bitter pain, tormenting her like the notes of shrill, discordant music, came the word "Enforcer."

Long ago, the Enforcers, the *Duuk-tsarith*, had come to take away her lover. It was a *Duuk-tsarith* who had turned him to stone. Now they were going to take away her child. As they had come once that other time. . . .

"No . . . Don't take my baby!" Anja cried wildly. "You mustn't. He'll be warm, soon. I'll warm him. Stillborn? No! You're wrong! Here, I'll hold him thus, next to my body. He'll be warm soon. Breathe, baby. Breathe, little one. You're lying, you bastards! My baby will breathe! My baby will live. The Vision was a lie . . ."

"Shut her up and call an Enforcer!" the overseer cried, turning away.

Father Tolban felt the conduit surge, energy was sucked from him with such force that he fell to his knees. With his last strength, he closed off the Life-giving force, but it was too late. Looking up, he watched helplessly as Anja's nails curled into strong, slashing talons, her teeth lengthened into fangs. The tattered dress changed to silken fur, her body rippled with muscles. Moving swiftly and silently in her giant catlike form, she leaped at the overseer.

The catalyst shouted an incoherent warning. The overseer, whirling, caught a glimpse of the raging wizardess. Flinging his arm up to protect himself, he reflexively activated a magical defense shield.

There was a crackling sound, a terrible, agonized scream, and Anja sank down to lie in a burned, crumpled heap on the newly plowed ground. The spell she had cast over herself ended. Relaxing into human shape, she looked up at Joram, tried to speak, then, shaking her head, she lay quite still, unmoving, her eyes staring up into the blue spring sky.

Weak and horror-stricken, Father Tolban crawled over and knelt beside her.

"She's dead!" murmured the catalyst in shock. "You've killed her."

"I didn't mean to," protested the overseer, staring at the lifeless body of the woman on the ground at his feet. "I swear! It was an accident! She . . . You saw her!" The overseer turned to face Joram. "She was crazy! You know that, don't you? She jumped at me! I —"

Joram didn't answer. The confusion was gone from his mind. Fear no longer blinded him. He saw everything with a startling, vivid clarity.

In my mother's body, the warmth of Life is gone. In me, it has never been. Now that the truth was spoken within him, he could accept it. The pain became a part of him, no different from any other.

Looking around, Joram saw the tool he needed, and reaching down, he picked up the heavy stone. He even paused a moment to notice the texture and feel of the stone as it lay in his palm. Rough and jagged, the stone's sharp edges bit into his skin. It was cold and lifeless, as Dead as he himself. He thought incongruously of the stone Anja had given him as a child, telling him "to make the air swallow it."

Balancing the stone for an instant, getting the feel of the weight, Joram straightened and, with all his strength, hurled it at the overseer.

The stone struck the man on the side of his face, caving in his head with a soggy sound, like the squashing of an overripe melon.

Father Tolban, still kneeling beside Anja's body, froze, as if turned to stone himself. The Field Magi slowly dropped to the ground, feeling the Life force ebb from them as shocked realization of what had occurred penetrated their minds.

Joram stood silently, unmoving, staring at the bodies on the ground.

Anja was a pitiable sight to her son. Thin and gaunt, clad in the rags of her former happiness, she died as she had lived, Joram thought bitterly. She died denying the truth. He spared a glance — and a glance only — for the overseer, who lay on his back, blood from the terrible wound forming a pool in the freshly turned dirt. The man had not seen the attack coming, he had not even imagined it possible.

Looking at his hands, then looking at the stone lying next to the man's crushed head, Joram's only thought was — how easy. . . . How very easy it had been to kill with that simple tool. . . .

He felt a touch on his arm. Whirling in fear, he grabbed Mosiah, who shrank back before the madness he saw in the dark, brown eyes.

"It's me, Joram! I'm not going to hurt you!" Mosiah raised his hands.

At the sound of the voice, Joram loosened his grip slightly, dim recognition dawning in his eyes, driving away the darkness.

"You've got to get out of here!" Mosiah said urgently. His face was pale, his eyes so wide that they seemed almost all white with only a tiny dot of color. "Hurry! Before Father Tolban opens the Corridor and brings the *Duuk-tsarith*!"

Joram stared at Mosiah blankly, then he looked back at the bodies on the ground.

"I don't know where," he muttered, "I can't —"

"The Outland!" — Mosiah shook him — "The border, where you wanted to go before. There are people who live there. Outlaws, rebels, Sorcerers. You were right. I've talked to them. They'll help, but you've got to hurry, Joram!"

"No! Don't let him escape!" Father Tolban cried. Pointing at Joram, the catalyst opened conduits full-force to the magi, sending Life flowing into them. "Stop him!"

Mosiah turned. "Father?" he cried urgently.

"Mosiah's right. Run, Joram," said the magus. "Take yourself to the Outlands. If you survive, those who live there'll watch over you."

"Don't worry about your mother, Joram," came a woman's voice. "We'll tend to the ceremony. You better run, young man, before the *Duuk-tsarith* get here."

Still Joram stood there, staring at the bodies.

"Take him partway, Mosiah," said his father. "He's addled. We'll see that he gets the time to make a fair start."

The Field Magi moved toward Father Tolban, who shrank backward, staring at them.

"You don't dare!" the catalyst whimpered. "I'll report you! An uprising . . ."

"No you won't report us," said Mosiah's father calmly, still advancing. "We tried to stop the boy, didn't we?"

The other Field Magi nodded.

"Your life has been easy enough here, Father. You wouldn't want that to change now, would you? Mosiah, get him going . . ."

But Joram had come to himself now, returning as if from a great distance. "Which way?" he asked Mosiah in a firm voice. "I don't remember . . ."

"I'll come with you!"

Joram shook his head. "No, you have a life here." He caught himself, adding bitterly. "You have a *life*. Now, which way?" he repeated.

"Northeast," Mosiah answered. "Cross the river. Once you're in the woods, be wary."

"How will I find those people?"

"You won't. They'll find you, hopefully before something nastier does." He held out his hand. "Good-bye, Joram."

Joram stared at the young man's hand for a moment, the only time he could remember seeing a hand held out to him in either help or friendship. Looking into Mosiah's face, he saw the pity in his eyes, pity and revulsion he could not hide.

Pity for a Dead man.

Turning, without a look behind, Joram ran across the plowed fields.

Mosiah's hand dropped to his side. For long moments, he stared after Joram, then, with a sigh, he went back to stand beside his father.

"Very well, Catalyst," said the magus, after Joram's figure had disappeared into the nearby woods. "Open the corridor and send for the Enforcers. And, Father," he added as the catalyst turned, cringing, to start back to his cabin, "remember the way of things, will you? The *Duuk-tsarith* will be here for only a few minutes. You'll be here a long, long time. . . ."

His head bowed in understanding, Father Tolban cast the magi a last, fearful glance, then hurried off.

Kneeling down beside Anja, one of the women moved her hands over the burned body, creating a coffin of crystal

around the corpse while the other magi levitated the body of
the overseer and sent it drifting toward the settlement.

"If the boy's truly Dead, you've done him no kindness,
sendin' him out there," remarked a woman, staring into the
dark regions of the forest. "He'll stand no chance at all
against the likes of what roams the Outland."

"At least he'll have a chance to fight for his life," Mosiah
answered hotly. Catching his father's eye, he choked and fell
silent.

Into each mind came the unspoken question.

What life?

12

Escape

Joram ran, though nothing chased him.

Nothing that he could see, that is. Nothing real. Nothing tangible. The Enforcers could not arrive this fast. The others would protect him, buy him time. He was in no danger.

Still, he ran.

It was only when spasms cramped his aching legs that he finally collapsed onto the ground and knew that he could never outrun the dark and tormented being who pursued him. He could never outrun himself.

How long Joram lay on the forest floor, he never afterward knew. He had no idea where he was. He had an indistinct impression of trees and tangled plant life. Somewhere, he thought he heard the low murmuring of water. The only thing real to him was the earth beneath his cheek, the pain in his legs, and the horror in his soul.

As he lay in the dirt, waiting for the pain to ease, the cold, rational part of his mind told him that he should get up and continue on. But beneath that cold and rational surface of

Joram's mind lurked a being, a dark creature that he managed, most of the time, to keep fettered and guarded. But on occasion it slipped its leash and took him over, mastering him completely.

Night blanketed the young man lying exhausted and frightened in the wilderness, and the coming of night loosed the blackness within Joram. Free again, it leaped out of its corner, sank its teeth into him, and dragged his soul away, to gnaw and ravage.

Joram did not get up. A numb, paralyzed sensation stole over his body, such as one feels upon first awakening from a deep sleep. The sensation was pleasant. The pain left his legs and soon all feeling left his body. He could no longer taste the dirt of the ground in his mouth, where his cheek pressed against the muddy trail. He no longer had any conscious thought of lying on the ground, or of the chill of the evening air, or that he was hungry or thirsty. His body slept, but his mind remained dreamily awake.

Once again he was a little child, crouched at the feet of the stone magus that was his father, feeling that hot, bitter tear splash upon him. Then the tear changed to his hair, tumbling and curling around his face and down his back, his mother's fingers ripping and tugging at it, tearing apart the tangles. And then his mother's fingers were the claws of animals, ripping and tugging at the overseer, tearing apart his life.

Then the stone that was his father became a stone in Joram's hand. Cold and biting, the stone shrank suddenly, becoming a toy, dancing in his fingers and appearing to disappear into the air. But all the while, the stone was safely palmed, concealed, hidden from view. Hidden, until today, when it grew so large in his hand that he could hide it no longer and he hurled it far away . . .

Only it kept coming back and, once again, he was a child. . . .

It was night. And it was day. Perhaps it was night again and day again.

Black spells, Anja called these times for Joram, when the darkness of his soul overwhelmed him. They had begun to afflict him when he was about twelve. He had no power over them. He could not fight them, but for days he would lie

upon his hard cot, staring at nothing, refusing to even ac-
knowledge his mother's frantic attempts to force him to eat or
drink or walk in the real world.

What roused him from these black times, Anja could
never tell. Joram would suddenly sit up, cast a bitter glance
about the hovel and at her, as if blaming her for his return.
Then, with a sigh, he would return to life, looking as if he had
wrestled with demons.

But so deep had he sunk this time that it seemed nothing
might rouse him. The cold and rational part of his mind appeared ready to give up the fight when it suddenly gained an
ally — danger.

Joram's first conscious thought was irritation at being
bothered. But his next was one of excruciating pain that exploded in his knee, tore through his body, and snatched his
breath away. Gasping and moaning, he rolled over in agony.

"It be live."

Through a haze of pain and the departing shadows of
darkness, Joram stared up toward the sound of the gruff
voice. He had a confused impression of greasy, matted hair
covering a face that once might have been human but now
had degenerated into something bestial and cruel. Hair covered human arms and a human chest as well. But it was not a
human foot that had kicked Joram. It was the cloven foot of
a beast.

The pain jolted his nerves, body, and mind back to reality.
Once again he could see and feel, and the first feeling he had
was one of terror. He saw sharp hooves standing close to his
head and, looking up, the powerful body of the creature that
was half-horse and half-man looming above him. A sudden
vision of that hoof slamming into his head caused fear to act
as the second stimulant to Joram's system. But it could only
do so much. His muscles were stiff from long disuse, his
body weak from lack of food and water. Gritting his teeth,
Joram managed to rise up on his hands and knees, only to
feel the hoof crash into his ribs, sending him sprawling head-
long into a thicket of underbrush.

Pain stabbed him. Unable to breathe, he fought for air as
the hooves clattered nearer. A huge hand gripped him by the
collar of his shirt and yanked him to his feet. Staggering on
legs that stung with returning circulation, Joram would have

fallen, but other hands held him up, binding his arms behind his back swiftly and skillfully.

A grunt. "Walk, human."

Joram took a step, stumbled, and fell as the blood tingled in his numb legs.

The hands jerked him to his feet again and shoved him forward. The pain in his side was a slow fire, the earth heaved beneath his unsteady steps, trees reached out to maul him. He stumbled ahead, then tripped and fell into the dirt, landing heavily. His arms bound, he was unable to catch himself and he rolled in the muck.

The centaurs laughed. "Sport," said one.

They hauled him to his feet again.

"Water," Joram gasped through cracked lips, his tongue swollen.

The centaurs grunted, the hairy faces splitting into yellow-toothed grins. "Water?" repeated one. Raising a massive arm, he pointed. Joram, barely standing on his shaking legs, turned his head. He could see the river ahead of him, sparkling through the leaves of the trees. "Run," said the centaur.

"Run! Human! Run!" shouted another centaur, laughing.

Desperately, Joram broke into a staggering run, hearing a cantering and thudding of hooves beating into the ground, feeling hot breath on his back, and choked by a foul, bestial odor. The river drew closer, but Joram felt his strength ebbing. He knew, too, with the certainty of despair, that the centaurs had no intention of letting him reach the river.

Once human, these creatures had been mutated by the *DKarn-Duuk*, the Battle Masters, and sent to fight in the Iron Wars. The wars had proved costly, devastating. The warlocks left alive were drained of their magic, their catalysts exhausted, having no more strength left to draw on the sources of Life. Unable to call upon the magic to change their creations back, the *DKarn-Duuk* abandoned their mutated soldiers, banishing them to the Outland. Here the centaurs lived their lives, breeding with animals or captured humans, creating a race whose human feelings and emotions were almost completely lost in the struggle to survive. Almost lost, but not quite. One emotion thrived among them, nurtured and cherished over the centuries — hatred.

Though the reason for that hatred had long since perished within the minds of these creatures who had no memory of their history, the centaurs knew one thing — torturing and murdering humans gave them a deep, inner satisfaction.

Stumbling to a halt, Joram turned with some idea of fighting. Immediately a hand crashed into his face, knocking him over. Lying on the ground, wracked by pain, the cold part of Joram's mind told him, "Die now. End it quickly. It doesn't matter, anyway."

He heard the hooves hitting the dirt around him. One thudded into his body. He didn't feel it, though he heard bones crack. Slowly, determinedly, he staggered to his feet. The centaurs knocked him down again. More blows from the sharp hooves broke his bones, cut into his flesh.

He tasted blood . . .

The coldness of a voice stung Joram back to consciousness as the coldness of water stung his lips.

"Can we do anything for him?"

"I don't know. He's pretty far gone."

"He's conscious, at least. That's something," continued the cold voice. "Any signs of a head wound?"

Joram felt hands upon his head. Rough and uncaring fingers ran over his skull, twitched open his eyes.

"No. I guess they wanted to enjoy him as long as possible." There was a pause, then the same voice continued, "Well, do we take him back to Blachloch or not?"

Another pause.

"Take him," said the cold voice finally. "He's young and strong. It'll be worth our trouble to haul him back to camp. Set his bones with the splints, the way the old man showed you."

"Do you 'spose he's the one killed the overseer?" a voice very close to Joram's ear boomed as rough hands gripped his limbs, making him gag with the sudden jolt of pain.

"Of course," said the cold voice dispassionately. "Why else would he have been out here? That makes him more valuable. If he proves troublesome, Blachloch can always turn him in. He still has his old contacts in the *Duuk-tsarith*."

A bone crunched. Blackness tinged with fiery red swirled around Joram. He caught hold of the cold voice, hanging on so that the darkness would not sweep him under.

"Be quick about it," the cold voice said irritably. "Get him on the packhorse. And stop him from screaming like that. There may be other centaur hunting parties on the border."

"I don't think you're going to have to worry about his yellin'. Look at him. He's finished."

Indistinguishable words, vanishing in a vast distance.

A sensation of being raised . . .

A sensation of falling . . .

Days and nights tumbled into one another with a noise of rushing water. Days and nights of the vague dreamlike awareness of traveling upon the water. Days and nights of struggling for consciousness, only to be assailed by pain and the bitter knowledge of being alone and forgotten. Days and nights of lapsing into unconsciousness and hoping bleakly never to waken.

Then there was the vague knowledge that the journey had ended and he was on land once more. He was in a strange dwelling, and Anja came to him, kneeling beside him and combing out his tangled black hair and whispering stories of Merilon, Merilon the Beautiful, Merilon the Wondrous. And he could picture Merilon in his mind. He could see the crystal spires and the boats with silken sails drawn by fabulous animals that drifted upon the currents of air. He was happy while these dreams lasted, and his pain eased. But when the pain returned, the dreams grew distorted and terrible. Anja became a creature of fangs and claws, trying to rip open his chest and tear out his heart.

Always, over and above the dreams and through the pain, came strange sounds, as of a giant breathing, and a banging, like an untuned bell, and a hissing, like a horde of snakes. Fire sprang up, burning before his eyes, burning away the beautiful, distorted images of Merilon.

But finally there was darkness and silence. Finally there was sleep, peaceful and restful. Finally there was a day when his eyes opened and he looked around him, and Anja was gone and Merilon was gone and there was only an old

woman sitting beside him and the banging sound ringing in
his ears.

"A long journey, you've had, Dark One," said the old
woman, reaching out her hand to smooth back his black hair.
"A long journey that almost took you Beyond. The Healer
did what she could, but without a catalyst to grant her Life,
her arts are limited."

Joram tried to sit up, but discovered that his arms and
legs were bound.

"Untie me," he cried hoarsely, trying to make himself
heard above the banging, bellowing sounds that came from
somewhere close, apparently outside the cabin.

"Nay, lad, you're not bound," said the old woman, smiling
in gentle amusement. "No, now lie still. You had a leg broke
in two places and an arm practically twisted off and ribs
smashed in. The bindings you feel are holding you together,
young man." Her smile changed to one of pride. "An inven-
tion of my husband, when he was younger. It's the best we
could do for you, without a catalyst to aid our Healer. Those
splints hold the bones in place while they knit themselves
back together."

Joram lay back, confused, and suspicious, but too weary
to either argue or fight. The incessant banging appeared now
to be coming from inside his head. Seeing him wince, the old
woman patted him.

"The sounds of the forge. You'll get used to it, in time. I
don't hear it at all now, except when it stops. Likely you'll
work there, lad," she added, rising to her feet. "You're a
strong one, I'll wager, and used to hard work. I can tell from
your callused hands. We can use a young man of your build
and girth. But don't worry about that now. I'll get you a bite
of broth, if you think you can stomach it."

Joram nodded. The bandages itched. It hurt to move.
But then he felt an arm beneath his head and a touch of
something on his lips. Opening his eyes, he saw the old
woman holding a bowl and an odd-looking implement in her
hand. With this implement, she carried the broth from the
bowl to his mouth. The taste was salty and delicious, filling
his body with warmth. Eagerly, he gulped it down.

"There, that's enough," said the old woman, settling him
back. "Your stomach's not used to it, yet. You must try to
sleep again."

How could he sleep with that infernal noise?

"What is a forge?" he asked wearily.

"You'll see, all in good time, Dark One," she said, bending over him with another kind smile. As she did, Joram noticed an object hanging from a silver chain around her neck that had slipped from the bodice of her dress and now dangled down before his eyes. It was a pendant of some sort, Joram recognized, remembering Anja telling him about the glittering jewels the people wore in Merilon. But this was not a glittering jewel. It was a crude, hollowed-out circle, carved in wood, with nine thin spokes running through it.

Seeing Joram's gaze upon the object, the old woman touched it with her hand, fondling it as proudly as the Empress might have fondled her rich jewelry.

"Where am I?" Joram asked drowsily, feeling as if he were back on that terrible journey and the water was once more sweeping him away.

"You are with those who practice the Ninth Mystery, those who would bring down death and destruction upon Thimhallan, according to some." The old woman's voice was sad, like the low murmur of the river. It came to him from a distance, muffled by the banging and bellowing sounds. Floating upon the water, he heard the old woman's voice once again, whispering as the wind.

"We are the Coven of the Wheel."

13

Saryon's Punishment

eventeen years had passed since Saryon had committed his heinous crime of reading forbidden books. Seventeen years had passed since he had been taken to Merilon. Seventeen years had passed since the death of the Prince. The people of Merilon and its small empire of surrounding city-states had just completed commemorating the holiday of that mournful occasion when Saryon was summoned once again to Bishop Vanya's chambers in the Font.

The arrival of the summons, coming as it did on the dark anniversary, brought such dreadful and unhappy memories to Saryon that he could not help but accept it with some trepidation. He had, in fact, returned to the Font from his current home in the Abbey of Merilon expressly to avoid the holiday that reminded him not only of his shattered hopes and dreams and of the Empress's bitter sorrow, but of the sorrow of others he had seen whose children had been born Dead.

Saryon always returned to the Font, if he could, during this time every year. He found comfort there, for no one at the Font was allowed to ever refer to the death of the Prince, much less celebrate it as a memorial. Bishop Vanya had forbidden it, an occurrence that everyone thought odd.

"Old Vanya really detests this holiday," remarked Deacon Dulchase to Saryon as the two walked the silent, peaceful corridors of their mountain fastness.

"I can't say that I blame him," Saryon replied, shaking his head with a sigh.

Dulchase snorted. Still a Deacon in his middle years, and knowing that he would undoubtedly die a Deacon, Dulchase had no compunction about speaking his mind — even in the Font where, it was said, the walls had ears, eyes, *and* mouths. Why he hadn't been sent to the fields long ago was due strictly to the intervention of the now elderly Duke of Justar, in whose household he had been raised.

"Bah! Let the Empress have her fancy. It's little enough, the Almin knows. You heard that Vanya tried to dissuade the Emperor from declaring the holiday?"

"No!" Saryon looked shocked.

Dulchase nodded, smug in his knowledge. He knew all the gossip of the court. "Vanya told the Emperor that it was sinful to remember one who had been born without Life, one who was obviously cursed."

"And the Emperor refused him?"

"They draped Merilon in weeping blue again this year, didn't they?" Dulchase asked, rubbing his hands. "Yes, the Emperor had guts enough to face up to His Holiness, even though it meant that His Holiness stalked out in a huff and now refuses to go near the Royal Court."

"I can't believe it," Saryon murmured.

"Oh, that won't last long. It's just for show. Vanya will be the winner in the end, no doubt about it. Just wait, the next matter that comes up, the Emperor will be only too happy to give in. They'll be reconciled, and Vanya will simply wait until next year to do it all over again."

"I didn't mean that," Saryon said, glancing around uneasily and drawing Dulchase's attention to one of the black-robed *Duuk-tsarith*, who was standing silently in the corridor, his face hidden in the depths of his cowl, his hands folded before him as was correct. Dulchase snorted again in disdain, but Saryon noticed that the Deacon crossed the corridor to walk upon the other side. "I mean, I can't believe the Emperor refused him."

"It was all due to the Empress, of course." Dulchase said, nodding knowingly and slightly lowering his voice, with a glance at the Enforcer. "*She* wanted it done, and so, of course, it was done. I tremble to think what might happen if she took it into her head to want the moon! But you should know that. You've been at court."

"No, not that much," Saryon admitted.

"In Merilon and doesn't attend court!" Dulchase flashed Saryon an amused glance.

"Look at me," Saryon said. Flushing, he raised his large, clumsy hands. "I don't fit in with the rich and the beautiful. You saw what happened during the ceremony seventeen years ago, when I got the color of my robe wrong? And I don't believe that I've once gotten it right since then! If the color was *Apricot Flambé*, I was *Rotting Peach*. Oh, you laugh, but it's true. Finally I left off changing it altogether. It was easier wearing the plain, untrimmed white of my rank and calling."

"I'll bet *you* were a hit!" Dulchase said caustically.

"Oh, wasn't I!" Saryon answered with a bitter smile and a shrug. "You know what they called me behind my back — Father Calculus. It was because all I could ever talk about was mathematics." Dulchase groaned. "I know. I bored them to tears, some to invisibility. One night the Earl simply dwindled away, before my eyes. He didn't mean to, poor man. He was frightfully embarrassed and apologized most handsomely. But he's getting old —"

"If you only made the effort . . ."

"I tried, I truly did. I joined in the gossip and the revelry." Saryon sighed. "But it proved too difficult. *I'm* getting old, I suppose. I'm asleep two hours before most people in Merilon even think about sitting down to dinner." He glanced around him at the stone walls that glowed softly with a magical radiance. "I enjoy living in Merilon. Its beauties seem to me as new and awe-inspiring as they did on that day I first saw them, seventeen years ago. But my heart is here, Dulchase. I want to pursue my studies. I need access to material here. There's a new formula I'm devising and I'm not quite certain about some of the magical theorems involved. You see, it's like this—"

Dulchase cleared his throat.

"Ah, yes. I'm sorry." Saryon smiled. "There goes Father Calculus again. I get too enthusiastic, I know. At any rate, I was planning to make my request to return here, then I received this summons from the Bishop. . . ." Saryon's face grew shadowed.

"Cheer up. Don't look so frightened," Dulchase said casually. "He's probably going to offer you condolences on the death of your mother. Then, like as not, he'll invite you back himself. You're not like me, after all. You've been a good boy, always eaten your vegetables, that sort of thing. Don't worry about anyone at court. Even as boring as you undoubtedly were, my friend, you could *never* outbore the Emperor." Dulchase glanced sharply at Saryon's averted face. "You *have* been eating your vegetables, haven't you?"

"Yes, of course," Saryon answered hastily, with an attempt to smile that was a dismal failure. "You're right. It's probably nothing more than that." Glancing at Dulchase, he found the Deacon staring at him curiously. Once again, the terrible burden of guilt for his crime assailed him. Feeling completely unable to stay around the shrewd, penetrating Deacon any longer, Saryon made his rather confused goodbyes and hastened away, leaving Dulchase to stare after him with a wry grin.

"I wish I knew what rats are crawling around in *your* closet, old friend. I'm not the first to wonder why you were sent to Merilon seventeen years ago. Well, whatever it is, I wish you luck. Seventeen years might as well be seventeen minutes as far as His Holiness is concerned. Whatever you've done, he won't have forgotten, nor forgiven either for that matter." Heading back to his own duties, Dulchase shook his head with a sigh.

Leaving Dulchase, Saryon fled to the haven of the Library, where he could count on being left alone. But he did not study. Burying himself beneath a mound of parchment, well out of sight from any who might chance by, the Priest put his tonsured head in his hands, feeling as miserable as he had when he had been summoned to Vanya's chambers seventeen years earlier.

He had seen Bishop Vanya on numerous occasions during the past years, since the Bishop always stayed at the Abbey when visiting Merilon. But Saryon had not spoken to him since that fateful time.

It was not that the Bishop avoided him or treated him coldly. Far from it. Saryon had received a very kind, very sympathetic letter on the occasion of his mother's death, expressing the Bishop's deepest sympathies and assuring him that she would rest in the same tomb as his father in one of the most honored places in the Font. The Bishop even approached him during the funeral ceremonies, but Saryon, under the guise of being deeply grieved, turned away.

He was not comfortable in the Bishop's presence. Perhaps it was because he had never truly forgiven His Holiness for condemning the small Prince to death. Perhaps it was because, whenever he looked at Vanya, Saryon could see only his own guilt. He'd been twenty-five years old when he had committed his crime. Now Saryon was forty-two, and he felt he'd lived more in these last seventeen years than he had in all those first twenty-five! What he'd told Dulchase about his life at court was only partially true. He *didn't* fit in. They *did* consider him a crashing bore. But that wasn't the real reason he avoided it.

The beauty and the revelry of court life was, he'd discovered, nothing but an illusion. As an example, Saryon had watched the Empress succumb, day by day, to a wasting illness that the Healers found impossible to treat. She was dying, everyone knew it. No one discussed it. Certainly not the Emperor, who never failed to comment nightly on how improved his lovely wife looked and how beneficial the spring air brought about by the *Sif-Hanar* (it had been spring a year in Merilon) was for her recovered health. Everyone in the court nodded and agreed. The magical arts of her ladies in waiting put color into the Empress's chalk-white cheeks and changed the hues of her eyes.

"She looks radiant, Your Majesty. Only grows more beautiful, Majesty. Never seen her in such delightful spirits, have you, Highness?"

They could not, however, add flesh to the sunken face or dim the feverish luster of her gaze, and the whispers around court were, "What will he do when she dies? The line runs through the female side. Her brother is visiting, heir to the throne. Have you been introduced? Allow me. Might be wise."

And through it all, through all the beauty and illusion, the only reality seemed to be Bishop Vanya — moving, working, lifting a finger to beckon someone here, motioning with his hand to smooth something out there, guiding, controlling, always in supreme control himself.

Yet Saryon had seen him shaken once, seventeen years ago. And he wondered, not for the first time, what it was that Vanya was keeping hidden from them. Once again, he heard the Bishop's words, *I could give you the reason* — Then the sigh that stopped the words, then the look of stern, cold resolution. *No. You must do what I tell you without question.*

A novitiate appeared before him, touching him gently on the shoulder. Saryon started. How long had the boy been standing there, unnoticed?

"Yes, Brother? What is it?"

"Forgive me for interrupting you, Father, but I have been sent to bring you to the Bishop's quarters, whenever it is most convenient."

"Yes. Right now will — uh — be fine." Saryon rose to his feet with alacrity. Not even the Emperor, it was said, kept Bishop Vanya waiting.

"Father Saryon, enter, enter." Vanya, rising to his feet, made a cordial motion with his hand. His voice was warm, though Saryon thought it seemed a bit strained, as if he were having a difficult time keeping the fires of his hospitality burning.

Starting to kneel to kiss the hem of his robes as was proper, Saryon was vividly and painfully reminded of the last occasion when he had performed this act, seventeen years earlier. Perhaps Bishop Vanya remembered as well.

"No, no, Saryon," Vanya said pleasantly, taking the priest by the hand. "We can dispense with obsequities. Reserve

those for the public for which they are intended. This is a
private, *quiet* little meeting."

Saryon looked at the Bishop sharply, hearing more said
in the tone of the words than in the words themselves.

"I am — am honored, Holiness," Saryon began in some
confusion, "to be summoned into your presence — "

"There is one here, Deacon, I would like you to meet,"
continued Bishop Vanya smoothly, ignoring Saryon's words.

Turning, startled, Saryon saw that there was another person in the room.

"This is Father Tolban, a Field Catalyst from the settlement of Walren," said Vanya. "Father Tolban, Deacon
Saryon."

"Father Tolban." Saryon bowed as was customary. "May
the Almin's blessing be yours."

It was no wonder Saryon had not noticed the man upon
first entering. Brown and dried and withered, the Field Catalyst disappeared into the woodwork as thoroughly as if he
had grown there.

"Deacon Saryon," Tolban mumbled, bobbing nervously,
his eyes darting from Saryon to Bishop Vanya and back to
Saryon again, his hands twitching and tugging at the long
sleeves of his untrimmed, mud-stained, and shabby green
robes.

"Please, everyone be seated," Vanya said kindly, indicating chairs with a wave of his hand. Saryon noticed that the
Field Catalyst waited a moment — to make certain he had
really been included in the invitation, he supposed. This
made things rather awkward, since by courtesy Saryon
could not really sit down without the Field Catalyst seating
himself as well. Starting to sit, he noticed that Tolban was
still standing, forcing him to catch himself and stand back up,
just about the same time as Tolban had finally decided it was
permissible for him to sit. Seeing Saryon standing, however,
the Field Catalyst leaped to his feet again, his face flushing
red in embarrassment. This time, Bishop Vanya intervened,
repeating the invitation to be seated in a pleasant but firm
tone.

Saryon sank into a chair, relieved. He'd had visions of
jumping around most of the afternoon.

After inquiring if anyone cared for refreshment — which they didn't — and some further polite talk about the difficulties of spring planting and the prospects for this year's harvest, all of which were answered weakly and somewhat confusedly by the obviously nervous Field Catalyst, Bishop Vanya finally came to the point.

"Father Tolban has quite an unusual story to relate, Deacon Saryon," he said, still in his same pleasant voice, as if they were three friends indulging in idle talk. Saryon's tension eased a bit, but his mystification increased. Why had he been called to Vanya's private chambers — a place he had not set foot in for seventeen years — to listen to a Field Catalyst relate a story? He looked at Vanya sharply, only to find the Bishop looking at him with a cool, knowing expression in his eyes.

Quickly, Saryon turned his attention to the Field Catalyst, who was drawing a deep breath as if about to plunge into icy water, now prepared to pay close attention to the little dried-up man's words. Though Bishop Vanya's face was smooth and placid as always, Saryon had seen a muscle twitch in the man's jaw, just as he had seen it twitch at the ceremony for the dead Prince.

Father Tolban began his tale, and Saryon discovered that he had no need to force himself to listen. He could not have torn himself away. It was the first time he heard the story of Joram.

The catalyst experienced several emotions during the telling, emotions ranging from shock to outrage and revulsion — the normal emotions one feels upon hearing such a grim, dark revelation. But Saryon knew, too, a stomach-clenching, bone-chilling fear, a fear that spread from his bowels through his body. Shivering, he huddled deeper into his soft robes.

What am I afraid of? he asked himself. Here I am, sitting in the Bishop's elegant chambers, listening to the halting, stumbling words of this withered old catalyst. What could possibly be wrong? Only later would Saryon recall the look in Bishop Vanya's eyes as he listened to the story. Only later would he come to understand why he shivered in terror. As it was, he decided at the time it was nothing more than the vicarious thrill of fear one enjoys listening to the stories of the nursery, stories of dead creatures who stalk the night. . . .

"And by the time the *Duuk-tsarith* arrived," Father Tolban concluded miserably, "the young man had been gone several hours. They tracked him as far as the Outlands, until it became obvious that he had vanished in the wilderness. We could see where his trail disappeared across the borders of civilization. They also found centaur tracks. There was little they could do, and in fact, they simply assumed him lost to this world, since all know that few who venture into those lands return. That is how I reported it."

Vanya frowned and the catalyst flushed, hanging his head. "I — I was premature, it seems, in my judgment, for now, a year later —"

"That will be sufficient, Father Tolban," Bishop Vanya remarked, still speaking very pleasantly.

But the Field Catalyst wasn't fooled. Clenching his hands, he stared down gloomily at the floor. Saryon knew what the wretched man must be thinking. After this disaster, he'd be a Field Catalyst for the rest of his natural existence. But that certainly wasn't Saryon's problem, nor was it why he had been asked to listen to this dark tale of insanity and murder. He glanced again, puzzled, at Bishop Vanya, hoping to find some answer. But Vanya was not looking at Saryon, nor was he looking at the poor Field Catalyst. The Bishop was staring out into nothing, his lips pursed, his brow furrowed, obviously grappling mentally with some unseen enemy. At last his struggles came to an end, or appeared to do so at any rate, for he turned to Saryon, his face once more smooth.

"A most shocking incident, Deacon."

"Yes, Holiness," Saryon replied, still feeling the shiver creeping over his body.

Placing the tips of his pudgy fingers together, Vanya tapped them delicately. "There have been several instances, over the past few years, where we have been able to locate those children who were born Dead and yet who, through the misguided actions of their parents, were allowed to remain in the world. When they were discovered, their terrible sufferings were mercifully relieved."

Saryon shifted uneasily in his seat. He had heard rumors of this, and though he knew what a tortured existence these poor souls must lead, he could not help wondering if such drastic measures were really necessary. Apparently his doubts were expressed upon his face, for Vanya frowned and, turning his gaze upon the innocent Field Catalyst, proceeded to expostulate.

"You know, of course, that we cannot have the Dead walking the land," Vanya said sternly to Father Tolban.

"Y-yes, Holiness," stammered the catalyst, shrinking before this undeserved and unexpected attack.

"Life, the magic, comes from all around us, from the ground we walk, the air we breathe, the living things that grow to serve us . . . yes, even the rocks and stones, crumbled remains of once great mountains, give us Life. It is this force we call upon and channel through our humble bodies that gives the magi the ability to mold and alter the raw elements into objects both useful and beautiful."

Vanya glared at the Field Catalyst, to see if he was paying attention. The catalyst, not knowing what else to do and looking thoroughly miserable, gulped, and nodded.

The Bishop continued, "Imagine this Life force as a rich, full-bodied wine, whose color, flavor, bouquet" — he spread his hands — "is perfect in every respect. Would you dilute this wonderful wine with water?" Vanya asked suddenly.

"No, oh no, Holiness!" cried Father Tolban.

"Yet you would permit the Dead to walk among us and, what is worse, perhaps allow their seed to fall into fertile ground and grow? Would you see the vines of weeds choke out the life of the grape?"

The Field Catalyst might have been a dried grape himself as he shriveled under this barrage. His brown face shrank, his wizened features twisted while he desperately protested that he had no intention of nurturing weeds. Vanya allowed him to babble, his gaze shifting to Saryon, who bowed his head. The reprimand was his, of course. It would not be proper for a Bishop to scold a Font Catalyst in the presence of an underling, so Vanya had chosen this method to rebuke him. Confused memories of hiccuping babies and weeping parents flitted into Saryon's mind, but he firmly repressed them. He understood. The Bishop was right, as always. Deacon Saryon would not be the one to dilute the wine.

But, he wondered, as he sat staring at his hands folded properly in his lap, where was all this leading?

With an abrupt gesture, Vanya squelched the Field Catalyst, cutting him off at the roots and leaving him on the ground to wither. The Bishop turned to Saryon.

"Deacon Saryon, you are no doubt wondering what this tale has to do with you. And now you will have your answer. I am sending you after this Joram."

Saryon could do nothing but stare, aghast. Now it was his turn to stammer and stutter, to the vast relief of Father Tolban, who seemed extremely grateful to find the attention shifted away from him at last.

"But. . . . Holiness, I — You said he was dead."

"N-no," Father Tolban faltered, cringing. "I — That was my mistake . . ."

"He's not dead, then?" Saryon said.

"No," Vanya replied. "And you must find him and bring him back."

Staring at Bishop Vanya, Saryon wondered what he could possibly say. That I'm not *Duuk-tsarith*. That I know nothing about apprehending dangerous criminals. That I'm middle-aged, that I'm a catalyst — a word synonymous with weak and defenseless. "Why me, Holiness?" he managed to ask feebly.

Bishop Vanya smiled, tolerant of his priest's confusion. Rising to his feet, he sauntered over to the window, waving his hand behind him as he went. This gesture was to the two underlings, indicating that they were to keep their seats, both of them having started to leap up when he stood.

Saryon relapsed into the soft cushions of the chair, but at the same time, he tried to shift his position in such a way that he could see Vanya's face as he talked. That proved impossible. Walking to the window, the Bishop stood with his back to Saryon, staring down at the courtyard below.

"You see, Deacon Saryon," he began, his voice still pleasant and nonchalant, "this young man, this Joram, presents rather a unique problem for us. He did *not* meet his physical death in the Outlands as was reported." At this juncture, Vanya half-turned, carefully examining a bit of the fabric of the curtain and scowling at it irritably. The Field Catalyst went deathly white. Finally muttering, "A flaw," Vanya continued imperturbably. "Father Tolban has since received word which leads us to believe that this young man, this Joram, has joined up with a group who call themselves the Coven of the Wheel."

Saryon glanced at Father Tolban, hoping for a clue, since Bishop Vanya had uttered these words in a tone of such dread that he could only suppose he was the only person in Thimhallan never to have heard of this group. But the Field Catalyst was no help, having shrunk back so far in his chair as to be practically invisible.

Receiving no response from his priest, Vanya glanced over his shoulder.

"You have not heard of them, Father Saryon?"

"No, Holiness," Saryon confessed, "but I lead such a retired life . . . my studies . . ."

"No need to apologize." Vanya cut him off. Clasping his hands behind his back, he turned to face him. "I would have been surprised if you had, as a matter of fact. As a loving parent keeps the knowledge of dark and wicked things from his children until they are strong and wise enough to deal with them, so we keep knowledge of this dark cloud from our people, bearing the burden upon ourselves in order that they may live in sunshine. Oh, the people are not in danger," he added, seeing that Saryon raised his eyebrows in alarm. "It is simply that we will not allow vague fears to disturb the beauty and tranquility of life in Merilon as it has been disturbed in other kingdoms. You see, Father Saryon, this coven is devoted to the study of the Dark Art — the study of the Ninth Mystery — Technology."

Once again, Saryon felt that cold fear grip his bowels. A shivering sensation starting at his scalp ran over his entire body.

"It seems that this Joram had a friend, a young man called Mosiah. One of the Field Magi, hearing noises in the night, woke and looked out his window. He saw Mosiah and a young man he is positive was Joram engrossed in conversation. He could not hear all of what was said, but he swears he overheard the words 'Coven' and 'Wheel.' He said

Mosiah drew back at this, but his friend must have been persuasive because the next morning, Mosiah was gone."

Saryon glanced over at Father Tolban just in time to see the Field Catalyst cast a furtive look at Vanya, who was studiously ignoring him. Tolban looked over at his fellow catalyst and caught Saryon looking at him. Flushing guiltily, Tolban returned to staring at his shoes.

"We have, of course, known of the existence of this coven for some time." Bishop Vanya frowned. "It is composed of every outcast and misfit who thinks the world owes him something in return for his birth. Not only do the Dead walk among them, but so do thieves and robbers, debtors, vagrants, rebels . . . Now a murderer. They come from all over the Empire, from Sharakan in the north to Zith-el in the east. Their numbers are growing, and while the *DKarn-Duuk* could deal with them easily enough, going in to take the young man by force would mean armed conflict. It would mean talk, upset, and worry. We cannot have that, not now, while the political situation in court is in such delicate balance." He cast a meaningful glance at Saryon.

"This — this is dreadful, Holiness," Saryon stammered, still too confused to catch more than one word in ten. But Vanya was looking at him, expecting a reply, so he said the first thing that came into his head. "Surely — er — something must be done. We cannot live knowing that this threat exists . . ."

"Something *is* being done, Deacon Saryon," Bishop Vanya said in soothing tones. "Rest assured, the matter is under control, another reason that apprehending the boy must be handled delicately. But, at the same time, we dare not allow this murder of an overseer go unpunished. Talk is already spreading throughout the Field Magi, who are, as you know, a discontented, rebellious lot. To let this young man go free after his heinous crime would encourage the spread of anarchy among this class. Because of this, the young man must be apprehended alive and made to stand trial for his crime. Apprehended alive," Vanya muttered, frowning. "That is most important."

At last, Saryon thought he was beginning to understand. "I see, Holiness." He had some trouble getting his words out past a bitter taste in his mouth. "You need someone to go in, isolate this young man, open a Corridor, and lead the *Duuk-tsarith* to him without anyone else being the wiser. And you chose me because I was once involved with the Dark —"

"You were chosen for the excellent mathematical knowledge you possess, Deacon Saryon," Bishop Vanya interrupted, sliding in under Saryon's words smoothly. A glance at the Field Catalyst and a slight shaking of the head were enough to remind Saryon that he was not to speak of the old scandal. "These Technologists, so we are led to believe, are extremely fascinated with the subject of mathematics, believing it to be the key to their Dark Art. This will provide you with ideal cover and lead them to accept you into their group most readily."

"But, Holiness, I am a catalyst, not a — a rebel, or a thief," Saryon protested. "Why should they accept me at all?"

"There have been renegade catalysts before," Vanya remarked wryly. "This Joram's father was one, in fact. I remember the incident quite well — he was found guilty of conceiving through the repulsive act of physically joining with a female. He was sentenced to the Turning to Stone . . ."

Saryon shuddered involuntarily. All his old sins were crowding in on him, it seemed. The lurid dreams of his youth returned to him, adding to his tension. The fate of Joram's father might well have been his own! For a moment, he was very nearly physically ill and leaned back against the cushions of his chair. When the blood quit pounding in his ears and his dizzy feeling abated, he could once more attend to Vanya's words.

"Surely you remember the incident, Deacon Saryon? It was seventeen years ago . . . But, no, I forgot. You were . . . absorbed . . . in your own problems at that time. To continue, upon being told that her child had failed the Tests, the mother — I believe her name was Anja — disappeared, taking the babe with her. We tried to trace her, but it proved impossible. Now, at last, we know what happened to her and her child."

"Holiness," Saryon said, swallowing the bile in his mouth, "I am not a young man. I do not believe I am suited for such an important task. I am honored in the confidence you repose in me, but the *Duuk-tsarith* are far better qualified—"

"You underestimate yourself, Deacon," Bishop Vanya said pleasantly, leaving the window and walking across the room. "You have been living too long among your books." Coming to stand directly in front of Saryon, he looked down at the priest. "Perhaps I have other reasons for choosing you, reasons that I am not at liberty to discuss. You have been chosen. I cannot, of course, force you to do this. But, do you not feel that you owe the Church something, Saryon, for— shall we say—past kindnesses?"

The Field Catalyst could not see the Bishop's face. Only Saryon could see it, and he would remember it to the day he died. The round, pudgy cheeks were placid and calm. Vanya was even smiling slightly, one eyebrow raised. But the eyes . . . the eyes were terrible—dark and cold and unyielding.

Suddenly, Saryon understood the genius of the man and, at last, he could give a name to his unreasoning fear. The punishment for the crime he had committed so many years before had been neither forgotten nor relaxed.

No, it had simply been deferred.

Seventeen years Vanya had waited patiently should an opportunity arise to use it . . .

To use him. . . .

"Well, Deacon Saryon," the Bishop said, still in that same, pleasant voice, "what do you say?"

There was nothing to say. Nothing but the ancient words Saryon had learned so long ago. Repeating them now, as he repeated them every morning in the Ritual of Dawn, he could almost see the white, thin-boned hand of his mother, tracing them in the air.

"*Obedire est vivere. Vivere est obedire.* To obey is to live. To live is to obey."

B O O K   T W O

The Outland

The border of the civilized lands and that region of Thimhallan known as the Outland is marked to the north of Merilon by a great river. Called the Famirash, or Tears of the Catalysts, its source is to be found in the Font, the great mountain that dominates the landscape near Merilon, the mountain where the catalysts have established the center of their Order. Thus the river's name—a daily reminder of the toil and sorrows suffered by the catalysts in their work for mankind.

The water of the Famirash is sacred. Its source in the mountain—a merry, bubbling brook—is a holy place, tended and guarded by the Druids. Water taken from this pure portion of the river possesses healing properties used by the Healers throughout the world. As the river runs upon its way, however, tumbling and laughing down the mountain like the child it is, the Famirash is joined by other streams and brooks, its innocence and purity diluted. By the time it reaches the city of Merilon, the river has grown up, becoming a wide, deep body of water.

Having gained in maturity and stature, the Famirash River, upon arriving in Merilon, becomes civilized. In the years following the Iron Wars, the *Pron-alban*, wizards skilled in the arts of shaping stone and earth, took hold of the river, rechanneled it and tamed it, split it and divided it, twisted it and turned it, sent it flowing up hills and down ornamental waterfalls, and caught it in quaint, small pools. Through their magical arts and those of their descendants, the river is forced up into the marble platforms where it bubbles in fountains and shoots high into the air in rainbow geysers. Magically heated, the river creeps demurely into perfumed bathing rooms or presents itself boldly, ready for work in the kitchens. Finally, allowed to venture into Merilon's Sacred Grove, where stands the tomb of the great wizard who founded this land, the Famirash nurtures the beautiful tropical plants and finds time to indulge in the artistic creations of the Illusionists. So vastly changed is the Famirash River in Merilon that most people forget it is a river at all.

After suffering itself to endure these civilized trappings, it is little wonder that once the river escapes the city walls of Merilon it churns and rages within its banks in a tumult of white-water confusion. Once the Famirash works this out of its system, it calms down, and by the time it meanders past the cleared fields and small farm villages, it is like a placid old Field Catalyst, plodding slowly and muddily along its tree-lined way.

Onward it flows through the croplands, quiet and hardworking until it leaves civilized lands behind. Then, once out of the sight of man, the Famirash River gives a final, great twist — like the back of a dragon — and plunges with a wild roar of exultation into the Outlands.

Free at last, the river becomes a raging torrent of white, foaming water that leaps over rocks and rushes through narrow cavern walls. There is an anger in the water, an anger it acquires as it surges past the dark places where lurk angry things — beings created by magic then tossed aside; beings wrenched from beloved homes, brought to a strange land, then left to fend on their own; beings who live here because their own, dark natures will not allow them to live in the light.

Strange sights the river sees, as it hurtles along its course. Trolls wash the bones of their victims in its waters in the manner that the creatures have, cleaning the bones to use them for ornaments upon the body or to decorate their dank caves. Giant men and women, fully twenty feet tall with the strength of rock and the brains of children, sit upon its banks, staring into the water in dim fascination. Dragons sun themselves upon its rocks like huge lizards, keeping one eye open always for signs of intruders into their secret caves. Unicorns drink from its pools, savage centaurs fish its streams, bands of faeries dance upon its waters. But the strangest sight of all, perhaps, comes within the deepest, darkest part of the river's journeying, within the very heart of the Outland — the camp of the Technologists.

By the time it reaches this region, the Famirash River runs deep and wide, dark and sullen. For here the river receives a rude shock. It flows into the clutches of the Sorcerers of the Ninth Mystery, who chain the river and force it to work for them.

The Technologists, or the Coven of the Wheel, as they call themselves, have dwelt peacefully within the shelter of the Outland for many years. Numbering several hundred people, their community is an ancient one, having been founded by those who escaped the purges that took place following the Iron Wars.

"They give Life to that which is Dead!" was the accusation of the catalysts then. "Their Dark Art will destroy us in this world, as it came close to destroying us in the ancient world. Look what it has done already! How many have died because of it and how many more will die if we do not remove this plague from our land!"

Hundreds of the practitioners of the Ninth Mystery were sent Beyond in what became known as the Casting Out. Their books and papers were, according to the catalysts, completely destroyed, though the catalysts secretly kept examples of many of them ("To fight the enemy, one must know him as well as one knows oneself.") The Sorcerers' terrible weapons and engines of war slowly became things of dark legend; the stories of machines that raise water from the river and carriages that crawl across the ground on round feet dwindled to the stuff of faerie tales that children laugh to hear repeated.

Those few who managed to escape the persecution fled into the Outland, where they waged a constant, bitter struggle for survival. Drawn to their ranks were all those who, as Bishop Vanya said, had a grudge against the world. Men and women of the lower classes who had rebelled against their lot, men and women of all classes whose greed led them to crime, men and women whose twisted passions led them into a thousand sins. Here too, in later years, came the Dead — those children who had failed the Testing. All were accepted because all were needed to help in the desperate battle against the wild and savage land and its inhabitants.

Finally, after centuries, the Technologists managed to create a haven in the wilderness where they could live more or less at peace. All they wanted was to be left alone, having neither the ambition nor desire left to force their ways upon others. They wanted to live as they chose, tinkering and puttering and building their waterwheels and grindstones and gristmills. Though still a haven for outcasts, the Sorcerers of the Ninth Mystery had their own laws, which were strictly enforced. Thus they managed to rid themselves of tainted blood. Thus they managed to live isolated and apart from the rest of Thimhallan for long, long years, eventually all but forgotten by the rest of the world.

The world, having forgotten the Sorcerers, might have left them alone. But, as often happens to mankind in his search for knowledge, the Coven chanced upon a discovery that could have led to great good but was, instead, perverted to evil.

They learned, once more, the ancient, lost art of forging iron.

Who knows by what chance this brought the evil men to them? Perhaps it was the discovery of a crude knife upon the body of a centaur. Perhaps it was the spear in the hands of some poor, pathetic giant, who babbled the name of those who had made it for him before he succumbed to torture. It doesn't matter now. The bandits found the Coven — a simple, peaceful people, isolated from the world. To enslave them was an easy task, for the leader of the bandits was a powerful warlock, a former *Duuk-tsarith*.

For the last five years, the Technologists have been ruled by a group who has taken the iron, taken that which is Lifeless, and given it a most deadly life of its own.

I

The Renegade

In less time than it takes to tell it, Saryon started on his journey. By the time he was ready to leave the Font, he was no longer afraid, nor was he bitter or angry. He was resigned. He had accepted his fate. After all, he had escaped punishment for seventeen years. . . . He left the Font under the cover of night, sped upon his way by the Enforcers, the black-robed *Duuk-tsarith*.

Only one person noticed Saryon was gone — Deacon Dulchase. When his inquiries among Masters and brethren brought only shrugs and blank looks, Dulchase, secure in the favor of his Duke, finally confronted Bishop Vanya himself.

"By the way, Holiness," said Dulchase in conversational tones, planting himself in front of the Bishop as he walked about one of the terraced gardens, "I have missed Brother Saryon of late. He and I were to have discussed a mathematical hypothesis concerning the possibility of fetching the Empress the moon. The last time I saw him, he spoke of being summoned to your chambers. I wondered —"

"Father Saryon?" interrupted the Bishop coldly, glancing around at several other catalysts, members of his staff, who were standing near. "Father Saryon . . ." the Bishop mused. "Yes, I recall now. I believe he and I discussed a mathematical theory of his, something about shaping stone. He seemed fatigued to me. Overworked. Don't you agree, *Deacon*?" An emphasis on the rank. "I recommended a . . . holiday."

"I'm certain he took your recommendation to heart, Holiness," the perennial Deacon returned, frowning.

"I hope so, Brother," Bishop Vanya said, turning away.

With a sigh, Dulchase went back to his cell to perform the Ritual of Night, seeing, in his mind's eyes, his poor friend slogging among the beans and cucumbers.

Dulchase was not far wrong in his imaginings. The Bishop had decreed that Saryon should establish a "reputation" as a renegade catalyst so that, when he vanished into the Outland, his story would be believed. He also advised Saryon to discover what he could about Joram, to gain information on the young man that might be of use later. What better way to accomplish both objectives then to live among the Field Magi in the village of Walren?

Saryon agreed to the arrangements calmly and quietly, a doomed man accepting his fate. He had decided, after serious reflection, that this business about Joram was all a sham. There seemed no other reasonable explanation. He simply could not fathom why the Bishop was going to all this trouble to track down one Dead young man, even if he was a murderer.

Saryon had simply outlived his usefulness to the Order and this was Vanya's way of eliminating him swiftly and silently. Such things were not unusual. Catalysts had disappeared before. The Bishop had even taken the trouble to establish a witness in this wretched Father Tolban, who would relate that Saryon had died in a heroic cause. Thus Saryon's mother's spirit would rest easy and not trouble Bishop Vanya in the night as spirits sometimes did now that the Necromancers were no longer in the world to propitiate them.

Saryon and Father Tolban arrived in the village of Walren within moments after leaving the Font, traveling through the Corridors whose magical halls made a journey of hundreds of miles seem little more than the placing of one foot in front of the other.

Though it was early night when they arrived, the Field Magi were in bed and asleep, according to Tolban, who was obviously nervous and ill at ease in Saryon's presence. Muttering something to the effect that he assumed Saryon would wish to rest as well, the Field Catalyst led the priest to an empty dwelling near his own.

"The old overseer lived here," Father Tolban said in gloomy tones, opening the door to a burned-out tree that had been converted to a dwelling like the others in the village. Slightly larger than the rest, it appeared on the verge of collapse.

Saryon glanced inside in bitter resignation. Nothing more, it seemed, could add to his misery. "The overseer who was murdered?" he asked quietly.

Tolban nodded. "I hope you don't mind," he mumbled, rubbing his hands. The spring air was chill. "But it — it's all that's vacant, at present.

What does it matter, thought Saryon wearily. "No, it's all right."

"I'll see you at breakfast, then. Would you care to eat your meals with me?" Father Tolban asked hesitantly. "There's a woman, too old to work in the fields, who earns her way by doing such chores."

Saryon was about to reply that he wasn't hungry and didn't expect to be, when he suddenly took notice of Tolban's anxious, pinched face. Something occurred to Saryon then and, remembering the pouch someone had thrust into his arms before he left the Font, he handed it to the Field Catalyst.

"Certainly, Brother," Saryon replied. "I would be pleased to share your table. But you must let me pay my way."

"Deacon . . . this — this is too much," stammered Tolban, who had been eyeing the hefty sack hungrily ever since they'd arrived. The fragrant aroma of bacon and cheese filled the air.

Saryon smiled wryly. "We might as well eat it now. I don't believe I will be needing it where I am going, do you, Brother?"

Flushing, Father Tolban muttered some incoherent reply and backed hurriedly out the door, leaving Saryon to stare around the dwelling. Once it might have been a relatively nice place to live, he thought bleakly. The wooden walls were polished, the branches that formed the roof gave some signs of having been skillfully mended and repaired. But its past owner had been dead a year, the dwelling allowed to fall into ruin. Apparently no one had entered it since the man's murder; there were remnants of its former owner scattered about in the way of clothes and a few personal items. Picking these up, Saryon tossed them into the firepit, then glanced about.

A bed, formed out of a bough of the tree, stood on one side of the small room. A crudely shaped table and several chairs huddled near the firepit. Branches formed a few shelves in the walls that had once been the tree's trunk, and that was all. Thinking of his comfortable cell in the Font, with its down mattress, warm fire, and thick stone walls, Saryon gave the bed where the murdered man had slept a shuddering glance. Then, wrapping himself in his robes, he lay down on the floor, and gave way to despair.

The next morning, after sharing Tolban's meager breakfast, Saryon was introduced to the cacklings and crowings of Marm Hudspeth, who considered him a wonder sent from the Almin himself. Then the catalyst was taken outside to meet the rest of his people and to begin his duties.

According to the part he was told to play, Saryon had been sent to the fields for some minor infraction committed against the Order, and was supposed to appear discontented and rebellious. He was not, as has been said, a very good liar.

"I don't know if I can play this part," he confided to Father Tolban as they trudged through the mud toward where the Field Catalyst stood patiently in line, waiting for the morning's Gift of Life.

"What — being angry at the Church? Angry at the fate that brought you here? Oh, you'll play it all right," muttered Father Tolban gloomily, the spring wind whipping his robes about his stick-thin, dried-up body. "For all the good it will do you."

And so Saryon discovered. He had not been in Walren a day before he lost some of his own despairing misery in his anger at the way these people were forced to live.

He had thought his own dwelling small and cramped until he found that entire families lived in shacks no larger. Food was plain and coarse and scarce after the harsh winter. Unlike the fortunate inhabitants of the cities where the weather is controlled, the Field Magi are subject to the whims of the varying seasons. In Merilon, surrounded by its magical dome, rain came only if the Empress decided that the sunlight had grown tiresome, snow fell only to glimmer beautifully in the moonlight on the crystal palaces. Here, on the border, there were terrible storms, the likes of which Saryon had never experienced.

"The nobles there" — Father Tolban glanced in the direction of distant Merilon — "fear these peasants. And with good reason." The Field Catalyst shuddered. "I saw them, the day that accursed boy murdered the overseer. I thought they were going to murder me, as well!"

Saryon shivered, too, but it was from the cold. The winds had been blowing steadily off the mountains and, until they switched, spring was more like winter. Opening a conduit to Marm Hudspeth, Father Tolban gave the magus sufficient Life to envelop the two catalysts in a cozy globe of warmth that made Saryon feel as though he were sitting in a bubble of flame. But it didn't help much. The cold seemingly defied magic. It had dwelt in this shack longer than mortals. Creeping from the floors and walls, it seeped up through Saryon's feet and into his very bones. He wondered if he would ever again be warm and sometimes thought, rather bitterly, that Bishop Vanya could at least have told him he intended to torture him before his execution.

"But if the Emperor fears rebellion, why doesn't he improve conditions?" Saryon asked irritably, endeavoring to wrap his feet up in the skirts of his white robes. "Give these people housing, enough to eat —"

"Enough to eat!" Tolban looked shocked. "Brother Saryon, these people are strong in magic to begin with. I've heard it said they're stronger than the *Albanara*, the noble wizards. How could we control them if they became stronger still? Right now, they are forced to depend upon us to provide them with Life. They must use all their energy to survive. If they ever gained the means to store it up . . ." He shook his head, then, glancing around fearfully, he drew close to Saryon. "And there's another reason," he whispered. "Their children aren't born Dead!"

A month passed, then two. Days and nights grew warmer, and Saryon learned the work of a Field Catalyst. Rising with the dawn, never feeling as though he'd had enough sleep, he mumbled wearily through the Ritual, joined Father Tolban for a frugal breakfast, then made his way into the fields where the magi were waiting. Here, the catalyst put into practice those mathematical exercises he'd been taught from childhood. He learned to measure out Life in exact and minute degrees, since it would never do to give a Field Magus too much. He trudged the rows with them — uncaring at first. It seemed nothing could penetrate the depths of his unhappiness. Even the sight of a small seedling, springing up from the earth, was like sunlight streaming through a break in storm clouds, cheering him for only a moment, then vanishing into darkness once more.

The catalyst had not forgotten, however, the real reason he was here. Mostly from boredom and to keep his mind off his own misery, Saryon spent the evenings talking with the people, and he had no difficulty in getting them to discuss Joram. They scarcely talked of anything else, in fact, the death of Anja and the murder of the overseer having been a high point in their lives. Over and over they related the story with relish during the brief hour they were permitted to socialize after their meager dinners.

"Joram was a fey one," said the father of the runaway Mosiah. "I saw him grow from a babe to a man. I lived with him in this village sixteen years, and the words he spoke to me I could count upon the fingers of this hand."

"How could he be among you all that time and you have no notion that he was Dead?" Saryon asked.

They shrugged. "If he *was* Dead," said a woman, with a contemptuous glance at Father Tolban. "Joram did the work, same as the rest of us. So he didn't have Life enough in him to walk the air. Neither do you, Catalyst." She said this with a sneer and the others laughed.

"He were a pretty babe," commented one.

"And a comely man," said another. At this Saryon saw a young girl nod so enthusiastically that she blushed red when she noticed him watching her. "Or he would have been," the older woman added, "if he ever smiled. But he didn't, nor laughed neither."

"Nor cried," said Mosiah's father. "Not even when he was little. I saw him take a bad spill once — Joram was always fallin' or stumblin' into things, seems like. Anyway, he split his head clean open. Blood ran down his face. It liked to knocked him silly for a bit. A growed man would have cried over that and not felt the least shamed. He had tears in his eyes, too. By the Almin, the lad was only eight or nine. But he gritted his teeth and blinked them back. 'Damn it, boy,' I said, running over to help him, 'let out a holler or two. I would if I'd taken a hurt like that.' But he only gave me such a look with those brown eyes of 'is it was a wonder I warn't turned to stone on the spot."

"It was his mother done it to him," said the older woman with a sniff. "She was moonstruck, was that one. Wearin' that fancy dress 'til it fell off her body. Fillin' his head with stories of Merilon and how he was better than the rest of us."

"He had beautiful hair," said the young girl, shyly. "And, I — I think I saw him smile . . . once. We were working together in the woods and I found a wild rose. He seemed so unhappy most of the time that . . . that I gave it to him." The young girl looked down at her hands, flushing. "I felt sorry for him."

"What'd he do?" The woman snorted. "Bite your hand?"

The others snorted derisively or snickered, causing the young girl to blush and fall silent.

"What did he do?" Saryon asked gently.

Glancing up at him, the girl smiled. "He didn't take it. He acted almost like it frightened him. But he smiled at me . . . I think he smiled. It was more with his eyes than his lips —"

"Foolish child," snapped the woman, who was her mother. "Go home and finish your chores."

"It's true, though," said one of the others. "I never seen hair so thick and black on the head of any living being. But if you ask me, it were a curse, not a beauty."

"It *was* a curse," Marm Hudspeth muttered, peering at the abandoned, tumbledown hovel that had been Joram's home with an eager gleam in her eye. "The mother was cursed and she passed it on to her son. She chewed at him, gnawing away at his soul. She dug her nails into him and sucked his blood."

Mosiah's father laughed derisively, causing Marm to glare at him. "Ye've little to laugh at, Jacobias," she cried shrilly. "Yer own boy's gone off to find him! Dead? Yes, Joram is Dead and it's my belief Anja took the Life from him. Drew it out of his body to use in her own! Ye've all seen the white scars on his chest . . ."

"What scars?" Saryon was about to ask. But the conversation ended abruptly when Jacobias, with a show of magical force Saryon found quite alarming considering the magus had worked a full day, angrily vanished into the air. Shaking their heads, the other Field Magi made their weary way to their shacks to get what sleep they could before daybreak found them back in the fields again.

Returning to his own dwelling, Saryon thought about what he'd heard, beginning to form a picture of this young man in his mind. Product of a cursed and unholy alliance, raised by an insane mother, the young man was probably half crazed himself. Add to the fact that he was Dead (Father Tolban had expressed no doubt whatsoever on this point), and it was a wonder he had not murdered or committed some other brutal act before this.

And this was the young man Saryon was supposed to go into the Outland and find?

The priest's bitterness increased. Anything — even the Turning to Stone — seemed better than this torture.

Saryon's life at this juncture was truly miserable. Accustomed as he was to spending his days in study, wrapped in the comforting, silent solitude of the libraries or his warm, secure cell, he found the life of a Field Catalyst one of bone-aching weariness, sore and swollen feet, and mind-numbing monotony. Day in and day out he and Father Tolban were in the fields, granting Life to the magi, walking along after them through the rows of wheat or corn or beets or whatever it was that grew there. Saryon never knew. It all looked the same to him.

At night, he lay on his hard cot, every joint and muscle hurting. Though desperately tired, he could not sleep. The wild wind howled around the mean shack, whistling in through cracks and chinks that all the magic of the magi could never keep closed. Above the wild sounds of the wind, he could hear other noises — living noises — and these frightened him more than anything else. They were the noises of the beasts of the Outland, who, he was told, sometimes felt bold enough or hungry enough to approach the village in hopes of stealing food. These howls and growlings made Saryon realize that bad as this life was here, it was nothing compared to the life he had to look forward to — life in the Outland. His stomach clenched every time he thought of it, and he often began to shake uncontrollably. His only bitter comfort was the knowledge that he probably would not survive long enough to suffer.

Four months passed thus — Saryon's allotted time to establish himself as a renegade catalyst. He didn't know whether he had fooled anyone or not. Supposedly sullen, rebellious, and hotheaded, Saryon generally came across as sickly and wretched. The magi were so lost in the drudgery of their own lives, however, that they didn't pay much attention to him.

As the day set for his departure in late summer drew near, Saryon had heard nothing from the Font, and he began to hope that perhaps Bishop Vanya might have forgotten him. Perhaps just sending me here is punishment enough, he thought. Surely one Dead young man doesn't matter that much.

Saryon determined that he would simply stay where he was until he heard something. Father Tolban still obviously considered himself Saryon's inferior, and would do whatever the priest told him.

But this was not to be.

Sitting alone in his cabin a few nights before he was supposed to leave, Saryon was startled and alarmed to see a Corridor suddenly open before him. He knew, even before the figure materialized, who had come to visit him, and his heart sank.

"Deacon Saryon," the figure said as it stepped from the Corridor.

"Bishop Vanya," Saryon said, bowing to the floor.

Saryon saw the Bishop glance around his poor surroundings, but, beyond a raised eyebrow, he didn't take much notice, his attention being centered on his Priest. "Soon you begin your journey."

"Yes, Holiness," Saryon replied. He was still on the floor, not so much from humility as from the fact that he simply did not believe he had the strength to rise.

"I do not expect to hear from you for some time," Vanya continued, standing near the Corridor's opening — a black void of nothingness. "Your situation among these — um — Sorcerers will be delicate and it will be difficult for you make contact . . ."

Especially if I am dead, Saryon thought bitterly, though he did not say it.

"Still" — Vanya was going on — "there are ways we have of communicating with those far distant. I will not elaborate, but do not be startled to hear from me if I deem it necessary. In the meantime, try to send a message through Tolban when you think you will be able to turn this Joram over to us."

Saryon stared up at the Bishop in amazement. The young man again! All Saryon's pent-up misery and anger over the last months found its outlet. Slowly, his bones creaking, the priest struggled to his feet and faced Vanya defiantly.

"Holiness," Saryon said respectfully but with an edge in his voice that was born out of fear and desperation, "you are sending me to my doom. At least let me die with what dignity I can. You know I cannot possibly survive even one night in the Outland. Keeping up the pretense of hunting for this . . . this Joram . . . was all very well before an inferior but we can at least dispense with it between ourselves —"

Vanya's face flushed, his brows contracted. Pursing his lips, he drew in a deep breath through his nose. "Do you take me for a fool, Father Saryon?" he bellowed.

"Holiness!" Saryon gasped, blanching. He had never seen the Bishop so angry. It was more frightening — at the moment — than the unknown terrors of the Outland. "I never —"

"I thought I had made myself clear. The importance of bringing this young man to justice cannot be over-emphasized." Vanya's pudgy fingers stabbed the air. "You, Brother Saryon, have a high opinion of yourself, it seems! Do you honestly think I would go to this considerable expenditure of time and effort simply to divest the Order of one foolish priest? I undertake nothing with an expectation of failure. I have information about these practitioners of the Dark Arts, Saryon. I know they need one thing, and that one thing I am sending them — a catalyst. No, you will be quite safe, I assure you, Father. *They* will see to that."

Saryon could not answer. He could only stare at the Bishop in utter confusion. One thought managed to rise to the top of the swirling waters of his mind. Once again he wondered, what was it that made this one Dead young man so vitally important?

Seeing his priest dumbfounded, Bishop Vanya shut his lips with a snap and, turning, prepared to take his leave. Then he hesitated, and turned back again to face the catalyst.

"Brother Saryon," the Bishop said in a peculiarly soft voice, "I have pondered long whether to tell you this or not. What I say now must not leave this room. Some of what I am about to reveal to you is known only to myself and the Emperor. The political situation in Thimhallan is not good. Despite our best efforts, it has been deteriorating for years. We have it on good authority that the kingdom of Sharakan has been influenced by certain members of this Coven of the Wheel. They have not yet embraced the Dark Arts that nearly destroyed us centuries ago, but their Emperor has been so rash as to actually invite these people to his kingdom. The Cardinal of the Realm, who sought to counsel against this, was dismissed from the court."

Saryon stared at him, transfixed. "But why — "

"War. To use them and their infernal weapons against Merilon," Vanya said with a heavy sigh. "Thus you see how vital it is that we take this young man alive and, through his trial, expose these fiends for what they are — murderers and black-hearted Sorcerers who would pervert dead objects by giving them Life. By doing this, we can show the people of Sharakan that their Emperor is in league with the powers of darkness, and we can then encompass his downfall."

"His downfall!" Saryon clutched at the back of a chair, feeling weak and dizzy.

"His downfall," Vanya repeated sternly. "Only then, Father Saryon, will we be able to prevent a catastrophic war." He looked grimly at the catalyst. "You see now, I hope, the extreme urgency and importance of your mission. We dare not attack the Sorcerers' camp. Sharakan would come instantly to their aid. One man must slip in, retrieve the boy . . . I chose you, one of my most intelligent brethren—"

"I'll try not to fail you, Holiness," Saryon murmured confusedly. "I only wish I had known, that I were better suited. . . ."

Reaching out, Vanya placed his hand upon Saryon's shoulder, his expression one of earnest caring. "I know you will not fail, Deacon Saryon. I have every confidence in you. I am only sorry you misunderstood the nature of your mission. I did not dare explain it more fully. The Font has ears, you know." He raised his hand in the ritual blessing. "The elements of earth and air, fire and water, grant you Life. The Almin be with you."

Stepping into the Corridor, the Bishop disappeared.

When he was gone, Saryon's strength gave out and he sank to his knees, overwhelmed by what he had heard. The thought of his own death had been terrifying. How much more frightening was it now to know that the fate of two kingdoms, perhaps, rested on his shoulders?

His mind in turmoil, he laid his head on the back of his clenched hands and tried to understand what was happening. But it was beyond him. How clear and simple and pure were the equations of his art. How neatly and logically the world of mathematics fell into place. How dreadful it was, to step into the world of chaos!

Yet, he had no choice. And he would be serving his country, his Emperor, his Church. How much better than believing himself a criminal! The thought gave him courage, and he was able to stand.

"I need something to do," he muttered to himself. "Something to keep my mind off this or I'll think myself into a panic again." In an effort to compose himself, Saryon began to perform the small household tasks around his dwelling that he had, in his despair, carelessly put off.

Taking the teapot from where it stood upon the table, he washed and dried it and put it upon the shelf. He swept the floor and even had the heart, finally, to begin packing a few possessions in preparation for the journey. When he realized he was tired enough that sleep would overtake him, he lay down upon the hard cot. Closing his eyes, he was just slipping into darkness when a thought suddenly occurred to him.

He didn't own a teapot.

2

Simkin

lachloch sat at a desk within his brick dwelling, the best and biggest in the camp, deeply absorbed in his work. Through an open window the morning sun shone bright upon a ledger spread open beneath the warlock's hand. Soft air, sweet with the smell of late summer, accompanied the sunshine, bringing with it sounds of rustling trees, the murmur of voices, the occasional shout of children at play or the harsh, deep laughter of his henchmen, who lounged about outside his cabin. And always, above and below the sounds of life and the seasons, rang the sounds of the forge, clanging rhythmically like the tolling of a bell.

Blachloch noticed all of this and none of it. The least change in one of any of those sounds, the switching of the wind's direction, a fight among the children, the lowering of a man's voice, and Blachloch's ears would have pricked like a cat's. A cessation of sound from the forge would have caused him to raise his head and, with a soft-spoken word of command, send one of his men to find out the reason why. This is what the *Duuk-tsarith* are trained for — to be aware of every-thing going on around them, to be in control of everything, yet manage to keep themselves above and apart from it. Thus Blachloch was aware of everything that occurred in the coven, thus he controlled it, though he seldom left his dwelling place, and then only to lead his men upon their silent deadly raids or, as had happened recently, on a trip to the northern lands.

Blachloch had just returned from Sharakan, and it was because of his successful negotiations there that he was penning figures in the ledger. He worked swiftly and accurately, rarely making a mistake, writing the numbers in neat, orderly fashion. Everything around him was arranged in neat, orderly fashion, from his furniture to his blond hair, from his thoughts to his clipped, blond mustache. All was neat, ordered, cold, calculated, precise.

A knock on the door did not interrupt Blachloch. Having been aware of his man's approach for some time, the former Enforcer did not stop his work. Nor did he speak. The *Duuk-tsarith* rarely speak, knowing well the intimidating value of silence.

"Simkin is back," came the report through the door.

This was unexpected, apparently, for the slender, white hand writing the figures paused an instant, hanging suspended above the page as the brain that guided it dealt swiftly with this matter.

"Bring him."

Whether these words were spoken or simply flashed into the guard's head was a question no one bothered to consider when addressed by one of the *Duuk-tsarith*, who were trained in mind reading and mind control, among other arts suitable to those who enforced the law in Thimhallan. Or, as in Blachloch's case, used the skills they had been taught to break it.

The warlock did not stop in his figuring, but continued to add up the long columns of numbers. By the time he had reached the end of a column, the knock sounded again. He did not answer immediately, but coolly and unhurriedly finished his work. Then, wiping the tip of his quill pen with a clean, white cloth, he laid it down next to the ledger, turning it so that the feather faced outward to his right. Then he made a motion with his hand and the door swung silently open.

"I've brought him. He's with me —" The henchman stepped inside, saw Blachloch's eyebrows raise slightly, and whipped around. No one was with him.

"Damn!" the guard muttered. "He was right behind —"

Darting out the door in search of his charge, the guard almost collided with a young man stepping inside, whose entry into Blachloch's cold and colorless dwelling might be likened to an explosion of flowers.

"Egad, you lout," cried the young man, stepping hastily out of the henchman's way and wrapping his cape around him protectively, "are you going in or out? Hah! A rhyme. I'll make another. Lout, out! There, charming, isn't it? Go bathe or butcher small children or whatever you do best. Come to think of it, bathing isn't in that category. You offend the snout, lout."

Drawing a bit of orange silk from the air, the young man held it to his nose, glancing about the room with the air of one who has just arrived at a dull party and can't decide whether to stay or leave. The henchman made it clear, however, that he was staying by laying a hand on the young man's purple sleeve and starting to shove him inside. Almost instantly, however, the guard snatched his hand back, yelping in pain.

"Ah, how sad. My fault entirely," said the young man, peering at the henchman's hand in mock dismay. "I *do* apologize. I call this color *Grape Rose*. I only thought it up this morning and I haven't had time to work on it. I fancy I've left a bit too much *Rose* in the *Grape*." Reaching out, he plucked something from the man's hand. "I thought so. A thorn. Suck on it, there's a good fellow. I don't *believe* it's poisonous."

Wafting past the angry henchman, a heady smell of exotic perfumes clinging to him like his own, personal suffocating cloud, the young man came to stand in front of the expressionless Blachloch.

"Do you like this ensemble?" the young man asked, turning this way and that, perfectly undaunted by the silent black-robed figure who sat unmoving, absorbing all around him into his dark void. "It's all the rage at court. 'Breeches' these are called. Damned uncomfortable. Chafe my legs.

But everyone's wearing them, even the women. Why, the Empress said to me — What was that? Did you mutter, O Mute Master? Thank you for the invitation, though it could have been phrased a bit more eloquently. I think I *will* be seated."

Dropping gracefully into a chair opposite Blachloch's desk, the young man lounged back in it comfortably, arranging himself to show off the outfit to the best advantage. It was hard to guess the young man's age, it might have been anything from eighteen to twenty-five. He was tall and well-formed. His hair fell in long chestnut curls upon slender shoulders. A soft, short beard the same chestnut color hid the weak lines of his chin. A soft mustache adorned his upper lip, apparently for the sole purpose of giving him something to play with when bored, which was generally, and he was dressed in an absolute bouquet of riotous color. His silken stockings were green, his breeches yellow, his waistcoat purple, his lacy blouse was green — to match the stockings — and a mauve cape hung from his shoulders to the floor, trailing behind him majestically.

As the young man sat there, twisting the ends of his mustache, the henchman moved over to stand behind the chair, but, at his approach, the young man promptly put the orange silk to his nose and gagged.

"Oh, I say, I can't stand this. I'm feeling nauseous . . ."

With a look, Blachloch told his man to back off. Grumbling, the guard obeyed, taking his place at the far end of the neat, orderly room. The young man, lowering the silk, smiled.

"Change your clothes," said Blachloch.

"Don't be such a boor . . ." the young man started to protest in aggrieved tones.

Blachloch neither moved nor spoke.

"You find my outfit highly ridiculous. You find *me* highly ridiculous," said the young man cheerfully, "but you use me anyway, don't you, my Lord of Benevolence?" Slowly, the colors of the young man's clothes deepened and darkened, their very shape and nature changing until he was dressed from head to toe in black robes that were an exact copy of Blachloch's, with only small exceptions. The sleeves were too long and the hood too big, the one completely engulfing his hands, the other drooping down over his eyes to touch his nose. Tilting his head back in order to see, the young man smiled.

"I say, 'Halt, miscreant!'" He waved his silk in the air. "Isn't that what you Enforcer chaps say all the time? I rather like this—"

"Where have you been, Simkin?" asked Blachloch.

"Oh, out and about, hither and yon, here and there," replied the young man in bored tones. Reaching over, dragging the long black sleeve across the desk, Simkin picked up the quill pen from beside Blachloch's ledger. Leaning back, he tickled himself on the nose with the feather, sniffed, snorted, and finally sneezed prodigiously with the result that the hood flew down, completely covering his head.

Blachloch's man in the back of the room made a kind of grunting sound, his hands clenching as though they had the young man in their grasp and were enjoying their work. Blachloch still neither moved nor spoke aloud, but Simkin, pushing back the hood, suddenly shifted uncomfortably and very carefully laid the quill back down on the desk.

"I went to the village," he said in a subdued voice.

"You should have told me you were going."

"I didn't think of it." Simkin shrugged. His nose twitched. "Ahch—" Starting to sneeze again, he caught Blachloch's eye, and hastily pinched his nostrils together with a delicate hand.

The warlock waited a moment before speaking.

Smiling in relief, Simkin removed his fingers from his nose.

"Someday you will go too far—" Blachloch began.

"*Choo!*" Simkin's sneeze descended like rain on the warlock's ledger.

Without a word, Blachloch reached out his white hand, shut the ledger, and stared coldly at the young man across from him.

"Frightfully sorry," Simkin apologized meekly. Taking the bit of orange silk, he began dabbing at the desktop. "Here, let me mop this up."

"*Dra-ach,*" spoke the warlock, freezing Simkin in place with a motion of his hand. "Continue."

Unable to move, Simkin made a most pathetic sound with his frozen mouth.

"You can talk," Blachloch said. "Do so."

Simkin did as he was told, his lips alone moving in his stiff face. His words coming slowly as he worked to form them, he looked very much like a man having a fit. "Where . . . was . . . I? The . . . village. It . . . is . . . true. Catalyst . . . there." Halting, he cast Blachloch a pleading glance.

The warlock relented. *"Ach-dra,"* he said, removing the spell. Sinking back in his chair, Simkin massaged his jaw and felt his face with his hands as though reassuring himself it was still there. Glancing at Blachloch out of the corner of his eyes like a punished child, he continued sullenly, "And he isn't going to be there long, from what I've heard."

Blachloch's face remained expressionless, giving the impression that it was only the sunlight glinting in his cold eyes that made them gleam. "He *is* a renegade, as we were informed?"

"Well, as to that" — Simkin, feeling the atmosphere thaw slightly, dared to lift the bit of silk and dab at his nose — "I don't think *renegade* quite describes the catalyst. *Pitiful* is much nearer the mark. But it is true that he intends to journey into the Outland. Bishop Vanya ordered him to go. Which leads me to believe" — Simkin leaned over the desk, lowering his voice conspiratorially — "that he is doing so under duress, if you take my meaning."

"Bishop Vanya." Blachloch sent a swift glance to his henchman, who grinned, nodded, and began to walk forward.

"Yes, he was there," Simkin returned, smiling charmingly and leaning back in his chair, perfectly at ease once more, "along with the Emperor and the Empress. It was quite a merry party, I assure you." He twirled one end of his mustache between his fingers. "At last, I felt I was truly in the company of my peers. 'Simkin' said the Empress, 'I adore the color of hose you are wearing. Please tell me the name of the shade, so that I may copy it . . .' 'Majesty,' I replied, 'I call it *Night of the Peacock*.' And she said — "

"Simkin, you are a liar," said Blachloch in an expressionless voice as the grinning henchman advanced.

"No, really, 'pon my honor," Simkin protested, hurt, "I truly do call it *Night of the Peacock*. But I assure you, I wouldn't dream of telling her how to copy it . . ."

Blachloch picked up his pen and returned to his work as his man drew nearer.

In a flash of color, Simkin changed back to his exotic clothes. Rising to his feet gracefully, he glanced around. "Don't touch me, lout," he said, sniffing and wiping his nose. Then, placing the silk in the sleeve of his coat, he looked down at the warlock. "By the way, Cruel and Pitiless One, would you like me to offer my services to this catalyst as guide through the wilderness? Something incredibly nasty's liable to snatch him otherwise. Waste of a good catalyst, wouldn't you say?"

Apparently absorbed in his work, Blachloch said without looking up, "So there really is a catalyst."

"In a few weeks, he'll be standing before you."

"Weeks?" The henchman snorted. "A catalyst? Let me and the boys go after him. We'll have him back here in minutes. He'll open the Corridors to us and—"

"And the *Thon-Li*, the Corridor Masters, will slam shut the gate." Simkin sneered. "Neatly trapped you'd be then. I can't think why you keep these imbeciles around, Blachloch, unless, like rats, they're cheap to feed. Personally, I prefer vermin. . . ."

The henchman made a lunge at Simkin, whose coat suddenly bristled with thorns.

Blachloch moved his hand; both men froze in place. The warlock had not even looked up but continued to write in the ledger.

"A catalyst," Simkin murmured through stiff lips. "What . . . power . . . give us! Combine . . . iron and magic. . . ."

Raising his head, ceasing to write, though he kept his pen poised, the warlock looked at Simkin. With a word, he removed the spell.

"How did you discover this? You weren't seen?"

"Of course not!" Lifting his pointed chin, Simkin stared down at Blachloch in injured dignity. "Am I not a master of disguise, as you well know? I sat in his very hovel, upon his very table—a very teapot! Not only did he *not* suspect me he even washed and dried me and set me on his shelf quite nicely. I —"

Blachloch silenced Simkin with a glance. "Meet him in the wilderness. Use whatever tomfoolery you need to get him here." The cold blue eyes froze the young man as effectively as the magical spell. "But get him here. Alive. I want this catalyst more than I've wanted anything in my entire life. Bring him and there will be rich reward. Return without him and I will drown you in the river. Do you understand me, Simkin?"

The warlock's eyes did not waver.

Simkin smiled. "I understand you, Blachloch," he said softly. "Don't I always?"

With a sweeping bow, he started to take his leave, his mauve cape trailing the floor behind.

"Oh, and Simkin," Blachloch said, returning to his work.

Simkin turned. "My liege?" he asked.

Blachloch ignored the sarcasm. "Have something unpleasant happen to the catalyst. Nothing serious, mind you. Just convince him that it would be unwise for him to ever think of leaving us. . . ."

"Ah . . ." remarked Simkin reflectively. "Now this *will* be a pleasure. Farewell, lout," he said, patting the guard on the cheek with his hand. "Igh . . ." Making a face, he wiped his hand on the orange cloth and swept majestically out the door.

"Say the word. . ." muttered the guard, glaring through the doorway after the young man, who was sauntering through camp like a walking rainbow.

Blachloch did not even deign to reply. He was, once more, working in the ledger.

"Why do you put up with that fool?" snarled the guard.

"The same might be asked of you," Blachloch answered in his expressionless voice. "And I might make the same reply. Because he is a useful fool and because someday I *will* drown him."

3

Lost

"What was that?" Jacobias, roused from a deep sleep, sat up in bed and looked around the dark hut, searching for the noise that had awakened him.

There it came again, a timid tapping sound.

"It's someone at the door," his wife whispered, sitting up beside him. Her hand clutched his arm. "Maybe it's Mosiah!"

"Humpf," the Field Magus grunted as he tossed aside the covers and drifted effortlessly across the floor on wings of magic. A soft word of command broke the seal on the door, and the magus peered out cautiously.

"Father Saryon!" he said in amazement.

"I—I'm sorry to awaken you," stammered the catalyst. "May I disturb you further and—and invite myself in? It's really quite urgent, imperative that I speak to you!" he added in a desperate tone, staring pleadingly at Mosiah's father.

"Sure, sure, Father," Jacobias said, backing up and opening the door. The catalyst stepped inside, his tall, spare figure in its green robes outlined for an instant in the light of a full moon that was rising in the sky. The moonlight shone for a moment on Jacobias's face as he exchanged glances with his startled wife, who was sitting up in bed, clutching the blankets to her chest. Then he shut the door, extinguishing the moonlight and plunging the room into darkness. A word from the magus, however, caused a warm light to glow among the branches of the tree that formed the ceiling.

"Please, put that out!" Saryon said, shrinking away from it and glancing fearfully out the window.

Completely mystified, Jacobias did as he was asked, dousing the light, leaving them in darkness once more. A rustling sound from the bed indicated that his wife was getting up.

"Can I get you some . . . something, Father?" she asked hesitantly. "A . . . a cup of tea?" What *did* one say to a catalyst who comes into your home at midnight, especially one who looks as if he were being pursued by demons?

"No — no, thank you," replied Saryon. "I . . ." he began, but cleared his throat and fell silent.

The three stood in the dark, listening to each other breathe for several moments. Then there was another rustle and a grunt from Jacobias in response to his wife jabbing him in the ribs with her elbow.

"Is there something we can do for you, then, Father?"

"Yes," said Saryon. Drawing a deep breath, he launched into his lines. "That is, I hope so. I'm — uh — desperate, you see, and — uh — I was told — that is I heard — that you had — that you might be able to —" At this point he dried up, the words he'd so carefully prepared flying completely out of his head. Hoping they would come home again, the catalyst latched onto a word he remembered. "Desperate, you see, and —" But it was useless. Saryon gave up. "I need your help," he said finally, simply. "I'm going into the Outland."

If the Emperor had appeared in his hut and said *he* was going into the Outland, Jacobias would have probably not been much more astonished. The moonlight had crept in through the window now and was shining on the balding, middle-aged catalyst standing stoop-shouldered in the center of the cabin, clutching a sack of what Jacobias realized must be all his worldly possessions. A noise from his wife, sounding suspiciously like a smothered, nervous giggle, brought a rebuking cough from her husband, who said sharply, "I think we'll take that tea, woman. You'd best sit down, Father."

Saryon shook his head, glancing out the window. "I — I must be gone, while the moon is full . . ."

"Moon'll be up for a while yet," Jacobias said complacently, sinking into a chair as his wife prepared the tea over a small fire she caused to spring up in the grate. "Now, Father Saryon" — the magus eyed the catalyst as sternly as he might have eyed his teen-aged son — "what is this nonsense about goin' into the Outland?"

"I must. I'm desperate," repeated Saryon, sitting down, still clutching his sack of belongings to his chest. And indeed, he did look desperate as he sat at the crude little table across from the Field Magus. "Please don't try to stop me and don't ask me any questions. Just grant me the aid I need and let me go. I will be all right. Our lives are in the hands of the Almin, after all — "

"Father," interrupted Jacobias, "I know that among your Order, to be sent here to the Fields is a punishment. Now, I don't know what sin you committed, nor do I want to know." He held up his hand, thinking Saryon might speak. "But, whatever it is, I'm certain 'tis not worth throwing your life away. Stay here with us, do your service."

Saryon simply shook his head.

Staring at him a moment, Jacobias frowned. Shifting in his chair, he appeared uncomfortable. "I — It's not in me to talk of such things as I'm goin' to say now, Father. Your god and I have been on fairly good terms, neither one of us askin' much from t'other. I never felt close to Him, nor He to me, and I figured that's the way He wanted it. Least, that's the way Father Tolban seemed to figure. But you're different, Father. Some of the things *you've* said have started me to wonderin'. When *you* say we're in the hands of the Almin, I can almost believe you mean me, too, not just yourself and t'Bishop."

Completely taken aback, Saryon stared at the man. He had certainly not expected this and felt ashamed, because it suddenly occurred to him that when he said, "We're in the hands of the Almin," he himself didn't really believe it. Otherwise, why would he be so frightened of venturing out into the wilderness? It's just as well I'm going, he thought bitterly. I'm a hypocrite now, too, apparently.

Seeing Saryon silent, obviously lost in reflection, Jacobias mistakenly assumed the catalyst was reconsidering. "Stay here with us, Father," the Field Magus urged gently. "It's not a good life, but it's not a bad 'un either. There's lots worse, believe me." Jacobias's voice lowered. "Go out there"—he nodded toward the window—"and you'll find it."

Saryon bowed his head, his shoulders slumping, his face pale and tight with fear.

"I see," said Jacobias after a pause. "So that's the way of it, is it? These words I'm sayin' are nothin' new to you, are they, Father. Ye've been hearin' them in yer own heart. Someone or something is making you go."

"Yes," said Saryon quietly. "Don't ask me any more. I'm a terrible liar."

Neither spoke as Jacobias's wife sent the tea floating to the table, where it spilled itself into cups shaped of polished horn. Sitting down beside her husband, she took his hand in hers and held onto it tightly.

"Is it because of our son?" she asked in a frightened voice.

Raising his head, Saryon looked at both of them, his face pale and drawn in the moonlight. "No," he said softly. Then, seeing her about to speak, he shook his head. "We do what we have to do."

"But, Father," argued Jacobias, "we do, or should do, what we are *suited* to do! Forgive me for speakin' blunt, Father Saryon, but I've seen you in t'field. If ye've been outdoors at all, it must've been in some royal lady's rose arbor! You can't take ten steps without fallin' over a rock! The first days you were here the sun burned you so bad we had to lay you in the creek to bring you 'round. You was fair roasted. And you jump at yer own shadow. Why I never in my life saw a man run so fast as you did when that locust flew up in your face."

With a sigh, Saryon nodded, but he did not answer.

"Ye're not a young man anymore, Father," Jacobias's wife said kindly, her heart softened by the catalyst's look of fear and despair. Reaching out her hand, she placed it over

Saryon's hand that rested, trembling, on the table. "Surely there must be some other way. Why don't you drink your tea and go back to your bed. We'll talk to Father Tolban . . ."

"There is no other way, I assure you," Saryon said softly, with a quiet dignity that was apparent even through the strained look of fear on his face. "I thank you for your kindness and . . . and your caring. It is something I—I didn't expect." Rising to his feet, leaving his tea untouched, he faced them. "Now, I must please ask you to give me the help I need. I know you have contacts out there. I don't ask you to name them. Just tell me where to go and what I must do to find them."

Jacobias, a look of indecision on his face, glanced at his wife. Leaving her tea untouched as well, she was staring into the coals of the fire. He squeezed her hand. Without turning her gaze to him, she nodded her head. Rumbling deep in his throat, Jacobias rumpled up his hair, scratched his chin, and finally said, "Very well, Father. I'll do what I can fer you, though I'd sooner send a man Beyond! I would indeed!"

"I understand," Saryon said, genuinely affected by the man's obvious pain. "And I truly thank you for your help."

"You are a kind and gentle man," said Jacobias's wife suddenly, still staring into the fire. "I've seen you look at us with something in your eyes that says we're not animals but people to you. If—if you see my son—"

She could not go on, but began to weep silently.

"You better be getting gone, Father," Jacobias said gruffly. "Moon's almost to the tops of the trees and ye've a ways to go. If you haven't made it to the river by the time she sets," he added sternly, "sit yourself down and wait till mornin'. Don't go bumblin' about in the dark. Ye're liable to tumble down a cliff."

"Yes," Saryon managed to say, drawing another deep breath and smoothing the folds of his robes around him with his shaking hands.

"Now, come here"—Jacobias led the catalyst to the door, which opened at his approach—"and look where I point and listen to my words careful, for they could mean life instead of death, Father."

"I understand," said Saryon, holding onto his courage as tightly as his hands gripped his sack.

"See that star yonder, the one at the tip of the stars they call the God's Hand. You see it?"

"Yes."

"That's the North Star. It's not called God's Hand fer nothin', 'cause it'll point yer way, if ye let it. Keep that star in yer left eye, as the saying goes. Know what that means?"

The catalyst shook his head, and Jacobias checked a sigh. "It means — Never mind. Just do this. Always make certain yer walkin' straight toward the star and just a bit to the right of it like. Never let the star get to the right of you. Understand? If so, you'll end up in centaur land. If they get hold of you, you can just pray to the Almin for the swiftest death there is."

Saryon stared up into the night sky, looking at the star, and felt suddenly dismayed. He had never looked up into the night sky before, he realized. At least, not out here, not where the stars seemed so close and so many. Overwhelmed at the vastness and immenseness of the universe and of his own tiny, tiny part in it, it seemed to Saryon terribly ironic that another tiny, cold, faraway and uncaring part was going to lead him. He thought of the Font, where the stars were studied as they affected a person's life from his birth. He saw the charts spread out on the table, he recalled the calculations he had made regarding them, and it occurred to him that he had never once really looked at the stars as he was looking at them now. Now that his life truly depended on them.

"I understand," he murmured, though he didn't, not in the slightest.

Jacobias looked at him dubiously. "Maybe I should take him," he muttered to his wife.

Saryon glanced around quickly. "No," he said. "No, there would be trouble. I've stayed too long as it is. Someone might have seen us. Thank you very much. Both for your help and — and your kind words. Good-bye. Good-bye. May the Almin's blessing be with you both."

"Maybe it's not right of me to say this, Father," Jacobias said roughly, "me not bein' a catalyst an' all, but may the Almin's blessing be with *you*." Flushing, he looked down at the ground. "There. I don't reckon He'll take offense, do you?"

Saryon started to smile, but the quivering of his lips led him to believe he might very well weep instead, and that would be disastrous. Reaching out, he shook hands earnestly with Jacobias, who appeared to be in the throes of some dilemma, for he was still staring at Saryon as though trying to make up his mind to speak further. His wife, hovering near him, suddenly lifted Saryon's hand in hers and pressed it to her rough lips.

"This is for you," she said softly, "and for my boy, if you see him." Her eyes filling with tears, she turned and hurried back inside the mean dwelling.

Saryon's own vision was dim as he started to walk away, only to feel Jacobias's hand on his shoulder.

"Listen," said the Field Magus. "I — I think you should know. It may make things a bit easier for you. There — there are some people who've been . . . making inquiries so to speak about you. They're in need of a catalyst, I fancy, so likely they'll be takin' an interest in you above the ordinary, if you get my meaning."

"Thank you," said Saryon, somewhat startled. Bishop Vanya had implied much the same thing. How had he known? "Where will I find these —"

"They'll find you," Jacobias said gruffly. "Just remember about the star, though, or the first thing that'll find you will be death."

"I'll remember. Thank you. Good-bye."

But Jacobias was still not easy in his mind apparently, for he held Saryon back one last instant.

"I don't approve of 'em," he muttered, frowning. "Not from anythin' I've seen, mind you, just from what I've heard. I hope the rumors mayn't be true. If they are, I pray my boy hasn't got hisself involved. I didn't approve him goin' out there, but we had no choice. Not when we heard the *Duuk-tsarith* was being sent to talk with him. . . ."

"*Duuk-tsarith?*" repeated Saryon, puzzled. "But I thought he ran off with that young man who killed the overseer, that Joram. . ."

"Joram?" Jacobias shook his head. "Dunno who told you this. That strange young man hain't been seen here in over a year. Mosiah was hopin' to find him, that's for certain; somethin' I wasn't hopeful of myself. A walkin' Dead man . . ."

He shook his head again. "But that's not what I meant to go on about." Holding onto Saryon's arm, Jacobias looked at him earnestly. "I didn't want to say nothin' about this round his mother. But if the boy *is* in bad company and is followin' ways of — ways of darkness, speak to him, will you, Father? Remind him that we love him and think of him?"

"I will, Jacobias, I will," Saryon said gently, patting the man's work-worn hand.

"Thank you, Father." Jacobias cleared his throat, and wiping his hand over his eyes and nose, he waited a moment to compose himself before he went back into the shack. "Good-bye, Father," he said.

Turning, he stepped back inside and shut the door behind him. Looking into the window, for a moment unwilling to leave, Saryon saw the Field Magus and his wife standing in the moonlight that beamed in through their window. He saw Jacobias take his wife into his arms and hold her close. He heard her muffled sobs.

Sighing, Saryon clutched his sack and started walking across the fields, his eyes on the stars and, occasionally, on the vast darkness to which the stars were drawing him. His feet stumbled over the uneven ground that was nothing to him but patches of white moonlight and black shadow. Reaching the edge of the village, he looked out over the fields of wheat that stirred gently in the breeze like a moonlit lake. Turning, Saryon glanced back one last time at the village, at his last contact, perhaps, with humanity.

The tree dwellings sat stolidly on the ground, their interlaced branches casting eerie, intricate shadows in the moonlight. There were no lights within the shacks; the faint light gleaming from Jacobias's window went out as Saryon watched. Too tired to dream, the Field Magi slept.

For an instant, the catalyst thought he might run back. But even as he gazed at the peaceful village, Saryon realized he couldn't. He might have, an hour earlier, when the fear inside of him had been very real. But not now. Now he could turn and walk away from them, turn and walk away from everything in his past life. He would walk into the night, guided by that tiny, uncaring star above. Not because he had discovered any newfound courage. No. It was a reason as dark as the shadows of the moonlit trees that rustled about him. He could not go back, not until he had the answer.

Bishop Vanya lied to him about Mosiah. Why?

That nagging question and its attendant dark shadow accompanied Saryon into the wilderness, proving a valuable companion, for it kept the catalyst's mind occupied and forced his other companion — fear — to straggle along behind. Keeping one eye on the star, a feat that proved increasingly difficult for the catalyst as he plunged deeper and deeper into the thick forests, Saryon pondered this question, trying to find excuses, trying to find explanations, only to be forced to admit to himself that there were no excuses and that he had no explanation.

Bishop Vanya had lied, that much was quite clear. What was more, it had been a conspiracy of lies.

Stopping for a moment to rest, Saryon sank down on a boulder to massage his aching and cramping leg muscles. The strange, ominous sounds of the forest growled and whispered about him, but Saryon was able to ignore them by going back, in his mind, to Bishop Vanya's chambers in the Font the day he had been called there to hear Father Tolban's story. Vanya's words came to him clearly, mercifully drowning out a low snarl from some predatory animal stalking its prey through the night.

It seems that this Joram had a friend — Saryon could hear Vanya quite plainly — *a young man called Mosiah. One of the Field Magi, hearing noises in the night, woke and looked out his window. He saw Mosiah and a young man he is positive was Joram engrossed in conversation. He could not hear all of what was said, but he swears he overheard the words "Coven" and "Wheel." He said Mosiah drew back at this, but his friend must have been persuasive because, the next morning, Mosiah was gone.*

Yes, Mosiah had gone. But not because of Joram. He had fled because of rumors that the *Duuk-tsarith* were interested in him.

A shrill scream behind Saryon, cut off suddenly by a furious growl, had the catalyst up off his boulder and running through the forest before he was quite aware of what had occurred. When he was once more master of himself, he drew several deep breaths to calm his rapidly beating heart.

Forcing himself to slow down, he took his bearings on the star that he could barely make out through the branches above him and discovered to his dismay that the moon was setting.

The catalyst recalled Jacobias's warning against wandering about in the dark at almost the same time he recalled, quite clearly, Father Tolban's furtive glance toward Bishop Vanya as the Bishop was relating the tale about Joram and Mosiah. Saryon recalled Tolban's guilty flush when he saw the catalyst looking at him. A conspiracy of lies.

But why? What were they hiding?

Suddenly Saryon had the answer. Hurrying forward with some vague idea of making his way to the river before the moon set, Saryon worked out the mystery much as he worked out his mathematical equations. Vanya *knew* Joram was in that coven. He had lied to conceal the true source of his knowledge. In fact, Saryon realized, Vanya knew lots of things about the coven — that they were in need of a catalyst, that they were dealing with the king of Sharakan. It was logical, therefore, that the Bishop had a spy planted within the coven. That much worked out. But, Saryon frowned, his equation lacked a final answer.

If Vanya had a spy in the coven, why did he need Saryon?

Distracted by these thoughts, the catalyst stumbled about in his mind nearly as badly as he was stumbling about in the gathering darkness. Coming to a halt, Saryon caught his breath, fixed his position by the star, and listened for the sound of the river. He did not hear it and, logic finally convincing him that he had not walked far enough to reach it, he decided to heed Jacobias's words and rest for the remainder of the night.

Saryon began to look for a place to spend the hours until dawn. He had not crossed the river yet, and naively assumed he was relatively safe. Not that it would have mattered much otherwise. The catalyst was so exhausted by both the unaccustomed exercise and the nervous strain and tension that he knew he could not go another step. Reasoning that it might be better to stay near the trail (without bothering to wonder who or what had made the trail), Saryon gathered his robes about his bony ankles and hunched down at the base of a gigantic oak tree, making a very uncomfortable bed between two huge, exposed roots. Drawing his knees up to his chin, he settled himself in the undergrowth and prepared to wait out the rest of the night.

Saryon had no intention of falling asleep. He would not have believed it possible that he *could* fall asleep, in fact. The moon had set and, though the stars shone brightly above him, the night was dark and frightening around him. Strange noises rustled and growled and snuffled. Wild eyes stared at him and, in desperation, he closed his own.

"I am in the hands of the Almin," he whispered to himself feverishly. But the words brought no comfort. Instead, they sounded stupid, meaningless. What was he to the Almin but just one of many wretched people in this world? Just one tiny being, not even as worthy of attracting the Almin's notice as one of those bright, gleaming stars. For he, poor mortal that he was, shed no light. Even some illiterate peasant could ask for the Almin's blessing with more sincerity than His catalyst! Saryon clenched his fists in despair. His Church, once as mighty and strong to him as the mountain fastness itself, was shaking apart and crumbling around him.

His Bishop, the man nearest his god, had lied to him. His Bishop was using him, for some dark, unseen purpose.

Shaking his head, Saryon sought to recall his studies in theology, hoping to catch hold of the faith that was slipping away from him. But he might as well have tried to stop the outgoing tide by putting his hand in the water and catching hold of a wave. His faith was bound up in men, and men had failed him.

No, be honest, Saryon told himself, quaking as the dreadful sounds of the night leaped out at him, dragging all the fears of his subconscious with it, your faith was bound up in yourself. It is *you* who have failed!

The catalyst covered his head with his arms in bleak hopelessness. Huddling beneath the tree, he listened to the horrible noises that were getting nearer and waited to feel sharp teeth sink into his flesh or to hear the harsh laughter of the centaurs. Slowly, however, the noises began to fade away. Or perhaps *he* was fading away. It didn't matter anymore. Nothing mattered.

Lost and wandering in a darkness vaster and more terrifying than the Outland, Saryon resigned himself to his fate. Worn out and despairing, no longer caring whether he lived or died, he slept.

4

Found

Lifting his head and blinking in the bright morning sunlight, Saryon stared around at his surroundings. Completely disoriented, he had the confused thought that something had spirited away his cabin in the night, leaving him to sleep upon the ground.

Then he heard a growling sound and everything came back to him in a rush, including his fear and the knowledge that he was alone in the wilderness. Panicked, Saryon leaped to his feet. At least — that's what he intended to do. As it was, he barely managed to move into a sitting position. Pain knotted his back muscles, his joints were stiff, and he seemed to have lost all feeling in his legs. His robes were wet with the morning dew, he was chilled and aching and thoroughly miserable. Groaning, Saryon laid his head back down on his knees and considered how easy it would be to stay here and die.

"I say," said a voice in admiration, "I know warlocks who don't dare spend a night in the Outland without ringing themselves round with fiery demons and such like, and here you are, a catalyst, sleeping like a babe in its mother's arms."

Starting up and staring around wildly, trying to blink the sleep out of his eyes, Saryon focused on the source of the voice — a young man sitting upon a tree stump, his eyes regarding Saryon with the same undisguised admiration as heard in his voice. Long brown hair curled upon his shoulders, matched by a soft brown beard and a sleek mustache. He was dressed to blend in with the wilderness in plain brown cloak and trousers and soft, leather boots.

"Who — who are you?" Saryon stammered, endeavoring, not very successfully, to stand up. Confused thoughts of the Field Magi having sent someone after him came into his half-asleep brain. "You're not from the settlement?"

"Let me give you a hand," the young man said, coming over and helping the catalyst rise stiffly to his feet. "Rather an elderly chap to be out wandering about in the woods, aren't you?"

Saryon jerked his arm out of the young man's solicitous grip. "I repeat, who are you?" he asked sternly.

"How old are you, if you don't mind my asking?" the young man inquired, looking at Saryon anxiously. "Forty-ish?"

"I demand —"

"Early forties," said the young man, studying the catalyst. "Right?"

"It's none of your concern," Saryon said, shivering in his damp robes. "Either answer my question or be on your way and let me go on mine . . ."

The young man's face grew solemn. "Ah there, that's just it. I'm afraid your age *is* a bit of concern to me, you know, because your way *is* my way. I'm your guide."

Saryon stared, too startled to reply. Then he recalled Jacobias's words: *There are some people who've been making inquiries about you. They're in need of a catalyst, so likely they'll be takin' an interest in you above the ordinary.*

"My name's Simkin," said the young man, reaching out his hand in a friendly manner. Weak with relief, Saryon returned the handshake, grimacing as he moved and bitterly regretting his night spent under the tree.

"If you feel up to traveling," Simkin continued placidly, "we really should be moving along. Centaurs caught two of Blachloch's men here a month ago. Ripped them into small pieces not fifty feet from where we're standing. Ghastly sight, I assure you."

The catalyst blenched. "Centaurs?" he repeated nervously. "Here? But we're not across the river. . . ."

"'Pon my honor," said Simkin, regarding Saryon with amazement, "you *are* a babe in the woods, aren't you? Here I thought you were incredibly brave and it turns out you're just incredibly stupid. This is a centaur hunting trail you've been sleeping on! And now, we've really wasted enough time. They hunt by day, you know. Well, I guess you *don't* know, but you'll learn. Let's be off." He stood looking at Saryon expectantly.

"What are you staring at me for?" Saryon asked shakily, the phrase *ripped them into small pieces* having made him go cold all over. "You're the guide!"

"But you're the catalyst," Simkin said ingenuously. "Open a Corridor for us."

"A C-corridor?" Saryon put his hand to his head, rubbing it in perplexity. "I can't do that! We'd be discovered. I—I'm desperate"—falling back on his script—"I'm a renegade . . ."

"Oh, come," Simkin said with a shade of coolness in his voice, "the farmers may believe that but I know better, and if you think I'm going to travel *months* through this godforsaken forest when you could get us where we're going in moments, then you are sadly mistaken."

"But the Enforcers . . ."

"They know when to look away," Simkin said, eyeing Saryon shrewdly. "I'm certain Bishop Vanya's given them their orders."

Vanya! Saryon's suspicions, doubts, and questions—momentarily forgotten in his predicament—flooded back. How did this young man know about Vanya? Unless he was the spy. . . .

"I—I have no idea what you are talking about," Saryon stammered, with an attempt at a perplexed frown. "I'm a renegade. A court of the catalysts sent me to this wretched village for my punishment. I've never spoken to Bishop Vanya—"

"Oh, this is such a complete waste of time," Simkin interrupted, stroking his brown curls with his hand and staring moodily down the trail. "You've talked to Bishop Vanya. *I've* talked to Bishop Vanya—"

"You've . . . talked . . . to Bishop Vanya?" Feeling his knees start to give way, Saryon grabbed hold of a tree branch to keep from falling.

"Look at you," Simkin said scornfully. "Weak as a cat. And this is the man you sent alone into the Outland!" he cried, appealing to some unseen being. "Of course I've talked to Vanya," Simkin said, turning back to Saryon. "His Tubbiness laid his plans out quite clearly before me. 'Simkin,' he said, 'I would be grateful, eternally grateful, if you would assist me in this little matter.' 'Bishop, old chap,' I replied, 'I'm yours to command.' He would have hugged me, but there are some things I draw the line at, and being hugged by fat bald men is one."

Saryon stared at the young man in amazed confusion, feeling dizzy and only half comprehending what he'd said. *This is insane,* was the first clear thought that came to him. *This . . . Simkin talking to Bishop Vanya? His Tubbiness! Yet Simkin knew . . .*

"You must be the spy!" Saryon blurted.

"I must, must I?" Simkin said, regarding him with a look both cool and mysterious.

"You've as much as admitted it!" Saryon cried, grasping hold of the young man's arm. Aching, frightened, and exhausted, the catalyst had reached his limit. "Why is Vanya sending me? I must know! You could bring him Joram, if that's all he wants! Why did he lie to me? Why the tricks?"

"Now look here, old boy, calm down," said Simkin soothingly. Suddenly serious, he laid his hand over Saryon's and drew him near. "If what you say is true and I *am* working for Vanya, and, mind you, I'm not saying I am—"

"No, of course not," Saryon muttered.

"—then you must know that my life would be worth less than that truly slovenly looking garb you're wearing if anyone back at"—he nodded in what Saryon presumed was the direction of the coven's settlement—"found out. Not that I care about myself," he added in a low voice, "but it's my sister."

"Sister?" Saryon asked weakly.

Simkin nodded. "They're holding her captive," he whispered.

"The Coven?" Saryon was growing more confused.

"The *Duuk-tsarith*!" hissed Simkin. "If I fail . . ." Shrugging, he grasped himself around the neck and twisted his hands. "Snap," he said gloomily.

"That's dreadful!" Saryon gasped.

"I could turn Joram over to them," Simkin continued with a sigh. "He trusts me, poor lad. I'm his best friend, in fact. I could tell them all they wanted to know about the negotiations with the Emperor of Sharakan. I could help expose these Technologists for the murderers and black-hearted Sorcerers that they are. But that's not what we're after, is it?"

Saryon deemed it safer not to reply, since he wasn't at all certain what he was after. He could only stare at Simkin dumbly. How did he *know* all of this? Vanya *must* have told him . . .

"It is a deep game we play, brother," said Simkin, clutching Saryon's arm. "Deep and dangerous. You are in it with me, the only one I can trust." He caught his breath in a choking sob. "I am thankful, thankful not to be alone anymore!"

Throwing his arms around the catalyst, Simkin laid his head on Saryon's shoulder and began to weep.

Taken aback by this unexpected development, Saryon could only stand helplessly in the middle of the forest, patting the young man awkwardly on the back.

"There, I'm all right," Simkin said bravely, straightening up and wiping his face. "Sorry for falling apart. It's this beastly strain. It will be better now that I have somebody to talk to. For the nonce, however, we really *must* be running along!"

"Yes," muttered Saryon, still feeling vastly confused, "but first please tell me why they sent *me* —"

"Listen!" said Simkin in a tense voice, grabbing hold of Saryon's arm again. "Did you hear that?"

Saryon froze, every sense alert. "No, I —"

"There it was again!"

"I didn't hear —"

"Centaurs! Not a doubt of it!" Simkin was pale, but controlled. "I was born in these woods! I can hear a squirrel's breath at fifty paces. Come on! Open the Corridor. Here, use my Life force. I know where we're going. I'll visualize the destination."

Saryon hesitated, still uncertain about using the Corridor when he knew the *Thon-Li*, the Corridor Masters, would certainly be monitoring it. He didn't trust this young man or his wild tales, although he had no other explanation for Simkin's extraordinary knowledge than that he must be a spy. Still, before he opened the Corridor—

Suddenly, Saryon *did* hear something, or thought he did! A crashing sound, as of hooves galloping down the trail! There seemed no choice now. Gripping Simkin's arm, the catalyst drew on the young man's Life force—never noticing, in his excitement, that it was unusually strong—and stammered out the words that opened the Corridor. The void opened, a patch of stark nothingness gaping in the middle of the trail. Simkin leaped inside, dragging the catalyst with him.

The void elongated, condensed, and shut, leaving the forest to murmur and rustle in peaceful, morning tranquility behind them.

"Where are we?" asked Saryon, stepping cautiously out of the Corridor.

"Deep, deep in the Outland," said Simkin softly, keeping his hand on Saryon's arm as he stepped out. "Watch every step, guard every word, search every shadow."

The Corridor closed behind them. Saryon glanced back at it nervously, half expecting the *Thon-Li* to leap out and apprehend them. Perhaps he was *hoping* someone would come out and apprehend them, he admitted to himself miserably. But no one did.

The two had reached their destination safely—that destination being, as far as Saryon could see, a swamp. Around them, tall trees with thick, black trunks rose up out of murky black water. The catalyst had never seen such trees in his life. Shining wet with slime, the trees' twisted limbs curled round and about each other until one tree was so entangled in the arms of another that it was impossible to tell where a single tree left off and its cousin began. The strange trees had no leaves, only twisting tentacles that shot out from the branches and dipped down into the water, like long, thin tongues.

"This . . . this isn't . . . the Coven?" Saryon asked nervously, feeling his feet sink into the boggy ground.

"No, of course not!" Simkin whispered. "It would never do now to appear suddenly in the middle of the Coven, stepping out of a Corridor, would it? I mean, people would ask questions. And believe me," he said, an unusually grim note hardening his voice, "you don't want Blachloch asking you questions."

"Blachloch?" Saryon lifted his foot from the muck, and immediately a puff of foul-smelling gas burbled to the surface where his foot had been. Gagging, the catalyst covered his mouth and nose with the sleeve of his robe, watching in horrible fascination as oozing ground rushed in to cover his tracks.

"Blachloch? Head of the Coven," said Simkin with a tight, strained smile. *"Duuk-tsarith."*

"An Enforcer?"

"Former Enforcer," Simkin said succinctly. "He decided his talents — and they are considerable — could be used more profitably for himself than his Emperor. So he left."

Shivering in the dank, chill air of the dark, tangled forest, Saryon gathered his robes closer around him and stood looking about despairingly, wondering if there were snakes.

"You'll learn more about him . . . much more . . . all too soon," Simkin said darkly. "Just remember, my friend" — he gripped the catalyst's arm — "Blachloch is a dangerous man. Very dangerous. Now, come this way. I'll lead. Keep behind me and step exactly where I step."

"We have to walk through this?" Saryon asked bleakly.

"Not far. We're near the village, this is part of the outer defenses. Mind where you step."

Looking at the black water gurgling up in the imprint left behind by Simkin's foot in the muck, Saryon was careful to obey the young man's instructions. Creeping along behind him, the blood pulsing in his throat and his heart beating painfully, the once sheltered and secluded catalyst stared around at his surroundings in a vague kind of dreamlike horror. Something stirred in his mind, memories of childhood stories told to him by the House Magus when she put him to bed at night. Stories of the creatures of enchantment that had been brought from the Dark Land of the ancients — dragons, unicorns, sea serpents. It was in places like this that they lived. They had terrified him then, lying safe in a warm bed. How much more terrifying were they now, perhaps watching at this very moment!

Saryon had never supposed himself an imaginative man, locked as he was into his cold, logical, and comfortable cell of mathematics. But now he realized that his imagination must have been hiding beneath the bed, because now it leaped out, ready to astound and frighten him.

"This is ridiculous," he told himself firmly, trying to remain calm, even as he was positive he saw the shining scaled tail of a dreadful monster slither away in the murky water of the swamp. Trembling from fear and damp and cold, he kept his eyes on Simkin, who was walking swiftly ahead of him, seemingly confident of every step. "Look at him. He's my guide. He knows where he's going. I have only to follow —"

The catalyst slowed, looking about him more intently, his senses now completely alert. Of course! How had he missed it at first?

"Simkin!" Saryon hissed.

"What is it, O Bald and Quivering One?" The young man turned around carefully, looking annoyed at being stopped.

"Simkin, this forest is under an enchantment!" Saryon gestured. "I can tell! I can sense the magic. It's unlike anything I'm used to!" So it was. The magic was so pervasive, Saryon almost felt smothered by it.

Simkin appeared uncomfortable. "I . . . I suppose you're right," he muttered, glancing about at the mist drifting up from the water and twining round about the twisting trees. "I . . . believe I did hear at one time that this forest was . . . er . . . enchanted, as you say."

"Who laid it? The Coven?"

"N-no," Simkin admitted. "They don't go in for that sort of thing, generally. Plus we haven't had a catalyst around, like yourself, you know, so it would have been rather difficult—"

"Then who?" Saryon came to a halt, staring at Simkin suspiciously.

"I say, old chap, I suggest you keep moving."

"Who?" Saryon repeated angrily.

Smiling and shrugging, Simkin pointed at the catalyst's feet.

Looking down, Saryon was alarmed to note that he was slowly sinking into the bog.

"Give me your hand!" said Simkin, tugging at the catalyst. It took considerable effort to drag Saryon's feet free of the muck and, when they did, the ground let loose with a sucking pop as though angry at having to release its prey.

Thoroughly frightened, there was nothing for the catalyst to do but keep stumbling after Simkin, though Saryon was so oppressed with the stifling sensation of the heavy enchantment that he could scarcely breathe. It seemed it was sucking the Life out of him unbidden, draining his strength.

"I must rest," Saryon gasped, staggering through the black water, his wet robes burdening him like a heavy weight.

"No, not now!" Simkin said insistently. Turning, he caught hold of Saryon's arm and pulled him on. "There's firmer ground, just a little farther . . ."

Clasped firmly in the young man's grip, Saryon trudged wearily on, noticing as he went that Simkin was having no trouble walking, but was moving lightly over the surface, his boots barely leaving any impression at all.

"After all, he *is* a magus," Saryon told himself bitterly, floundering after him. "Probably a wizard. . . ."

"Here we are," said Simkin brightly, coming to a halt. "Now you can rest a bit, if you must."

"I must," Saryon said, thankful to feel solid ground beneath his feet. Following Simkin up onto a small round knoll that rose out of the bog, Saryon wiped the chill perspiration from his face with his sleeve and, shivering, glanced about their surroundings. "How far—" he began when suddenly, his breath catching in his throat, he made a strangled sound. "Run!" he cried.

"What?" Simkin whirled around, crouching, prepared for any enemy.

"Get . . . out!" Saryon managed to gasp, trying to move his feet but feeling the enchantment drawing him slowly and inexorably down.

"Get out of what?" Simkin's voice seemed to come from far away. The mist was rising and swirling around them.

"Ring . . . mushrooms!" Saryon shouted, falling to his hands and knees as the ground shivered and quaked beneath his feet. "Simkin . . . look . . ."

With a last, desperate lunge, the catalyst tried to escape from the magical ring by flinging his body outside it. But as he lurched forward, the ground gave way and he fell. His fingers scrabbled for an instant among the mushrooms as he sought frantically to hold on, but the enchantment was irresistible, drawing him down, down . . .

The last thing he heard was Simkin's voice, sounding ghostly through the whirling mist.

"I say, old boy, I believe you're right. Frightfully sorry. . . ."

"Simkin?" whispered Saryon into the impenetrable darkness.

"Here, old boy," came a cheerful response.

"Do you know where we are?"

"I'm afraid so. Try to be calm, will you? Everything's under control."

Calm. Saryon closed his eyes and drew a deep breath, seeking to slow the beating of the heart that was lurching unsteadily in his chest. His mouth was dry, it hurt to breathe. He was standing on firm ground, however, which was some comfort, even though when he put his hands out and groped about in the darkness he could feel nothing around him. He could *sense* nothing around him either — nothing living, that is. For, oddly enough, his entire being pulsed and throbbed with magic — the source of the enchantment . . . as Simkin must have known.

When he thought he could speak in a relatively normal sounding voice, with only the hint of a quiver, he began, "I demand to know —"

At that moment, Saryon's vision literally exploded with light and sound. Torches flared, stars seemed to shout from the sky and go flitting about him. Specks of green fire zoomed before his eyes and danced in his head. Brilliant bursts of white phosphorus blinded him as trumpet blasts deafened him. Reeling backward, he covered his eyes with his hands and heard laughter tingle and sparkle around him, while other, deeper laughter, boomed and shouted.

Blinking and rubbing his eyes, trying to see in the dazzling, smoky atmosphere that was somehow light and dark at the same time, Saryon heard a deep, low voice flowing out of the laughter like a cool river running through a vast, echoing cave.

"Simkin, my sweet, pretty boy, you have returned. And have you have brought me my desire?"

"Well, er, not exactly. That is . . . perhaps. Your Majesty is so difficult to please. . . ."

"I am not difficult to please. I would have settled for you."

"Ah, come, come, now, Your Majesty. We've been over that, you know," Simkin answered with a catch in his breath, or so it seemed to Saryon, who was still trying to see through the bursting blaze of light. "You know I would be . . . be honored, but if I left the Coven, Blachloch would come searching for me and he'd find me. And then he'd find you. He's a powerful warlock —"

Saryon heard a throaty growl of impatience.

"Yes," said Simkin hastily, "I know you could handle him and his men, but it would be so ugly. They have iron, you know —"

At this, the darkness was filled with hissing and yammering, dreadful to hear, while the lights blinked and flared, causing Saryon to shield his eyes with his hand.

"Someday," said the deep, low voice, "we will deal with this matter. But now there are more urgent needs."

Saryon heard a rustling sound, as if someone had moved, and instantly silence fell. The dazzling, brilliant lights winked out, the horrible noise stopped, and the catalyst was, once more, left standing in the darkness. But this darkness was alive, he could hear it breathing all around him — light, quick, shallow breaths; deep, even, rumbling breaths; and, above them all, a soft, whispering, throaty breathing.

He had no idea what to do. He dared not speak or call Simkin's name. The breathing continued all around him — coming closer, it seemed — and the tension built inside him until he knew that any moment he would fling himself into the darkness and begin to run aimlessly, probably dashing himself to pieces among rocks —

Light flared again, only this time it was a pleasant, yellow light that did not blind him or hurt his eyes. He could see by it, he discovered, once his eyes became accustomed to it. And, looking around, he saw Simkin.

The catalyst blinked in astonishment. It was the same young man who had found him in the wilderness, the same brown hair curled upon his shoulders, the same brown mustache adorned his upper lip. But the brown robes were gone, so were the leather boots. Simkin was now dressed in nothing but shining green leaves that twined about his body like ivy. He was facing Saryon and regarding the catalyst with a pleading look on his expressive face — a look that changed the next instant when a figure emerged from where it had been standing in the darkness behind Simkin.

The figure stepped into the pool of shimmering light, and Saryon forgot about young men, forgot about Bishops, forgot about enchanted traps. He very nearly forgot about breathing and it was only when he felt light-headed and faint did he remember to draw a deep, quivering breath.

"Father Saryon, may I present Her Majesty, Elspeth, Queen of the Faeries."

It was Simkin's voice, but Saryon could not look at him. He could look at only one thing.

The woman drifted closer.

Saryon felt his throat close and an aching sensation spread through his chest.

Golden hair cascaded in undulating waves to the floor, casting a halo of light about the woman as she walked. Silver eyes shone brighter and colder than the stars Saryon had looked upon in the night. She did not walk, that he could see, but she came closer and closer to him, filling his vision. Her naked body — and Saryon had never in his life imagined anything so soft and white and smooth — was wreathed in flowers. And these blossoms, which might have been used to modestly conceal her nakedness, had precisely the opposite effect. Hands of roses and lilacs cupped her white breasts, seeming to offer those breasts to the spellbound catalyst. Fingers of morning glories traced across her sleek stomach and caressed her shapely legs as if saying to Saryon, "Don't you envy us? Cast us aside! Take our place!"

Nearer and nearer, her fragrance intoxicating him, she drifted toward him until she came to rest before him, her slim feet barely touching the ground. Saryon could do nothing, say nothing. He could only stare into her silver eyes and smell the lilacs and tremble at her nearness.

Tilting her beautiful head to one side, Elspeth studied him intently, earnestly, her sweetly curving lips puckering with the seriousness of her regard. Raising her hands, she laid them on Saryon's shoulders. The movement of her arms lifted her breasts from their rose and lilac garden. . . . Saryon shut his eyes, swallowing painfully, holding himself rigid and stiff as her fingers traced along his shoulders, down over his chest, and around his back.

"How old is he?" the low, throaty voice asked suddenly.

Saryon opened his eyes.

"Forty or so," answered Simkin cheerfully.

Elspeth frowned, almost a pout, her lips curving downward. Saryon swallowed again as her hands came to rest lightly on his shoulders. "That is not too old for humans?"

"Oh, no!" Simkin said hastily. "Not old at all. Many consider it to be the ideal age, prime of life."

Saryon, finally able to withdraw his gaze from the lovely woman before him, started to ask Simkin what was going on — if he could find his voice, that is. But the young man scowled so fiercely and nodded so emphatically at the Queen that the catalyst kept quiet.

Elspeth's frown deepened. "He is thin. He is not strong."

"He is a scholar, a wise man," answered Simkin quickly. "He has spent his life in study."

"Indeed?" Elspeth said with interest. Saryon found himself in the silver-eyed gaze once more. "A wise man. We like that. There is much we would learn."

Pausing a moment longer, her head tilted to one side, keeping Saryon in her enchanting gaze, Elspeth at last nodded slowly to herself. "Very well," she murmured.

Clasping Saryon's hand in her own, she drifted up, turned to face her people, and floated down to stand beside him. Her golden hair floated about him, enveloping him, her touch tingled through his body like a sweet, burning poison. Lifting the catalyst's unresisting hand, Elspeth cried out, "Faeriefolk, bow down! Prepare for the celebration! Do homage to the one we have chosen to father our child!"

5

The Wedding Feast

Saryon paced back and forth, back and forth, back and forth, in the small cavern chamber until, too exhausted to take another step, he collapsed onto a soft, leafy bower and, groaning, let his head sink into his hands.

"I say, old boy, cheer up! You're the bridegroom, the reason for the feast — not its main course."

At the sound of the cheerful voice, Saryon raised his haggard face.

"What have you gotten me into! You have —"

"There, there, calmly, old boy, calmly," Simkin said with a laugh and a grin as he entered the room. Nodding his head casually behind him, he gripped Saryon's wrist tightly and jerked him up off the bed. "Company," he muttered under his breath. "We can talk back here," he added, steering the catalyst toward the far end of the cavern.

Glancing over his shoulder, Saryon saw several of the faeriefolk standing or flitting about the doorway, leering at him, giggling, and winking. With the arrival of the faeries, the cavern that up until now had been dark and peaceful erupted into chaos. Highly sensual beings, faeries live literally from moment to moment. Their only object in life is to indulge themselves in any sensation that will give them an instant's gratification. The magic of the world flows through them like wine, they live in a constant state of intoxication. Neither rules nor morals govern their actions; no conscience guides them. Each does as he or she pleases without regard to others. Their only bond, and the only force that keeps their small band together, is their unswerving loyalty to their Queen. When her mind is with them, there is some semblance of order. But once it is withdrawn . . .

Saryon stared in shock. Where previously a leafy, fragrant bower had filled one corner of the shadowy cavern, now a great pool of water stood there, lilies and swans floating upon its surface. An instant's time changed the swans to horses, splashing frantically to escape the water, the lilies were parrots, screeching raucously and flapping about the caverns. And then the pool was a coach, drawn by the horses, who came charging straight at the catalyst. Shutting his eyes and flinging his arms over his head with a shriek, Saryon felt the steeds' hot breath and heard the thunder of their hooves, expecting to be crushed at any second. Laughter hooted around him. Opening his eyes, he saw the horses change to lambs that gamboled at his feet while he screamed in terror. His breath catching in his throat, Saryon staggered backward, only to feel Simkin's arm embrace him firmly.

"Don't look," said the young man, forcibly turning Saryon around.

Closing his eyes, Saryon drew in a deep breath, only to regret it immediately. Every smell conceivable flew up his nostrils and down his lungs—delicate perfumes, foul odors of decaying bodies, the smell of freshly baked bread.

"What must I do now? Quit breathing?" he asked Simkin. But the young man ignored him.

"That's better," said Simkin, patting Saryon's hand solicitously. Turning to the faeries crowded in the doorway, he added by way of explanation, "Touch of nerves. Man of the cloth. Never been with a woman . . . if you know what I mean . . ."

The faeries obviously *did* know by the raucous noise they
made.

Blood rushed to Saryon's head. He felt dizzy, burning
with fever, and chilled, all at the same time. Snatching his
hand away from Simkin, he groaned again and tried to force
himself to think clearly.

"Best sit down, old chap," said Simkin, guiding Saryon to
the mossy cushion that changed to a fainting couch and then
to a giant toadstool before they were even halfway near it.
"I'll see if I can induce the wedding guests to go inflict their
attentions on more deserving personages."

Numbly following Simkin's direction, Saryon cast the
toadstool a shuddering glance and sank down upon the floor,
only to find himself sitting upon the soft, leafy bower once
more.

He thought of all the dangers he had expected to face in
the Outland — everything from being ripped apart by centaurs to falling under a dragon's terrible enchantment. Being
taken captive by the Faerie Queen and expected to . . . to
. . . Well, this was something he'd never considered.

"I don't even *believe* in the faeries!" he muttered to himself. "Or I didn't. It's all nursery tales!"

"The mushroom ring! That is how faeriefolk trap mortals." The voice of the old House Magus sang in his ears like
the laughter of the faeries. "Anyone foolish enough to step
into the enchanted ring will fall down, down, down into their
caves far beneath the ground. And there the poor mortal, be
he ever a wizard so powerful, will find himself enthralled by
the faerie spells and so he will lose his own magic and become
a prisoner, spending his days in luxury, his nights in unspeakable acts, until he goes mad from the pleasure."

As a child, Saryon had a confused idea of what "unspeakable acts" might be. He recalled thinking dimly that it had
something to do with cutting out someone's tongue. Even so,
it had been a sufficiently frightening story to set the small
boy running away in gleeful panic at the sight of a mushroom
in the grass.

But I forgot. I lost the wonder of that little boy. Here I
am, lounging on a cushion of sweet-smelling grasses and
clover and moss, softer than the finest couches of the Emperor. Here I am, my blood burning every time I conjure up

a vision of Elspeth, part of me longing to commit those "unspeakable acts."

Half-turning, peering out through half-open lids, Saryon's unwilling gaze was drawn, fascinated, to the faeriefolk in the doorway, whom Simkin was trying unsuccessfully to shoo away.

"I know I am not dreaming," Saryon whispered to himself, "because even in my dreams, I do not have the imagination to conjure up such as these."

Sprouting up in his doorway like their enchanted mushrooms, the faeriefolk shifted and changed before his eyes like their mad, magical creations. Some were nearly four feet tall, with brown, laugh-crinkled, mischievous faces, like children grown old but not wise. Others were tiny, small enough to fit in the palm of Saryon's hand. These appeared as little more than balls of light, each a slightly different color. But, on staring at them closely, Saryon thought he could detect delicate, naked, winged bodies surrounded by a magical radiance. And in between these two extremes was an entire range of other faerie species, some short, some squat, some thin, some all, some none. There were children, too — smaller copies of the adults — and animals of every description who wandered about freely, many appearing to serve as mounts or servants to the larger faeries.

None of the faeries were as tall or looked as human as Elspeth. But that wasn't unusual, according to Saryon's nursery tale remembrances. Just as the queen bee is the largest and most pampered in the hive, so the Faerie Queen is tall and voluptuous and beautiful. For the same reason, he guessed, his face burning — to continue her species. Without a Queen to guide them, the irresponsible faeries would die. The Queen must, therefore, mate with a human male and produce a child. . . .

Saryon put his head in his hands, trying to blot out the sight of the leering grins and the flitting lights.

But he couldn't blot out their voices.

So different are the varieties of faeriefolk and so varied their voice range and pitch — from squeaking sounds like mice to deep rumblings like frogs — that Saryon was bewildered and even uncertain as to whether or not they were all speaking the same language. He couldn't understand a word but, he noticed, Simkin could. Simkin could not only understand them, but he could converse with them as well. He was doing so now, sending them into gales of merriment. Writhing in embarrassment, Saryon could just imagine what he was telling them.

Explain this logically, Saryon, he told himself. Explain this, catalysts, with all the books in your libraries. Explain these people away, and then explain to yourself why you are watching them dance in your flower-filled bower. Explain why you are thinking of losing yourself in this sweet prison, of yielding to that soft, white flesh. . . .

No! The yammering and twittering and giggling was beginning to tear his nerves to shreds. I've got to get out of here! Saryon realized wildly, getting a grip on reality. I'm going mad, as the old stories said. But how? Simkin is in league with them! He brought me here! But even as Saryon thought this, a vision of Elspeth came to his mind — swelling breasts, soft skin, warmth, sweetness, perfume . . . Frantically, Saryon started up from the cushion of moss, the look on his ashen face one of such panic and determination to flee that Simkin, catching a glimpse of him, shoved the faeriefolk unceremoniously out into the hallway and slammed shut the oaken door.

"Let me out!" Saryon cried in a hollow voice.

"Now do be reasonable, my dear fellow," began Simkin, standing in front of the door.

Saryon did not answer. Grabbing hold of the young man with a strength born of desperation, he threw him to one side.

"Sorry to do this, but you must listen to reason," Simkin said with a sigh. Speaking several words in the birdlike language of the faerie, he watched with a sigh as the oaken door began to dissolve and reshape itself into part of the cavern wall just as the catalyst lunged against it.

Groaning in pain, feeling his reason start to slip away, the catalyst let his body slide slowly to the floor.

"Don't take it so hard, old chap," Simkin said, squatting down beside him and laying a reassuring hand on Saryon's shoulder. "I'm going to get us out of this predicament. You've just got to give me a little time, that's all."

Casting the leafily clad young man a bitter glance, Saryon shook his head and did not reply.

Simkin's voice quavered. "I see. You don't trust me. After everything I've done for you . . . What we've been to each other . . ." Two great tears rolled down into his beard. "I've thought of you as my father . . . My poor father. He and I were very close, you know," the young man said in choked tones, "until the Enforcers came and dragged him away!" Two more tears trickled down his face. Covering his face with his hands, Simkin stumbled across the room and landed on the cushion of leaves, sending up a shower of fragrant blossoms. "You know what they'll do to my sister if I don't get you back to the Coven!" he sobbed. "Oh, this is too much to bear! Too much!"

Staring at the young man in amazement, Saryon was completely at a loss. Finally, the catalyst stood up and walked across the cavern floor. Coming near the weeping young man, Saryon clumsily patted Simkin on the shoulder.

"There, now," the catalyst said awkwardly, "I didn't mean to hurt you. I — I'm just distraught, that's all."

No response.

"Can you blame me?" Saryon asked feelingly. "First you lead us into an enchanted forest —"

"That was an accident," came a muffled voice from amid the flowers.

"Then the mushroom ring —"

"Anyone can make a mistake."

"Then the next thing I see you are dressed like one of *them!*"

"Only being hospitable —"

"The Queen calls you by name, you speak their language. You even joke with them, for 'Min's sake," Saryon concluded in exasperation, losing his patience and committing an unforgivable sin by taking the god's name in vain. "What am I supposed to think?"

Sitting up, Simkin peered at him with red-rimmed eyes. "You might have given me the benefit of the doubt," he said, sniffing. "It can all be explained, I assure you. Only . . . well . . . there isn't much time now," he added hastily, wiping away his tears. "You don't have a comb, do you?" Glancing at Saryon's bald head, he sighed. "Stupid question. I'll have to make do, I guess, though I look a perfect fright." Picking twigs out of his hair and beard, Simkin began combing through his curls with a forked stick that he plucked from the bower.

"You'd better get ready, too," he stated, glancing at Saryon. "I say, can't you come up with anything better than those drab robes? I've an idea! Open up a conduit to me! I'll have you decked out in no time! Leaves from the . . . um . . . copper maple. That would do quite nicely. Not ostentatious in the least. A pine bough in the strategic location. Perfect thing. The pine needles itch a little at first, but you'll get used to it. Oh, come on! After all, you *are* getting married —"

"I am not!" cried Saryon, springing to his feet and pacing feverishly about the sealed cavern chamber.

"Well, of course not," Simkin said with a light little laugh that cracked about halfway through. Clearing his throat, he glanced hopefully at the pale-faced catalyst. "I mean, it wouldn't be unthinkable, would it? Elspeth is really quite charming, don't you know? A great personality, not to mention —"

Saryon shot him a vicious glance.

"Yes, you're right. Unthinkable," Simkin said firmly. "Therefore, I have a plan. Everything all arranged. My sister . . . you know . . ." he added in low tones. "Life at stake. I believe I mentioned how they are holding her captive —"

"What do we do?" Saryon asked, wearily cutting Simkin off in mid-tragedy.

"Wait for my signal," said Simkin, standing up and arranging his leaves in a fashionable manner. "Ah, here they are, come to escort the bridegroom to his blushing bride."

"What will the signal be?" Saryon whispered as the stone door began to dissolve. Outside, he could see flaming torches surrounded by thousands of dancing, blinking lights and he could hear hundreds of shrill, deep, soft, loud voices raised in eerie, enchanting song. At the far end of the vast, flower-decked cavern, he could barely make out the figure of Elspeth, seated on a throne made of a living oak tree, her golden hair glistening in the torch light.

Saryon swallowed. "The signal?" he repeated hoarsely.

"You'll know it," Simkin assured him. Taking the catalyst by the arm, he led him forward into the presence of the Faerie Queen.

*   *   *

"More wine, my love?"

"N-no, thank you," stammered Saryon, putting his hand over the golden goblet. Too late. With a word, Elspeth caused the cup to fill to overflowing with the sweet, blood-red liquid. Grimacing, Saryon snatched his hand away and wiped it surreptitiously on his robes.

"More honeycomb?" Some appeared on his golden plate.

"No, I'm—"

"More fruit, meat, bread?" Within seconds, the plate was heaped with delicacies, their rich aroma blending with the other smells—smoke of torches, steaming platters of roast meat, and, near him, the fragrance of Elspeth herself, dark, musky, more intoxicating than the wine. "You've eaten nothing!" she said to him, leaning so close that he could feel her hair brush against his cheek.

"Really, I'm—I'm not hungry," Saryon said in a faint voice.

"I expect you are nervous," Elspeth said, her lips curving into a smile, her eyes inviting him to draw nearer still. "Is it true that you have never lain with a woman?"

Saryon flushed redder than the wine and cast an irritated glance at Simkin, who was sitting next to him.

"I had to tell them *something*, old boy," Simkin muttered out of the corner of his mouth, draining his goblet. "They simply couldn't understand why you carried on so when their Queen made the announcement about you fathering the child and so forth. All that hand-waving and shouting. You were lucky they just put you in that little room to cool off. Once I explained—"

"Why are you bothering with that fool? Pay attention to me, my love," Elspeth said in a soft voice, catching hold of the fabric of Saryon's robe and tugging him toward her. She moved in a playful manner, her voice was soft and sultry, yet her words chilled Saryon. "I will be very good to you, my own, but remember—you *are* my own! I need, I demand, your complete attention. At all times, day and night, every thought you think must be *of* me. Every word you speak must be *to* me." Lifting his hand, she rubbed it against her petal-smooth cheek. "Now, my *own*, since you will not eat and since it is too early to go to the bridal bower—"

"When — when is that?" Saryon asked, flushing.

"Moonrise," said Simkin, watching the wine level rise in his goblet again with appreciative eyes.

Elspeth gave him an angry glance but, at that moment, a riotous clamoring broke out on the other side of the Faerie Queen, momentarily distracting her. Taking advantage of the opportunity, Saryon grabbed hold of Simkin's shoulder.

"Moonrise! That's less than an hour!"

"Yes," said Simkin, staring into the wine.

"We've got to get out of here!" Saryon whispered frantically.

"Soon," murmured Simkin.

Saryon dared not pursue the matter further, for the quarrel or joke or whatever it had been was quieting down. Trying to keep hold of himself, all the while feeling as if he was about to scream and fling himself into the center of the table, Saryon decided that a sip of wine might be beneficial.

Lifting the goblet to his lips, trying to keep his hand from shaking, he stared about him with the dazed look of a sleepwalker. He had attended revels in court. He had attended what were considered wild revels in court — All Fools' Day, for example, when supposedly all propriety is cast to the wind. But staring at the madness and mayhem going on before him, his senses were literally so overwhelmed that he could not comprehend it completely, but saw it in blurs of color and bursts of noise and flares of light.

Every conceivable activity was going on around him, from pitched battle being fought in the center of the table to shameless lovemaking on couches. Bears danced in the aisles, acrobats juggled flaming brands, children sang bawdy songs, food splattered on the walls and floors and ceilings. Looking over here, he was horrified; looking over there, he was embarrassed; looking somewhere else, he was nauseated.

"Are you thinking of me?" whispered a sweet voice in Saryon's ear.

The catalyst started. "Of course," he answered hastily, turning to face Elspeth, who smiled and, inserting her hand up the sleeve of his robes, softly caressed his arm. And as he looked at her, the catalyst noticed something. Though all might be chaos around her, she herself was a haven of peace, of restfulness. He felt drawn to her to escape the madness.

"And now," she said, slightly pouting. "You will tell me why you have never been with a woman. You enjoy my touch, I can tell," she added, feeling Saryon's muscles tense involuntarily.

"It — it is not the . . . custom . . . of my people," stammered Saryon, licking his dry lips and breaking free of her grasp to reach for his wine goblet again. "Such . . . mating . . . is done by animals, but not by civilized . . . men and — uh — women."

"I had heard something of this," said Elspeth, her silver eyes gleaming with laughter and amazement, "but I did not believe it." She shrugged, her breasts, decked with lilies-of-the-valley, rising and falling with her soft breath. "How, then, do you have children?"

"When the will of the Almin was made known to the people regarding this matter," Saryon said, his voice shaking, "we catalysts, together with the *Theldari*, the shamans skilled in such medicines, were given the knowledge to perform this rite. The granting of a life, after all, is a sacred gift and should be entered into only in the most . . . most reverent frame of mind." Oh, how silly this sounded, so close to her soft body . . .

"A truly beaut — beaut — bu'ful speech," blubbered Simkin, causing his wine goblet to fill again. "You're going to make a wonderful father. Just like mine!" Breaking down, he laid his head on Saryon's arm and wept.

"Simkin!" hissed Saryon, shaking him, aware of Elspeth's glittering-eyed gaze upon them. "Stop this! Sit up!"

Simkin sat up, but only to wrap one arm around Saryon's neck and drag him down with him, causing the catalyst to bang his head smartly on the table.

"What are you doing?" Saryon demanded, trying to free himself and nearly choking from the wine fumes exhaling from Simkin's mouth.

"Thish . . . shignal," Simkin said in a loud whisper, wrapping his other arm around the catalyst's neck and smiling up at him drunkenly. "Time to" — he belched — "'shcape."

"What?" demanded Saryon, still trying to break Simkin's hold. But every time he loosened one of the young man's hands, the other entwined itself around him again. Simkin was hanging onto his neck, then — falling forward — around his waist, then — leaning his head on his chest — lolling around his shoulders.

"Shcape," whispered Simkin, frowning solemnly. "Now."

"How?" Saryon muttered, dimly aware that there was singing going on in the background. To his dismay, he saw moonlight filtering down onto the table through the rifts in the high cavern ceiling. Elspeth was rising to her feet, her beautiful face as cold and pale as the light shining on it.

"Tell . . . tell them I'm shick," said Simkin, belching again. "Hor — hor — hor'ble illness. Plague."

"But you're drunk!" Saryon snarled furiously.

Suddenly Simkin lurched forward, his dead weight dragging Saryon to the floor. The faeries laughed and cheered. Elspeth was shouting something. Completely tangled up in Simkin, his robes, and the chair, Saryon lay on his back on the floor, Simkin on top of him, as feet of every shape and description danced and darted about him.

Lifting his head from where it rested on Saryon's chest, Simkin looked at the catalyst with round, solemn, unfocused eyes. "You shee . . ." he breathed in a grape-laden whisper, "faeries never get drunk. Physh . . . ically im-possible. They'll b'lieve I'm shick. Shcape. Shee?"

Saryon stared at the young man hopefully. "Then, you're only pretending to be drunk?"

"Oh, no!" said Simkin solemnly. "N'ver do anythin' half-way. Jush . . . help me to my . . . feet. All . . . four of 'em."

At that moment, several of the stronger male faeries grasped hold of Simkin and dragged him off the catalyst. Several more helped Saryon to his feet, the catalyst stalling as long as possible to try to think what to say and do, wondering if he might not be able to get out on his own.

Simkin, meanwhile, was being held upright by the combined forces of four faeries, two holding his feet and two more flying over his head, gripping him firmly by the hair. Looking at the young man's rolling eyes, crazed grin, and wobbly legs, Saryon suddenly went calm with despair. Leave without Simkin? Impossible. Saryon had no idea where he was and he guessed, from what little he had seen, that the Faerie Kingdom was a vast catacomb of twisting, winding tunnels and caverns. He would be lost by himself. Besides, if he did make it back into the wilderness, his life was worth nothing anyway.

Stay here . . . with Elspeth . . . He would go mad, soon. But what sweet madness. . . .

Sighing softly, Saryon turned to the Faerie Queen. "Send for your Healer," he commanded in his sternest voice.

"What?" She appeared astonished and, raising her hand, instantly quieted the clamor and commotion of the faeries. Darkness descended suddenly on the great hall except for a light that gleamed from her golden hair. "A Healer? We have no Healer."

"What, none?" Saryon was shocked. "No *Mannanish* at least?"

"What for?" Elspeth responded scornfully. "We are never sick. Why do you think we avoid human contamina—"

Pausing, she looked at Simkin more intently, her eyes narrowing.

"Until now," Saryon said grimly, pointing to Simkin, who was looking worse all the time. His face had turned an unbecoming green beneath the beard, his eyes were rolling in his head. The faeries supporting the weak and reeling young man stared at their Queen in alarm.

"Here," offered Saryon, stepping over and putting his arm firmly around Simkin's sagging body, "I'll take him to his chambers—"

"I'll take care of him!" said Elspeth calmly. "At once!"

Saryon's heart leaped into his throat as he saw her preparing to cast a magic spell that would probably have sent Simkin to the bottom of the river.

"No! Wait!" the catalyst cried, hanging onto the foolishly grinning Simkin. Peacefully swaying from side to side, he was humming a little ditty. "No, you mustn't send him away. We—we need to know what he's got!" Saryon finished in a burst of inspiration. "To see if it's . . . catching."

"Fatal," said Simkin mournfully, and was promptly sick all over the floor. The faeries who had been attending him screeched and jabbered in fear and anger, backing up until there was a clear circle around the catalyst and his guide.

"Are humans subject to such frailties?" Elspeth asked, frowning.

"Yes, oh yes!" Saryon said breathlessly, seeing a ray of hope drift down among the moonbeams. "It happens to me constantly!"

Looking at him, Elspeth smiled. "Then it is well that we mingle the blood of your child with mine. In time, perhaps we will wipe out this weak, human trait. Take him to his chambers, then. You four"—she detailed four of the tallest of the tall faeries—"accompany them. When Simkin is settled, bring my beloved to my bed."

Moving closer, she brushed her lips against Saryon's cheek. Her warm flesh, soft and curving, pressed against his and for an instant the catalyst was as weak as Simkin. Then she was gone, her cloud of golden hair shimmering around her.

"Let the merriment continue!" she shouted and the darkness came alive.

Saryon turned, his despair complete, and proceeded to half-walk, half-drag the drunken Simkin through the hall, followed by four dancing faerie guards.

"Well, it was a good try," Saryon whispered to Simkin with a sigh. "But it didn't work."

"It didn't?" asked Simkin, looking about in amazement. "Did they catch us? I don't remember running!"

"Running!" Saryon said, puzzled. "What do you mean— running? I thought we were trying to convince them to let us go because you were sick?"

"I shay, that'sh a good idea!" said Simkin, regarding Saryon with misty-eyed admiration. "Letsh try it."

"I did," snapped Saryon tensely, his arms and back aching with the strain, his hands pricked by the leaves Simkin was wearing. He was growing increasingly nauseated from the smell of forest, wine, and vomit. "It didn't work."

"Oh." Simkin appeared downcast, then almost immediately cheered up. "I guessh we'll have to . . . to make . . . makearunforit."

"Shhh!" cautioned Saryon, glancing back at the guards. "That's nonsense! You can't walk, let alone run."

"You forget," said Simkin with a lofty air, "I am a skilled wizard. Class *Albanara*. Open a con . . . duit to me, Catalysht, and I . . . will walk the wings of air."

"You really know the way out?" Saryon asked dubiously.

"Coursh."

"How do you feel?"

"Much better . . . since I was shick."

"Very well," Saryon muttered nervously, glancing back at the guards, who weren't paying the least attention to them. "Which way?"

Simkin stared around, swiveling his head like an owl. "That way," he indicated, nodding at a dark, unused corridor branching off to their right. Glancing behind him, Saryon saw the four guards lagging behind, staring back wistfully at the revelry they were missing.

"Now!" Simkin cried.

Saryon started to whisper a prayer to the Almin. Remembering bitterly that he was on his own now, he opened a conduit to the magic around him. Drawing it into his body, he hastily made the mathematical calculations necessary to give the young man Life, but not enough to completely drain himself. Filled with the magic he could never use, he extended the conduit to Simkin and felt the surge as the young wizard drew it from him.

Suffused with magical energy, Simkin took to the air with the grace of a drunken loon.

Seeing the young man safely on his way, Saryon broke into a run, the pent-up fear and nervousness surging in his blood giving him an unusual burst of strength as he dashed down the cavern corridor. He heard their guards cry out, but he dared not risk looking behind him to see what was happening. He was having enough trouble staying on his feet as it was. Though here and there a torch sputtered on the wall, the cavern corridor was shadowy, the floor was strewn with rocks and rubble. He had no idea where they were headed. Corridors branched off in all directions, but Simkin flew past them without pausing, his leaves fluttering around him like those of a tree in a high wind.

The shouting behind them grew louder, echoing down the cavern walls in an alarming fashion. Saryon thought he could hear Elspeth's furious voice rising shrill and harsh above them all. The torches winked out, plunging them into a darkness so complete that Saryon instantly lost all sense of what was ahead of him, above him, or below him.

"Ouch! Drat!"

"Simkin?" Saryon cried fearfully, coming to a halt, not daring to take another step in the darkness, though he could hear the shouts of the faeries exulting loudly.

"More Life, Catalyst!" Simkin called out.

His breath coming in gasps, his heart lurching in his chest, Saryon opened the conduit once again. Immediately the corridor was lit with a faint light, shining from Simkin's hands. The young magus hovered before him, rubbing his nose.

"Bashed into a wall," he said ruefully.

Glancing back, Saryon saw lights leaping down the corridor, gaining on them rapidly. "Let's go!" he gasped and ran forward, only to stumble very quickly backward with a cry.

A huge black spider, nearly as large as the corridor itself, hung in a gigantic web spun across their path. A sudden vision of having plummeted into that web in the darkness, of hairy legs crawling over his body, of stinging poison paralyzing him crowded into Saryon's mind, leaving him so weak and drained that he could barely stand.

Leaning back against the wall, he stared at the hideous spider that was watching them with fiery red eyes. "It's useless," he said quietly. "We can't fight them!"

"Non . . . sense!" Simkin remarked. Flying over to Saryon, he grabbed the catalyst by the arm and tugged him down the corridor, heading for the web.

"Are you mad?" Saryon gasped.

"Come on!" Simkin insisted. Dragging the terrified catalyst along after him, he lunged straight for the body of the huge spider.

Frantically, Saryon tried to break free of Simkin's hold, but the young man, now filled with magical energy, was too strong. The spider's red eyes loomed larger than twin suns, its hairy legs reached out, the web was wrapping round, suffocating him. . . .

Saryon closed his eyes.

"I say, old friend, I can't keep this up for ever," came an aggrieved voice.

Opening his eyes, Saryon saw, to his amazement, nothing.

The dark corridor stretched ahead of them, empty except for Simkin, who hovered in the air near him.

"What? The spider —" Saryon glanced around wildly.

"Illusion," Simkin said scornfully. "I was . . . fairly certain . . . it wasn't real. Elspeth's good . . . not that good. Real spider in the wink of a . . . finger? Hah!" He snorted. "Coursh," he added, struck by a sudden thought, his eyes widening. "Always possibility, I'spose . . . real spider . . . posted to guard corridor. Never occurred to me. Almin's blood, we dashed right into the middle of the web!" Seeing Saryon's horrified expression, the young magus shrugged and clapped Saryon on the shoulder. "Could have been a bit sticky for us, couldn't it, old fellow?"

Too exhausted to speak, Saryon could only draw in painful breaths and try to push the terror out of his mind. Shouts behind him helped considerably.

"How far do we have to go?" he managed to ask, stumbling forward.

"Round . . . bend." Simkin pointed. "I think. . . ." Glancing at the catalyst staggering wearily along the ground beside him, the young man asked, "You going to make it?"

Saryon nodded his head grimly, though his legs had long ago lost any sensation of feeling and seemed to be just so much dead weight for him to carry around. The shouts were getting closer. Glancing behind again, he could see the dancing lights, or perhaps it was spots bursting before his eyes. He wasn't certain and, at that moment, he didn't care. "They're gaining," he croaked, his voice catching in his throat as a sharp, swift pain tore through his side.

"I'll stop that!" Simkin said. Whirling about in midair, he raised his hand. Lightning shot from his fingers, exploded on the cavern ceiling, and immediately the air around them was filled with booming thunder, falling rock, and the choking smell of sulfur.

Blinded, deafened, and in dire peril of being struck on the head by the collapsing cavern roof, Saryon hurled himself forward, assisted by Simkin. "That ought to keep them busy," the young man muttered in pleased tones as they dashed down the corridor.

The catalyst had no idea what happened after that. He ran and stumbled and fell, and had the vague impression of Simkin hauling him to his feet, and ran some more. He had the hazy remembrance of pleading with Simkin to let him lie

down and die in the darkness and end the burning pain that
was tearing through his body. He heard shouts behind him
and then the shouts stopped and he wanted to stop, but Simkin wouldn't let him and then there were shouts again and
finally . . . sunlight.

Sunlight. It was the only thing that could have penetrated
the darkness of fear and pain that was closing over Saryon.
They had escaped! Fresh air blew on his face, giving him
added strength. With a final burst of energy that came from
somewhere unknown inside him, the catalyst made a lunge
for the opening he could see now, shining brightly at the end
of the tunnel.

What would he do once he was outside? Would the faeries follow them into the forest? Pursue them, hunt them
down, drag them back? Saryon didn't know and he didn't
care. If he could just feel the sun on his face, grass beneath
his feet, see sheltering trees spread their boughs above him —
everything would be all right. He knew it.

Victory and exultation flooding through him, Saryon
reached the end of the tunnel, burst out into the sunlight . . .

. . . and nearly fell off the edge of a sheer cliff.

Grabbing hold of the catalyst, Simkin dragged Saryon
away from the end of the ledge, stumbling backward into a
rock wall. Saryon sank to his knees, at first too exhausted
and confused to comprehend what had happened. When the
dizziness cleared and he was able to look around, he saw that
he and Simkin were perched on a small ledge of rock that
extended out from the tunnel about ten feet before it ended
in a drop of a hundred feet or more straight down into a
heavily wooded river canyon.

His body aching, his hope dashed as effectively as if it
had leaped off the rock edge and tumbled to the ground
below, Saryon could do nothing but look at Simkin, too exhausted even to speak.

"This *is* rather unexpected," the young man admitted,
stroking his beard as he stared down into the tops of the trees
below. "I know!" he said suddenly. "Damn! I should have
taken a right at the second fork instead of a left. I *always*
make that mistake."

Saryon closed his eyes. "Go ahead and save yourself," he
said. "You have Life enough to float down on the wind currents."

"And leave you behind? No, no, old fellow," Simkin said. He floated over to stand before the catalyst, still weaving slightly from the effects of the wine. "Couldn't think of abandon . . . doning you. Like a . . . a father to me. . . ."

"Don't start crying!" Saryon snapped.

"No, sorry." Simkin choked and wiped his nose. "We're not done for yet, if you have a bit more strength left?" He peered at the catalyst hopefully.

"I don't know." Saryon shook his head. He wasn't certain he had strength enough to even keep breathing.

"It's this sort of talent I've got," Simkin said persuasively. "I can change myself into inanimate objects."

Saryon stared at him, uncomprehending. "That's crazy," he said finally. "I know the mathematical calculations involved. It'd take six catalysts, with full strength, to give you enough Life —"

He heard the shouts behind him then, mingled with harsh, raucous laughter as the faeries realized their prey was trapped.

"No!" Simkin said eagerly. "I said, it's my talent. I can do it at will, with just my own force generally. Now, I'm a bit flagged and somewhat muddled from the wine, so if you could help . . ."

"I don't —"

"Quickly, man!" Simkin cried, grabbing hold of Saryon and pulling him to his feet.

Too spent to argue, not caring anyway, Saryon opened the conduit and expended his last energy. Magic flowed through him like blood from an open vein and then he was empty, drained. He had no more to give, not having the strength required to draw in any more from the world around him. The shouts grew louder and louder. They'd be here soon. Perhaps he should just jump, he thought, and stared dreamily out over the ledge.

He pictured himself falling through the air, the ground leaping up to meet him, his body crashing onto sharp rocks, smashing, breaking. . . .

Feeling his stomach clench, Saryon backed up precipitously . . . and walked right into a tree. Whirling, he looked at the tree in amazement. It hadn't been there before. The ledge had been bare. . . .

"Up! Climb up!" the tree said in a muffled voice.

Staring in wonder, Saryon reached out a trembling hand to touch the tree's rough bark. "Simkin?"

"There's no time to waste! Hide in the boughs! Quickly!"

Too tired to think clearly or even to marvel at this strange occurrence, Saryon hitched his robes up around his waist and, catching hold of a low-hanging bough, pulled himself up into the tree that was standing on the edge of the rock ledge.

"Higher! You've got to climb higher!"

Clinging to the trunk, Saryon managed to scrabble his way up a little farther. Then he came to a stop. Pressing his cheek against the limb, he shook his head. "I . . . can't . . . go . . . any further. . . ." he murmured brokenly.

"All right!" The tree sounded irritated. "Hold still. Thank goodness you're wearing green."

This won't fool them, Saryon thought, listening to the voices echoing in the cavern. All it will take is one of them to look up here or fly up here and —

A gust of wind hit the tree and a limb beneath Saryon's feet gave way with a sudden snap. Grasping hold of a branch, pulling himself up, the catalyst stared down at the splintered limb and hope vanished completely. Brown and dried up inside, the limb was dead, as dead as he himself was going to be soon. Another gust swirled about the mountain, another dead branch fell to the ledge. Beneath him, Saryon could feel the entire tree shaking and shivering. There was a crack, then a snapping and rending sound. Finally, with a heartrending shudder, the tree toppled over the edge of the cliff.

Clinging to Simkin's bark and leaves, Saryon heard the young man murmuring to himself as they fell.

"Strike me dead! I'm rotten."

6

The Coven of the Wheel

"**S**o this is the catalyst."

"Yes, dear boy. Not a very imposing specimen, is he? Still, there must be more to him than was readily apparent to *me* after our little outing. He's been sent here after you, Joram."

"Sent? Who sent him?"

"Bishop Vanya."

"Oh, and the catalyst told you that, did he, Simkin?"

"Of course, Mosiah. I'm in the old chap's complete confidence. He thinks of me as the son he never had. Told me so many times. Not that I trust him. After all, he *is* a catalyst. But I heard the same thing from Bishop Vanya — about Joram, that is. *Not* about me being the son he never had."

"And I suppose the Emperor sent along his regards . . ."

"I'm sure I don't know why he would. Not to *you* peasants. Go ahead and laugh. I have merely to await the day of my vindication. This Saryon is after you, Dark One."

"He looks in fairly bad shape. What did you do to him?"

"Nothing! 'Pon my honor. Is it my fault, Mosiah, that it is a cruel and vicious world out there? A world into which, I daresay, our catalyst will not soon dare to venture by himself."

Saryon awakened with a sneeze.

His head was clogged and aching, and he was afflicted with a sore, raw throat. Coughing, the catalyst huddled into his robes, afraid to open his eyes. He was lying in a bed, but where? In my own bed, in my cell in the Font, he told himself. When I open my eyes, that's what I'll see. This has all been a dream.

For several pleasant minutes he lay wrapped in his blankets, pretending. He even pictured all the old familiar objects in his room, his books, the tapestries he'd brought from Merilon, all would be there, just as it was.

Then he heard someone moving about. Sighing, Saryon opened his eyes.

He was in a small room, the likes of which he had never seen before. Pale sunlight filtering through a cracked window illuminated a scene the catalyst might have pictured existing Beyond. The walls of the room were not shaped of stone or of wood, but were made up of perfectly formed rectangles arranged one on top of the other. It had a most unnatural appearance and, looking at it, the catalyst shuddered. Everything in the room appeared unnatural, in fact, he noticed with growing horror as he propped himself up to look around. A table in the center had not been crafted lovingly from a single piece of wood, but was made up of several different pieces of wood brutally forced together. Several chairs were formed the same way, looking misshapen and fiendish. If Saryon had seen a human being walking about whose body had been made from the bodies of other dead humans, he could not have been more appalled. He imagined he could almost hear the wood screaming in agony.

But there was the sound again. Saryon peered uncertainly into the shadows of the small room.

"Hello?" he wheezed.

There was no reply. Puzzled, he lay back down again. He could have sworn he heard voices. Or had that been a dream? He'd had so many dreams lately, terrible dreams. Faeries and the most beautiful woman and a dreadful tree—

With another sneeze, he sat up in bed, groping about for something to wipe his streaming nose.

"I say, O Bruised and Battered Father, will this do?"

A bit of orange silk materialized out of the air, fluttering to lie on the blanket near Saryon's hand. The catalyst drew back from it as though it had been a snake.

"'Tis I. In the flesh, so to speak."

Looking behind him, toward the sound of the voice, Saryon saw Simkin standing at the head of the bed. At least the catalyst supposed it was the young man who had "rescued" him in the Outland. Gone were the plain brown robes of a woods ranger, gone were the leaves of the faerie. A brocade coat of the most startling blue, combined with a paler blue waistcoat, covered a red silken blouse that glowed brighter than the watery sun. Green skintight breeches were buckled with red jewels at the knees, his legs were wrapped in red silken hose, while green frothy lace peeped out from everywhere — wrists, throat, waistcoat. His brown hair was sleek and shiny, his beard combed smooth.

"Admiring my ensemble?" asked Simkin, smoothing his curls. "I call it *Corpse Blue*. 'Dreadful name, Simkin,' said the Countess Dupere. 'I am aware of that,' I replied with feeling, 'but it was the first impression that came into my mind and things so *rarely* come into my mind at all that I thought I'd better latch hold of it, so to speak, and make it feel welcome.'"

Simkin sauntered over to stand beside Saryon as he talked. Gracefully lifting the orange silk scarf from the blanket, he handed it to the astounded catalyst with a flourish. "I know. The breeches. Never seen anything like them, I suppose? Latest fad at court. Quite the rage. I must say I'm fond of them. Chafe my legs, though . . ."

Another sneeze and a fit of coughing from the catalyst interrupted Simkin who, motioning a chair to come to his side, sat down upon it, crossing his legs so that he might better admire his hose.

"Feeling a bit rotten? Nasty cold you've caught. Must have been from when we tumbled into the river."

"Where am I?" croaked Saryon. "What is this place?"

"I say, you're positively froglike. And as for where you are, it's where you wanted to be, of course. I was your guide, after all." Simkin lowered his voice. "You're among the Technologists. I've brought you to their Coven."

"How did I get here? What happened? What river?"

"Don't you remember?" Simkin sounded hurt. "After I risked my life, changing into a tree and then leaping over the precipice, holding you in my branches — er, arms — as tenderly as a mum holds her child."

"That was real?" Saryon peered blearily at Simkin through watery eyes. "Not . . . a nightdream?"

"I am cut to the quick!" Simkin sniffed, looking deeply wounded. "After everything I've done for you and you don't remember. Why, you're like a father to me . . ."

Shivering, Saryon pulled the blankets up around his neck. Closing his eyes, he blotted out everything, Simkin, *Corpse Blue* coats, the abysmal room, the voices he'd heard or dreamed. The young man prattled on, but Saryon ignored him, too sick to care. He almost dozed, but a horrifying feeling of falling came over him and, with a catch in his breath, he started awake again. Then he became aware of a sound in the distance, a sound that had seemed a thumping, rhythmic undercurrent to his nightdevils.

"What's that?" he asked, coughing.

"What's what?"

"That . . . noise . . . That banging. . . ."

"The iron forge . . ."

The iron forge. Saryon's soul shrank within him. Vanya had been right. The Sorcerers of the Coven *had* relearned the ancient, banished art — the art of darkness that had nearly caused the destruction of the world. What kind of people were these who had lost their souls to the Ninth Mystery? They must be fiends, devils, and he was alone among them now. Alone, except for Simkin. Who was Simkin? What was he? If Saryon hadn't dreamed the tree and the faeries, then perhaps the voices he had heard had been real, too, and that meant Simkin had betrayed him. *He's been sent here after you, Joram.* There had been no frippery in the voice that said those words. *Is it my fault that it is a cruel and vicious world out there? A world into which, I daresay, our catalyst will not soon dare to venture by himself.* There was no green lace, no orange silk, no sleek, shining smile. Corpse Blue. As cold and cutting as the iron.

Joram knows who I am and why I am here, Saryon realized, shuddering. He will kill me. He has done murder before. But perhaps they won't let him. They need a catalyst, after all. At least, that's what Vanya said. Yet how can I help these fiends, these foul Sorcerers? Will I not be helping them further their dread art? Didn't Vanya foresee that?

Saryon sat up in bed, struggling to breathe, his thoughts coming sluggishly through the cold in his head. I won't! he determined. The first time this Joram and I are alone together, I will open a Corridor and return with him. Though he may be Dead, he and I together possess Life enough between us to effect the magic. I will take him back and rid myself of him, let Vanya do to him what he will. Then I will leave their Font and their spies, their lies and their pious, empty teachings. Perhaps I will return to my father's house. It is empty, the Church owns it. I will shut myself up with my books. . . .

Saryon lay back down, tossing feverishly. He had the vague impression that Simkin had left the room, flying through the air like some gaudy, tropical bird, but he was too ill and too distraught to pay any attention.

The catalyst sank into a troubled sleep. A vision of a Sorcerer rose up before him, emerging from the flame and smoke of the iron forge — a man whose face was twisted by every evil passion, whose eyes burned red from having stared into the fire day after day, whose skin was coated with the foul soot of his black art. As Saryon stared in petrified fear, the Sorcerer drew near him. In his hand, he held a glowing rod of iron . . .

"Easy, Father. Do not be alarmed."

Sitting up without any conscious remembrance of doing so, Saryon found himself trying desperately to throw off his blankets and escape from his bed. The bright glare of flame blinded him in the darkened room. He couldn't see . . . He didn't want to see . . .

"Father!" A hand on his shoulder shook him. "Father, wake up. You're having a fever dream."

Shuddering, Saryon came to himself. Sanity returned. He'd been dreaming again. Or had he? Blinking his eyes, he stared into the flame. The voice that spoke wasn't Simkin's. It was older, deeper. The Sorcerer. . . .

As his eyes became accustomed to the light, Saryon saw the glowing rod of iron diminish into nothing but a flaming torch, held in the hand of an old man, whose wrinkled face peered at him benignly. The touch of the hand upon his shoulder was gentle. With a shivering sigh, Saryon sank back down onto his pillow. This was not a Sorcerer. Nothing but a servant, perhaps. Glancing about, he saw that the room was dark. Was it night, he wondered vaguely, or had the blackness of this evil place finally blotted out the light?

"There, that's better, Father. The lad said you were restless. Lie back and relax. My wife is coming with the Healer —"

"Healer?" Saryon stared at the old man, puzzled. "You have a Healer?"

"A Druid of the *Mannanish* class, nothing more, I'm afraid. She is quite skilled in herb lore, however, having much knowledge that has been lost in the outside world. Such skills are not needed among the Druids, I suppose, with you catalysts to assist them in their work."

Padding over to the far end of the room, the old man used the flame of the torch to start a fire in the grate, then doused the torch in a bucket of water. "Perhaps we will not need to rely upon the gifts of nature now since you are among us, Father," the old man continued. Taking up what appeared to be a slender stick of wood, he thrust one end of it into the blaze, caused it to burn, and carried it over to the table, talking all the while about the Healer and her skill.

Lying back, Saryon followed the old man's movements about the firelit cabin with a strange sense of euphoria, his mind only half attending to the conversation. Even the sight of the old man using the end of the flaming stick to set fire to the top of several tall, thick sticks that stood on crude pedestals did not disturb the catalyst's strange sense of uncaring relaxation. He was rather startled to notice that the fire did not die out or immediately consume the sticks. A small flame remained burning steadily at the top of each, filling the room with a soft, glowing light.

"The *Mannanish* is a good woman, very dedicated to her calling. Her healing arts have saved the lives of more than one person in our settlement. But how many more could have lived if her powers of magic had been enhanced? You have no idea," the old man said with a sigh, returning to his seat and smiling down at Saryon, "how long I have prayed to the Almin to send us a catalyst."

"Pray to the Almin?" Saryon was confused for a moment, then the truth penetrated his slow-moving mind. "Ah, of course. You're not one of *them*."

"One of whom, Father?" the old man asked, his smile broadening slightly.

"The Sorcerers"—Saryon gestured outside, coughing—"these Technologists. Are you a slave?"

Reaching beneath the collar of his long gray robes, the old man brought forth a strange-looking pendant attached to a finely wrought golden chain that hung about his neck. Made of wood, the pendant was carved into the shape of a hollowed-out circle connected by nine spokes.

"Father," said the old man simply, a look of pride coming into his wrinkled face, "I am Andon, their leader."

"Steady, Father. That's right. Lean on my arm. This is your first day out. We don't want to overdo it."

Walking slowly beside the old man, his hand on Andon's arm, Saryon blinked in the bright sunshine as he gratefully drew in a breath of fresh air, fragrant with the smells of late summer.

"Your adventures must have been quite terrifying," Andon continued as they proceeded slowly out of the cabin's small yard and into the dirt road that ran through the settlement. Noting the stares of the villagers, the old man acknowledged them with a nod of his head. No one spoke to them, however, although many regarded the catalyst with unabashed curiosity. Their respect and veneration for the old man was obvious, however, and they did not disturb them.

So these are Dark Sorcerers, Saryon thought. Faces of twisted evil passions? Faces of young mothers, nursing small babies. Red, glowing eyes? Tired, weary, work-worn eyes. Chants to the powers of darkness? The laughter of children, playing in the street. The only difference that he saw between these people and those in the village of Walren, or even between these people and those in Merilon, was that these people used little or no magic. Forced to conserve Life since they had no catalysts to replenish it for them, the Sorcerers walked, trudging through the mud of the refuse-strewn street, wearing soft, leather boots.

Saryon's gaze went to a group of men working busily, shaping a dwelling place. But these were not magi of the *Pron-alban*, lovingly drawing the stone up out of the earth, skillfully molding it with their magical spells. These men used their hands, stacking the rectangular blocks of unnatural stone one on top of the other. Even the stones themselves were made by the hands of men, so the old man said. Clay put into molds and baked in the sun. Pausing a moment, Saryon watched in grim fascination as the men placed the stone in neat and orderly rows, joining them together with some sort of adhesive substance that they spread between them. But this was not the only use of Technology. Everywhere he looked, in fact, he was confronted with the Dark Arts.

None were more in evidence than the symbol of the coven itself, the pendant the old man wore around his neck—the wheel. Small wheels caused laden carts to roll across the ground, a huge wheel stole Life from the river, using it—so Andon said—to run other wheels inside a brick building. These wheels caused great stones to rub together, grinding wheat into flour. Marks of the Sorcerers were even carved into the land itself.

Across the river, the catalyst could see the dark eyes of man-made caves glaring at him as if in reproach. Here, long ago, so Andon told him, the Technologists tore the stone containing iron out of the earth, using some sort of devilish substance that could literally blast rock to fragments. A skill now lost, Andon mentioned sadly. The Sorcerers now had to rely on iron ore left from that distant past.

And over and above every sound, the talking, the laughing, the crying, was the eternal, never-ending clanging that came from the forge, sounding through the village like a huge, dark bell.

Perversion of Life, screamed the catalyst in Saryon. *They are destroying the magic!* But the logical part within him answered, *Survival*. And perhaps it was that same logical part that Saryon caught toying with wonderful new mathematical concepts using this art. He had already noticed that the brick dwelling in which he lived was warmer and snugger than the dead, hollowed-out trees used by the Field Magi. Might not something be done . . .

Shocked to find himself thinking such things, Saryon forced his attention back to the old man.

"Yes, your adventures must have been quite terrifying. Captured by giants, fighting centaur, Simkin saving your life by transforming himself into a tree. I'd enjoy hearing your version someday, if it wouldn't upset you to talk about it." Andon smiled indulgently. "One hesitates believing Simkin."

"Tell me something about Simkin," Saryon said, glad to turn his mind to other matters. "Where did he come from? What do you know about him?"

"Know about Simkin? Nothing, really. Oh, there's what he tells us, but that's all nonsense, I suppose, like his tales about Duke So-and-So and the Countess of d'Something-or-Other." Glancing at the catalyst, Andon added in a mild tone, "We don't ask questions of those who come to make their home among us, Father. For example, one might wonder what a catalyst of the Font — as you so obviously are, if you forgive my saying so — was doing trying to cross the border into the Outland by himself."

Flushing, Saryon stammered, "You see, I —"

The old man interrupted him. "No, I'm not asking. And you needn't tell me. This has been our custom here — a custom that is as old as this settlement." Sighing, Andon shook his head. His eyes were suddenly old and weary. "Perhaps it is not such a good custom," he murmured, his gaze going to a large building that sat apart from the others on top of a small rise. Taller than the others, built out of the same rectangular, unnatural rock, the structure appeared newer than most in the settlement. "If we had asked questions, we might have avoided much sorrow and pain."

"I don't understand." Saryon had noticed, during his recovery, a shadow lying over those who came to visit him — Andon, his wife, the Healer. They were nervous, talking in low voices sometimes, glancing about warily, as if fearful of being overheard. He had thought of asking, more than once, what the matter might be, recalling certain words of Simkin's. But he still felt a stranger among them and uncomfortable in his strange and dark surroundings.

"I told you I was the leader of my people here," Andon said in such a low tone that Saryon had to bend down to hear him. The street they walked wasn't crowded, but the old man seemed unwilling to risk the chance of even the few people hurrying along on their various errands overhearing his words. "That isn't precisely true. I was once, years ago. But now another leads us." He looked at Saryon out of the corner of his eye. "You will meet him soon. He's been asking about you."

"Blachloch," said Saryon before he thought.

Stopping, the old man stared at him. "Yes, how did you—"

"Simkin told me . . . something of him."

Andon nodded, his face darkening. "Simkin. Yes. Now there's someone — Blachloch, I mean — who could tell you more about the young man, I believe. Simkin seems to spend a great deal of time with the warlock. Not that Blachloch would answer your questions, mind you. A true *Duuk-tsarith*, that one. I have often wondered what he did to cause them to cast him out of that dread Order." The old man shivered.

"But" — Saryon looked around at the numerous dwellings and small shops that lined the streets of the village — "there are many of you here and only one of him. Why—"

"—didn't we fight him?" The old man shook his head sadly. "Have you ever been apprehended by the Enforcers? Have you ever felt the touch of their hands upon you, draining you of Life like a spider drains it victim of blood? No need to reply, Father. If you have, you understand. And — as to us? Yes, we are many, but we are not one. That you may not understand now, but you will come to in time." The old man changed the subject abruptly. "But if you're still interested in Simkin, you might discuss him with the two young men who share his dwelling place."

Seeing that Andon was obviously intent on leading the conversation away from the former Enforcer, Saryon let the matter drop and returned once more, and not reluctantly, to Simkin, saying that he would be interested to meet his friends.

"Joram and Mosiah are their names," remarked Andon. "You might have heard of Mosiah from his father since you lived for a time in Walren—" Glancing at the catalyst, he stopped suddenly in concern. "Why, how pale you are, Father. I was afraid this outing might be overdoing things a bit. Would you like to sit down? We're near the park."

"Yes, thank you," Saryon said, though he wasn't in the least tired. So Simkin had been telling the truth when he said he and Joram were friends. And those voices in his room he'd heard when he had been ill. Joram . . . Mosiah . . . Simkin. . . .

"They're working now — Mosiah and Joram, that is. Simkin's never turned a hand that anyone's seen," Andon said, helping Saryon to a seat on a bench in the cool shadow of a large spreading oak tree. "Are you feeling better, Father? I can send for the Healer . . ."

"No, thank you," Saryon murmured. "You were right. I have heard of Mosiah. I've heard of Joram, too, of course," he added in a low voice.

"An unusual young man," said Andon. "I presume that since you are from Walren, you heard about the murder of the overseer?"

Saryon nodded, afraid to speak, afraid of saying too much.

The old man sighed. "We knew of it, too, of course. Word spread rapidly. Some among us viewed him as a hero. Some thought he would be a useful tool." Andon glanced darkly at the large brick building on the hill. "That, in fact, was why he was brought here."

"And you?" Saryon asked. He had come to have a profound respect for this gentle, wise man. "What do you think of Joram?"

"I fear him," Andon admitted with a smile. "That may sound strange to you, Father, coming from a Sorcerer of the Dark Arts. Yes" — he patted Saryon's hand — "I know much of what you have been thinking. I see the horror and revulsion on your face."

"It — it is just hard for me to accept —" Saryon stammered, flushing.

"I understand. You are not alone. Many who come to us feel the same way. Mosiah, for example, still finds it difficult, I think, to live among us and accept our ways."

"But, about Joram," Saryon said hesitantly, wondering if his interest seemed too suspicious. "Were you right? Is he to be feared?" The catalyst felt chilled, and waited anxiously for the response. But when it came, it wasn't what he had expected.

"I don't know," Andon said softly. "He has lived among us a year, and I feel I know less about him than I do you, whom I have known only a few days. Fear him? Yes, I fear him, but not for the reason you might think. And I'm not the only one." Andon's gaze went, once again, to the brick building on the hill.

"An Enforcer? Afraid of a seventeen-year-old boy?" Saryon looked skeptical.

"Oh, he wouldn't admit it, maybe not even to himself. But he does or, if not, he should."

"Why?" asked Saryon. "Is the young man so formidable? Has he such a violent nature?"

"No, none of that. There were extenuating circumstances to the murder, you know. Joram had just seen his mother killed. He doesn't have a wild or violent nature. If anything, he is *too* controlled. Cold and hard as stone. And alone . . . so very alone."

"Then — "

"I think . . ." Andon frowned, trying to give word to his thoughts. "It is because — Have you ever walked into a crowd of people, Father, and noticed one person almost immediately? Not for anything he might do or say, but just for his presence alone? Joram is such a one. Perhaps because he took a life, he has been marked by the Almin. There is an intensity about him, a sense of destiny. A sense of dark destiny." The old man shrugged, his face grave. "I can't explain it, but you can judge for yourself. You will soon meet this young man, if you want. That's where we're headed. Joram, you see, works in the iron forge."

7

The Forge

According to the catechism, "To deal in the Dark Art of the Ninth Mystery is to deal in Death."

According to the catechism, "The Souls of those who deal in Death shall be cast in the fiery pit and shall dwell there forever in agony eternal and unending."

Thus do they act out their own doom, Saryon thought as he stared into the fire-lit, red-tinged darkness of the forge.

Andon had entered the cavern ahead of him, saying something to the men who worked there, gesturing behind him at the catalyst. Now, aware that Saryon had not followed him, the old man turned around. Saryon saw his lips moving, though the noise of the forge was such that he could hear nothing. Andon gestured. "Step in. Step in."

Yellow and orange, the heat of the fire beat upon the old man's face, the red heart of the forge burned in his eyes, the wheel he wore at his breast blazed with a flaming light. Consumed with horror, seeing the Sorcerer of his fevered dreams spring up before him, Saryon drew back from the gaping entryway. Andon might truly have been the Fallen One, rising up to drag the catalyst to the flames.

At the sight of Saryon's fear, an expression of puzzled hurt creased Andon's face. But it was followed almost immediately by understanding.

"I am sorry, Father." Saryon saw Andon's lips form the words. "I should have realized how this would affect you." The old man came toward him. "Let us return home."

But Saryon could not move. Transfixed, he stared at the scene. The iron forge was located in a cave in the side of a mountain. A natural chimney carried away the noxious fumes and heat from vast quantities of glowing red charcoal banked in the center of a vast, round stone ledge. Crouched over it like a wheezing monster, a large baglike contraption breathed air on the coals, giving them fiery life.

"What . . . what are they doing?" Saryon asked, wanting to leave, yet drawn to it by a terrible fascination.

"They are heating the iron ore until it becomes a molten mass," Andon shouted over the banging and hissing and wheezing, "that contains refuse of the ore and the charcoal as well."

As Saryon watched, one of the young men working in the forge walked over to the ledge and, using what appeared to be a hideous extension of his arm made out of metal, lifted a lump of the red-hot iron from its bed among the coals. Setting it down on another ledge — this not of stone but of iron itself — he took a tool and began pounding the hot iron.

"There he is — that is Joram," said Andon.

"What is he doing?" Saryon felt his lips shape the words, he couldn't hear himself speak.

"He is hammering the iron into the form he wants," Andon continued. "He does it this way or else he could pour the hot iron into a mold and let it cool first, then work it."

Destroying the Life within the stone. Shaping the iron with a tool. Perverting its god-given qualities. Killing the magic. Dealing in death. The thoughts pounded in Saryon's head with each strike of the hammer.

He started to turn away, but at that moment, the young man working in the black shadows of the forge lifted his head and looked out at him.

It is written that the Almin knows the hearts of men but does not rule them. Thus man is free to choose his own destiny, but thus also can the Almin foresee how each man will act to fulfill that destiny. By making themselves one with the mind of the Almin, the Diviners were able to predict the future. It is also said that two souls destined to touch each other for good or for evil will know this in the instant of their meeting.

At that moment, two souls met. Two souls knew.

As the hammer's ringing blows cracked the black slag covering the smoldering red iron, Joram's dark-eyed stare sent a shivering blow through Saryon. Shaken to the very core of his being, the catalyst turned away from the forge and its fire-lit shadows.

Andon was hovering near him. "Father, you're not well. I'm sorry. I should have realized how shocking . . ."

But the old man's voice was lost in the pounding of the hammer blows and in the steady, intense gaze of those brown eyes. For Saryon knew those eyes, he knew that face.

Stumbling through the streets of the settlement, having the dim impression that Andon was with him but unable to see or hear the old man, Saryon saw only the clear cold eyes that not even the reflected fire of molten iron could heat. He saw the heavy black brows tracing a line of bitterness across the sweat-covered forehead. He saw the grim, unsmiling mouth, the high planed cheekbones, the shining black hair tinged a burning red.

I know that face! he said to himself. But how? Not in that aspect. Sorrow, not bitterness, came to his mind. A sorrow that never quite left the face, not even in gaiety. Perhaps he had seen the face seventeen years ago, in the Font. Perhaps he had known this boy's accursed father. Only the vaguest recollection of hearing about the renegade catalyst's trial came to Saryon. The scandal had been talked of for weeks, but he had been too involved in his own torment to be interested in another man's. Perhaps he had taken note of him unconsciously, without realizing it. That must be the explanation. It had to be and yet, yet. . . .

Visions of the face drifted into his mind. He could see it smiling, laughing yet always tainted, always haunted by a shadow of sorrow. . . .

He recognized it! He knew it! He could almost put a name to it. . . .

But it vanished before he could grasp it, drifting from his mind like smoke upon the wind.

8

The Warlock

Picking his way through the mud streets of the Technologists' village, Simkin looked very much like a bright-plumaged bird wandering through a dreary brick jungle. Many of the people working about the area regarded him with looks of wary wonder, much as they might have regarded a rare bird appearing suddenly in their midst. Several scowled and shook their heads, muttering unflattering comments, while here and there a few called out cheerful greetings to the gaudily dressed young man as he walked through the streets, careful to keep his cape out of the mud. Simkin responded to both imprecations and greetings the same — with a casual wave of his lace-covered hand or the doff of a pink feathered cap that he had just added, as an afterthought, to top off his wardrobe.

The village children, however, were delighted to see him again. To them, he was a welcome distraction, easy prey. Dancing about him, they tried to touch his strange clothes, made fun of his silk-covered legs, or dared each other to sling mud at him. The boldest among them — a hefty child of eleven who had the reputation as the town tough — was urged to go for a solid hit between the shoulder blades. Creeping up behind the young man, the child was prepared to throw when Simkin turned around. He did not speak to the child, he simply stared at him. Shrinking away, the child hurriedly withdrew, and promptly beat up the next smaller child he encountered.

Sniffing in disdain, Simkin drew his cape protectively around him and was continuing on his way when a group of women accosted him. Coarsely dressed, uneducated, their hands reddened and callused from hard labor, they were, nevertheless, the leading ladies of the town; one being the wife of the blacksmith, another the wife of the mine foreman, the third the wife of the candlestick maker. Crowding around Simkin, they eagerly and somewhat pathetically demanded to know the news of a court they had never seen except through the young man's eyes. A court they were as far removed from as the moon from the sun.

To their delight, Simkin readily complied. "The Empress said to me, 'What *do* you call that shade of green, Simkin, my treasure?' To which I replied, 'I don't *call* it at all, Your Majesty. It simply *comes* when I whistle!' Ha, ha, what? Drat, what did you say, my dear? I can't hear a thing above the infernal banging!" He cast a scathing glance toward the forge. "Health? The Empress? Abysmal, simply abysmal. But she *insists* upon holding court every night. No, I'm not lying. In frightfully poor taste, if you ask me. 'You don't suppose she has anything *catching?*' I said to old Duke Mardoc. Poor man. I didn't mean to upset him. Grabbed his catalyst, he did, and disappeared in the wink of an eye. Wouldn't have supposed the old boy had it in him. What did you say? Yes, this is the *absolute latest* in fashion. Chafes my legs, though. . . . And now I must be getting along. I am running errands for our Noble Leader. Have you seen the catalyst?"

Yes, the ladies had seen him. He and Andon had been visting the forge. The two had returned to Andon's home, however, the catalyst having been taken suddenly ill.

"I don't doubt it," Simkin murmured into his beard. Doffing his cap and bowing deeply to the ladies, he proceeded on his way, eventually arriving at one of the larger and older homes in the settlement. Knocking at the door, he twirled his cap in his hands and waited patiently, whistling a dance air.

"Enter, Simkin, and welcome," said an old woman pleasantly as she opened the door.

"Thank you, Marta," Simkin said, pausing to kiss the wrinkled cheek as he passed. "The Empress sends her best wishes and thanks for your inquiry about her health."

"Get along with you!" Marta scolded, waving her hand to dispel the strong wave of gardenia fragrance that enveloped her as Simkin walked past. "Empress indeed! You're either a liar or a fool, young man."

"Ah, Marta," said Simkin, leaning near her to whisper in confidence. "The Emperor himself posed that very question, 'Simkin,' he said, 'are you a liar or a fool?'"

"And what was your answer?" Marta asked, her lips twitching, though she tried to sound severe.

"I said, 'If I say I am neither, Your Majesty, then I am one. If I say I am one, then I am the other.' Do you follow me so far, Marta?"

"And if you say you're both?" Marta tilted her head, putting her hands beneath the apron of her dress.

"Precisely what His Majesty inquired. My reply: 'Then I am either, aren't I?'" Simkin bowed. "Think about it, Marta. It kept His Majesty occupied for at least an hour."

"So, you've been to court again, have you, Simkin?" asked Andon, coming over to greet the young man. "Which one?"

"Merilon. Zith-el. It doesn't matter," returned Simkin with a gaping yawn. "Let me assure you, sir, they're all alike, 'specially this time of year. Preparing for Harvest Revels and all that. Quite boring. 'Pon my honor, I'd be more than happy to stay and chat. Especially"—he sniffed hungrily—"since dinner smells positively heavenly as the centaur said of the catalyst he was stewing, but—What was I saying? Oh, catalyst—Yes, that's the very reason I've come. Is he about?"

"He is resting," said Andon gravely.

"Not taken ill, I suppose?" Simkin asked nonchalantly, his gaze wandering about the room and just happening to fix on the figure stretched out upon a cot in a shadowy corner.

"No. We walked rather farther this morning than he was up to, I am afraid."

"A pity. Old Blachloch's sent for him," said Simkin coolly, twirling his cap in his hand.

Andon's face darkened. "If it could wait—"

"'Fraid not," Simkin replied with another yawn. "Urgent and all that. You know Blachloch."

Moving to stand near her husband, a worried look on her face, Marta put her hand on his arm. Andon patted it. "Yes," he said quietly. "I know him. Still, I—"

The figure on the bed roused itself. "Do not worry, Andon," said Saryon, getting to his feet. "I am feeling much more myself. I think it must have been the fumes or the smoke, it made me feel light-headed—"

"Father! You've no idea," cried Simkin in a choked voice, leaping forward and throwing his arms around the startled catalyst, "how perfectly wonderful it is to see you up and about. I was so worried! So frightfully worried—"

"There, there," Saryon said, flushing in embarrassment and trying to disengage the young man, who was sobbing on his shoulder.

"I'm all right," Simkin said bravely, stepping backward. "Sorry. Forgot myself. Well . . ." He rubbed his hands together, smiling. "All ready? If you're tired, we could take a cart . . ."

"A what?"

"Cart," said Simkin patiently. "You know. Moves over the ground. Drawn by a horse. Thing with wheels—"

"Uh, no. I'd really prefer walking," Saryon said hastily.

"Well, up to you." Simkin shrugged. "Now, must be off." Herding the catalyst along in front of him, the young man practically pushed him out the door. "Good-bye, Marta, Andon. Hopefully we'll be back in time for dinner. If not, don't wait up."

Before he quite knew what was happening, Saryon found himself standing in the street, rubbing the sleep from his eyes. He'd napped almost all afternoon, he realized, seeing the sun starting to set behind the trees that lined the riverbank. But he didn't feel any better, and he wished he hadn't fallen asleep. Now his head ached; he felt incapable of thinking clearly.

Of all times to see Blachloch—the man everyone from Andon to the devil-may-care Simkin seemed to hold in quiet terror. I wonder what Joram thinks of him? Saryon wondered. Then he shook his head angrily. What a stupid thought. As if it mattered. Hopefully, the walk will wake me, he told himself, falling into step with Simkin, who was prodding him along.

"What can you tell me about this Blachloch?" Saryon asked Simkin in a low voice as they moved among the lengthening shadows cast by the buildings in the slowly gathering gloom of twilight.

"Nothing I haven't already. Nothing you won't find out soon enough," Simkin replied nonchalantly.

"I hear you spend a good deal of time with him," Saryon commented, glancing at Simkin sharply. But the young man returned the glance with a cool and sardonic smile.

"They'll be saying the same of you shortly," he remarked.

Shivering, Saryon drew his robes around him. The thoughts of what this warlock, this Enforcer turned outlaw, might ask him to do alarmed him. Why had he never considered this before?

Because I never expected to live long enough to get here before, Saryon answered himself bitterly. Now I am here, and I have no idea what to do! Maybe, he said to himself hopefully, it won't be any more than giving these people sufficient Life so that they can go about their work easier. The thought of the new mathematical calculations he'd made occurred to him. Surely that would be all they could expect of him . . .

"Tell me," Saryon said to Simkin abruptly, glad to change the subject and take his mind off one worry by investigating another, "how do you manage to work that . . . that magic you do? . . ."

"Oh, you've been admiring my hat?" Simkin inquired with a pleased air, twirling the cap's feather. "Actually, the difficult part comes not with conjuring up the article but in deciding upon just the right shade of pink. Too much, and it makes my eyes look swollen—so the Duchess of Fenwick told me, and I rather fancy she's right—"

"I don't mean the hat," Saryon snapped irritably. "I meant the . . . the tree. Turning yourself into a tree! It's quite impossible," he added. "Mathematically speaking. I've been over and over the formula . . ."

"Oh, I don't know a thing about math," Simkin said with a shrug. "I just know it works. I've been able to do it since I was a small tyke. Mosiah says it must be like lizards changing their skin color to match rocks and jolly things like that. I'll tell you how it came about, if you like. We've got a ways to go, I'm afraid." His gaze went to the tall building. Standing black against the reddish light of the setting sun, it cast a stark, dark shadow over the entire settlement.

"I was abandoned as a babe in Merilon," Simkin was saying in a subdued voice. "Dumped in a doorway. Left on my own. I never knew my parents. I probably wasn't supposed to have happened, if you know what I mean." Shrugging, he gave a short, forced laugh. "I was taken in by an old woman. Not out of charity, I assure you. By the age of five I was working, picking through refuse for anything valuable that she could sell. She beat me regularly, for good measure, and finally, I ran away. I grew up in the streets of Lower City, the part you *don't* see from the Crystal Spires. Do you have any idea what the *Duuk-tsarith* do with abandoned children?"

Saryon was staring at him in amazement. "Abandoned children? But—"

"Me either," Simkin continued with his tight, little laugh. "They just . . . disappear . . . I saw it happen. Friends of mine. Vanished. Never seen nor heard from again. One day, the Enforcers suddenly materialized in the street right before me. I couldn't escape. I can still hear"— Simkin's eyes grew dreamy —"the rustle of their black robes, so near me, so near . . . I was terrified. You can't imagine . . . My one thought was that they mustn't see me and I concentrated on that thought with my whole being." He smiled suddenly. "And, you know what? They *didn't* see me. The *Duuk-tsarith* walked right past me . . . as they would have walked past any other water pail on the street."

Saryon rubbed his head. "You're saying that out of sheer terror, you were able to—"

"Perform a remarkable transformation? Yes," Simkin replied with a touch of modest pride. "Later, I learned to control it. Thus, I survived many, many years."

Saryon was silent a moment, then he said grimly, "What about your sister?"

"Sister?" Simkin glanced at him in bemusement. "What sister? I'm an orphan."

"The sister the Coven is holding captive, remember? And then there's your father? The one the Enforcers dragged off. The one I remind you of. . . ."

"I say, old fellow" — Simkin looked at him in deep concern — "you must have received a smart blow to the head when we jumped off the cliff. Whatever are you talking about?"

"We didn't jump," Saryon said through clenched teeth. "We fell because *you* were rotten —"

"Rotting!" Simkin stopped dead in the street, his face stricken. "I am wounded, wounded deeply. Here, take my dagger" — one materialized in his hand — "and stab me in the heart!" Yanking aside his brocade coat, he revealed a broad expanse of green shirt. "I can live no longer with the stain of this dishonor!"

"Oh, come on!" Saryon said, aware that everyone in the vicinity was staring at them.

"Not until you have apologized!" Simkin said dramatically.

"Very well, I apologize!" Saryon muttered, staring at the young man in confusion so vast he couldn't even begin to frame questions.

"I accept," Saryon said graciously, and the dagger disappeared, replaced by a flutter of orange silk.

Looking into Joram's eyes, Saryon had seen a soul — tormented, dark, burning with anger — but a soul nonetheless, its very passions giving it life. Looking into the eyes of the warlock, Saryon saw nothing. Flat, opaque, the eyes regarded him fixedly for several moments, then, with a flicker of the thin lids, Blachloch bade him be seated.

Saryon obeyed, his will drained from him by those eyes quite as effectively as by any spell.

Duuk-tsarith. A privileged class. Their black-robed presence in Thimhallan granted security and peace. This did not come cheaply, but the people, remembering the old days, were willing to pay the price.

Though vastly different, in many ways the warlock class mirrored that of their opposites, the catalysts. As powerful in magic as the catalysts are weak, the children born to the Mystery of Fire are a rarity in the world. They, too, are taken from their homes at an early age and placed in a school whose very location is secret. Here the powerful magic skills of the young witches and warlocks are developed and channeled. Here they are taught the strict, severe discipline that will henceforth govern their lives. The training is harsh and demanding, for it is necessary to leash this power and keep it under control. That was what started the trouble long ago in the old Dark World, so legend tells. Witches and warlocks, not content with keeping their magic art hidden, went abroad into the land to try to claim it as their own. They brought down the wrath of the populace upon their race. The persecutions began that would eventually force many of their people to flee the land and seek a new home among the stars.

Most of those born with the Mystery of Fire become *Duuk-tsarith*, the Enforcers, the lawkeepers of Thimhallan. A few, the most powerful, become *DKarn-Duuk*, the War Masters. There are, of course, those who fail. Nothing is said of these. They do not return to their homes. They simply vanish. It is widely believed that they are sent Beyond.

What is their reward for this strict, dark life? Limitless power. The knowledge that even the Emperors themselves, though they do their best to hide it, look with fear upon those black-robed figures that glide silently about the Royal Palaces. For the *Duuk-tsarith* possess a magical spell that is theirs and theirs alone. As the catalyst has the power to grant Life, the Enforcer has the power to take that Life away. Rarely seen, rarely speaking, the *Duuk-tsarith* walk the streets or halls or fields, cloaked in invisibility, armed with the Null-magic that can drain the Life from mage or wizard, leaving him as helpless and powerless as a babe.

Blachloch was one of the failures. Not content with power, the story had it that he sought richer, more material reward. No one knew how he had managed to escape. It must have been no easy task, and proved the man's extraordinary skill and cool courage, for the *Duuk-tsarith* live together, isolated in their own small community, keeping themselves under a surveillance as strict as the surveillance of the populace.

Saryon considered all of this as he sat, chilled and nervous, in the presence of the black-robed warlock. Blachloch had been working in his ledgers again and had, indeed, only laid such work aside once the catalyst and Simkin had been introduced by one of the henchmen.

Wrapped in the accustomed silence of his kind, Blachloch stared at Saryon, learning more from the way the man sat, from the lines on the face, from the position of the hands and arms, than he could have learned in an hour of interrogation.

Though he fought to remain calm and unmoved, Saryon fidgeted under the scrutiny. Terrifying memories of his own brief encounter with the Enforcers in the Font at the time of his crime made his throat dry and the palms of his hands sweat. Part of their effectiveness lay in their ability to intimidate by their presence alone. The black robes, the folded hands, the enforced silence, the expressionless face — all this was carefully taught. Taught to engender one emotion — fear.

"Your name, Father," was Blachloch's first spoken words, not so much a question as a verification.

"Saryon," the catalyst replied after a first unsuccessful attempt to speak.

The warlock's hands rested on his desk, the fingers interlacing. Silence as thick and heavy as the black robes he wore blanketed the room. Blachloch stared at the catalyst impassively.

Gradually becoming more and more unnerved, feeling those penetrating eyes plunging deep into his soul, Saryon was not comforted by the fact that even Simkin appeared subdued, the gaudy colors of his attire seeming to fade in the dark shadow of the warlock's presence.

"Father," said Blachloch at last, "it is a custom in this village that no one questions a man's past. I allow this custom to continue, generally because a man's past doesn't mean a damn thing to me. But there is something in your face I don't like, Catalyst. In the lines around your eyes I see scholar, not renegade. In the sunburned skin I see one who is accustomed to spending long hours in libraries, not fields. In the mouth, the set of the shoulders, the expression of the eyes, I see weakness. Yet you are a man, so I am told, who rebelled against your Order and ran into the most dangerous, deadly place in this world — the Outland. Therefore, tell me your story, Father Saryon."

Saryon glanced at Simkin, who was toying with the bit of orange silk, affecting playfully to tie it around the feather in his cap that sat on his lap. The young man neither looked at him nor appeared the least bit interested in the proceedings. There was no help for it but to play this bitter game to its conclusion.

"You are right, *Duuk-tsarith* —"

Blachloch did not appear disturbed at this use of a title he had no claim to. Saryon had adopted it, hearing one of his henchmen address him as such.

" — I am a scholar. My special field of study is mathematics. Seventeen years ago," continued Saryon in a low voice that surprised himself with its steadiness, "I committed a crime brought about by my thirst for knowledge. I was caught reading forbidden books —"

"Which forbidden books?" interrupted Blachloch. As *Duuk-tsarith* he would, of course, be familiar with most banned texts.

"Those dealing with the Ninth Mystery," Saryon replied.

Blachloch's eyelids flickered, but otherwise he made no sign. Pausing to see if the warlock had any further questions, Saryon felt rather than saw that Simkin was listening attentively, with unusual interest. The catalyst drew a breath. "I was discovered. Due to my youth, but due more to the fact, I believe, that my mother was cousin to the Empress, my crime was hushed up. I was sent to Merilon, in hopes that I would soon forget my interest in the Dark Arts."

"Yes, so much I know to be true, Catalyst," said Blachloch, his hands unmoving, still folded together, still resting on his desk. "Continue."

Saryon blanched, a tightening sensation gripping his stomach. He had assumed correctly that Blachloch would already know something about him. The man undoubtedly still had contacts among the Enforcers, and such information would not be hard to acquire. Then, of course, there was always Simkin. Who knew what game of his own he was playing?

"I — I discovered that I could not help myself, however. I am . . . fascinated by the Dark Arts. I was . . . an embarrassment to my Order at Court. It was a simple thing to have myself transferred back to the Font where I hoped to continue — in secret, of course — my studies. That was not to be, however. My mother had just recently died. I had formed no strong ties nor attachments at court. I was, therefore, considered a threat and so I was sent to the settlement of Walren."

"A wretched life — Field Catalyst, but a secure one," Blachloch remarked. "Certainly better than life in the Outland." Moving slowly and deliberately, the two index fingers of the warlock's hands unfolded and extended themselves. It was the first sign of movement the man had made since they entered, and both Simkin and Saryon could not help but watch, fascinated, as the fingers came together, a flesh-and-bone dagger, pointing at the catalyst. "Why did you leave?"

"I heard about the Coven," Saryon answered, maintaining his steady tone. "I was rotting in that village. My mind was turning to mush. I came here to study and learn . . . the Dark Arts."

Blachloch did not move or speak. The fingers remained pointed at Saryon and, if they had been a dagger held to his throat, he could have felt no greater pain or fear than he experienced staring at them as they rested upon the desk.

"Very well," Blachloch said suddenly, the sound of his voice making the near-hypnotized catalyst start. "You will study. Only you must learn not to faint at the sight of the iron forge."

Blood rushed to Saryon's face. Lowering his head before the gaze of those flat eyes, he hoped it would be taken for confusion, not for guilt. It hadn't been the sight of the forge itself that upset him — not nearly as much as the sight of Joram.

"You will be given a house in the village and share in our food. But, like everyone else here, you will be expected to work for us in return . . ."

"I will be more than happy to provide my services to the people of the settlement," Saryon said. "The Healer tells me that the mortality rate among the children is very great. I hope — "

"We will be leaving within the week," pursued Blachloch, completely ignoring the catalyst's words, "to lay in stores for the winter. Our work in the forge and the mines takes up so much manpower that, as you might imagine, we are unable to devote ourselves to raising food. The Field Magi settlements provide us with what we need, therefore."

"I will accompany you, if that is what you want," said Saryon, somewhat mystified, "but I think I could be of much more use here —"

"No, Father. You will be of much more use to *me*," said Blachloch expressionlessly. "You see, the villages do not know that they are going to be helping us through the long winter. In the past, we were forced to depend on raids, stealing food by night. Demeaning work that generally acquires very little. But" — he shrugged and moved his fingers up to rest upon his lips — "we had no magic. Now, we have you. We have Life. What is more important, we have Death. This winter should be a good one for us, will it not, Simkin?"

If this sudden question was intended to startle the young man, it did not succeed. Apparently absorbed in now trying to untie the orange silk from around the feather, Simkin discovered that the knot was too tight. After tugging at it without result, he irritably consigned both hat and silk to the ethers.

"I really don't care what kind of winter you have, Blachloch," he said with a bored air, "since I'll be spending most of it in court. Robbing the natives does sound a bit of a lark, though . . ."

"I — I cannot help you do that!" Saryon stammered. "Robbing — Those people have barely enough to live on as it is —"

"The penalty for running away, Catalyst, is the Turning. Have you ever seen it done? I have." The fingers on the lips moved, descending slowly to point once more at Saryon. "I can see your mind working, scholar. Yes, as you surmised, I have contacts still among *my* Order. Telling them where to find you would be simplicity itself. I would even receive money. Not as much as I can earn using you, but enough to make the thought one that I can consider with equanimity. I suggest you spend the remaining days learning how to ride a horse."

The hands unfolded and separated, one stretching out to grip the catalyst's arm. "It is a pity there is only one of you," Blachloch remarked, his eyes holding Saryon in their imprisoning gaze. "Had we more catalysts, I could mutate some of the men and give them wings, allowing them to attack from the air. I studied the skills of the *DKarn-Duuk* for a time." The grip tightened painfully. "It was thought I might qualify as a War Master, but I was considered . . . unstable. . . . Still, if all goes well in the North Kingdom, who knows. Perhaps I may be War Master yet. And now, Catalyst, before you leave, grant me Life."

Staring at the man in horror, Saryon was so shaken that he could not, for the moment, remember the words of his ritual prayer.

Blachloch's grasp tightened still further, fingers of iron closing over the catalyst's arm. "Grant me Life," he said softly.

Bowing his head, Saryon complied. Opening his being to the magic, he drew it into him and let a portion of it flow through him into the warlock.

"More," said Blachloch.

"I can't — I am weak —"

The grip grew tighter, enhanced by magical energy. Sharp needles of pain darted through the catalyst's arm. Gasping, he let the magic surge through him, suffusing the warlock with Life. Then he collapsed, drained, back in his chair.

His face expressionless, Blachloch released him. "You are dismissed."

Though he did not speak and made no gesture, the door to the room opened and one of the henchmen stepped inside. Rising unsteadily to his feet, Saryon turned numbly and walked toward the door with faltering steps. Simkin, yawning, rose too, but subsided into his chair again upon noticing an almost-imperceptible flicker of the warlock's eyelids.

"If you can't find your way back, O Bald One," called Simkin languidly, "wait for me. I'll just be a moment."

Saryon did not hear him. The rushing of blood in his ears was too loud, unbalancing him. It was all he could do to walk.

∘ ∘ ∘

Glancing out the window, into the darkening evening, Simkin saw the catalyst stagger and nearly fall, then lean wearily against a tree.

"I really should go help the poor chap," Simkin said. "You were rather brutal with him, after all."

"He's lying."

"Egad, my dear Blachloch, according to you *Duuk-tsarith*, there isn't a person alive on this planet from the age of six weeks on up who ever breathes a word of truth."

"You know the real reason why he is here."

"I told you already, O Merciless Master. Bishop Vanya sent him."

The warlock stared at the young man.

Simkin blanched. "It's the truth. He's after Joram," he muttered.

Blachloch raised an eyebrow. "Joram?" he repeated.

Simkin shrugged. "The young man they brought from the settlement half-dead. The dark one with the hair. . . . Chap who killed the overseer. He works in the forge—"

"I know him," Blachloch said with a shade of irritation. He continued to stare intently at the young man, who was gazing out the window at Saryon. "Look at *me*, Simkin," the warlock said softly.

"Very well, if you insist, although I find you extremely uninteresting," Simkin replied, attempting to stifle a yawn. Lounging back in his chair, one silk-clad leg thrown over the armrest, he gazed at Blachloch obligingly. "I say, do you use a lemon rinse on your hair? If so, it's starting to go a bit dark at the roots—" Suddenly, Simkin stiffened, his playful voice grew harsh. "Stop it, Blachloch. I know what . . . you're trying to do. . . ." His words trailed off drowsily. "I've been . . . shrough thish be . . . bevore . . ."

Shaking his head, Simkin tried to break free, but the flat blue eyes of the Enforcer held him fast in their unblinking, unwavering stare. Slowly, the eyelids of the young man fluttered, blinked, opened wide, then fluttered, blinked, fluttered, and closed.

Murmuring words of magic, ancient words of power and spellbinding, Blachloch rose slowly and silently to his feet and walked around the desk to stand near Simkin. Chanting the words over and over again in a soothing refrain, he rested his hands upon Simkin's smooth, shining hair. The warlock closed his eyes and, throwing his head back, exerted all his powers of concentration upon the young man. "Let me see into your mind. The truth, Simkin, tell me everything you know . . ."

Simkin began to whisper something.

Smiling, Blachloch stooped low to hear.

"I call it . . . *Grape Rose*. . . . Mind the thorns. . . . I don't believe . . . they're poisonous. . . ."

9

The Experiment

Night flowed into the village like the dark waters of the river, submerging fears and sorrows in its gentle current. Around the brick houses it crept, its shadows growing deeper and deeper, for it was a cloudy, moonless night. Gradually almost every light in the village was engulfed by the rising darkness, nearly everyone let sleep wash over him, sinking down into the murky depths of dreams.

But when night was at its flood, when the silent waters of sleep were at their deepest, light from the forge continued to glow red, burning away sleep and dreams for one person at least.

The firelight glistened in black curling hair, flickered in brown eyes, and beat upon a face now neither sullen nor angry but intent and eager. Within the fires of the forge, Joram heated iron ore in a crucible, iron that he had ground as finely as he could. The mold for a dagger sat to one side of the young man, but he did not pour the molten iron into it. Instead, he lifted another crucible from the fire, this containing a molten liquid similar in appearance to the iron except for its strange white-purple color.

Joram regarded the second crucible thoughtfully, a look of frustration causing the thick, black brows to contract.

"If I only I knew what they meant," he muttered. "If only I understood!" Closing his eyes, he called to mind the pages of ancient writing. He could see the letters, could see every shape and twist and idiosyncrasy of the hand that had formed them, in fact, so often had he mulled over and studied the page. But it did not help. Again and again before his eyes rose those strange symbols that might have been another language to him for all the meaning they conveyed.

Finally, with a bitter shrug and a shake of his head, Joram tilted the contents of the second crucible into the first, watching as the hot liquid streamed into the burning pool of iron. He continued pouring until he had nearly doubled the measure of iron, then stopped. Looking at the mixture, he shrugged again and added a bit more for no particular reason except that it felt right. Putting the second crucible aside carefully, Joram stirred the molten mixture, examining it with a critical eye. He saw nothing out of the ordinary. Was this good or bad? He didn't know and, with another frustrated shrug, poured the alloy into the dagger mold.

It would cool quickly, the text had noted, minutes compared to the hours it took to cool iron. Still, it did not seem quick enough to Joram. His fingers itched to strike off the mold and see the object he had created. To take his mind off it, he lifted the second crucible and returned it to its hiding place among a pile of cast-off, broken tools and other refuse of the smithy's. This done, he walked to the front of the cavern and peered through the cracks of the crude wooden door. The village was silent, drowned in sleep. Nodding his head in satisfaction, Joram returned to the forge. It must be ready now. His hands shaking in anticipation, he struck aside the wooden forms that held the mold, then broke the mold itself.

The object within had only the very crudest resemblance to the weapon it would become. Lifting it out with the tongs, he plunged it into the fires of the forge, heating it until it glowed red hot, as the text had instructed. Carrying the dagger to the anvil, he lifted his hammer and, with practiced blows, pounded it into shape. He hurried, being not too par-

ticular as to the weapon's construction since this was only a
test. What happened next was critical, and he was anxious to
proceed. At last, deeming the dagger good enough for his
purposes, he lifted it by the tongs again and, drawing a deep
breath, plunged the hot weapon into a bucket of water.

Steam billowed up in a cloud, momentarily blinding him.
But with the hiss of the red-hot iron in the water came another sound, a sharp crack. Joram's heavy brows drew together in a scowl. Impatiently waving his hand to clear the
air, he jerked the weapon from the water — and brought up
only a shattered fragment. Hurling it onto the refuse pile
with a bitter curse, he was about to dump out the worthless
alloy he had produced when a prickling feeling at the base of
his neck made him turn around quickly.

"You work late, Joram," said Blachloch. The warlock's
face was visible as he stepped into the light of the forge,
along with the hands that he held clasped in front of him in
the manner of the Enforcers. Other than those, he was a
patch of night within the red-lit forge, the black of his robes
absorbing the light and even the warmth of the fire.

"It was my punishment," said Joram coolly, having had
this matter arranged beforehand. "I was negligent in my
work today and the master ordered I stay until the dagger
was finished."

"It appears that you will be here most of the night," the
warlock stated, his cold-eyed gaze going to the refuse pile.

Joram shrugged, his face flowing into its embittered, angry lines much as the molten iron had flowed into the mold.
"I will if I am not permitted to get on with my work," he said
sullenly, walking around to pump the bellows. Deliberately
turning his back upon the warlock, he almost, but not quite,
shouldered the black-robed man aside.

A tiny line creased Blachloch's smooth forehead, his lips
pressed together, but there was no sign of annoyance or irritation in his voice. "I understand that you claim to be of noble
birth."

Grunting from the exertion of his labors, Joram did not
bother to reply. Not appearing surprised or disconcerted by
this, Blachloch moved to where he could see the young man's
face.

"You can read."

Joram paused in his work for an instant, but continued almost immediately, the muscles in his back and arms rippling and knotting with the exertion as he operated the device that sent a blast of air onto the coals of the forge.

"I hear you have been reading the books."

Joram might have been deaf. His arms moved in unceasing, rhythmic motion, his dark hair fell forward, curling about his face.

"A little knowledge to one who is otherwise ignorant is like a dagger in the hands of a child, Joram. It can hurt him very badly," Blachloch continued. "I would have thought you had learned your lesson when you committed murder."

Glancing at Blachloch through the tangle of his black hair, Joram smiled a smile only visible in the dark, fire-lit eyes. "I would have thought there was a lesson there you could learn," he said.

"You see? You are threatening me." From his calm, even tone, Blachloch might have been speaking of the weather. "The child brandishes the dagger. You will cut yourself upon its sharp edges, Joram," the warlock murmured. "You really will. Either yourself"— Blachloch lifted his shoulders —"or someone else. Can your friend . . . What's his name . . . Mosiah? Can he read?"

Joram's face darkened, the steady pumping of the bellows slowed slightly. "No," he answered. "Leave him out of this."

"I thought not," Blachloch said blandly. "You and I are the only ones in the village who can read, Joram. And I think that is one too many of us, but there is nothing I can do about it — short of melting your eyes in your head."

For the first time, the warlock moved his hands, unclasping them and bringing one up to stroke the thin blond mustache that ran across his upper lip. Joram had ceased to work. Keeping his hands on the handles of the bellows, he stared fixedly into the fire.

Blachloch drew nearer. "It would grieve me to destroy the books."

Joram stirred. "The old man will never tell you where they are."

"He would," Blachloch said with a smile, "in time. In time, he would be searching for things to tell me. I have not pressed him before on the matter because it simply wasn't worth upsetting these people by resorting to violence. It would be a pity if I were forced to change my policy, particularly now that I have the magic."

Joram's face flushed, burning in the light of the glowing coals. "You won't have to," he muttered.

"Good." Blachloch clasped his hands together once again. "We *Duuk-tsarith* know something of these books, you know. There are things written in them that the world is better off for having lost." The warlock stared intently at Joram, who remained standing where he was, looking into the fire.

"You remind me of myself, young man," Blachloch said. "And that makes me nervous. I, too, hated authority. I, too, believed myself above it" — the faintest tinge of sarcasm colored his otherwise gray voice — "though I am *not* of noble blood. To rid myself of those I believed were oppressing me, I, like you, committed murder without guilt, without remorse. You liked that taste of power, didn't you? And now you crave more. Yes, I see it, I feel it burn in you. I've watched you learn, this past year, to manipulate people, to use them and get them to do what you want. You got the old man to show you the books that way, didn't you?"

Joram did not answer or raise his gaze from the flame. But his left fist clenched.

Blachloch smiled, a smile that was dark in the firelight. "I see great things before you, Joram. In time you will learn how to handle this lust that consumes you. But you are a child still, as young as I was when I committed my first impetuous act — the act that drove me here. There is one difference, though, between you and me, Joram. The man I sought to displace was not aware of me or of my ambition. He turned his back upon me." Unclasping his hands, the warlock laid one upon the young man's arm. Even in the warmth of the forge, Joram shivered at the chill touch. "I *am* aware, Joram, and I will not turn my back upon you."

"Why don't you just kill me," Joram muttered with a sneer, "and have done with it."

"Why not indeed," Blachloch repeated. "You are of little use to me now, though you may be when you are older. Whether you *grow* older will depend upon you and those who take an interest in you."

"What do you mean, 'those who take an interest in me'?"
Joram glanced at him.

"The catalyst."

Joram shrugged.

"He is here for you. Why?"

"Because I am a murderer—"

"No," Blachloch said softly. "Enforcers hunt murderers,
not catalysts. Why? What is he here for?"

"I have no idea," Joram replied impatiently. "Ask him . . .
or ask Simkin."

Blachloch's eyes stared searchingly into Joram's. The
warlock began speaking words of magic. He saw the brown
eyes glaze, the lids droop. Moving his hand up to touch
Joram's face, the warlock raised an eyebrow. "You are telling
the truth. You *don't* know, do you, young man. What's more,
you don't believe Simkin. I'm not certain I do either, and
yet — How can I risk it? What is Simkin's game?"

Irritably, the warlock dropped his hand.

Feeling as though he had awakened from a disturbed and
fitful sleep, Joram blinked and glanced quickly around the
forge. He was alone.

10

The Spy

"**B**ishop Vanya has retired to his private chambers for the evening," was the message the Deacon who acted as secretary gave to all who asked to see His Holiness.

These were not many; everyone living in the Font, and a good majority of those who did not, being very familiar with the Bishop's habits. He retired to his chambers to have the evening meal in private or with those few fortunate enough to be invited as guests. While in his chambers, he was not to be disturbed for anything short of the assassination of any of the Emperors. (Death of the Emperors by natural causes could wait until morning.) *Duuk-tsarith* stood outside the Bishop's chambers, their sole task to make certain that His Holiness remained undisturbed.

There were several reasons for this well-guarded privacy, reasons both public and private. Publicly it was known all over Thimhallan that Bishop Vanya was something of a gourmand and refused to allow any sort of unpleasantness to interrupt his dinner. Guests at his table were carefully selected to provide interesting and noncontroversial dinnertime conversation, which was viewed as important to the digestion.

Publicly it was known that Bishop Vanya worked extremely hard during the day, devoting himself completely to matters of the Church (and state). Rising before the sun, he rarely left his office until it had set. After such a rigorous day, it was important to his health to have these hours of unbroken rest and relaxation in the evening.

Publicly it was known that the Bishop used these quiet hours in meditation and discussion with the Almin.

These were the public reasons. The real reason, of course, was a private one, known only to the Bishop. Vanya used these quiet hours for discussion — but not with the Almin. Those to whom he talked were of a more worldly nature. . . .

There had been guests to dinner this autumn night, but they had left early, the Bishop indicating that he felt unusually tired that evening. After the guests had gone, however, Vanya did not proceed to his bedchambers as might have been expected. Instead, moving with a swiftness and an alacrity that accorded ill with pleas of exhaustion, the Bishop removed the spell that sealed off a small, private chapel, and opened the door.

A beautiful and peaceful place, the chapel was built along ancient lines and traditions. Its dark interior was illuminated by stained glass windows conjured up many centuries ago by the most skilled of artisans whose speciality lay in glass shaping. Benches of rosewood stood before an altar of crystal, also centuries old, decorated with the symbols of the Nine Mysteries.

Here Vanya performed the Ritual of Dawn, the Evening Prayers, and sought guidance and counsel of the Almin — something he did infrequently, if at all, it being Bishop Vanya's private opinion that it was the Almin who could use the guidance and counseling of his minister, not the other way around.

Vanya entered the chapel, which was illuminated by a perpetual gleam of light shining from the altar, as pale and restful as moonbeams, gracing the chamber with an air of peaceful tranquility.

There was neither peace nor tranquility in the Bishop as he walked through the chapel, however. Moving swiftly, without a glance at the altar, Vanya crossed the room and came to stand before one of the handsomely decorated wooden panels that formed the interior of the small chapel. Laying his hand upon the panel, the Bishop murmured secret, arcane words and the panel dissolved beneath his fingertips. Before him opened up a vast void, empty and dark — a Corridor. But it was not an ordinary Corridor, not part of that vast network of time-dimensional tunnels created long ago by the Diviners that crossed and crisscrossed Thimhallan. This Corridor had been created by the Diviners, but it connected to no other Corridor. Only one man knew of its existence — the Bishop of the Realm — and it went to only one place.

It was to that place that Bishop Vanya proceeded, arriving there within the space of a heartbeat. Stepping out of the Corridor, the Bishop was in a pocket made of the very material of the Corridors themselves, a pocket that existed only in the warped fabric of space and time. It seemed to Vanya that whenever he entered this place he was entering some dark and inner part of his own mind.

He could see nothing within this place, nor could he touch walls or feel a floor, though he had the sensation that he walked in it. He had the impression that the pocket of time and space was round. There was a chair in the center where he could sit down, if his business proved long. But the chair may have well been in his mind, for it seemed to have armrests when he wanted them and to lack them when he didn't. At times it was soft, at others times firm, and sometimes, when he was irritated or pressed for time or felt like walking as he talked, the chair wasn't there at all.

This evening, the chair was there and, this evening, it was soft and comfortable. Sitting in it, Vanya relaxed. This was not a meeting that demanded the application of subtle pressures, threats, or coercion. It was not one of delicate negotiation. This was a meeting of an informative nature, clarification, reassurance that all was proceeding according to plan.

Settling back, Vanya allowed himself a moment to absorb and activate the magic in the room that permitted this communication to work, then he spoke aloud into the darkness.

"My friend, a word with you."

The magic pulsed around him, he could feel it whisper against his cheek and stir across the fingers of his hand.

"I am at your service."

It was the darkness that spoke to Vanya, though human lips well over hundreds of miles distant formed the words. Because of the magic within the room, the Bishop heard the words as his own mind formed them, not necessarily as the person on the other end of his conscious thought spoke them. Thus the room was known as the Chamber of Discretion, for two people could converse with each other, neither knowing the other's identity unless it was revealed, neither ever being able to recognize the other by sight or sound. In the ancient days, so legend had it, there had been several of these chambers built — each of the Royal Houses, for example, had one, as did the various Guilds. Following the Second Rectification, however, the catalysts had moved swiftly to see that the other pockets in the Corridors were sealed up, giving as pretext the reasoning that in a world of peace, no one need have secrets from each other.

It was assumed by all parties that when the catalysts sealed off the other Chambers of Discretion, they sealed off their own in the Font as well. Which only goes to prove the old adage that assumptions are lies believed by the blind.

"Are you alone?" Vanya's mind queried his unseen minion.

"For the moment. But I am busy. We ride within the week."

"I am aware of that. Did the catalyst arrive?"

"Yes."

"Safely?"

"In a manner of speaking. He is better now, if that is what you mean. At least he has no desire to venture by himself into the Outland."

"Good. He will perform adequately?"

"I see no problem. He *seems*, as you described him, naive and weak, easily intimidated, but —"

"Bah! The man is a mass of quivering jelly. He may cause trouble once, but that will be dealt with harshly, I presume. Once he has learned his lesson, I foresee no further problems."

"I hope not." The voice in Vanya's head sounded skeptical, causing the Bishop to frown.

"Where are the Technologists in terms of the forging of the weapons?" Vanya continued.

"With this catalyst's help, production should accelerate rapidly."

"How are matters progressing in Sharakan? Have you contacted His Majesty there?"

"You probably know more about that than I do, Holiness. I must move cautiously, of course. I cannot afford to reveal my hand. It is a dangerous game I play. His Majesty has been discreetly informed of the acquisition of a catalyst and how it will affect us. That is the best I could do."

"Adequate. His Majesty must be confident of you. His demeanor is becoming increasingly warlike. We are, of course, attempting to quell this storm" — Vanya made a gesture with his hand as of smoothing turbulent water — "and when the time comes we will be grieved to admit our failure. Things are moving here. The Empress's brother is becoming a nuisance, but he is easily dealt with. When war is declared, we will be ready to act. Is there anything else?"

"Yes. What about Joram? What does this catalyst intend to do with him?"

"What does it matter to you? The boy is a cat's-paw, nothing more. The only thing you need concern yourself with is keeping him alive."

"What are the catalyst's instructions? What will he do?"

"Do? I doubt if he has the guts to do anything. I have recommended caution to him. He is to report to me in a month or so. I will entreat him to move slowly in the matter. But make your preparations. When I give you the word, you will need to move swiftly. You have your orders. Do I need to remind you of them?" Vanya's frown deepened. "I sense dissatisfaction in you, my friend. I am not accustomed to this questioning. What is wrong? Has your disguise been penetrated?"

"Of course not, Bishop." The voice grew cold. "We both know my talents. That was why you chose me. But certain matters have arisen that were unexpected. Someone is taking a greater interest in this than I like."

"Who?" Vanya demanded.

"I think you know." The voice inside Vanya's head was smooth. "I think, in fact, that you have dealt me marked cards."

"How dare —"

"I dare because of who I am. And now, I must go. Someone is coming. Remember, Holiness, in my hand, I hold the king."

The magical link between the two broke, leaving Vanya sitting, staring into the darkness, his lips pursed, his fingers crawling spiderlike over the arm of his chair. "King? Yes, my friend. But I hold swords."

BOOK THREE

The Scianc

We *are many, but we are not one.*

If the Technologists had risen in a group and rebelled against Blachloch, the warlock and his henchmen must have fallen. Without a catalyst to grant him Life, the Enforcer's magical powers were limited. His henchmen, few in number, could not have held out long against hundreds. These hundreds did not arise, however. Most of the Sorcerers were, in fact, in complete agreement with Blachloch's plans for joining with the people of Sharakan and declaring war. It was time for the Sorcerers to bring the power of the Ninth Mystery back to the world, to once more take their rightful place among the inhabitants of Thimhallan. And if they had to bring death and destruction back to the world as well, wouldn't this be mitigated by the wonders they would introduce, wonders that would improve life?

There were those among the Technologists who were wise enough to see that in this kind of dream, the Sorcerers were simply repeating the tragic mistakes of the past. But these people were in the minority. It was all very well for Andon, an old man, to talk of patience and peace. The young were sick and tired of skulking about in the wilderness, leading dreary lives of drudgery when the riches and wealth of the world could be theirs, *should* be theirs.

Thus they followed Blachloch wholeheartedly, abandoning their farms, working with a will in the mines and the forge to craft the weapons that were to carve them a future.

This future came to be embodied for them in the monument that stood in the center of the village — the Great Wheel. Older than the village itself, the Wheel had been rescued from the destruction of the Sorcerers' Temples by the persecuted Technologists following the Iron Wars. They brought it with them as they fled for their lives into the Outlands, and now it hangs in the center of an arch formed of black rock. The huge wheel with its nine spokes has become the center of a ritual known in the village as the Scianc.

Who knows how the ritual began? Its roots are buried in the mud and blood of the past. Perhaps, long ago, when the Sorcerers saw the knowledge they had worked so hard to acquire sinking into the darkness of their harsh lives, they used this method to try to pass on what they had learned to the next generations. Unfortunately, next generations remembered only the words, the knowledge and the wisdom dwindled and burned out like the flame of a guttered candle.

On the seventh night of every week, the entire population of the village gathers around the Wheel and recites the chant that each learns as a child. Accompanied by the music of instruments of iron, tortured wood, and stretched animal skins, the chant begins by paying homage to the three major forces in the Sorcerers' lives — Fire, Wind, and Water. With voices that rise higher and higher as the music of the instruments becomes more frenetic, the people sing of the construction and building and development of wonders that no one now remembers or understands.

On the night before the men of the village were to leave with Blachloch on the raid of the farming communities, the Scianc was particularly wild, the former *Duuk-tsarith* cleverly using it as the *DKarn-Duuk* uses the war dance — to heat the blood until human conscience and compassion is burned away. Round and round the great Wheel the chanters danced, the beating and strumming of the instruments adding their inhuman voices to the melee. Torches lit the darkness and in their light, the Wheel — forged of some type of shiny metal, the knowledge of whose making had been lost — shone in the torchlight like an unholy sun. Occasionally one of the dancers leaped up onto the black stone platform that supported the monument. Grabbing hold of one of the forge's hammers, he would strike the center of the nine-spoked Wheel, causing it to join in the chanting with a voice of iron that seemed to shout from the bowels of the earth itself.

Most of the Sorcerers took part in the Scianc, men, women, and children, chanting the words no one understood, dancing in the flaming light, or watching with mixed emotions.

Andon watched in sorrow, hearing in the words of the chant the voices of the ancients crying out to their children to remember the past.

Saryon watched in a horror so vast it was a wonder he did not go mad. The flaring lights, the shrieking music, the leaping figures of men and women drunk with bloodlust — all seemed sprung from his carefully taught visions of Hell. He paid no attention to the words of the chant, he was too sickened. Here dwelt Death, and himself in the midst of it.

Blachloch watched in satisfaction, his black-robed figure standing well outside the circle of dancers, calm, observant, unnoticed. He heard the words of the chant, but he'd heard them often, and they didn't matter anymore.

Joram watched in frustration. He heard the words. What's more, he listened to them and he understood them — in part. He alone had read the hidden books. He alone, of all those there, saw the knowledge those ancient Sorcerers had hoped to impart to their children. He saw it, but he didn't understand it. The knowledge remained locked up in those words, locked up in the books. And he couldn't find the key — the key that was in strange, unfathomable symbols.

Simkin watched, bored.

With the rising of the moon, the Scianc ended. Standing in a ring of flame made by the flaring torches, Blachloch wielded the hammer that struck the Wheel nine times. The people raised their voices in nine wild shouts, then the fiery ring broke apart as the Sorcerers walked to their homes, talking of the great deeds they would do when, once again, the Ninth Mystery ruled the world.

Soon the black rock arches stood alone, casting eerie shadows as the moon rose higher, its pale light shining on the Wheel nothing more than a ghostly reflection of the brilliant torchfire. In the moonlit darkness, the village slept, wrapped in a silence that was broken only by the sounds of autumn's dry, dead leaves — blown by a chill wind — skittering and rustling through the empty streets.

Choose Three Cards...

On a bright, sunny day in late autumn, most of the men and boys of the Sorcerers' village rode out to take, as they saw it, what the world owed them. Andon watched them go with eyes that held the sadness of centuries. He had done what he could to stop them but he had failed. They had to learn their lesson, he supposed. The old man only hoped it would not be too bitter. Or too costly.

The first days of the journey were days of sunshine and clear weather — warm and pleasant during the hours of light, cool and crisp with the hint of the coming winter at night. Blachloch's band was lighthearted and merry; the young men, especially, enjoying the break from the drudgery of work in the forge or the gristmill, the mines or bricklaying. Led by the riotous Simkin, who was again dressed in his ranger clothing in honor of the occasion ("I call this color *Dirt and Dung*"), the young men laughed and joked and teased each other about their difficulties in riding the shaggy, half-wild horses that were raised in the village. At night they gathered around a blazing fire to swap stories and play games of chance with the older men, wagering winter rations of food and losing them so consistently that it seemed likely none of them would eat until spring.

Even the usually morose Joram appeared better for the change, astonishing Mosiah by his willingness to talk, if he did not share in the horseplay and joking. But then, Mosiah reflected, this may have had something to do with the fact that Joram had just come out of another one of his black melancholies.

By the second week, however, the fun had gone out of the ride. A chill rain dripped from the yellowing leaves, soaking through cloaks and trickling down the back. The soft plopping of the drops formed a monotonous rhythm with the horses' plodding hoofbeats. The rain settled in, falling steadily for days. There were no fires by Blachloch's orders. They were in centaur country now, and the watch had been doubled, which meant many lost half a night's sleep. Everyone was miserable and grumbling, but there was one person so much more obviously miserable than the rest that Mosiah couldn't help noticing.

Joram noticed too, apparently. Every now and then Mosiah saw a look of shadowed pleasure in Joram's dark eyes and there would be almost a half-smile upon the lips. Following Joram's gaze, Mosiah saw him looking at the catalyst, who rode ahead of them, jouncing uncomfortably in the saddle, his tonsured head bowed, his shoulders slumped. The catalyst was a pathetic sight on horseback. The first few days he had been stiff with fright. Now he was just plain stiff. Every bone and muscle in his body hurt. Just sitting in the saddle was obviously painful.

"I feel sorry for the man," Mosiah said on the second week of their journey north. Chilled and soaked, he, Joram, and Simkin were riding together down a stretch of trail that was wide enough for a cavalry brigade to have ridden six abreast. Giants had blazed this trail, Blachloch said, warning them all to be alert.

"What man?" Joram asked. He had been listening to Simkin elaborate on how the Duke of Westshire had hired the entire Stone Shapers Guild, together with six catalysts, to completely redo his palatial dwelling in Merilon, transforming it from crystal to rose-colored marble streaked with flecks of pale green.

"The court can talk of nothing else. Such a thing has never been done before. Imagine, marble! It looks quite . . . ponderous . . ." Simkin was saying.

"The catalyst. What's his name? I feel sorry for him," Mosiah said.

"Saryon?" Simkin appeared slightly confused. "Pardon me, dear boy, but what has he to do with rose-colored marble?"

"Nothing," returned Mosiah. "I was just watching the expression on Joram's face. He seems to be enjoying the poor man's misery."

"He's a catalyst," Joram replied shortly. "And you're wrong. I don't care enough to think about him one way or the other."

"Mmmm," Mosiah muttered, seeing Joram's dark eyes grow darker as they stared at the man's green-robed back.

"He's from your village, you know," Simkin commented, leaning over his horse's neck to talk confidentially in a loud voice that could be heard by nearly everyone in line.

"Keep your voice down! He'll hear us. What do you mean, he's from our village?" Mosiah asked, astonished. "Why didn't you say anything before? Maybe he knows my parents!"

"I'm certain I said something," Simkin protested with an aggrieved air, "when I told you about his coming for Joram—"

"Shh!" Mosiah hissed. "That nonsense!" Biting his lip, the young man stared at the catalyst with a wistful air. "I wonder how my parents are? It's been so long . . ."

"Oh, go ahead! Talk to him!" snapped Joram, his black eyebrows drawing a straight, hard line across his face.

"Yes, go have a chat with the old boy," Simkin said languidly. "He's not a bad sort, really, as catalysts go. And I've got no more cause to love them than you, O Dark and Gloomy Friend. I told you they stole away my baby brother, didn't I? Little Nat. Poor tyke. Failed the Testing. We had him hidden away until he was five. But they found out about him—one of the neighbors snitched. Grudge against my mother. I was Nat's favorite, you know. The little fellow clung to me, when they were dragging him off."

Two tears rolled down Simkin's face into his beard. Mosiah heaved an exasperated sigh.

"That's it!" said Simkin, sniffing. "Mock my affliction. Make light of my sorrow. If you'll excuse me," he muttered, more tears streaming down his face, mingling with the rainwater, "I will indulge my grief in private. You two go on. No, it's no use trying to comfort me. Not in the slightest . . ." Mumbling incoherently, Simkin suddenly wheeled his horse around and left the trail, galloping back toward the rear of the line.

"Mock his affliction! How many brothers is that who've met some appalling fate?" Snorting in disgust, Mosiah glanced back at Simkin, who was wiping tears from his face and calling out a rude remark to one of Blachloch's henchmen at the same time. "To say nothing of assorted sisters held captive by nobles or hauled off by centaurs, not counting the one who ran away from home because she was enamored of a giant. Then there's the aunt, who drowned in a public fountain because she thought she was a swan, and his mother, who has died five times of five different rare diseases and once of a broken heart because the *Duuk-tsarith* arrested his father for conjuring up offensive illusions of the Emperor. All of this happening to an orphan who was discovered floating in a basket of rose petals down the Merilon sewer system. He's a monumental liar! I don't see how can you put up with him!"

"Because he's an amusing liar," Joram replied, shrugging. "And that makes him different."

"Different?"

"From all the rest of you," Joram said, glancing at Mosiah from beneath his heavy, dark brows. "Why don't you go talk to your catalyst," he suggested coolly, seeing Mosiah's face flush in anger. "If what I hear is true, he's in for a lot worse punishment than saddle sores."

Digging his heels into the horse's flanks, Joram galloped ahead, riding past the catalyst without a glance, his horse flinging up mud from its hooves. Mosiah saw the catalyst raise his head and stare after the young man, whose long black hair, whipped free from its bindings, glistened in the rain like the plumage of a wet bird.

"Why do I put up with *you?*" Mosiah muttered, gazing after the figure of his friend. "Pity? You'd hate me for that. But it's true, in a way. I can understand why you refuse to trust anyone. The scars you bear aren't only from wounds on your chest. But, some day, my friend, those scars are going to be nothing — nothing — compared to the scar from the wound you're going to get when you find out you've been wrong!"

Shaking his head, Mosiah urged his horse forward until he rode next to the catalyst.

"Excuse me for interrupting your thoughts, Father," the young man said hesitantly, "but would — would you mind if I kept you company?"

Saryon looked up fearfully, his face strained and tense. Then, seeing only the young man, he appeared to relax. "No, I'd like it very much, in fact."

"You — you weren't praying or anything like that, were you, Father?" Mosiah asked in some confusion. "I can leave, if you —"

"No, I wasn't praying," Saryon said with a wan smile. "I haven't done much praying lately," he added in a low voice, glancing about the wilderness with a shiver. "I'm used to finding the Almin in the corridors of the Font. Not out here. I don't think He lives out here."

Mosiah didn't understand but, seeing a chance for an opening, remarked, "My father talks like that sometimes. He says the Almin dines with the rich and throws scraps to the poor. He doesn't care about us, so we must get through this life on our own honor and integrity. When we die, that's the most important thing we leave behind."

"Jacobias is a very wise man," Saryon said, looking at Mosiah intently. "I know him. You are Mosiah, aren't you?"

"Yes." The young man flushed. "I know you know him. That's why I came — That is, I didn't know or I would have come sooner — I mean, Simkin just now told me —"

"I understand." Saryon nodded gravely. "I should have come to see you. I have messages from your parents, but . . . I haven't been well." It was now the catalyst's turn to flush uncomfortably. Grimacing in pain, he shifted in his saddle, his gaze going to the figure of Joram disappearing among the trees.

"My parents . . ." nudged Mosiah, after several moments of silence.

"Oh, yes, I'm sorry," Saryon roused himself. "They are well and send their love. They miss you very much," the catalyst said, seeing a look of hunger and longing sweep across the young man's face. "Your mother gave me a kiss for you, but I don't suppose I need pass that along personally."

"No, that's all right. Thank you, Father," Mosiah murmured, blushing. "Did — did they say anything else? My father . . ."

Glancing at the young man, Saryon's face grew grave and he did not immediately reply.

Mosiah saw the look and understood. "That's it, isn't it," he said bitterly. "I'm in for a lecture."

"Not a lecture," Saryon answered, smiling. "He said only that he'd heard some things about these people that he didn't like to hear. He hoped the rumors weren't true but, if they were, that you would remember what you were brought up to believe, and that he and your mother loved you, and that you were in their thoughts."

Looking at the young man, Saryon saw crimson stain the smooth cheeks, where there was just the faintest growth of beard. But the shame — if that's what it had been — was gone almost immediately, replaced by anger. "What he's heard is wrong."

"What about this raid?"

"These people are good people." Mosiah glared at Saryon defiantly. "All they want is to have the same chance at life others have. All right," he said quickly when it seemed Saryon would speak, "maybe I don't like some of what they do, maybe I don't think it's right. But we have a right to survive."

"By doing this? By robbing others? Andon tells me —"

Mosiah made an impatient gesture. "Andon is an old man —"

"He tells me that before the coming of Blachloch, the Technologists were able to provide for themselves," Saryon continued. "They farmed the land, using tools instead of magic."

"We don't have time now. We're working too hard. We have to eat this winter!" Mosiah retorted angrily.

"So do the people we're robbing."

"We don't take much. Joram said so. We leave them plenty—"

"Not this year. This year you have me, a catalyst. This year Blachloch can use me to enhance his powers. Have you ever seen the magic a warlock can summon?"

"Then, why are you here?" Mosiah asked abruptly, turning to look at Saryon, his face grim. "Why did you run to the Outland if you're full of such righteous notions?"

"You know," replied the catalyst in a low voice. "I heard Simkin tell you."

Mosiah shook his head. "Simkin can't tell you the time of day without lying," he said scornfully. "If you mean that nonsense about you coming for Joram—"

"It isn't nonsense."

Mosiah blinked, staring. Saryon's face, though pale and haggard with weariness, was composed. "What?" he repeated, not certain he had heard correctly.

"It isn't nonsense," the catalyst said. "I was sent here to take Joram back for justice."

"But . . . Why? Why are you telling me this?" Mosiah demanded in confusion. "Do you want something from me, is that it? Do you want me to help you? Because I won't! Not Joram! He's my—"

"No, of course not," Saryon interrupted, shaking his head with a sad smile. "I don't want anything from you. What I do about Joram, I must do alone." Sighing, he rubbed his eyes wearily. "I told you because I promised your father I would speak to you if I found you involved in this . . ." He waved his hand.

The two rode together in silence through the dreary rain. Faintly, behind them, above the jingle of the harness and plodding hoofbeats, Mosiah heard Simkin's raucous laughter.

"You could have preached me your sermon without telling me the truth about yourself, Father. I didn't believe Simkin anyway. No one ever does," Mosiah muttered, his hand twisting the reins, his eyes on the horse's tangled mane. "I don't know what you mean about taking Joram in for justice. I don't see how you could," he added, glancing at the catalyst with contempt. "I'll warn Joram, of course. I still don't understand why you told me. You must have realized this would make us enemies, you and me."

"Yes, and I am sorry," Saryon answered, hunching deeper into his soggy cloak. "But I was afraid you wouldn't have paid attention to me otherwise. My 'sermon' wouldn't have had much impact if you thought I was talking out one side of my mouth as the saying goes. Now, at least, I hope you will think about what I have told you."

Mosiah did not answer, but continued to stare down at the horse's mane. His expression hardened; the hand twisting the reins gripped them firmly. "Your conscience can feel eased now," he said, raising his head. "You've done your duty to my father. But, speaking of conscience, I don't see you hesitate to obey Blachloch when he tells you to grant him Life. Or perhaps you're thinking of disobeying," Mosiah said with a sneer, recalling the punishment at which Joram had hinted. Expecting the weak-appearing catalyst to cower and cringe, the young man was startled to see him meet his gaze with quiet dignity.

"That is my shame," Saryon answered steadily, "and I must deal with it as you must deal with yours."

"I have no need to deal —" began Mosiah angrily, but was interrupted by Simkin's lilting voice, rising above the sound of rain and hooves.

"Mosiah, Mosiah! Where are you?"

Irritably, the young man turned around in the saddle, looking behind him and waving his hand. "I'll be there in a moment," he shouted. Then he turned back to the catalyst. "One last thing I don't understand, Father. Why did you tell Simkin about Joram? Preaching him a sermon, too?"

"I didn't tell Simkin," Saryon said. Awkwardly kicking at his horse with his big, ungainly feet, the weary catalyst urged the animal forward. "You better go, they're calling for you. Good-bye, Mosiah. I hope we can talk again."

"Didn't tell him! Then how —"

But Saryon shook his head. Pulling his hood low over his eyes, he rode on, leaving Mosiah to stare after him in confusion.

"You're too gullible."

"You weren't there," Mosiah muttered. "You didn't see him, the look on his face. He's telling the truth. Oh, I know how you feel about that"—seeing the bitter half-smile in Joram's dark eyes—"but you have to admit that Simkin *did* tell us the catalyst was here for you. And if the catalyst claims he didn't tell Simkin, then how—"

"What does it matter?" Joram snapped impatiently, staring moodily into the small fire they had built to dry their clothes. The group had found shelter for the night in a huge cave they'd discovered in the hillside near the river. Since it was rare to find a cave in the Outland unoccupied, Blachloch had entered it cautiously, keeping his catalyst with him. Upon investigation, it proved empty, however, and the warlock decided it was a safe place in which to stay. The only drawback was an atrocious smell coming from a pile of refuse in a dark corner; refuse no one wanted to examine too closely. Though they had burned it, the smell lingered on. Blachloch said the cave had probably been inhabited by trolls.

"Of course it doesn't matter to you about the catalyst," Mosiah said bitterly, starting to get to his feet. "Nothing ever matters to you. . . ."

Reaching out, Joram gripped his friend's hand. "I'm sorry," he said in a tight voice, the words coming with difficulty. "I thank you . . . for the warning." The half-smile twisted his lips. "I don't consider one middle-aged catalyst much of a threat, but I'll be on my guard. As for Simkin"—he shrugged—"ask him how he found out."

"But you can't believe that fool!" Mosiah said in exasperation, sitting back down.

"Fool? Did I hear someone taking my name in vain?" came a dulcet-toned voice from the darkness.

Sighing in disgust, Mosiah winced and shaded his eyes as the gaudily clad figure stepped into the firelight.

"What, dear boy, don't you like this?" Simkin inquired, raising his arms to show off his new robes to their most garish advantage. "I was so bored, wearing that drab ranger garb, that I decided a change was in order, as the Duchess D'Longeville said when she married her fourth husband. Or was it her fifth? Not that it matters. He'll be dead like the others before long. *Never* take tea with the Duchess D'Longe-

ville. Or, if you do, make certain she doesn't serve you from
the same pot that she serves her husband. Don't you like this
shade of red? I call it *Smashed Vermilion*. What's the matter,
Mosiah? You look in a worse humor than our friend the
Dark One today."

"Nothing," Mosiah mumbled, twisting to his feet to peer
into a crude iron pot perched precariously in a bed of hot
coals.

"Smells like it's burning on the bottom," said Simkin,
bending down and sniffing. "I say, why don't you ask that
jolly old catalyst for some Life? Use our magic, like everyone
else now that he's here. Am I invited for dinner?"

"No." Lifting a stick, and ignoring the suggestion about
the catalyst, Mosiah began to stir the bubbling contents of
the pot.

"Ah," said Simkin sitting down, "thanks. Now, what are
we in such a pet over? I know! You rode with Father
Skinhead today. He have anything interesting to say?"

"Shhh," Mosiah cautioned, gesturing to where Saryon
was seated alone, trying without much success to build a fire.
"Why ask? You probably know more about what we discussed than either of us."

"Probably I do," Simkin said gaily. "Look at the poor
chap, he's freezing to death. Old fellow like that shouldn't be
roaming about in the wilderness. I'll invite him over to share
our stew." The young man looked around at his friends.
"Shall I? I believe I will. Don't scowl, Joram. You really
should meet him. After all, he's here to apprehend you. I say,
Catalyst!"

Simkin's voice echoed in the cave. Saryon started and
turned, as did nearly everyone else in the cavern.

Mosiah reached out and tugged at Simkin's sleeve. "Stop
it, you fool!"

But Simkin was calling out once again and waving, his
red robes flaming in the firelight. "Over here, Catalyst.
Look, we've got this nice squirrel stew . . ."

Many of the men were glancing at them, snickering and
making muttered comments. Even Blachloch raised his
hooded head from the game of cards he was playing with
some of his men, regarding the group with a cold, impassionate stare. Slowly, Saryon rose to his feet, his face flushed,

and walked toward them, obviously hoping to shut Simkin up.

"Damn!" groaned Mosiah, leaning close to Joram. "Let's go. I'm not hungry anymore. . . ."

"No, wait. I want to meet him," Joram said softly, his dark eyes on the catalyst.

"I'll escort you, Father," Simkin cried, leaping to his feet and running over to the catalyst. Bowing gracefully, he grabbed the embarrassed man by the hand and led him to the fire, performing a quadrille on the way. "Shall we dance, Father? One, two, three, hop. One, two, three, hop . . ."

There was laughter. Everyone in the cave was watching now, grateful for the diversion. The exception was Blachloch, who returned to his card game.

"Not a dancer, Father? Probably frowned upon, isn't it."

Saryon was trying, unsuccessfully, to shake Simkin loose.

But Simkin was having far too good a time. "Undoubtedly His Tubbiness just prohibits it because he's jealous. I mean, with him, 'one, two, three, hop' would be closer to 'one, two, three, bouncey, bouncey, bouncey.'" Puffing his cheeks and throwing out his stomach, Simkin did a credible impression of the Bishop that brought roars of laughter and scattered applause.

"Thank you, thank you." Placing his hand over his heart, Simkin bowed. Then, with a flourish of orange silk, he led the red-faced catalyst to the fire. "Here you are, Father," he said, bustling about and dragging over a rotted log. "Wait! Don't sit down yet. I'll bet you suffer from piles. Curse of the middle-aged. My grandfather died of them, you know. Yes," he continued mournfully as he tapped the log once with his hand and transformed it into a velvet cushion, "poor old gentleman went for nine years without sitting down. Then he tried it once, and *bam* — keeled right over. Blood rushed to his — "

"Please, Father, won't you be seated?" Mosiah interrupted hurriedly. "I — I don't believe you have met Joram. Joram, this is F-father — "

Mosiah stammered himself into confused silence as Joram gazed steadily at the catalyst without speaking.

Sitting down awkwardly on the cushion, Saryon tried to give some polite greeting to the young man, but the look of cool disdain in Joram's brown eyes sucked the air out of his body and the words from his mind. Only Simkin was at ease. Hunching down on a rock, he rested his arms on his bent knees, leaned his bearded chin on his hands, and smiled on all three mischievously.

"I'll bet the squirrel's cooked by now," he said, reaching out suddenly to give the catalyst a playful shove with his hand. "Wouldn't you say so, Father? Or maybe it's your goose we've cooked?"

His face flushing so that it appeared fevered, Saryon looked as though he could cheerfully sink through the floor. Casting Simkin a vicious glance, Mosiah moved hastily over to the iron pot. He started to lift it by the handle, when Joram caught hold of his arm.

"It will be hot," he said. A stick materialized in Joram's hand. Sliding it through the handle, he lifted the pot from the blaze. "The heat from the flame heats not only the pot but the handle itself."

"You and your damn technology," muttered Mosiah, sitting back down.

"I will be happy to open a conduit to you and provide you with Life —" Saryon began, then his eyes met Joram's.

"That wouldn't be of much use to me now, would it, Father?" Joram said evenly, his heavy brows slashing a dark line across his forehead. "I'm Dead. Or didn't you know?"

"I knew," said Saryon quietly. The flush was gone from his face, leaving it pale and composed. No one was watching them now. The rest of the men in the cavern, seeing that the show was apparently over, had gone back to their own concerns. "I will not lie to you. I was sent to bring you to justice. You are a murderer —"

"And one of the walking Dead," Joram snapped bitterly, setting the stewpot down on the ground with a thud.

"I say, careful there," Simkin remonstrated, leaning over hastily to rescue the pot. Lifting the spoon, he began to ladle out portions of the grayish, lumpish mixture into rough-hewn wooden bowls. "Forgive the use of the tools, Father, but —"

"Are you?" asked Saryon, gazing steadily at Joram. "I have been watching you. I have seen you use the magic. That stick you produced from thin air, for example . . ."

To Saryon's amazement, Joram's dark eyes flashed, but it was not with anger. It was with fear. Puzzled, his words forgotten, the catalyst stared at him. The look was gone in an instant, covered by the hard, stone facade. But it had been there, Saryon was certain.

Taking a dish from Simkin, Joram sat down upon the stone floor and began to eat, using the tool to shovel food into his mouth, never raising his eyes from his dish. Accepting his dish, Mosiah did the same, manipulating the unfamiliar spoon awkwardly. Simkin offered a dish to the catalyst, who took it and a spoon. But Saryon did not eat, he was still looking at Joram.

"I have been thinking," he said to the scowling young man. "Since no records exist of your Testing, it is possible that Father Tolban might have, in the excitement of the moment, made a mistake in your case. Return with me of your own accord and let the case be examined. There were extenuating circumstances involved in the murder, I've heard. Your mother—"

"Do not speak of my mother. Let us talk of my father, instead. Did you know him, Catalyst?" Joram asked coldly. "Were you there, watching, when they turned his body to stone?"

Saryon had picked up his bowl, but now he set it down with shaking hands.

"I say, Mosiah," remarked Simkin, chewing vigorously, "this squirrel didn't happen to stagger in here and die of old age in your arms, did it, dear boy? If so, you should have given it a decent burial. I've been chewing on this piece for ten minutes—"

"No, no . . . I wasn't present during your father's execution," replied Saryon in a low voice, his eyes on the stone floor. "I was a Deacon, then. Only the higher-ranking of my Order—"

"Got to see the show?" Joram sneered.

"Water! I need water!" Simkin gestured, and a waterskin, hanging in a cool part of the cavern, floated over to them. "I must have something to wash down this elderly party." Taking a drink, he wiped his mouth with the bit of orange silk, then gave a prodigious yawn. "I say, I'm frightfully bored with this conversation. Let's play tarok." Reaching into the air, he produced a pack of colorful, gilt-edged cards.

"Where did *you* get a deck?" Mosiah demanded, thankful for the interruption. "Wait a minute, those aren't Blachloch's, are they?"

"Of course not." Simkin looked hurt. "He's playing over in the corner, didn't you notice? As for this"— he spread the cards out on the ground with an expert flick of his hand — "I picked it up at court. This is the newest deck. The artisans did a superb job. The court cards are drawn to look like everyone in the Royal House of Merilon. It was quite the rage, I assure you. Overly flattering to the Empress, of course. She doesn't look nearly this good now, especially up close. But the artisans have no choice in the matter, I suppose. Notice the lovely azure color to the sky around the Sun card? Crushed lapis lazuli. No, truly, I assure you. And see the Kings? Each suit is a different Emperor of one of the realms King of Swords — Emperor of Merilon. King of Staves is Zith-el. King of Cups is the notorious lover, Emperor of Balzab. A perfect likeness, and the King of Coins is that money-grubber Sharakan —"

"We'll play, won't we, Joram?" Mosiah interrupted hurriedly, seeing Simkin about to proceed to the Queens. "What about you, Father? Or is playing tarok against your vows or something?"

"Only three players," Simkin said, shuffling the deck. "The catalyst will have to wait his turn."

"Thank you," said Saryon. Gathering his robes around him, he started to rise, leaving his untouched stew on the floor. "We are permitted to play but I would not break up your game. Perhaps another time . . ."

"Go ahead, Catalyst." Shoving his plate away, Joram stood up, his face dark and sullen, a wild, strange look in his eyes. "I don't want to play. You can have my place."

"Don't, Joram!" Mosiah said in low tones. A note of anxiety in his voice, he caught hold of Joram's muscular arm.

"See here," said Simkin cheerfully, cutting the deck and stacking it back with a swift gesture of his hand. "We won't play if Joram's going to go off into one of his sulking fits. Look, I'll tell your fortunes. Sit back down, Catalyst. I think you will find this interesting. You first, Joram."

Anciently, the Diviners had used the tarot deck to enable them to see into the future. Brought from the Dark World, the cards were originally cherished as a sacred artifact. The Diviners alone, it was said, knew how to translate the complex images painted on the cards. But the Diviners were no more, having perished in the Iron Wars. The cards still existed, preserved for their quaint beauty, and after a time someone recalled that they had once been used in an ancient game known as tarok. The game caught on, particularly among the members of the noble houses. The art of fortune-telling did not die out either, but dwindled (with the encouragement of the catalysts) into a harmless pastime suitable for entertainment at parties.

"Come, Joram. I'm quite skilled at this, you know," said Simkin persuasively, tugging at Joram's sleeve until the young man sat down. Even Saryon hesitated, regarding the cards with the fascination all feel when they try to lift the veil that hides the future. "The Empress simply dotes on me. Now, Joram, using your left hand — the hand closest to your heart — choose three cards. Past, present, future. This is your past."

Simkin turned up the first card. A figure robed in black riding a pale horse stared out at them with the grinning face of a skull.

"Death," said Simkin softly.

Despite himself, Saryon could not repress a shiver. He glanced quickly at the young man, but Joram was staring at the cards with nothing but a half-smile upon his lips, a smile that might have been a sneer.

The second card pictured a man in royal robes, seated on a throne.

"The King of Swords. Oh, ho!" Simkin said, laughing. "Maybe you're destined to wrest control from Blachloch, Joram. Emperor of the Sorcerers!"

"Hush! Don't even joke about that!" Mosiah said with a nervous glance into the corner of the cavern where Blachloch and his men played their own game.

"I'm not joking," Simkin said in aggrieved tones. "I'm really quite good at this. The Duke of Osborne said—"

"Turn over the third card," Joram muttered. "So we can get to bed."

Obediently, Simkin turned over the card. At the sight of it, Joram's eyes flickered with amusement.

"Two cards exactly alike! I might have known you'd have a crooked deck," Mosiah said in disgust, though Saryon noted the relief in the young man's voice as he saw the wild look fade from Joram's face. "Fortune-telling! Turn over the Fool card for yourself, Simkin, and I'd believe it. Come on, Joram. Good night, Father." The two left, heading for their bedrolls.

"Good night," Saryon said absently. His attention was caught by Simkin, who was staring at the cards in bewilderment.

"That's impossible," Simkin said, frowning. "I'm certain that the last time I looked at this deck, it was perfectly normal. I recall it quite well. I told the Marquis de Lucien that he was going to meet a tall, dark stranger. He did, too. The *Duuk-tsarith* picked him up the next day. Mmm, very odd. Oh, well." Shrugging again, he draped his bit of orange silk over the cards and, tapping them once on top, caused them to disappear. "I say, are you going to eat your stew, Bald One?"

"What? Oh . . . no," Saryon answered, shaking his head. "Go ahead."

"I hate to see it go to waste, though I do wish Mosiah had more respect for the aged." Simkin said, picking up the bowl and spooning in a mouthful of squirrel. Lying back on the velvet cushion, he began to chew resignedly.

Saryon did not reply. Walking away, the catalyst went to a corner of the cavern that was in relative shadow. Wrapping himself in his robes and his blanket, he lay down on the cold stone and tried to get as comfortable as possible. But he could not sleep. He kept seeing the cards spread out on the stone floor.

The third card had been Death again; this time, though, the grinning figure had been reversed.

2

Grant Me Life...

The rain and the journey continued, as did Saryon's misery. Only now, it was misery tempered with growing fear as they drew nearer and nearer their goal—the small Field Magi settlement of Dunam north of the border of the Outland, about one hundred miles from the sea coast. At least once a day Blachloch called upon the catalyst to grant him Life; never much, just sufficient for defensive purposes or to give his men the magical power to rise above the tops of the trees on the wings of the air to scout the trail ahead.

But, although minor in nature, Saryon knew these for what they were—conditioning, the conditioning of a slave to obey his master's voice. Each command was always a little more difficult, each required more expenditure of energy on the catalyst's part, each drained him a little more every day. And always the cold, impassionate eyes of the warlock stared at him from the shadows of the black hood, watching him for the least sign of weakness, of hesitation or resistance.

What Blachloch would have done had his slave rebelled, Saryon did not know. Not once during the entire month-long

journey through the Outland did the catalyst ever see th
warlock mistreat, threaten, or even speak harshly to anyone
The *Duuk-tsarith* had no need to resort to such measures. Th
warlock's presence alone commanded respect, his eye
turned toward anyone filled them with a vague feeling of ter
ror. To be included as one of the threesome of Blachloch
nightly tarok games — the warlock's only indulgence and on
to which he was passionately addicted — took either grea
fortitude or large quantities of fiery spirits. Some simpl
could not take playing cards for hours in the gaze of thos
blue, expressionless eyes. Saryon saw men slink into th
shadows when evening came and Blachloch drew forth hi
pack of cards.

Saryon's guilt and misery deepened. Day after day, th
catalyst rode through the rain, his head bowed almost as lov
as his horse's. Nothing occurred to mar the drudgery of th
ride. Though the bandits saw centaur tracks, they were no
attacked. Centaur prefer catching one or two lone humar
and will think twice about striking such a large, wel
equipped group. Once Saryon thought he caught a glimps
of a giant peering at them from above the treetops, the hug
shaggy-haired head seemingly at variance with the poppin
childlike eyes and the gaping mouth that grinned in the d
light at this tiny parade through his homeland. Before th
catalyst could speak or shout an alarm, the figure was gon
Saryon might have doubted his senses, but he felt the groun
tremble beneath the thuds of gigantic feet. Later, he was gla
he had not mentioned it, listening to some of Blachloch's me
tell stories about the sport they had when they caught one o
these big, gentle, dim-witted creatures.

The only sips of pleasure in the catalyst's bitter cup wer
the few moments he spent each day with Mosiah. The youn
man took to riding with Saryon for short spells, most of th
time by himself, occasionally (when Mosiah couldn't get ri
of him) with Simkin. Joram, of course, never joined then
although Saryon always noticed the young man riding
short distance behind them, within hearing range. But whe
the catalyst started to mention this to Mosiah, he only re
ceived a quick shake of the head, a swift backward glanc
and the whispered words "Don't pay any attention to him" i
return.

The two were an unlikely pair — the tall, stoop-shouldered, middle-aged priest and the fair-haired, handsome youth. Their talk ranged over a wide variety of subjects, nearly always starting with the small doings of the people in Mosiah's village, which the homesick youth never tired of discussing. After that, however, it ranged far afield, Saryon finding himself talking about his studies, about life in court and the city of Merilon. It was during these times, particularly when he talked about Merilon or when he was discoursing on mathematics (his favorite topic), that he saw, out of the corner of his eye, Joram edging his horse nearer.

"Tell me, Father" — Mosiah's voice carried clearly over the thudding of the horses' hooves and the dripping of the water from the trees beneath which they rode — "when Simkin talks about the court at Merilon . . . You know, when he mentions those Dukes and Duchesses and Earls and all that, is he . . . well . . . making these people up? Or do they really exist?"

"Is he lying?" Joram muttered to himself as he rode behind them, that strange inner smile lighting his eyes. "Of course he's lying. Still trying to catch the wily Simkin, are you, Mosiah? Well, give up. Better people than you have tried, my friend."

"I really can't say," Joram heard the catalyst reply in a perplexed tone. "You see, I wasn't at court much myself and . . . I'm terrible at names. Some of them he mentions *do* sound familiar, yet I can't ever seem to call them to mind. I suppose it's entirely possible . . ."

"See there?" Joram said to Mosiah's back. He often made such comments during the course of the conversation. But they were always made to himself, always unheard by the principals involved. For Joram never joined them, and if either glanced back, he always feigned looking at his surroundings to the exclusion of all else.

But he was listening, listening carefully and with intense interest. A change had come over Joram in the months he had spent living among the Sorcerers of Technology. Sick and exhausted upon his arrival, it had been easy for the young man to fall into his old, accustomed ways of leaving people severely alone and expecting them to leave him alone.

But he discovered after long weeks of this that being left alone was . . . lonely. Worse than that, he realized that if his self-imposed solitude continued, he would soon end up as insane as poor Anja.

Fortunately, Simkin had returned at this time from one of his frequent and mysterious disappearances. Acting some say upon a suggestion of Blachloch's, Simkin appeared on Joram's doorstep, introduced himself, and moved in before the morose young man could utter a word. Joram, intrigued and amused by the older youth's conversation, allowed Simkin to stay. Simkin, in turn, introduced Joram to the world.

"You have a gift, dear boy," said Simkin banteringly to Joram one night. "Don't scowl. Your face will freeze like that someday and you'll spend all of your life frightening dogs and small children. Now, about this gift, I'm serious. I've seen it at court. Your mother was *Albanara*, right? They're born with this ability, charisma, charm, whatever you want to call it. Now, of course, you have all the charm of a pile of rocks, but stay with me and you'll learn. Why should you bother? you ask. The best reason in the world. Because, dear boy, you can make people do anything you want. . . ."

Venturing out into his small world, Joram found, to his surprise and pleasure, that what Simkin said was true. Perhaps it was the "noble blood," the hereditary abilities of the *Albanara* that ran in his veins, perhaps it was nothing more than the fact that he was educated. Whatever the reason, Joram discovered the ability to manipulate people, to use them and still keep them at a comfortable distance from himself.

The one person this failed to work upon was Mosiah. Although he had been extremely glad to see his longtime friend when the young man came into camp, Joram resented Mosiah's continued attempts to break apart the carefully crafted stone exterior of his being. Simkin entertained Joram. Mosiah demanded something in return for his friendship.

Back off, Joram often thought in exasperation. *Back off and let me breathe!*

Despite this, Joram was more truly content among these people than he had once thought possible. Although he still had to keep up the pretext of possessing a certain amount of magic, he was able to do this easily with his sleight-of-hand illusions. There were others in this camp who had failed the Testing, and he wasn't made to feel like a freak or an outcast.

Through hard, physical labor, he had grown strong and muscular. Some of the bitterness and anger that scarred his face was eased, though the slashing black brows and the dark, brooding eyes made many uncomfortable in his presence. The beautiful black, shining hair was generally unkempt and tangled, there being no Anja to comb it for Joram every night. But he refused to cut it, wearing it in a long thick braid that extended down his broad back, almost to his waist.

He enjoyed his work in the iron forge, as well. Shaping the shapeless ore into useful tools and weapons gave him the satisfaction he imagined other men must feel when they summoned the magic. In fact, Joram became fascinated by Technology. He spent hours listening to Andon tell of the legends of the ancient days when the Sorcerers of the Ninth Mystery had ruled the world with their terrible and wonderful engines and machines. Through some mysterious means, the young man was able to discover the location of the hidden texts that had been written after the Iron Wars by those who fled the persecution. Intrigued with the wonders described, Joram fumed that so much had been lost.

"We could rule the world again if we had such things!" he told Mosiah more than once, his thoughts always turning to this direction in the feverish, talkative state that followed his black periods of melancholia. "A powder, fine as sand, that could blast down walls; engines that hurled balls of molten fire—"

"Death!" cried Mosiah, aghast. "That's what you are talking about, Joram. Engines of Death. That is why the Technologists were banished."

"Banished by whom? The catalysts! Because they feared us!" Joram retorted. "As for death, people die at the hands of the War Masters, the *DKarn-Duuk*, or, worse, they're mutated, changed beyond recognition. But just think, Mosiah, think what we could do if we combined magic and technology . . ."

"Blachloch's thinking of it," Mosiah muttered. "There's our ruler, Joram. A renegade warlock."

"Maybe . . ." Joram murmured thoughtfully with that strange half-smile in his eyes. "Maybe not. . . ."

Joram had made a discovery in one of the ancient books. It was this discovery that led him to work late nights in the forge with such frustrating results. He lacked the key yet to complete understanding. That was why his experiment had failed. But now he thought he might have found it in an unlikely place — the catalyst. At last he had an idea what those strange symbols were in the text. They were numbers. The key was mathematics.

But now Joram was torn. He hated the catalyst. With Saryon came the bitter memories — Anja's stories, the stone statue, the knowledge that he was Dead, the knowledge that he had murdered. His peaceful life was shattered. Old dreams returned to plague him, the black moods threatened once more to engulf him in their madness. When the catalyst first arrived, he had thought more than once of ending the man's life as he had so easily ended another's. Often he found himself standing, a large, smooth stone in his hand, remembering how easy it had been. He recalled clearly how it had felt to hurl the stone, how it had sounded when it struck the man's head.

But he did not kill the catalyst. The reason being, he told himself, that he discovered the man knew mathematics. A plan began to take shape within Joram, becoming as sharp and strong as the iron blades he hammered.

The catalyst would be of use to him. Joram smiled inwardly. The catalyst would grant *him* Life — of a sort. I'll have to wait and see what type of man he is, Joram said to himself. Weak and ignorant, like Tolban, or does he have something more in him? One thing was in the catalyst's favor — the man had, surprisingly, been honest with him. Not that Joram trusted him. The young man almost laughed at the absurdity. No, he did not trust the catalyst, but he allowed him a grudging respect.

The true test would come soon. Joram was waiting, along with nearly everyone else in the group of bandits, to see how Saryon would react when Blachloch ordered him to help rob the villagers.

"Do you think what we're doing is right?" Mosiah asked one night as they lay on a pile of dead, wet leaves beneath a tree. Even wrapped in their blankets, it seemed impossible to keep warm.

"What's right?" muttered Joram, trying unsuccessfully to get comfortable.

"Taking food . . . from these people."

"So you've been talking to that pious old man again?" Joram asked, sneering.

"It's not that," Mosiah returned. Propping himself up on one elbow, he turned to face his friend, who was nothing more than a black shapeless form in the starless, moonless darkness. "I've been thinking about it myself. These people are like us, Joram. They're like my father and mother and your mother." He ignored a sudden angry, rustling sound. "You remember how hard winters were. What if bandits had stolen from us?"

"It would have been our tough luck, just like it'll be theirs," Joram said coldly. "It's us or them. We have to have food."

"We could trade for it . . ."

"What? Arrowtips? Daggers? Spearheads? The tools of the Ninth Mystery? Do you think those farmers would barter with Sorcerers who have sold their souls to the Powers of Darkness? Hah! They'd sooner die than feed us."

The conversation ended, Joram rolling over and refusing to talk, Mosiah hearing those last, disturbing words echo in his head.

They'd sooner die. . . .

3

The Raid

A strong, chill wind blowing from the ocean swept apart the storm clouds, blowing them back southward into the Outland. The rain stopped and the sun appeared, its meager autumn warmth doing little, however, to counter the cutting cold of the wind through wet clothing. The men's spirits did not rise. With the cessation of the rain, Blachloch pushed them forward rapidly, sometimes riding into the evening hours if the night was clear. The thick stands of oak and walnut trees of the Outland gave way to pines. The riders grew more cautious, for they were nearing the borders of civilized lands. Stopping at last on the banks of the river, they made camp and then spent three days cutting trees and lashing logs together to form crude flatboats.

The catalyst was kept busy giving Life to the men to enable them to complete the work swiftly. He did as he was told, though he watched the building of the boats with increasing despondency, In his mind, he could already see them loaded with booty, ready to be transported upriver back to the settlement.

At last the boats were finished, and there came a night without a moon. The wind blew stronger and fiercer, buffeting Blachloch's men as they mounted their horses. Riding swiftly, their black cloaks billowing in the gusts like the sails of a ghostly armada, the bandits swept down upon the village of Dunam, intending to strike them in the evening when, worn out from their long labors in the fields, the magi were settling down to rest.

On the outskirts of the village, Blachloch reined in his horse, calling a halt. Open land stretched out before them, fields already harvested, lying fallow. Stacked at the far end were the disks used by the Ariels to transport the fruits of the harvest to the landowner's granaries. Seeing these, the men grinned at each other. They were in time.

The wind blew chill from the ocean waters to the north, carrying with it, even at that distance, a faint, salty tang. Facing into the biting wind, the horses shook their heads, setting the harnesses to jingling, and causing a few of the more skittish to shift nervously in place. Their riders, no more comfortable than their mounts, muffled up to the eyebrows in thick cloaks still damp from the soaking ride, sat stolidly in a line awaiting the orders that would send them into action.

Sitting apart from them, alone, hunched in his green cloak, Saryon shivered from fear and the cold, the credo of his upbringing ringing in his ears, its irony twisting in his bowels.

Obedire est vivere. Vivere est obedire.

"Catalyst, to my side."

The words were not heard so much as they penetrated Saryon's mind. Gripping the reins in his shaking hand, the catalyst rode forward.

"To obey is to live . . ."

Where was the Almin? Where was his God at this desperate time? Back in the Font, probably, attending Evening Prayers. Certainly He was not in this wild and windswept night, riding with bandits.

"To live is to obey. . . ."

Riding forward, Saryon was dimly aware of a face turned to look at him. His hood dragged back, the young man was barely visible in the bright starlight. But the catalyst recognized Mosiah, looking troubled and distraught. The dark shrouded figure beside him would undoubtedly be Joram. Saryon caught a glimpse of the young man's eyes behind a tangle of matted hair, staring at him with cool, appraising speculation. Muffled laughter came from behind the two along with a bright flash of color — Simkin.

Seemingly of its own volition, Saryon's horse carried him past the young men, past the rows of waiting, grim-faced Sorcerers and their nervous mounts up to the front of the line. Here Blachloch sat upon his steed — a thick-bodied charger.

The moment had come. Half-turning in the saddle, the warlock looked at Saryon. Blachloch did not speak, his face remained impassive, expressionless, but the catalyst felt courage drain from him as surely as if the warlock had slit his throat. Saryon bowed his head and, at that, Blachloch smiled for the first time.

"I am glad we understand each other, Father. You have been trained in the art of warfare?"

"It was a long time ago," Saryon said in a low voice.

"Yes, I can imagine. Do not worry. This will soon be over, I think." Turning around, Blachloch spoke a few words to one of his guards, apparently going over last-minute instructions. Saryon did not listen, he could not hear for the wind and the blood pounding in his head.

The warlock rode forward; a gesture brought the catalyst to ride beside him.

"The important thing to remember, Catalyst," Blachloch murmured, "is to keep to my left and stand slightly behind me. Thus I can shield you if need be. I want to see you out of the corner of my eye, however, so make certain to keep within my visual range. And, Father" — Blachloch smiled again, a smile that sent a shudder through the catalyst — "I know that you have the ability to drain Life as well as give it. A dangerous maneuver, but one not unheard of if the catalyst feels like avenging himself upon his wizard. Do not try it with me."

There was no threat, the words were spoken in an expressionless, even tone. But the last tiny flicker of hope within the catalyst died. Not that it had ever burned very brightly. Draining the Life from Blachloch would leave

Saryon at the mercy of the Sorcerers, for such an action drains the catalyst as well. And, as Blachloch said, it was extremely dangerous. A powerful wizard could shut off the conduit, then deal swift retribution to his attacker. Still, it had been a chance, and now it was gone.

Had Bishop Vanya considered this? Had he known Saryon was going to be forced into committing these vile crimes? Surely Vanya had never intended it to go this far! Even if he had lied to him, there must be some reason, some purpose . . .

"Hail, strangers in the night," came a voice.

Saryon started so that he nearly fell from his saddle. Blachloch reined in his horse and the catalyst hastily did likewise, positioning himself, as the warlock had instructed, to Blachloch's left and slightly behind.

Glancing around, the catalyst saw that while he had been lost in his dark thoughts, they had ridden into the village. Light shone from the windows of the shaped stone homes where the Field Magi lived. It was a large settlement, Saryon noticed, larger than Walren. Hope rose again. Surely Blachloch with his small band of thirty or so would never dream of attacking a village that must have at least a hundred magi.

The door of one of the dwellings had opened and a man stood there, outlined in firelight that glowed softly behind him. He was tall and muscular, Saryon could see. Undoubtedly the overseer, it was he who had called out the greeting.

"Catalyst," the man shouted. "We have visitors."

The door to the stone dwelling next to his opened and another man stepped out — a catalyst by his green robes. As he hurried to take his place beside the overseer, Saryon saw the catalyst's face reflected in the light. He was young, probably no more than a Deacon. This must be his first assignment.

The overseer peered into the night, trying to see who rode into his village at this hour. He was wary, cautious. Blachloch had not spoken nor had he replied to the hail as was customary.

We must look like nothing more than black windows cut into the night, Saryon realized. Then he felt a cold hand touch his wrist and he blenched, his stomach quaking.

"Grant me Life, Catalyst."

The words were not spoken, they reverberated through Saryon's head. Closing his eyes, he blotted out the lights of the hovels, the puzzled, suspicious face of the overseer, and the tense face of the young catalyst. I could lie, he thought desperately. I could say I am too weak, too frightened to sense the magic . . .

The cold hand tightened its grip painfully. With a shudder, feeling the magic rise from the ground, from the night, from the wind, and flow through him, Saryon opened the conduit.

The magic surged from him to Blachloch.

"I said 'Hail, stranger.'" The overseer's voice grew gruff. "Are you lost? Where do you ride from and where are you bound?"

"I ride from the Outland," Blachloch said, "and this is my destination."

"The Outland?" The overseer folded his arms across his chest. "Then you can turn around and ride back to that god-cursed territory. We want none of your kind around here. Go on, get out of here. Catalyst —"

But the young Deacon was quick-thinking, opening a conduit to the overseer before he asked.

By this time the sound of talking had roused other villagers living nearby. Some looked out of windows, several of the men came to their doors, and a few stepped into the roadway.

Sitting calmly on his steed, Blachloch might have been waiting for this audience, for he smiled again, as if in gratification.

"I said, Begone!" the overseer began, taking a step forward.

Blachloch removed his hand from Saryon's arm, breaking the conduit so swiftly that the catalyst gasped as some of the magical power surged back through him.

Pointing his hand at the overseer, Blachloch whispered one word. The overseer began to glow with an eerie aura that surrounded his body, giving off a faint greenish glow — the magus was of the Mystery of Earth. The aura grew brighter and stronger, and by its light, Saryon saw the overseer's face contort in astonishment, then fear, as he realized what was happening to him. The light was his own magic, his own Life. When the glow died, the man's body slumped to the ground.

Saryon's throat constricted, he could not breathe. All his life he had heard of the terrible power of Nullmagic, but he had never seen it used. The overseer was not dead, but he might as well have been. He lay on his doorstoop, more helpless than a newborn child. Until the spell was reversed or until such time as he might train his body to live without the magic, he would be able to do nothing but stare about him in impotent fury, his arms and legs twitching feebly.

Several of the magi were running toward their overseer, shouting in alarm. Kneeling beside the fallen man, the young Deacon raised his head to look at Blachloch. Saryon saw the catalyst's eyes widen in fear, his lips open in a plea, a protest, a prayer . . .

Blachloch moved his hand again, spoke again. This time there was no light, no sound. The spell was swift and efficient. Compressed air slammed into the young catalyst like an ocean wave, surging over him, smashing his body up against the stone wall of the overseer's house.

The shouts of alarm became anger and outrage. Sickened and horrified, Saryon swayed in the saddle, the lights of the village swam about him, the shadows leaped and danced in his dazed vision. He saw Blachloch raise his hand, saw it burn with flame and heard the answering sounds of horses' hooves thudding behind him. The band was riding to the attack. He had the vague impression that some of the Field Magi appeared ready to fight Blachloch with their own magic, weakened though it might be after a day in the fields, when the warlock lifted his fiery hand and pointed.

A dwelling place burst into an inferno of flame. Sounds of screaming came from within, a woman and several children rushed outside, their clothes ablaze. The Field Magi stopped, hesitating, fear and confusion replacing the anger on their faces. A few came nearer, a few turned, stumbling, to help the victims of the fire. But there were two who kept coming toward Blachloch and Saryon, one already raising his hands, calling upon the forces of the earth to aid him. His eyes were on Saryon, who could not move.

He found himself hoping bitterly that the man would smite him down where he sat. But Blachloch, without undue haste, moved his hand slightly, pointing to another shack. It, too, burst into flame.

"I can destroy this entire village in minutes," he said in his expressionless voice to the approaching magi. "Cast your spell. If you know anything of the *Duuk-tsarith* you know that I can protect both myself and my catalyst from it. And where will you get the energy to cast another? Your catalyst is dead. Mine lives." Extending his hand to Saryon, he said, "Catalyst, grant me Life."

Obedire est vivere.

Saryon still could not move. In a dreamlike horror, he looked from the magi to the body of the young Deacon lying in the doorway beside the helpless overseer.

Blachloch did not turn, he did not look at Saryon. He merely repeated.

"Catalyst, grant me Life."

Again, there was no threat made, not even in the tone. Yet Saryon knew he would be made to pay for his lapse in duty. Blachloch never gave an order twice.

Obedire est vivere.

And he had no doubt the price would be high.

"No," said Saryon softly and steadily, "I will not do it."

"Well, well," Joram murmured, "the old man has more guts than I'd imagined."

"What?" Mosiah, his face pale and strained, was staring at the burning homes of the Field Magi with wide eyes. Dazedly he turned to Joram. "What did you say?"

"Look." Joram pointed to where the warlock sat astride his horse not far from them, the two young men having ridden in the vanguard. "The catalyst. He's refused Blachloch's command for more Life."

"He'll kill him!" Mosiah whispered in horror.

"No, Blachloch's smarter than that. He won't kill his only catalyst. Still, I'll bet the man will soon wish he was dead."

Mosiah put his hand to his head. "This is dreadful, Joram," he said thickly. "I had no idea— I didn't know it would be like this . . . I'm leaving!" He started to turn his horse.

"Get hold of yourself!" Joram snapped, grasping his friend's arm and jerking him back sharply. "You can't run! The villagers might attack us . . ."

"I hope they do!" Mosiah shouted furiously. "I hope they kill you all. Let go of me, Joram!"

"Where will you go? Think!" Joram held onto him with the firm grip of the iron forge.

"I can get into the woods!" Mosiah hissed, trying to twist free. "I'll hide there until you're gone. Then I'll come back here, do what I can for these people —"

"They'll turn you over to the Enforcers," snarled Joram through clenched teeth, maintaining his grip on his friend with difficulty. Their horses, alarmed by the fire and the smoke, the yelling and the young men's struggles, were milling round and round, churning up the ground with their hooves. "Listen to reason — Wait —" He glanced up. "Look, your catalyst . . ."

Mosiah turned, his gaze following Joram's in time to see two of Blachloch's henchmen drag Saryon from his horse and hurl him to the ground. Staggering, Saryon tried to stand, but two other men, at a gesture from the warlock, leaped from their horses, grabbed hold of the catalyst, and held him, arms pinned behind his back. Seeing his commands being obeyed, Blachloch cast a last glance at the catalyst, saying something to him Joram could not hear. Then the warlock galloped off, yelling more commands to his men and gesturing toward a large building where the crops were stored. As he passed, other huts burst into flame, lighting the night like a dreadful sun fallen to earth.

All around Joram and Mosiah, the bandits rode to do their commander's bidding, some heading for the granary, others keeping watch on the Field Magi, some of whom were fleeing in terror, others were trying in vain to save their homes from the magical fires. But Joram's and Mosiah's attention was on the men holding Saryon.

By the light of the burning dwellings, Joram saw a hand clench, then he heard the sound of a fist thudding into flesh. The catalyst doubled over with a groan, but the guard who held him hauled him upright. The attacker's next blow smashed into Saryon's head. His face suddenly dark with blood, the catalyst's choked cry was cut off as the guard drove his fist once again into the priest's stomach.

"My god!" whispered Mosiah. Feeling his friend's body stiffen, Joram turned to him in alarm. Mosiah's face had gone ashen, sweat stood on his forehead, and he was staring at the catalyst with white-rimmed eyes. Looking back, Joram saw the catalyst slumped in his captor's grasp, moaning, flinching as more blows landed on the unresisting body with ruthless efficiency.

"No! Don't— Are you mad?" Joram shouted, hanging onto Mosiah. "They'll do worse to you if you interfere . . ."

But he might have been talking to the air. Giving his friend a bitter, angry look, Mosiah kicked his horse violently in the ribs and dashed forward, nearly dragging Joram out of his saddle in his wild plunge.

"Damn!" Joram swore, searching around for help to try to catch Mosiah.

"I say," came a lilting voice in his ear, "grand conflagration this. I'm quite enjoying myself. What about toodling over to the granary and watching them load sacks— Almin's blood, what's the matter, dear boy?"

"Shut up and come on!" Joram shouted, gesturing. "Look!"

"More jollity," said Simkin with enthusiasm, riding after Joram. "I'd completely missed that. What *are* they doing to our poor catalytic friend?"

"He refused one of Blachloch's commands," Joram said grimly, urging his excited horse to a gallop. "And look, there's Mosiah! Going to get himself mixed up into this."

"I feel I should point out that from the looks of things, Mosiah is *already* mixed up in this," panted Simkin, jouncing along behind as he tried to keep up. "Now, I enjoy beating up a catalyst as much as the next man, but Blachloch's boys seem to be having quite a good time and I don't think they'd appreciate us horning in on their sport— Almin's blood and brains! What *is* our friend doing?"

Leaping off his horse, Mosiah had hurled himself bodily at the man who was beating Saryon, knocking the henchmen to the ground. As the two went down in a struggling heap, the other guard, who had been holding Saryon while his companion inflicted the blows, flung the catalyst to one side.

Conjuring up a huge branch in his hand, the guard started to smash it down on the young man's head.

"Mosiah!" Joram called, sliding off his horse and dashing madly toward them. But he knew, with an aching in his heart that startled him, that he must be too late. The blow was falling that would split the young man's skull. Then Joram stopped, staring in astonishment as a brick appeared out of nowhere, materializing in the air right above the guard's head.

"I say, take that!" shouted the brick. Dropping down, it rapped the guard smartly on the head, then tumbled into the grass. The guard took a staggering step, swayed drunkenly, and keeled over, landing on top of the brick.

Jumping forward, Joram grabbed hold of Mosiah, who had his hands around the guard's throat.

"Let him go!" Joram grunted, wrenching his friend from his victim. The man rolled over, gasping for air. Struggling to escape Joram's hold, Mosiah lashed out with a booted foot and kicked the guard in the head. The guard lay still.

"He's finished! Leave him alone!" Joram ordered Mosiah, shaking him. "Listen! We've got to get out of here!"

Glancing up at his friend, his eyes burning with blood-lust, Mosiah shook his head dazedly. "Saryon," he gasped, wiping blood from a cut lip.

"Oh, for the love of —" Joram began in disgust. "There he is, but I think he's past helping." He gestured to the catalyst's inert body, which was lying crumpled on the grass. "Get him on a horse then, if you insist. Damn it, where the devil's Simkin . . ."

"Help!" shouted a muffled voice. "Joram! Get this cad off me! I'm suffocating from the stench!"

Seeing Mosiah bending over the catalyst, Joram reached down and grabbed the henchman by his collar, heaving the man off the brick. The brick disappeared, transforming itself into Simkin. Holding a bit of orange silk over his nose, the young man stood staring down at the henchman in disgust.

"Egad, the lout! I'm quite nauseated. Where's Mosiah and the jolly old catalyst? . . ." Looking around, Simkin's eyes widened. "Oh, I say." He gave a low whistle. "Here comes trouble."

"Blachloch!" Joram muttered, seeing the black-robed figure approaching through the smoke and flame. "Simkin! Use your magic. Get us out of here — Simkin?"

The young man was gone. In Joram's hand was a blood-spattered brick.

4

Prisoners

"**F**ather . . ."

Saryon started, roused from some dark dream that seemed loath to let him loose from its clutches.

"Father," said the voice again. "Can you hear me? How are you feeling?"

"I can't see!" Saryon moaned, clutching at the source of the voice with groping hands.

"It's because of the gloom in this foul place, Father," said the voice gently. "We feared light might disturb your rest. Here, now, can you see?" The soft glow of a single candle illuminated Andon's kindly face, and brought inestimable relief to the catalyst.

Sinking back on the hard bed, Saryon put his hand to his head where he felt a heaviness. Something was obscuring his vision in his left eye. He tried to pull it off, but Andon's hand intercepted his.

"Don't disturb the bandages, Father," he instructed, holding the candle above Saryon, examining him by its light.

"The bleeding will start again. It will be best for you to lie quietly for a few days. Is there pain anywhere else?" he asked, a shadow of anxiety in his voice.

"My ribs," answered the catalyst.

"But not the stomach, the back?" Andon pursued.

Wearily, Saryon shook his head.

"Thank the Almin," murmured the old man. "And now I must ask you some questions. What is your name?"

"Saryon," answered the catalyst. "But you know that . . ."

"You have had a severe head injury, Father. How much do you remember of what happened?"

The dreams. Had they been dreams at all? "I—I remember the village, the young Deacon . . ." Shuddering, Saryon covered his face. "He slaughtered him, using my help! What have I done?"

"I did not mean to distress you, Father," Andon said gently. Setting the candle on the floor by his feet, he placed his hand on the catalyst's shoulder. "You did what you had to do. None of us thought Blachloch would go this far. But that is neither here nor there at the moment. Do you remember anything else, Father?"

Saryon searched his memory, but it was all flame and pain and darkness and terror. Seeing the catalyst's agonized face, the old man patted his shoulder and sighed. "I am truly sorry, Father. Thank the Almin you are safe."

"What happened to me?" Saryon asked.

"Blachloch had you beaten for disobeying him. His men were . . . overzealous. They would have killed you, if it had not been for him." Andon turned, his gaze going to another part of the dark room.

Slowly, conscious now of a dull aching in his head, Saryon followed Andon's glance. A young man sat on a chair beside a crude window, his head resting on his arms, his eyes staring out into the night sky. A half-moon shed its pale, cold light upon the face, emphasizing with sharply defined shadows the stern, sullen harshness, the heavy black brows, the full-lipped, unsmiling mouth. Black, curling hair shown purple in the moonlight, falling in a tangle around the young man's broad shoulders.

"Joram!" Saryon breathed in astonishment.

"I must admit, I was as amazed as you, Father," Andon said, speaking softly, though it appeared as if the young man was completely oblivious to their presence. "Joram has never seemed to care for anyone before, not even his friends. He did not even taken a stand against Blachloch's wickedness when I tried to talk to him about it. He said the world cared nothing for us, why should we care what happened to it." Shrugging helplessly, Andon seemed perplexed. "But according to Simkin, when Joram saw you being beaten, he hurled himself into the fray, wounding one guard severely. Mosiah helped rescue you, too, I believe."

"Mosiah. . . . Is he all right?" Saryon asked anxiously.

"Yes, he is fine. Nothing happened to him. A warning to mind his own business, that is all."

"Where are we?" Saryon asked, examining his bleak surroundings as well as the dim light and the pain in his head permitted. He was in a small, filthy brick building, no bigger than a single room with one window and a thick, oaken door.

"You and Joram are being held prisoner. Blachloch put you both in here together, saying that there was something going on between the two of you and he intended to find out what."

"This is the village prison. . . ." Saryon remembered vaguely having seen it on one of his walks.

"Yes. You are back in the settlement. They carried you here by boat up the river with the stolen supplies. May they choke on them," the old man muttered.

Saryon glanced at him in some surprise.

"My followers and I have taken a vow," Andon said softly. "We will not eat the food that they wrested from those unfortunate people. We would sooner starve."

"It is my fault. . . ." Saryon murmured.

"No, Father." The old man sighed and shook his head. "If it is anyone's fault it is ours, we Sorcerers. We should have stopped him when he came to us five years ago. We let him intimidate us. Or maybe it wasn't even that so much, although it is a comfort to look back and say we were frightened of him. But were we? I wonder." Andon's wrinkled hand lifted from Saryon's shoulder, going to the pendant of the wheel that hung around his neck. Fingering it absently, he stared into the flickering light of the candle that sat upon the stone floor near his feet. "I think that, in truth, we welcomed him. It was satisfying, to strike back at the world that reviled us." His mouth twisted bitterly. "Even if it was only stealing a few bushels of grain by night.

"His talk of supplying weapons of our Dark Arts to Sharakan seemed a fine thing, once." Andon's eyes glimmered with unshed tears, the rims grew red. "The legends tell much about the ancient days, about the glories of our art. Not all was evil. Much that was good and beneficial was developed by those of the Ninth Mystery. If we could just have a chance to show people what wonders we could build, how we could save the use of magical energies, allowing those to be devoted to the creation of beautiful, marvelous things . . . Ah well, such was our dream," he said wistfully. "And now it has been perverted by this evil man into a nightmare! He has led us to our doom. The destruction of that village will not be allowed to go unpunished. At least that is what *I* believe. Blachloch laughs at me when I tell him my fears. Or rather, he doesn't laugh, the man never laughs. But he might as well. I can see the scorn in his eyes."

"'They dare not seek us out,' he tells me."

"He may be right," Saryon muttered, thinking of Bishop Vanya's words. *The Sorcerers numbers are growing and, while we could deal with them easily enough, still, going in to take the young man by force would mean armed conflict. It would mean talk, upset, worry. We cannot have that, not now, while the political situation in court is in such delicate balance.* "What are his plans?"

The catalyst shivered. The prison was chill. A small fire flickered in a firepit at the end of the room, giving little light and less warmth.

"He intends us to work through the winter, making weapons. In the meantime, he will pursue his negotiations with Sharakan." Andon shrugged. "If we *are* attacked, Sharakan will come to our defense, he says."

"But it all means war," Saryon said thoughtfully, his gaze going once again to Joram, who was still staring fixedly out the window into the moonlit night. Once again, he heard Vanya's words. *Thus you see how vital it is that we take this young man and, through him, expose these fiends for what they are — murderers and black-hearted Sorcerers who would pervert Dead objects by giving them Life. By doing this, we can show the people of Sharakan that their Emperor is in league with the powers of darkness, and we can then encompass his downfall.*

But it wasn't the Sorcerers. He looked back at Andon, an old man with a dream of bringing waterwheels to the world so that magic could be used to create rainbows instead of rain. He looked at Joram. He had come to think of this young man differently, too, now that he knew him.

He is not a spawn of demons as I had imagined him. Confused, bitter, unhappy, certainly, but so was I in my youth. He committed murder, that is true. But what provocation! His mother, lying dead before him. And am I any better? Closing his eyes, Saryon shook his head restlessly. Am I not responsible for the death of that young catalyst? If I take Joram back as I was instructed to do, will I bring about the downfall of these people? What must I do? Where can I find help?

"I will leave now, Father," Andon said, picking up his candle and rising. "You are tired. I have been selfish in worrying you with my troubles when you have enough of your own. We will put our faith in the Almin and ask for His help and guidance. . . ."

"The Almin!" Saryon repeated bitterly, sitting up. "No, I'm all right. Just a little dizzy." He swung his feet over the edge of the bed, waving off Andon's offer of help and ignoring his worried cluckings. "You talk as if you knew the Almin personally!"

"But I do, Father," Andon replied, glancing at the catalyst in some embarrassment. Setting the candle on a crude wooden table in the center of the prison, the old man knelt down and did what he could to stir up the fire, using his magic to add to the warmth. "I know that we are supposed to talk to Him only through you priests, and I hope what I say will not offend you. But it has been many, many years since a catalyst was among us to intercede with the Almin in our behalf. He and I have shared many problems. He is our refuge in these troubled times. His guidance led us to take the vow that we will not eat food gained by blood and flame."

Saryon gazed at the old man in perplexity. "He speaks to you? He answers your prayers?"

"I realize I am not a catalyst," Andon said humbly, fingering the pendant around his neck as he stood up, "but, yes, He communicates with me. Oh, not in words. I do not hear His voice. But a feeling of peace fills my soul when I know that I have made a decision, and I know then that I have received His guidance."

A feeling of peace, Saryon thought despondently. I have experienced religious fervor, ecstacy, the Enchantment, but never peace. Did He ever talk to me? Did I ever listen?

The catalyst groaned. His head ached, his body hurt. Memories of flame danced in his vision, he could see clearly the look of fear on the young Deacon's face right before Blachloch —

"The Almin give you rest." There was the sound of a door closing softly. Saryon shook his head to clear it of the fuzziness and instantly regretted the action that only caused the aching to change to a swift, sharp pain. When he was able to look around, he saw that Andon was gone.

Standing on unsteady feet, Saryon tottered across the room and sagged into a chair at the table. He knew he should probably lie back down but he was frightened, afraid to close his eyes again, afraid of what he would see.

A pitcher of water made him realize he was terribly thirsty. Reaching out an unsteady hand, trying to combat the dizziness that threatened to overwhelm him, he was going to pour water into a cup that sat nearby when a voice startled him.

"They will starve to death this winter, the fools."

Nearly dropping the pitcher, Saryon turned to Joram, who had not spoken a word the entire time Andon had been in the prison.

The young man did not move from his place beside the window. His back was to Saryon now, since the catalyst had risen from his bed on the other side of the room. But Saryon could picture the brown eyes staring into the moonlight, the sullen face.

"And, Catalyst," Joram continued coldly, still not turning around, "I did *not* save your life. They could beat the whole lot of you, and I wouldn't lift a finger to stop them."

"Then, what happened? Why —"

"More of Simkin's lies," Joram said, shrugging his shoulders. "The soft-hearted, soft-headed Mosiah rushed in to save your precious skin, and I went to get him out of it. It was none of our affair, after all, if you were stupid enough to defy Blachloch. Then Simkin — But, what does it matter?"

"What did Simkin have to do with it?" Saryon asked, trying to pour the water into the cup and slopping most of it over the table.

"What does Simkin ever have to do with anything?" Joram replied. "Nothing. Everything. He got Mosiah off, which was more than the idiot deserved."

"What about you?"

Throwing his arm indolently over the back of the chair, Joram turned back to face the catalyst. "What does it matter about me? I'm Dead, Catalyst, or had you forgotten? In fact," he continued, spreading his arms wide, "this is your big chance. Here we are . . . alone. No one to stop you. Open a Corridor. Send for the *Duuk-tsarith*."

Sinking into a chair, feeling his strength give way, Saryon murmured, "You could stop me." He had, in fact, been considering that very idea and was appalled to find the young man had penetrated so far into his mind. "Even the Dead have magic enough to stop a catalyst. I know. I've seen what you can do. . . ."

For long moments, Joram stared at Saryon in silence as though considering something. Then, rising suddenly, he approached the table and leaned down over it, looking directly into the catalyst's pale, drawn face. "Open a conduit to me," he said.

Puzzled, Saryon drew back, reluctant to give this young man any additional strength. "I don't think —"

"Go on!" Joram demanded harshly. Muscles in the young man's arms twitched, the blood veins stood out beneath the brown skin as his hands gripped the edges of the table, the dark eyes flared in the candlelight.

Mesmerized by the suddenly feverish gaze of the young man, Saryon hesitantly opened a conduit to Joram . . . and felt nothing. The magic filled him, tingled in Saryon's blood and his flesh. But it went nowhere. There was no pleasant rush of transference, no surge of energy between the two bodies. . . . Slowly the magic began to seep out of him as he stared at Joram in disbelief.

"But this is impossible," he said, shivering uncontrollably in the chill prison cell. "I have seen you work magic . . ."

"Have you?" Joram asked. Letting go of the table, he stood up straight and folded his arms across his chest. "Or have you seen me do this?" With a sudden movement of his hand, he produced a rag with which he proceeded to mop up the spilled water. Clapping his hands, he made the rag disappear, an ordinary occurrence to Saryon — until he saw the young man pull the damp rag out of a cunningly concealed pocket in his shirt.

"My mother called it sleight-of-hand," Joram said coolly, seeming to enjoy Saryon's discomfiture. "Do you know of it?"

"I have seen it at court," Saryon said, leaning his head on his hand. The dizziness had passed, but the aching in his temples made it difficult to think. "It is a . . . game. . . ." He gestured feebly. "Young . . . people play it."

"I wondered where my mother learned it," Joram said, shrugging. "Well, it is a game that has saved my life. Or perhaps I should say it is a game that *is* my life — all life being a game, according to Simkin." He gazed down upon the catalyst with a sort of bitter triumph. "Now you know my secret, Catalyst. You know what no one else knows about me. You know the truth, something that even my mother couldn't face. I am Dead. Truly Dead. No magic stirs within me at all, less than what is in a corpse, if we believe the legends of the ancient Necromancers, who were able to communicate with the souls of the dead."

"Why have you told me?" Saryon asked through lips so stiff he was barely able to shape the words. A memory came to his aching mind, a memory of one other who had been Dead, truly Dead; one who had failed the Tests utterly as no one has failed them before or since. . . .

Joram leaned down again, close to him. The catalyst found himself cringing away from the touch of the young man as he would have cringed at the touch of dead flesh. No! Saryon told himself, staring at the young man in horror, his mind incapable of handling the rush of thoughts that burst over him in a crashing wave. Feeling himself drowning beneath them, the catalyst banished them, blocked them out. No. It was impossible. The child was dead. Vanya had said so.

The child was dead. The child is dead.

Seeing the catalyst's confusion, Joram drew a little nearer.

"I tell you this, Catalyst, because it would have been only a matter of time before you found out anyway. The longer I stay here, the greater my peril. Oh"—he gestured impatiently—"there are walking Dead among us, yet they have some magic. I am different. Completely, unspeakably, horribly different! Have you any idea, Catalyst, what Blachloch and these people—yes, even the Sorcerers of the Ninth Mystery—would do to me if they found I was truly Dead?"

Saryon could not answer. He could not even comprehend what the young man was talking about. His mind had shut its doors, refusing admittance to these dark and terrifying thoughts.

"You must make a decision, Catalyst," Joram was saying, his voice coming to Saryon as through a dark fog. "You must either take me to the Enforcers now or you will stay with me here and help me."

"Help you?" Saryon blinked in astonishment, this statement jolting his aching brain back to reality. "Help you do what?"

"To stop Blachloch," said Joram coolly, the half-smile shining in his dark eyes.

5

Tempted...

"**I** regret the incident, Father, as I am certain you do," said Blachloch in his expressionless voice. "And now that the punishment has been administered and the lesson learned, we will speak no more of it."

The warlock sat at the wooden table in the prison. Evening's gray and dismal light — the same color as the damp walls — came through the small window, along with a chill wind that rattled the ill-fitting casement, blowing out the candle flame and rendering the meagre fire practically worthless. Standing beside the window, Joram cast a glance at the catalyst. Though bundled in his cloak and his robes, Saryon was gray himself with the cold. Joram smiled inwardly. Clad only in his rough woolen shirt and soft doeskin breeches, the young man leaned against the wall and stared out the cracked window, ignoring both the catalyst and the warlock.

"Does this mean I can return to Andon's?" Saryon asked, his teeth chattering.

Blachloch smoothed the thin blonde mustache upon his upper lip. "No, I am afraid not."

"I am to be kept a prisoner, then."

"Prisoner?" Blachloch raised an eyebrow. "There are no magical spells laid upon this house. You are free to come and to go as you choose. You have visitors. Andon was here last night. The young man"—he gestured toward Joram—"continues to work in the forge daily. With the exception of the guard, who is here for your own protection, this in no way resembles a prison."

"You can't expect us to live in this wretched place during the winter!" Saryon snapped. The cold must be giving the catalyst courage, Joram thought. "We'll freeze."

Blachloch rose to his feet, his black robes falling in soft folds about his body. "By the time winter comes, I am certain you will have proven your loyalty to me, Father, and you can move to quarters more suitable for a man of your age. Not back with Andon." Blachloch's black hood stirred slightly as he moved to depart. "I have often wondered if it was the old man's influence that caused you to defy me. I have, in fact, heard some rumor to the effect that he and his people refuse to eat the food I provided." Joram had the impression the warlock was looking at him. "Starvation is a slow and uncomfortable way to die, as is freezing to death. I trust this rumor is untrue."

His black robes brushing the dirt floor, Blachloch came to stand beside Saryon and laid his hand upon the catalyst's shoulder.

"Grant me Life, Father," he said.

Glancing back, Joram saw the catalyst shudder at the touch of the thin fingers that seemed the embodiment of the biting wind. Involuntarily Saryon sought to free himself and the fingers closed over his shoulder. Bowing his head, the catalyst opened a conduit to the warlock and, suffused with magic, Blachloch vanished from sight.

Clenching his hands into fists, Saryon wrapped his arms close to his body. "The man must be stopped. What help can I give you?" he asked Joram abruptly.

Joram's face showed no reaction to the catalyst's question. But within himself, he was exultant. His plan was progressing. But he must proceed carefully. After all, he thought grimly, he had to lure the man into the ways of the Dark Arts. Giving Saryon one cool, appraising glance, Joram returned to looking out the window, his arms folded across his chest as he leaned against the brick wall. "Is he gone?"

"Who?" Saryon glanced around, startled. "Blachloch?"

"The *Duuk-tsarith* have the power to make themselves invisible. Still, I would suppose you have the power to sense his presence."

"Yes," Saryon replied after a moment's concentration. "He is gone."

Joram nodded and continued leading the unsuspecting catalyst toward darkness. "Simkin told me that you had once read some of the forbidden books about the Ninth Mystery."

"Only one," Saryon admitted, flushing. "And I—I just had a glimpse of it. . . ."

"How much do you know about the Iron Wars?"

"I have read and studied the histories—"

"Histories written by the catalysts!" Joram interrupted coldly. "I knew those histories, too, when I came here. I read the books. Oh, yes"—this in reply to a rustling sound he heard behind him—"I was raised as a child in a noble house. My mother was *Albanara*. But surely you knew that?"

"Yes, I knew. . . . Where did she get the books?" Saryon asked.

"I've wondered," Joram said softly, as if answering some often-asked, inner question. "She was disgraced and outcast. Did she come to her home in the night, traveling the Corridors of time and space? Did she float through the hallways she had known as a child, returning to the site of her lost youth and shattered life like a ghost doomed to haunt the place where it died?"

Joram's face darkened. He fell silent, staring out the window.

"I'm sorry for distressing you—" Saryon began.

"Since then," Joram interrupted coldly, "I have read other books, their information is far different from what we were taught. Always remember, Andon says, it is the winners of the war who write the histories. Did you know, for example, that during the Iron Wars, the Sorcerers developed a weapon that could absorb magic?"

"Absorb magic?" Saryon shook his head. "That's ridiculous. . . ."

"Is it?" Joram turned to look at him. "Think about it, Catalyst. Think about it logically as you are so fond of doing. For every action, there is an opposite and equal reaction, isn't that what you had said?"

"Yes, but —"

"Therefore, it stands to reason that in a world that exudes magic there must be some force that absorbs it as well. So the Sorcerers of long ago reasoned, and they were right. They found it. It exists in nature in a physical form that can be shaped and formed into objects. You don't believe me."

"I am sorry, young man," said Saryon through clenched teeth. He sounded disappointed. "I gave up believing in the House Magi's tales when I was nine."

"Yet you believe in faeries?" Joram said, regarding the catalyst with the strange half-smile that rarely touched his lips, only the brown eyes.

"I was with Simkin," Saryon muttered, flushing. Drawing as near the fire as possible, he hunched down over it. "When I'm around him, I'm not certain whether I believe in myself, much less anything else."

"Yet you saw them? You talked to them?"

"Yes," Saryon admitted grudgingly. "I saw them . . ."

"Now you see this."

Joram plucked the object from the air — so it appeared — and laid it on the table before the catalyst. Picking it up, Saryon regarded the object suspiciously.

"A rock?"

"An ore. It is called darkstone."

"It seems similar to iron, but what a strange color," Saryon said, studying it.

"You've a good eye, Catalyst," said Joram, pushing a chair over with his foot and seating himself at the table. Picking up the other small piece of rock, he studied it himself, frowning. "It has many of the same properties as iron. But it is different." His voice grew bitter. "Vastly different, as I have reason to know. What knowledge do you have of iron, Catalyst? I wouldn't have thought you had much to do with ores."

"If you do not want to call me by my proper title, which is 'Father,' I wish you would call me by my name," said Saryon gently. "Perhaps that would remind you that I am a person like yourself. It is always easier to hate than it is to love, still more easy to hate a class or race of people because they are faceless and nameless. If you are going to hate me, I prefer that you do it because you hate *me*, not what I represent."

"Keep your sermons for Mosiah," Joram answered. "What I think of you or you of me doesn't matter in this, does it?"

Seeing Joram's lip curl in disdain, Saryon sighed and looked back at the small stone he held in his hand. "Yes, I studied ores," he said. "We study all the elements of which our world is composed. It is knowledge valuable in and of itself, plus it is knowledge that is useful and necessary to those of our Order who work with the *Pron-alban*, the Stone Shapers, or the *Mon-alban*, the Alchemists." Saryon's brow creased in puzzlement. "But I don't recall seeing or reading about any mineral that looked like this, particularly one with the same properties as iron."

"That's because all references to it were purged after the wars," Joram said, regarding the catalyst hungrily, his hands twitching as though he would tear knowledge from the man's heart. "Why? Because the Sorcerers used it to form weapons, weapons of tremendous power, weapons that could —"

"— absorb magic," Saryon murmured, staring at the stone. "I'm beginning to believe you. Inside the Chamber of the Ninth Mystery, there are books scattered about the floor and stacked in piles against the walls. Books of ancient and forbidden knowledge."

Watching the catalyst intently, Joram saw that Saryon had forgotten the chill wind that wailed mournfully through the window, that the catalyst had forgotten his own fear and discomfort and unhappiness. Joram looked into his eyes and saw there the same hunger he knew was in his own — the hunger for knowledge. The words came almost reluctantly from Saryon's lips: "How did they do it?"

I have him, thought Joram. Once, the man came close to selling his soul for knowledge. This time I will see to it that he completes the bargain.

"According to the texts," Joram said, careful to speak calmly and suppress his rising excitement, "the ancients mixed darkstone with iron to form an alloy —"

"What?" Saryon interrupted.

"An alloy, a mixture of two or more metals."

"Was this done by alchemy?" Saryon asked, a note of fear in his voice. "By changing the base form of the metal through magic?"

"No." Joram shook his head, noticing the catalyst's increasing pallor with amusement. "No. It is done according to the rituals of the Dark Arts, Catalyst. The ores are ground, heated to their melting points, then physically joined together. They are then cast in molds, beaten and tempered, and formed into swords or daggers. Quite deadly"— Joram's gaze went back to the stone he held in his hand — "as you can imagine. First the sword drains a wizard of his magic, then is able to penetrate his flesh."

Beside him, Joram felt the catalyst's body shudder. Saryon set the stone down hastily. "You have tried this?" he asked in a low, trembling voice.

"Yes," Joram answered coldly. "It didn't work. I formed the alloy and poured it into a mold. But the dagger I created shattered when I put it into water . . ."

Closing his eyes, Saryon sighed. It may have been with relief, certainly that's what he told himself. But the young man watching closely wondered if there was not an underlying tinge of disappointment.

"Perhaps this rock is nothing more than some strange-looking stone," Saryon said after a moment. "Perhaps it is not the ore you read about in the texts. Or perhaps the texts themselves lied. You would not be able to tell if it could absorb magic —" He hesitated.

"— since I am Dead," finished Joram. "No, you are right." He pushed the ore across the table toward the catalyst. "Yet you should be able to tell. Try it, Catalyst. What do you sense about this ore?"

Saryon lifted the stone in his hand. For long moments he looked at it, then, shutting his eyes, he sensed for the magic.

Watching closely, Joram saw the catalyst's face grow peaceful, the man's concentration turning inward. His expression became one of awe and bliss, he was absorbing the magic. But then, slowly, the catalyst's expression changed to one of horror. Quickly he opened his eyes, and set the stone down upon the table, hurriedly withdrawing his hand from it.

"This is the darkstone!" Joram said softly.

"I do not see why it should excite you," Saryon said. He licked his lips as though he had a bitter taste in his mouth. "The secret to forming the ancient alloy is apparently one you cannot unlock."

"Not me," said Joram softly. "You, Catalyst. You see"— he leaned near—"the formula for the alloy is given in the text, but I cannot read it. It is—"

"—mathematics." Saryon's lips twisted.

"Mathematics," Joram repeated. "Something my mother never taught me, of course, since it is an art of the catalysts." Shaking his head, the young man clenched his fist, forgetting himself in his earnestness. "The texts are filled with mathematical equations! You cannot know, Saryon, how frustrating this was to me! To be so close, to have found the ore they spoke of, and then to have my way blocked by what is so much gibberish dancing across the page. I did all I could. I thought maybe by experimenting I could come across the right answer by accident. But my time was short, and Blachloch began to suspect. He is having me watched." Picking up the rock, Joram held it in his open palm, then slowly closed his fingers over it, as though he would crush it in his hand. "I don't believe I would have ever gotten it right anyway," he continued with growing bitterness. "There's a lot about catalysts in there. Directions to them. I thought I could ignore that, but apparently not."

"You called me 'Saryon,'" the catalyst said to Joram quietly.

Looking up, Joram flushed. He hadn't meant to do that, this wasn't part of his plan. There was something about this man, something he hadn't counted on finding, particularly not in a catalyst. Someone who understood.

Angrily, Joram's face hardened; the black brows drew together threateningly. No, he must stick to the plan. This man was a tool, nothing more.

"If we're going to be working together, I suppose I must call you by name," he said sullenly. "I will *not* call you 'Father'!" he added with a sneer.

"I haven't agreed to work with you," Saryon replied steadily. "Tell me, if you create this . . . this weapon, what will you do with it?"

"Stop Blachloch," Joram answered with a shrug. "Believe me, Cata — Saryon — it is only a matter of time before he destroys me. He has so much as told me so already. As for you — Well, do you want to be part of another raiding party?"

"No," Saryon said in a low voice. "Will you take over leadership of the coven then?"

"Me?" Joram shook his head with a mirthless laugh. "Are you mad? Why should I want such responsibility? No, I will give the leadership of the coven back to Andon. He and these people can live in peace once more. As for me, I want only one thing. To return to Merilon and claim what is mine. With this weapon," he said grimly, "I can do it."

"You forget one thing," Saryon said. "I was sent to bring you back to . . . to stand trial."

"You are right," Joram said after a pause, "I had forgotten. Very well" — he shrugged — "open a Corridor. Call the *Duuk-tsarith*."

"I cannot open a Corridor without the assistance of a magic-user," Saryon replied. "If you had sufficient Life, I could use yours . . ."

"That was the plan?"

"Yes," Saryon murmured inaudibly.

"A pity it didn't work out, Catalyst," Joram answered coolly. "Weak though you may be, I am weaker yet. Now, that is. Once I have the weapon, however . . . Well, you will do what you have to do when the time comes. Perhaps your Bishop might consider Blachloch an acceptable trade for me. As for now — Saryon — are you with me? Will you help free us both, and help free Andon and his people? You know they will keep their vow, and you know what Blachloch will do to them."

"Yes," Saryon said. Clasping his hands, he looked down at them, noticing the blueness in his fingernails. "I'm losing the feeling in my fingers," he murmured. Rising to his feet, he walked from the table to the feeble fire. "I wonder what the Almin is doing now," he said to himself, holding his hands to the warmth. "Getting ready to attend Evening Prayers in the Font? Preparing Himself to listen to Bishop Vanya praying for guidance that he probably doesn't need? No wonder the Almin stays there, safe and secure, within the walls of the Font.

"What an easy job."

6

Fallen

"**I**t cannot be done," said Saryon, looking up from the text he was reading, his face pale and strained.

"What do you mean, it can't be done?" Joram demanded, ceasing his restless pacing and coming to stand next to the catalyst. "Don't you understand it? Can't you read the math? Is there something we lack? Something we're missing? If so—"

"I mean it cannot be done because I will not do it," Saryon said wearily, leaning his head upon his hand. He gestured at the text. "I understand it," he continued in a hollow voice. "I understand it all too well. And I will not do it!" He closed his eyes. "I will not do it."

Joram's face twisted in fury, his fist clenched, and for an instant it seemed as though he might strike the catalyst. With a visible effort, the young man controlled himself and, taking another turn about the small, underground chamber, forced himself to calm down.

As he heard Joram walk away, Saryon opened his eyes, his wistful gaze falling on the volumes and volumes of leather, hand-bound texts that stood neatly arranged on wooden bookshelves, so crudely fashioned that it appeared they might have been the work of children. An early example of woodworking without the use of magic, the catalyst guessed. He felt Joram's anger — it radiated from him like a wave of heat from the forge — and Saryon sat tense and expectant, waiting for the attack, either verbal or physical. But none came. Only a seething silence and the steady, measured pacing of the young man walking out his frustration. Saryon sighed. He would almost have preferred an outburst. This coolness in one so young, this control over a nature so obviously in turmoil, was frightening.

Where did it come from? Saryon wondered. Surely not from his parents, who — if reports were true — gave way to passions that encompassed their downfall. Perhaps this was some sort of attempt at reparation, Joram's father reaching out to him with his stone hands. Or then there was that other possibility, the one that had come to Saryon out of the darkness, out of the pain of his injury. The one he had shut out, the one he would never think of again. . . .

Saryon shook his head angrily. What nonsense. It was the influence of this room, it had to be.

Joram sat down in a chair beside him.

"Very well — Saryon," he said, his voice cool and even, "tell me what must be done and why you will not do it."

The catalyst sighed again. Raising his head, he looked back at the text that lay before him on the table. Smiling sadly, he ran his hand over the pages with a touch almost caressing. "Do you have any idea of the wonders within these pages?" he asked Joram softly.

Joram's eyes devoured the catalyst, watching every nuance of expression upon the man's tired, lined face. "With these wonders, we could rule the world," he replied.

"No, no, no!" Saryon said impatiently. "I meant wonders, wonders of learning. The mathematics . . ." His eyes closed again in exquisite agony. "I am the best mathematician of this age," he murmured. "A genius they call me. Yet here, within these pages, I find such knowledge that makes me feel like a child crouched at my mother's knee. I don't begin to understand them. I could study for months, years . . ." The look of pain faded from his face, replaced by one of longing. His hand stroked the pages of the text. "What joy," he whispered, "if I had found *this* when I was young. . . ." His voice died.

Joram waited, watching, as patient as a cat.

"But I didn't," Saryon said. Opening his eyes, he moved his hand away from the pages of the text swiftly, as another might move his hand from a burning brand. "I have found them now that I am old, my conscience fixed, my morals formed. Perhaps those morals are not right," he added, seeing Joram frown, "but, such as they are, they are fixed within me. To deny them or fight them might drive me mad."

"So you are saying that you understand what this means" — Joram gestured toward the text — "and that you could do what must be done except that it goes against your conscience?"

Saryon nodded.

"And did it go against this conscience of yours to kill that young catalyst in the village —"

"Stop!" Saryon cried in a low voice.

"No, I won't stop," Joram returned bitterly. "You're so good at preaching sermons, Catalyst. Preach one to Blachloch. Show him the evil of his ways as he ties old Andon by his hands to the whipping post. You watch while his men flail the flesh from that old man's bones. You watch, and comfort yourself with the knowledge that it may be wrong but it isn't going against *your* conscience —"

"Stop!" Saryon's fist clenched. He glared angrily at the young man. "I don't want to see that happen anymore than you —"

"Then, help me to stop it!" Joram hissed. "It's up to you, Catalyst! You're the only one who can!"

Saryon shut his eyes again, resting his head in his hands, his shoulders slumped.

Sitting back, Joram watched and waited. The catalyst raised a haggard face. "According to the text, I must give Life . . . to that which is Dead."

Joram's face darkened, the thick brows drew together. "What do you mean?" he asked tightly. "Not to me —"

"No." Drawing a deep breath, Saryon turned to the text. Moistening a finger, he carefully turned one of the brittle parchment pages, his touch gentle and reverential. "You have failed for two reasons. You have not been mixing the alloy in the correct proportions. According to this formula, that is quite important. A deviation of a few drops can mean the difference between success and failure. Then, once it is taken from the mold, the metal must be heated to a extremely high temperature —"

"But it will lose its form," Joram protested.

"Wait . . ." Saryon raised his hand. "This second heating is not done in the fires of the forge." Licking his lips, he paused a moment, then continued, speaking slowly and reluctantly. "It is heated within the flame of magic. . . ."

Joram stared at him in confusion. "I don't understand."

"I must open a conduit, take the magic from the world, and infuse it into the metal." Saryon looked at Joram steadily. "Can't you understand, young man? I must give the Life of this world to something Dead, made by the hands of men. This goes against everything I have ever believed. It is truly the blackest of the Dark Arts."

"So what will you do, Catalyst?" Joram asked, sitting back and regarding Saryon with triumph.

But Saryon had lived over forty years in the world. Sheltered years, as he had come to learn, but he had lived them nonetheless. He was not the fool Joram thought him, walking near the edge of the cliff, his eyes staring at the sun shining above him instead of at the reality of the world around him. No, Saryon saw the chasm. He saw that in a very few steps he would fall over the edge. He saw it because this was a familiar path he walked, one he had trod before, though it had been a long time ago.

A soft knocking upon an overhead door caused both men to start up in alarm.

"Well?" said Joram insistently.

Looking at him, seeing the eager intensity of the face, Saryon drew a breath, shut his eyes, and leaped off the cliff. "Yes," he answered inaudibly.

Nodding to himself in satisfaction, Joram hurried across the floor to the center of the small room and peered upward as the door in the ceiling above him opened a crack.

"It is Andon," came the whisper. "The guard is looking for you. You must return."

"Let down the ladder."

A rope ladder tumbled down in response, Joram catching it as it fell.

"Catalyst . . ." He motioned.

"Yes." Gathering his robes about him, Saryon came over to stand beneath the ladder, not without a final, hungry glance at the storehouse of treasure that surrounded him.

"Should we take the book with us?" Joram asked, starting back to pick it up.

"No," Saryon said tiredly. "I have the formula memorized. You had best put it back in its place, however."

Hastily Joram set the book on the shelves, then snuffed out the candle. Thick darkness buried the chamber, musty with the smell of the ancient texts lying in their hidden sepulcher.

Did the spirits of those who had written them live in this place as well, Saryon wondered as he fumbled clumsily with the rope ladder in the dim light from a candle Andon held above them. Perhaps *my* spirit will return here when I am dead, the catalyst thought, unable to refrain from a backward look as he clamored up the ladder with Joram's impatient assistance. Certainly, here, I could remain happily for centuries.

"Here, Father, give me your hand."

He was at the top. Clasping him by the wrist, Andon pulled him through the trapdoor, helping Saryon climb up into the old mineshaft that ran beneath Andon's house. "Hold the light," the old man told him, handing him the candle in its wrought-iron holder. Shadows leaped and danced about the rock walls as Saryon took the light.

Joram pulled himself up easily; Saryon looked at the strong, muscular arms with envy. Bending down, the young man made certain the trapdoor was closed tightly, then he and Andon between them fastened it with something the old man called a lock, inserting a piece of oddly shaped metal into it and turning it with a clicking sound. Returning the key to his pocket, Andon stepped back and, after a brief inspection, nodded to Joram.

Placing his hands upon a gigantic boulder, the young man slowly and with obvious effort rolled the rock into place over the trapdoor, effectively concealing it from sight.

Andon shook his head. "It generally takes two grown men to move that rock," he said to Saryon, watching Joram and smiling in admiration. "At least so I remember from my youth. The rock had not been moved in years, not until the young man here insisted on seeing the ancient texts." He sighed. "There was no need to move it, no need to go down there. None of us can read them, nor could they in my father's day. I saw that rock moved only once, and then I suppose it was just to check to make certain the texts were surviving without damage."

"They are well preserved," Saryon murmured. "The room is dry. They should last for centuries if they are undisturbed."

His face soft with sympathy, Andon laid his hand upon the catalyst's arm. "I am sorry, Father. I can imagine how you must feel." His brow creased in irritation. "I tried to tell Joram—"

"No, do not blame him," Saryon said steadily. "It was my decision to come here. I am not sorry I did."

"But you seem upset. . . ."

"So much knowledge . . . lost," the catalyst replied, his gaze going to the boulder, his thoughts with what lay beneath it.

"Yes," agreed Andon sadly.

"Not lost," said Joram coming over to them, his eyes burning brighter than the flame of the candle. "Not lost . . ." he repeated, rubbing his hands.

"'Pon my honor, it's devilishly cold in here. Or is that a contradiction in terms? You'll forgive me, I trust," Simkin said, slipping into a fur cape that he conjured up with a negligent wave of his hand, "but I have a tendency to weakness in the lungs. Sister died of pneumonia, you know. Well, not actually. She died of being rather badly squashed from falling off one of the platforms in Merilon, but she wouldn't have fallen if she hadn't been wandering about delirious from the fever that she ran on account of the pneumonia. Still—"

"Not now," snapped Mosiah, sitting down at the table near the young man. "We can't stay long. The guard didn't want to let us in at all, but Simkin got Blachloch to agree to it. Why did you send for us?"

"I need your help," Joram said, sitting down near the young men.

"Oh, I say, a conspiracy! How frightfully fearful sounding. I am all ears. I *could* be all ears, you know," Simkin added in sudden inspiration. "If it would help."

"All mouth is nearer the mark. Shut up," muttered Mosiah.

"I won't say another word." Muffled to the eyes in fur, Simkin obligingly snapped his lips shut and gazed at Joram with grave intensity that was, however, rather spoiled by a gaping yawn. "Beg pardon," he said.

Huddled, shivering, in a corner as close to the feeble fire as he could get, Saryon snorted in disgust. Joram glanced at him irritably, making a motion as if to reassure him. Then he turned back to his friends.

"The catalyst and I have to get out of here tonight . . ."

"You're escaping?" Mosiah asked eagerly. "I'll come with you—"

"No, listen!" Joram said in exasperation. "I can't tell you what we're doing. It's better you don't know, anyway. In case anything goes wrong. We have to get out of here and back in without the guard knowing and, more important, we have to be free to do . . . what we have to do without being interrupted."

"That should be easy." Mosiah appeared disappointed. "You went to Andon's last night—"

"And the guard escorted us there and back, just like he escorts me to the forge every day," Joram finished grimly.

"In other words," said Simkin coolly, "you want the guard to be in the land of Bidey-Bye whilst you two perform dark and treacherous acts. In the morning you want him to find you slumbering peacefully in your little beds when he himself awakes."

Glancing at Simkin, Saryon stirred uneasily. The young man was near the mark with his playful guessing. Too near. The catalyst hadn't wanted to involve these two at all— Mosiah because it was dangerous and Simkin because he was Simkin.

"In addition," the fur-covered young man was continuing
languidly, "you do not want interruptions by one person in
particular — our Blond and Baleful Leader. My dear boy" —
Simkin snuggled comfortably into his cape — "nothing simpler. Leave everything to me."

"What do you intend to do?" Saryon asked, his voice
rasping.

"I say, old fellow. You're not taking cold, are you?" Simkin asked anxiously, twisting around to look over at the catalyst. "A bit dangerous for one of your advanced years.
Carried off the Earl of Mooria in a matter of days, and he
was your age to the year. Sneezed his head off. Quite literally. It landed — splat — in the baked custard. Oh, Duke
Zebulon *said* it was just his little joke — a sort of after-dinner
entertainment for the amusement of his guests — and that he
never *meant* his catalyst to take him seriously and grant him
such an excessive amount of magic. But we all wondered. He
and the Earl had quarreled over Swan's Doom just the day
prior. Something about cheating. At any rate, the guests were
highly diverted. Nothing else was talked of for weeks. It's
quite the thing, now, to land a dinner invitation from the
Duke —"

"I am not taking cold!" Saryon snapped when he could
get a word in edgewise.

"Delighted to hear it," Simkin said earnestly, leaning over
to pat the catalyst's hand.

"Let's get on with this," Joram said impatiently. "The
guard and Blachloch?"

"Ah, yes. I knew we were talking about something else.
The guard. I'll handle him," said Simkin.

"How?" asked Mosiah suspiciously, glancing at the catalyst. It was obvious he and Saryon shared the same opinion
of the bearded young man.

"A mild sedative — recipe known only to myself and the
Marchioness of Lonnoni, who had fourteen children. So
much for the guard. Now, as to Blachloch. I am engaged to
play tarok with him this evening anyhow. He will not disturb
you. 'Pon my honor."

"Honor!" Mosiah sneered. "I'm coming with you."

"Oh, no. Quite impossible," Simkin said with another yawn. Stretching his feet out toward the fire, he lounged back in the chair at a seemingly impossible angle, shifting around until he got himself completely comfortable. "Not to sound unfeeling, but you are a bit of a bumpkin, dear boy. I mean, I don't dare take you anyplace in polite society. Table manners quite shocking. Besides," he added, ignoring Mosiah's glare, "someone should stay here in this wretched shack and keep up the illusion that Father and Son are within."

"That's not a bad idea," said Joram, placing his hand on Mosiah's clenched fist restrainingly. "What would he have to do?"

"Nothing much," said Simkin, shrugging his fur-cloaked shoulders like a dainty bear. "Build up the fire. Move back and forth in front of the window now and then so that his shadow is visible. I say, Mosiah," he added with a yawn so wide his jaws cracked, "I could even conjure your hair to look like Joram's. Just a little help from our Life-giving friend here and your tresses would be the envy of every woman in the settlement. Long, thick, luxuriant . . ."

Mosiah turned to Joram. "He's a buffoon," the young man said quietly. "You're staking your life on a fool!"

The bored expression on Simkin's bearded face changed suddenly to a look so shrewd and penetrating that Saryon could have sworn, for an instant, that a stranger sat there. Mosiah had his back turned to the young man; Joram was scowling at Mosiah. No one saw the look but the catalyst, and before he could realize it or absorb it, the look was gone, replaced by the playful, negligent smile.

The fur cape vanished, as did the silken breeches and waistcoat. There was a blur of color and, in an instant, Simkin was dressed from head to toe in motley. Rainbow colors wildly clashing, his ribbons fluttering, and bells tinkling, Simkin slithered out of his chair and crawled on hands and knees across the floor to Joram. Sitting cross-legged before him, he shook the bells on his cap.

"A fool, yes, I am a fool," cried Simkin gaily, waving his arms in a grand flourish, the ribbons floating about him like a swirling, multicolored fog. "I am Joram's fool. Remember the tarok reading? The king of Swords was your card! You will be Emperor someday and you will need a fool, won't you, Joram?" Leaning forward, Simkin put his hands together in a mockery of prayer. "Let me be your fool, sire. You need one, I assure you."

"Why, idiot?" asked Joram, the half-smile in his dark eyes.

"Because only a fool dares tell you the truth," Simkin said softly.

Joram stared at Simkin in silence for as long as it took to draw a breath, then — seeing the bearded face split into a grin — he lifted his booted foot and placed it firmly on the young man's chest, shoving him backward. Tumbling head over heels, laughing wildly, Simkin performed a graceful somersault and came up on his feet.

Ignoring Simkin, who was dancing about the room, Mosiah put his hand on Joram's shoulder, almost shaking him in his earnestness. "Listen to me," he said urgently. "Forget this! Forget the cards, forget whatever idea you have of challenging Blachloch. Oh, come on, Joram! I know you! I've heard you talk. I'd be a fool myself not to figure it out. Let's take this chance to escape! Let Simkin use his potion on the guard, and we'll try our luck in the Outland. We can make it. We're young and strong, plus we'll have the catalyst along to give us Life. You'll come, won't you, Father?"

Saryon could do nothing but nod. The idea of losing himself in the wilderness was suddenly so appealing that he would have rushed out the door then and there if but one person had led the way.

Joram did not immediately answer, and Mosiah, seeing the thoughtful expression on his friend's dark face and mistaking it for interest, hurried on. "We could go north, to Sharakan. There'll be work for us there. No one knows us. It's dangerous, but not as dangerous as staying around here, not as dangerous as fighting Blach —"

"No," said Joram quietly.

"Joram, think —"

"You think!" Joram said. Flame flickered in the brown eyes as he shook Mosiah's hand from his shoulder. "Do you believe for one instant that Blachloch would just let his catalyst escape without doing everything in his power to bring him back? And his power is pretty damn extensive. What are the *Duuk-tsarith* trained for — hunting, tracking people down! He knows the Outland! We don't. And when he caught us, he'd kill us, you and I. What are we, after all? But what about the catalyst? What do you think he would do to him?"

"Cut off his hands," said Simkin, divesting himself of the fool's clothing with a gesture. Dressed once more in his habitual garish costume, he conjured up the fur cape and draped it gracefully around his shoulders. "It's what they used to do to them in the old days, I understand," he continued with an apologetic glance at Saryon. "Doesn't affect their usefulness, you see."

Scowling, Mosiah kept his eyes on Joram. "And what happens if he catches us now?"

"He won't."

Mosiah turned away. "Come on," he said to Simkin. "We've been here long enough. The guard will get suspicious."

"Yes, we must be running along," Simkin said, following. "I think I feel a definite stuffiness in my nose. I — Ah-choo! There, what did I tell you! The catalyst has given me his cold! I'm — Ah-choo! quite put out!" The orange bit of silk fluttered in the air. Applying it to his nose, Simkin sniffed gloomily. "And such a strenuous evening ahead of me, too. Blachloch cheats, you know."

"No, he doesn't. He's too good. *You* cheat," said Joram dryly.

"Because he always wins! Even when I cheat, I never seem to manage that. I suppose I should keep my mind on the game. See you in a bit, dear boy. Must go pick the pretty flowers and mix up the potion." Simkin winked. "Be ready. You'll hear my voice . . ." Nodding toward the guard, who could be seen watching from the doorway of a house across the street, Simkin sauntered out of the prison.

"What about you?" Joram asked, stopping Mosiah in the doorway.

"Maybe, maybe not," Mosiah answered without looking at him. "Maybe I'll leave by myself, before you all get caught."

"Well . . . good luck, then," Joram said coldly.

"Thanks." Mosiah gave him a hurt, bitter glance. "Thanks very much. Good luck to you, too."

Slamming the door shut behind him, he left abruptly.

Looking out the window, Saryon could see him walking away, his head bowed.

"He cares a lot for you," the catalyst said quietly, turning from the window to Joram, who was mixing a bowl of gruel over the coals of the fire.

The young man did not reply, he might not have even heard.

Crossing their small, cold prison, Saryon lay down on the hard bed. How long had it been since he'd slept? Truly peaceful sleep? Would he ever be able to sleep again? Or would he always see that young Deacon, the look of fear as he saw death in the warlock's eyes?

"Do you trust Simkin?" Saryon asked, staring up at the rotting beams of the ceiling.

"As much as I trust you, Catalyst," Joram replied.

7

The Storm

"C'mon, old hag, be brisk there. Take any longer and supper'll be breakfast!"

The old woman to whom this was addressed made no reply, nor did she appear to move faster. Shuffling back and forth between table and fireplace, carrying vegetables in her apron, she tossed them into a pot hanging by a hook over the fire. Slumped in a chair by a table he had dragged over near the window, the guard watched these proceedings with a growl, his attention divided between the old woman, the pot bubbling over the fire — from which came a strong smell of onions — and the prison across the street.

The very faintest light shone in the window of the prison, the light of a feeble fire. Occasionally the guard could see shadowy figures cross back and forth in front of the window. There was no one on the streets this night; no one came to visit the prisoners. The prisoners had made no move to leave, for which the guard was grateful. This was no night to be out. A cold slanting rain drove into the mud street like spears, arrowtips of sleet rattled against the windows of the houses, while the wind leading this onslaught shrieked and howled like a demon horde.

"It's stupid, keepin' a man here this night," muttered the guard. "Not even the Prince of Devils would be out in a storm the likes of this. A'nt that ready yet, you old bitty?" Half-turning in his chair, he raised his hand as if to cuff the woman. Being slightly deaf and dim of vision, she still paid no attention to him, and the guard was just getting to his feet when he was startled by the rattle of the door lock.

"Open up in there!" came an eerie voice as shrill as the wind.

The guard cast a swift glance across the street. The feeble light still burned in the prison, there were no shadows at all to be seen in the windows.

"Hullo! Hullo!" cried the voice. This was followed by a battering and banging on the door that seemed likely to stave it in.

The guard was not overburdened with imagination, but then neither was he overburdened with intelligence. Having summoned the Prince of Devils to mind, so to speak, the guard found, like many conjurers, that it was difficult to banish him. That this gentleman might have arrived to claim his soul seemed not unlikely, having been told by a mother he only dimly recalled that this was undoubtedly going to be his fate. Rising to his feet, he peered out the window in an attempt to see the visitor, but could make out nothing but an indistinct shadow.

"Answer the door!" the guard shouted at the old woman, having some vague idea that the Prince might not be particular about whose soul he claimed. But the old woman's attention was fixed solely upon the stew, for she heard neither shout nor door.

"Is anybody home?" came the voice, and the rattling increased.

At this, hope glimmered within the guard. Shrinking back from the window so that he couldn't be seen, he judged it likely that the unwanted visitor would go away. To insure this, he made several signs to the old woman, indicating she was to go on about her work undisturbed.

Unfortunately, this frantic hand-waving did what all the shouting in the village could not have done — it caught the old woman's attention. Seeing the guard pointing at the door, she nodded and, with shuffling gait, walked over and opened it.

A blast of chill wind, a flurry of rain, a stinging spray of sleet, and a huge furry figure all burst into the room simultaneously. Only one of these nocturnal visitors was permitted to stay however. Turning around, the furry figure put his shoulder against the door and, with the old woman's help, slammed it shut upon the icy intruders.

"Almin's death," swore a sepulchral voice, slightly muffled by frost-rimed fur, "I might have perished out there on that doorstoop! And here I've come for you 'specially."

At this confirmation of his fears, though he had expected something more fiery with tails and horns, the guard could only stammer incoherently until the figure removed its hat and hurled it upon the floor with another oath.

This was matched by an oath from the guard. "Simkin," he muttered, sinking back down in his chair in weak-kneed relief.

"So this is the thanks I get, after nearly perishing of the cold to bring you a bit of cheer," said Simkin with a sniff, tossing an aleskin upon the table in front of the guard.

"What's that?" the man demanded suspiciously.

"A little something from dear old Blachloch," said the young man, with a casual wave of his hand as he went to stand near the fire. "Sharing in the captured spoils, commendation for job well done, a toast drunk to rape, pillage, and plunder, and all that sort of thing."

The guard's face lit up. "Well, that's fine, that is," he said, eyeing the aleskin greedily and rubbing his hands. A sudden thought occurred to him. His eyes narrowing, he turned around. "Here, now," he said surlily, glancing at Simkin who was, it seemed, taking an uncommon interest in the stew. "You can't stay. I'm on guard duty and I'm not to be bothered."

"Believe me, dear chap, I wouldn't stay here for all the pet monkeys in Zith-el." Simkin sniffed and, grabbing the bit of orange silk from the air, put it to his nose. "I assure you, the smell of onion and unbathed lout hold no attraction for me. I am an errand boy, that is all, and I will remain here long enough to warm myself or until I pass out from the odor, whichever comes first. As for your guard duty"—he cast a disdainful glance out the window—"it's a complete waste of time, if you ask me."

"I didn't, but you're right there," said the guard, sitting back comfortably, not at all disconcerted by Simkin's insults once assured the young man would not be sharing his repast. "I c'n understand puttin' up with the catalyst, makin' sure he toes the mark. But a clunk over t'head and a dip in t'river would settle that black-haired bastard of a kid. Why Blachloch puts up with 'im is beyond me."

"Why indeed," murmured Simkin in bored tones, his eyes on the guard, who was pulling the cork on the aleskin. "Well, back into the night, as they say. You take care, Grammie," the young man whispered. "Get to bed early, and when you do, be certain to put out the light."

Simkin emphasized this last with a wink and a nod toward the guard, who was sniffing at the ale and licking his lips. Looking at him with eyes suddenly shrewd and penetrating, the old woman smiled and bobbed her white cap, then shuffled back to dish up the stew, her ears deaf to all but whispers, it would seem.

Cheered by the sight of the guard putting the neck of the aleskin to his lips, Simkin hurried out the door into the teeth of the storm and dashed across the street. Blinded by darkness, rain, sleet, and his huge fur hat, he promptly collided with someone.

"Simkin! Watch where you're going!" snarled a voice in irritated relief.

"I say, Mosiah! So you didn't venture into the wilderness, after all. No, not the door, the lout's still watching. Come over here in the shadows. Wait . . ."

"For what? I'm freezing! Didn't you—"

"Ah, there's the signal." The light in the guard's house blinked out, leaving it dark except for the reflected gleam of the fire. Darting out from behind the corner of the prison, Simkin tapped upon the door, which opened at his knock.

Darting inside, Simkin dragged Mosiah with him, and Joram slammed the door shut behind them. "A fine night you've picked for this," Simkin said through clicking teeth.

"I know," remarked Joram coolly from the depths of the shadows in the chill room. "With the fog and the rain, the light from the forge won't be seen."

"It won't matter if it is," muttered Mosiah, standing hunch-shouldered and shivering near the door. "I talked to the smith. He's let the word out among Blachloch's men that some of his people might be working tonight — make up for the time lost because of the raid. Don't worry," Mosiah returned in answer to Joram's frown, "I didn't tell him anything and he didn't ask. His sons were with us when the village burned. They've taken the vow. You — Well, never mind." Mosiah stopped.

"You what?" said Joram.

"Nothing," Mosiah mumbled. *You can trust him* had been on Mosiah's lips, but, looking at Joram's dark, cold expression, he shook his head.

The half-smile lit the brown eyes like the light from the dying embers. Joram knew what his friend had intended to say and why he hadn't said it.

"What about the guard?"

"The lout is out on his snout," reported Simkin, highly pleased with his rhyme that he had been composing all evening. "I — Oh, good evening, Father. I didn't see you, lurking about the shadows. Getting in practice? I say, you don't look at all well. Cold still bothering you? I got over mine, fortunately. Blachloch *and* a cold in the head would simply be too much to deal with. . . ."

Saryon said nothing. He hadn't even heard Simkin. He couldn't hear anything above the sound of the wind, prowling about the prison like a beast of prey yearning for the blood it smelled inside.

Once, long ago, Saryon had heard the wind talk. Only then it had whispered, "The Prince is Dead. . . . The Prince is Dead. . . ." and its tone had been sad and sorrowful. Now it shrieked and yammered, "Dead, Dead, Dead!" in a kind of mad triumph, delighting to torment him in his downfall.

"Saryon . . ."

The wind spoke to him, calling him by name, summoning him —

"Saryon!"

Blinking, he started.

"I — I'm sorry," he murmured. "I was . . . just . . . Is it time?"

"Yes." Joram's voice was cool and toneless. The wind seemed more alive. "Simkin's gone. We should delay no longer."

"Here, Father, you'll need more wraps than that," said Mosiah, struggling out of his own wet cloak.

"He'll warm up quick enough in the forge," muttered Joram, irritated at the delay.

Paying no attention to Joram, Mosiah overrode Saryon's confused protests and helped the catalyst put the young man's cloak on over his shabby robes.

"Are you finally ready?" Joram asked and, without waiting for a reply, cautiously opened the door and peered into the street. Not surprisingly, its only occupants were the rain, the sleet, and the wind. Grabbing a cloak Mosiah handed to him at the last moment — or he might have gone out into the bitter weather without any protection — Joram carelessly tossed it around his shoulders and stepped out into the storm whose fierceness seemed reflected on the young man's face.

Moving more slowly, Saryon followed.

"May the Almin go with you," came Mosiah's soft whisper.

Saryon shook his head.

As though waiting for him to emerge, the wind pounced on the catalyst with a snarl. Chill talons of rain ripped through his cloak and robes with ease; teethlike sleet bit into his flesh. But the wind wasn't intent on devouring him, it seemed. Dogging his heels, it panted behind him, driving him forward, its breath cold upon the back of his neck. Saryon had the vague impression that if he tried to veer from this dark path he walked, the wind would leap to intercept him and block him, nipping at his bare ankles, its slashing fangs a threat and a reminder.

Death, Death, Death . . .

"Confound it, Father, watch where you're going!"
Joram's voice cracked impatiently, but his strong arm stead-
ied Saryon, who, in his misery and bleak despair, had nearly
walked into a gully filled with icy water.

"It's not much further," said Joram. Glancing at the
young man through the driving rain, Saryon saw that
Joram's teeth were clenched, not against the chill of the
storm but against the excitement that raged within him. And,
as though conjured up by the young man's voice, the cavern
of the forge suddenly rose up out of the darkness, its red-
glowing embers staring at the catalyst like the eyes of the
creature that had been pursuing him.

Joram dragged aside the heavy, wooden door to let them
in. Saryon started to step inside, the warmth and peace of the
fire-lit darkness beckoning him. Then he hesitated. He could
turn and run. Go back to his Church. *Obedire est vivere. Vivere
est obedire.* Yes! It was so simple! He would obey. Hadn't catalyst done that for centuries, obey without question?

But the wind only laughed at him, mocking him, and
Saryon realized that the storm had been building all his life,
rising from that first whisper to this shriek of triumph. Lifting the skirts of his robes, the wind tugged at him from the
sides and pushed him from behind until, with a final, wild
shriek, it shoved him over the small rock ledge and sent him
staggering into the red-tinged blackness.

Behind him, Joram dragged the heavy door shut again,
then hurried to his work. Standing in the forge, relaxing in
the warmth, Saryon stared around in the fascination he could
no longer deny. Strange tools gleamed in the reflected glow
of the coals that burned brighter as Joram, operating the
bellows, gave them life. The children born of this fiery union
cluttered the floor — horseshoes, bits, broken nails, half-
finished knives, iron pots. Absorbed in his work, Joram paid
no attention to the catalyst. Sitting down, careful to keep out
of the young man's way, Saryon listened to the harsh breath
of the bellows and realized suddenly that he could no longer
hear the wind.

The storm raged still, its fury increasing, perhaps, in its
triumph at its victory over the catalyst. The wind roared
through the streets, tore limbs from trees, tiles from roofs,

Rain knocked threateningly at every door, sleet tapped against the windows. Those inside the large brick dwelling upon the hill overlooking the Technologists' settlement were able to ignore the storm, however. Absorbed in the intricacies of their games—and there was more than one game being played—they paid scant attention to the vagaries of nature without, being far more concerned with those within.

"Queen of Cups, high trump card. That takes your Knight, Simkin, and the next two tricks are mine, I believe." Blachloch laid a card upon the table and, sitting back, stared at Simkin expectantly. "How are our prisoners getting along?" the warlock asked casually.

Looking at the card before him in some consternation, Simkin regarded his hand thoughtfully. "Plotting against you, O Winning One," he said with a shrug.

"Ah"—Blachloch smiled slightly, rubbing the tip of his finger along his blond mustache—"I guessed as much. What are they plotting?"

"Doing you in, that sort of thing," Simkin replied. Looking up at Blachloch with a sweet smile, he laid a card down upon the warlock's queen. "I'll sacrifice this to protect my Knight."

Blachloch's expressionless face tightened. The lips compressed, drawing the mustache into a straight, thin line. "The Fool! That card has been played!"

"Oh, no, dear boy," said Simkin with a yawn. "You must be mistaken—"

"I am never mistaken," Blachloch retorted coldly. "I have followed the fall of the cards with the utmost attention. The Fool has been played, I tell you. Drumlor sacrificed it to protect his King . . ." The warlock looked at his henchman for confirmation.

"Y-yes," stammered Drumlor. "I—I . . . That is—"

Having been invited to play simply so there would be three, Drumlor had neither love for nor interest in the game. Like many of the other guards, Blachloch had taught him to play in order that the warlock would have someone with which to game. These nights were nerve-racking experiences to poor Drumlor, who barely remembered the last card he had played, much less a card ten tricks earlier.

"Really, Blachloch, the only Fool this imbecile remembers is the one he saw this morning when he looked into the mirror. I say, if you're going to get into a snit, go back through the tricks! It doesn't matter anyway"— Simkin tossed his cards on the table —"you have defeated me. You always do."

"It isn't the winning," Blachloch remarked, turning over Simkin's cards and sorting through them, "it is the game itself — the calculating, the strategy, the ability to outwit your opponent. You should know that, Simkin. You and I play the game for the sake of the game, do we not, my friend?"

"I assure you, dear fellow," said Simkin languidly, leaning back in his chair, "the game is the only reason I continue to exist on this wretched patch of grass and gravel we call a world. Without it, life would be so boring one might as well curl up into a ball and drop oneself into the river."

"I will save you the trouble one day, Simkin," Blachloch said mildly, sorting back through the tricks, flipping the cards over with skilled, rapid motions of his slender hands. "I do not tolerate those who mistakenly believe they can outwit me." With a flick of his wrist, the warlock tossed a card in front of Simkin. There were now two Fool cards upon the table.

"It isn't *my* fault," said Simkin in aggrieved tones. "It's your deck, after all. I shouldn't wonder if *you* weren't trying to cheat *me*." The young man sniffed and the orange silk appeared in his hand. Delicately, Simkin wiped his nose. "Frightful night out there. I think I have caught cold."

An unusually strong gust of wind hit the house, causing timbers to creak. From somewhere nearby came a crash, a tree limb breaking off and falling to the ground. Shuffling the cards, Blachloch glanced out the window. His gaze suddenly became fixed.

"There's a light in the forge."

"Oh, that," said Drumlor, starting. He had been nodding off to sleep, his body slowly sliding out of his chair to Simkin's infinite amusement. Catching himself, the man struggled upright. "The smith's got some men . . . workin' late."

"Indeed," said Blachloch. Stacking cards neatly, he slid them across to Simkin. "Your deal. And remember, I am watching. Which of the men is working?"

"Joram," said Simkin, sliding the cards over to Drumlor to cut.

A muscle twitched in Blachloch's cheek, the eyes narrowed. The hand that had been negligently lying upon the table tensed, the fingers curling in upon each other slightly. "Joram?" he repeated.

"Joram. An inauspicious gameplayer, by the way," Simkin said, yawning. "Too impatient. Quite often he can be inveigled into playing his trump cards early on, instead of holding them until later in the game, when they'll do him more good."

Preparing to deal, Simkin's attention was on Blachloch's face, not the cards.

"What about the catalyst?" Blachloch asked, gazing out the window at the red spot of flame in the cavern that winked on and off, obscured by the driving rain and sleet.

"A much more skilled player, though you might not think so to look at him," Simkin replied softly, absently shuffling the cards again. "Saryon plays by the book, my friend." A smile lingered upon Simkin's lips. "I say, let's not play anymore. I begin to find this game deadly dull."

Drumlor cast Simkin a look of profound gratitude.

"I'll tell your fortune instead, shall I?" the young man asked Blachloch nonchalantly.

"You know I don't believe in that—" Turning from the window, Blachloch caught a glimpse of Simkin's face. "Very well," he said abruptly.

The wind rose again. Rain tried to enter by the chimney, hissed as it fell into the fire. Sitting back into his chair, Drumlor crossed his hands over his belly and drifted off to sleep. Simkin handed the cards to Blachloch.

"Cut them . . ."

"Skip that nonsense," the warlock replied coldly. "Get on with it."

Shrugging, Simkin took the cards back.

"The first card is your past," he said, turning it over. A figure in a miter sat upon a throne between two pillars. "The High Priest." Simkin raised an eyebrow. "Now, that's a bit strange . . ."

"Continue."

Shrugging, Simkin turned over the second card. "This is your present. The Magus Reversed. Someone who's magic but isn't . . ."

"I'll interpret them for myself," Blachloch said, his eyes on the cards.

"Future" — Simkin turned over the third card — "King of Swords."

Blachloch smiled.

8

The Forging
of the Darksword

"**W**hat a strange color it
burns," Saryon mur-
mured. "Iron glows red. This is white. I wonder why? The
difference in properties, undoubtedly. How I wish I could
study it — Now, be careful. Measure it precisely. There." He
scarcely breathed, lest even that should cause Joram to slip
and pour too much of the molten liquid.

"This doesn't seem enough," Joram remarked, frowning.

"No more!" Saryon said urgently, his hand darting forward to stop the young man. "Add no more!"

"I'm not," Joram replied coldly, lifting the crucible and
setting it aside.

The catalyst felt he could breathe again. "Now you
must —"

"This part I know," Joram interrupted. "This is my
craft." He poured the fiery liquid into a large mold made of
clay, held in place by wooden boards.

Looking at it, Saryon swallowed nervously. His mouth
was dry, tasting of iron, and he thirstily drank a cup of water.

The heat in the forge was stifling. His robes were black with soot and wet with sweat. Joram's body glistened in the firelight. Held back by a leather band around his forehead, his black hair curled tightly around his face. Watching the young man as he worked, Saryon felt that tug upon his memory, a sliver of pain as sharp as a thorn.

He had seen hair like that, admired it. It had been long ago in . . . in . . . The memory was almost there, then it was gone. He sought for it again but it would not return and remained lost in the leaves of musty books, buried beneath figures and equations.

"Why are you staring at me? How long is the cooling period?"

Saryon came back to the present with a start. "I — I'm sorry," he said. "My thoughts were . . . far away. What did you ask?"

"The cooling . . ."

"Oh, yes. Thirty minutes." Rising stiffly to his feet, he suddenly realized he had not moved for an hour, and decided to see if it was still storming. Out of the corner of his eye, he saw Joram reach for a timekeeping device, and it was a mark of Saryon's abstraction that he gave it no more than a glance, although, when he had first seen what Andon called an "hourglass," he had been lost in fascination at its remarkable simplicity.

He felt the cold before he even neared the cavern entrance. Bitter as it had been before, it was worse now, contrasted with the warmth of the forge. Once again, Saryon could hear the howling of the wind but it sounded distant, as though the beast were chained outside, wailing to get in.

Shaking his head, Saryon hastily returned to the forge, where Joram was busy cleaning up all traces of their strange work.

"How much darkstone exists?" the catalyst asked, watching Joram carefully brush the fine grains of the pulverized ore into a small pouch.

"I don't know. I found these few rocks in the abandoned mines below Andon's house. According to what I read in the texts, there was a large deposit of the ore located around here. Of course, that's why the Technologists came to this place after the war. They planned to forge their weapons anew, return, and take their revenge on those who persecuted them."

Saryon felt the accusing, penetrating gaze of the dark eyes, but he did not flinch before it. From what he had seen in the books, the members of his Order had been right in banishing this Dark Art and suppressing this dangerous knowledge. "Why didn't they?" he asked.

"They had too many other things to worry about," Joram muttered, "such as staying alive. Fighting off the centaurs and the other mutated creatures created and then abandoned by the War Masters. Then there was hunger, sickness. The few catalysts who had come with them died, leaving no heirs behind. Soon, all the people cared about was survival. They stopped keeping records. What for? Their children could not read. They didn't have time to teach them — the fight to live was too desperate. Eventually, even the memories and the old skills died, and with them died the idea of going back and seeking their revenge. All that remain are the chants of the Scianc and a few rocks."

"But the chants carry the tradition, surely they could have been used to carry on the knowledge," Saryon argued mildly. "What if you are wrong, Joram? What if these people realized the horror they had come near bringing upon the world and chose to deliberately suppress it themselves?"

"Bah!" Joram snorted, turning around from where he had hidden the crucible in the refuse pile. "The chants preserve the key to the knowledge. It was the only way the wise could hope to pass it on, when they saw the darkness of ignorance beginning to close in around them. And that is what refutes your sanctimonious theory, Catalyst. There *are* clues in the litanies to those who truly listen to them. That is where I got the idea of searching in the books. To the Sorcerers" — he gestured out beyond the cavern walls at the settlement — "the chants are nothing but mystical words, words of magic and power maybe, but, when you get right down to it, only words."

Saryon shook his head, unconvinced. "Surely there would have been those before now who recognized that."

"There have been," Joram said, the half-smile burning deep in his dark eyes. "Andon, for one. Blachloch for another. The old man knew the clues were there, he knew they led to the books that had been so carefully preserved." Joram shrugged. "But he couldn't read. Ask him sometime, Saryon, about the bitter frustration that gnawed at him. Hear him tell about going down into the mine shaft and staring at the books, cursing them even, in helpless fury, because he knew that in them was the knowledge to help his people, more precious than the treasure of the Emperor, and just as impossible to acquire — to those without the key."

Joram spoke with a low, passionate intensity Saryon found quite remarkable in the usually reticent, sullen young man. When Joram mentioned the key, his hand closed over some unseen object, his eyes flamed with a feverish excitement. The catalyst stirred uncomfortably. Yes, now he had the key, the key to the treasury. And Saryon himself had shown him how it fit the lock.

"What did you say about Blachloch?" he asked, trying to banish his uncomfortable thoughts and trying also to keep his mind from the fact that the sand in the bottom of the hourglass was accumulating rapidly.

"The first time he heard the chanting, so Andon says, he heard the clues and deduced the existence of the books. But the old man — who feared Blachloch from the beginning — refused to tell him where to find them. That must have been frustrating for the warlock." The half-smile almost touched Joram's lips. "A master in the art of 'persuasion' and he doesn't dare use it, knowing that the entire camp would rise against him."

"He's biding his time, that's all," Saryon said softly. "He has the people so firmly in his grip now that he can take what he wants."

Joram did not answer; his gaze was fixed on the clay box, though he glanced impatiently at the hourglass now and then. Saryon, too, fell silent, his thoughts leading him places he would just as soon not wander. The silence grew so deep that he became aware of the difference in the sound of their breathing — his somewhat rapid and shallow as opposed to Joram's deeper, more even breaths. He began to fancy he could hear the swishing of the sand falling through the neck of the glass.

The sands ran out. Slowly, almost reluctantly, Joram rose to his feet and reached for a hammer. Grasping it in his hands, he stood above the mold where it rested on the stone floor of the cavern, staring down at it.

"What about you?" Saryon asked suddenly. "Why did Andon show the books to you?"

Looking up at the catalyst, the dark eyes dark no longer but glowing as if their cold ore had been heated among the coals, Joram smiled — a smile of victory, triumph, a smile that touched his lips, if only with darkness. "He didn't. Not the first time. Simkin did."

Raising the hammer, Joram hit the clay box, shattering it at one blow. The firelight gleamed orange on his skin as he crouched over the dark object lying in the midst of broken clay and splintered wood. His hand shaking with eagerness, he cautiously reached out to pick it up.

"Careful, the heat . . ." warned Saryon, moving nearer to it, drawn by a fascination he refused to explain to himself or even to admit.

"It isn't hot," whispered Joram in awe, holding his hand above the object. "Come nearer, Saryon! Come look! See what we have created!" Forgetting his enmity in his excitement, he grasped the catalyst's arm and dragged him closer.

What had he expected? Saryon wasn't certain. There had been illustrations of swords in the ancient text — detailed drawings of gracefully curved blades, ornately carved handles, done with the loving remembrance of those who had once held these tools of darkness in their hands. Saryon was surprised he recalled the illustrations with such clarity, having told himself repeatedly that these *were* tools of darkness, instruments of Death. Yet now he realized, when he felt the pangs of disappointment, that he had been picturing them in his mind, secretly admiring them for their delicate efficiency. He had been eager — maybe as eager as the young man — to see if he couldn't emulate this beauty.

They had failed. Recoiling, Saryon jerked his arm from Joram's grasp. This thing that lay upon the stone floor was not beautiful. It was ugly. A tool of darkness, an instrument of Death, not a bright and shining blade of light.

It occurred to Saryon that centuries of craftsmanship had been behind the making of the swords portrayed in the ancient texts. Joram was a beginner, untrained, without skill, without knowledge, with no one to teach him. The sword he had fashioned might have been wielded a thousand years before by some savage, barbaric ancestor.

It was made of a solid mass of metal — hilt and blade together, possessing neither grace nor form. The blade was straight and almost indistinguishable from the hilt. A short, blunt-edged crosspiece separated the two. The hilt was slightly rounded, to fit the hand. Joram had added a bulbous protrusion on the end in some attempt to weight it, Saryon having reasoned that this would be necessary in order to handle the weapon effectively

The weapon was crude and ugly. Saryon might have been able to deal logically with that. But there was something more horrifying about the sword, something devilish — the rounded knob on the hilt, combined with the long neck of the hilt itself, the handle's short, blunt arms, and the narrow body of the blade, turned the weapon into a grim parody of a human being.

The sword lay like a corpse at his feet, the personification of the catalyst's sin.

"Destroy it!" he gasped hoarsely, and was actually stretching out his hand to take hold of it, with some wild notion of hurling it into the very heart of the blazing coals, when Joram knocked him aside.

"Are you mad?"

Losing his footing, Saryon stumbled backward into a stack of wooden forms. "No, I am sane for the first time in days," he cried in a hollow voice, picking himself up. "Destroy it, Joram. Destroy it, or it will destroy you!"

"Going into the fortune-telling business?" snarled Joram angrily. "You'll rival Simkin!"

"I do not need cards to see the future in that weapon," Saryon said, pointing at it with a trembling hand. "Look at it, Joram! Look at it! You are Dead, but life beats and pulses in your veins! You care, you feel! The sword is *dead!* And it will bring only death."

"No, Catalyst!" Joram said, his eyes as dark and cold as the blade. "For you will give it Life."

"No." Saryon shook his head resolutely. Gathering his robes about him, he sought for the words to argue with Joram and make him understand. But he could look at nothing, think of nothing, but the sword lying upon the stone floor, surrounded by the refuse of its making.

"You *will* give it Life, Saryon," Joram repeated softly, lifting the weapon clumsily in his hand. Bits of clay clung to its surface. Thin tentacles of metal, from where the molten alloy had run into small crevices within the mold, branched out from the body. "You talk very righteously of death, Catalyst. And you are right. This"—he shook the sword awkwardly, almost dropping it, its weight twisting his wrist—"is dead. It deals death. But the blade cuts both ways, Saryon. It deals life as well. It will be life for Andon and his people, to say nothing of the others out there Blachloch plans to exploit."

"You don't care about any of that!" Saryon accused, breathing heavily.

"Perhaps I don't," Joram said coldly. Straightening, tossing the curly mane of black hair back from his face, he stared at Saryon, the dark eyes expressionless. "Who does? The Emperor? Your Bishop? What about your god even? No, just you, Catalyst. And that is your misfortune, not mine. Because you care, you will do this for me."

Saryon's tongue clove to the roof of his mouth. Words seethed in his brain, but found no utterance. How could this young man see into the very darkness of his soul?

Seeing the catalyst's agonized face and wide, staring eyes, Joram smiled once again, that eerie smile in which there was no light.

"You say we have brought death into the world," he said, shrugging. "I say death was already in the world, and we have brought life."

The sword lay upon the anvil. Joram had placed it once again into the coals, heating it until the metal was malleable. The weapon glowed red, taking on the properties of the iron in the alloy rather than the white-glowing darkstone. Now, with ringing blows of his hammer, the young man beat the edges of the blade thin. Once the weapon was tempered, he would use a stone wheel to grind the point and edges to cutting sharpness.

Saryon watched Joram work, his mind in turmoil, his eyes glazed and stinging. His head pounded with the hammer blows that jolted through his body.

Life . . . death . . . life . . . death . . . Every hammer blow, every heart beat, struck it out. Saryon had been wrong. The sword wasn't dead, he realized now. It was alive, terribly alive, twisting and jerking, seeming to revel in every blow. The noise was unnerving, but when Joram finally cast the hammer aside, the terrible silence was louder and more painful than the hammer's pounding. Gripping the sword firmly with long iron tongs, Joram looked grimly over at the catalyst. Hunched miserably in his robes, Saryon shivered with a chill sweat.

"Now, Catalyst," said Joram. "Grant me Life." He spoke in a mocking voice, imitating Blachloch.

Saryon closed his eyes, but he could still see the red fire of the forge imprinted upon the lids. It seemed his vision swam with blood. Joram's image was there, an indistinct patch of darkness, while the weapon he held glowed a garish green. Visions appeared amidst the flame and blood — the young Deacon, dying; Andon, bound to a wooden stake, his body sagging beneath the blows; Mosiah, running, but not fast enough to shake off his pursuers.

I say death is in the world. . . .

Saryon hesitated. Other visions came to his mind — the Bishop carrying the tiny Prince to his death, all the children he himself sent to their deaths "for the sake of the world."

Perhaps the world had existed only in each one of those children.

All around Saryon was stillness and silence. He could hear his own heart beating, like muffled hammer blows, and he knew that for him, the world existed now only in Mosiah, in Andon, in the children of that small farming village who had watched their homes burning. Drawing a deep breath, Saryon summoned the magic.

The catalyst felt it flow into his body, filling him with the Enchantment and, at the same time, demanding an outlet. Slowly he rose from the chair where he had been sitting and came forward to stand before Joram.

"Place the weapon on the floor before me," Saryon tried to say, but the words were inaudible.

Obeying more by instinct than because he understood, Joram laid the weapon at the catalyst's feet.

As he knelt for the Ritual of the Dawn, as he knelt for Evening Prayers, as he knelt before the Almin who was far away, attending services at the Font, Saryon knelt on the stone floor before the sword. Reaching out a trembling hand, he grasped hold of the hilt. His flesh shriveled as he touched it; he feared it might burn him, but the magical alloy had already grown cold and rigid. The bitter chill of the iron shot through his arm, striking a blow to his heart. But Saryon held the sword fast, exalted by a strength of spirit that overcame the weakness of the flesh.

With a soft sigh, Saryon repeated the prayer that accompanied the granting of Life and felt the magic flow from the world, through his body, into the dead hunk of man-begotten metal.

In his hand, the sword began to glow again, this time with the white radiance of the molten darkstone. Brighter and brighter it shone, appearing hot enough to melt through the very rock upon which the blade rested, but it was still cool to the touch; the catalyst still held the hilt in his hand.

He couldn't let go! He couldn't close the conduit he had opened to the weapon! Like a Living being, the sword sucked the magic from him, drained him dry, then used him to continue to absorb magic from all around it. Gasping for breath, feeling himself growing weaker and weaker, Saryon tried to wrench his hand free from the weapon, but he couldn't move it.

"Joram!" he whispered, "help me!"

But Joram was staring at the sword, its cold, white glow was so bright it seemed the moon had escaped the storm clouds and come here to rule.

Fainting, Saryon sank onto the floor, his mind in a stupor as the magic surged into him, through him, and out of him with a force that was carrying his own Life force with it. Darkness closed around him even as the light grew brighter and brighter.

And then strong arms lifted him and strong hands were dragging him across the cold floor, propping him up against something he was too sick and dizzy to recognize. He could not see, a brilliant white light blinded him. Where was the sword? The white light was far from him, halfway across the cavern it seemed, yet it also seemed to him that he still held the cold metal in his hand and would always hold it, forever and ever.

Outside, Saryon could hear the wind again, and feel its cool breath upon his cheek. He must be lying near the cavern entrance, he thought dimly, and then the sound of the wind was swallowed by a hissing noise. Opening his eyes in horror, he saw Joram plunge the cold, burning sword into the water trough. A cloud of white, foul-smelling steam rose up around him, like a ghost fleeing its lifeless body.

Saryon closed his eyes again, his brain too weary to absorb any more. The light, the fog, Joram's white face, everything merged together into a swirling, suffocating vortex. Nausea swept over him, his stomach clenched. He was going to be sick. Slumping down, he pressed his fevered cheek against the cold stone, longing for a breath of fresh air.

Above the hissing of the boiling, bubbling water, he heard Joram's voice whispering an almost reverent invocation.

"The Darksword . . ."

9

Simkin's Deal

The journey back from the forge through the gray of early morning was one of furtive stumbling, bone-chilling cold, and mind-numbing exhaustion. The gale had blown itself out. The wind died, the rain ceased. The only sounds in the still-sleeping town were the dripping rainwater from the eaves of the houses and the half-awake bark of some unusually dedicated house dog. But the cold was bitter. Even the prison began to seem a haven of peace and warmth to Saryon as he staggered through the strange, dark streets, supported by Joram's arm. With him as well, the young man carried the Darksword, pressed close against his body, hidden beneath his cloak.

Both Joram and Saryon were worn out, drained by excitement and terror. But now rose up to haunt them the sudden fear—all but forgotten in the turmoil of the sword's creation—that something might have gone wrong. Had the guard awakened and decided to investigate? Had Mosiah been caught? Was Blachloch sitting, waiting for them as a cat waits patiently for the mouse? These fears grew as the two drew nearer and nearer the prison. When they reached the street where the building stood, both stopped, shrinking into the shadows, staring at it intently before they dared go further.

All seemed quiet. No light burned in the guard's window as must have been the case had he been aroused. No light shone in the prison window.

"Everything's all right," said Saryon with a sigh of relief, starting forward.

"It could be a trap," cautioned Joram, his hand on his sword.

"At this point, I don't care," said the catalyst wearily, but he stayed with Joram.

Gripping his sword clumsily, not at all certain what he would do with it if attacked, Joram continued down the street. For him, too, the exhilaration was fading, leaving him feeling unusually tired and drained. The old dark despondency was rapidly claiming him.

Nothing had turned out as he had hoped. The sword was heavy and awkward. He felt no surge of power when he held it, only an aching in his wrist and arm from the unaccustomed weight. He had tried to grind an edge to it, but the hands that could be so delicate performing his "magic" had proved clumsy and unskilled in this. He had botched the job, he feared. The blade was uneven and marred, not curved and sharp as those he had seen in the ancient texts. He was a fool to think this crude, ugly weapon could ever overcome Blachloch's wizardry, and so on and on his mind turned, spiraling downward. The blackness was coming over him; he recognized the symptoms. Well, what did it matter, he thought darkly. Let it come. He had achieved his goal, such as it was.

With a last, furtive glance at the guard's window across the way, and seeing no sign of movement, Joram pressed softly on the door. Opening it, he motioned Saryon to come inside.

Mosiah slept sitting at the table, his head buried in his arms. Hearing movement, he started up, partially rising out of the chair in sleepy alarm.

"What — Father!" The young man came forward to catch the catalyst, whose knees were giving way beneath him. "My god, you look awful! What happened? Where's Joram? Is everything all right?"

Saryon could only nod wearily as Mosiah led him to his bed. "I'll get you some wine . . ."

"No," Saryon murmured. "I couldn't keep it down. I just need rest. . . ."

Helping the spent catalyst lie down, Mosiah covered the man's shivering body with a worn blanket, then turned as Joram shut the door behind him.

"Saryon looks terrible. Is he hurt? You don't look much better. What happened?"

"Nothing. We're fine, both of us. Just tired. Did everything go all right here?" Joram spoke with obvious effort. Seeing Mosiah nod, he walked to his bed and, lifting the straw mattress, pulled something from beneath his cloak and slid it underneath.

The words were on Mosiah's lips to ask what it was, but, recognizing the symptoms of the impending melancholia on Joram's grim face, he thought better of it. He wasn't certain he wanted to see it anyway.

"Everything was quiet here," he answered instead. "No one even walked down the street that I saw. The storm was fierce. It didn't end until early this morning. I — I must have dozed off when the wind quit howling . . ."

Mosiah quit talking when it became apparent Joram wasn't listening. Casting himself on the bed, the young man stared at nothing with unseeing eyes. Saryon had already fallen into a restless sleep. His body twitched and jerked. Once he moaned and muttered something incoherent. Feeling alone and disquieted, a strange, unreasoning fear growing within him, Mosiah was walking softly across the room when a whispering voice from outside made every nerve tingle.

"I say, open the door!"

A cold, shivering sensation flashed down Mosiah's spine at the sound of an unusual tenseness in the usually carefree voice. Glancing swiftly at Joram, Mosiah flung the door open and Simkin darted inside.

"Shut it quickly, there's a good boy. I trust I wasn't seen."
Slipping to the window, keeping in the shadows, Simkin
peered outside. The foolish, negligent look was gone, the
skin beneath the beard was pale, the lips white.

"All quiet," he murmured. "Well, that won't last long."

"What's the matter? What's gone wrong?"

"Rather bad news, I'm afraid," Simkin said, turning to
Mosiah with a strained imitation of his playful smile. "I've
just been to check on the guard—see if he spent a restful
night. He did. *Very* restful, if you take my meaning."

"Well, I don't," Mosiah said irritably. "What's the matter?"

"You see," began Simkin, biting his lip. "It's like this. The
great lout has actually been inconsiderate enough to go and
die on us."

"Die!" Mosiah's mouth sagged open. For an instant he
was struck dumb, and could do nothing but stare at Simkin.
Then, he stumbled across the room. "Joram!" he whispered
urgently, shaking him. "Joram! Please! It's urgent, I—we
need you! Joram!"

Slowly Joram tore his gaze from the ceiling. Mosiah
could almost see him struggling to the surface of the blackness that washed over him. "What?"

"The guard, Simkin's killed him!"

Joram's brown eyes opened wide. Sitting up, he stared
coldly at Simkin. "You were supposed to just drug him."

"That's precisely what I did," said Simkin, hurt.

"What did you give him?"

"Henbane," Simkin muttered.

"Henbane?" repeated Mosiah in horror. "But that's nightshade! It's poisonous."

"To chickens," Simkin remarked with a sniff. "I had no
idea it would affect louts, though he was a foul sort of fellow
now that I think of it."

Mosiah sat down at the end of Joram's bed, trying to
think. "Are you sure he's uh—uh—dead? Maybe he's just a
heavy sleeper . . ."

"Not unless he goes cold and limp as a mackerel and
sleeps with his eyes wide open. No, no, he's quite dead, I
assure you. The skin of ale was still full, lying beside him.
Probably keeled over after the first mouthful. I wonder, come

to think of it, if I didn't get that potion mixed up with one from the Duchess de Longeville? As I recall, they found her second husband in much the same state —"

"Shut up!" Moisah cried tersely. "What can we do? Joram? We've got to think." He wiped chill sweat from his face. "I know! We'll hide the body. Take it into the woods . . ."

Joram said nothing. Sitting on the edge of the bed, his head sank into his hand, the black shadows gathering about him.

"That's an excellent plan, dear boy," said Simkin, looking at Mosiah with admiration. "Truly. I'm quite impressed. But" — he raised a hand as Mosiah leaped to his feet — "it won't work. I wasn't . . . um . . . alone, you see, when I made my little discovery. One of Blachloch's henchmen, Drumlor by name, was keeping me company along with this skin of remarkably fine wine." Simkin heaved a sigh. "I'm afraid he took the demise of his compatriot rather hard. Hotfooted it back to the warlock's. Quite amazing how fast he could run considering how drunk —"

"You mean Blachloch knows about this?"

"If he doesn't now, I should say he will in a matter of moments."

"Damn you!" Jumping up, Mosiah leaped at Simkin, catching hold of him by his lace-covered lapels and hurling him back against the wall. "Damn you for a fool! What do we do now?"

"Well, to me it would seem advantageous to wake up the slumbering bald party there," replied Simkin, smoothing out his crumpled lace with injured dignity. "Though how he can sleep through your screaming is beyond me. Then we have to rouse our dark friend from his fit of sulks. . . ."

"I'm all right. Wake up Saryon," said Joram. Seeing Mosiah take another step toward Simkin, he stood up. "Stop it! Both of you, calm down. We've done nothing wrong."

"We haven't?" Simkin appeared dubious.

"No. Go on, Mosiah! Wake up the catalyst. We've got to get our stories straight. . . ."

Shaking his head, Mosiah hurried over to the bed where the catalyst was sleeping fitfully. "Father!" Bending over him, he shook him by the shoulder. "Father!"

"Now," said Joram coolly, "The catalyst and I—"

His voice died.

Turning around, his hand still on the catalyst's shoulder, Mosiah saw the black-cloaked warlock materialize in the center of the room, his hands clasped before him as was customary, his eyes hidden by the overhanging black cowl.

"You and the catalyst what, young man?" said the expressionless voice.

"—have been in all night," Joram continued coolly. "You could ask your guard, but that might be difficult now unless you are a Necromancer."

"Yes, I figured Simkin would tell you of the guard's death," Blachloch said, glancing at the bearded young man.

"Frightful shock to me, I assure you," remarked Simkin. Snatching the orange silk from the air, he dabbed delicately at his forehead. "I'm quite unstrung, as the Baron of Esock said when he mistakenly transformed himself into a mandolin. What do you suppose he died of?" Simkin asked casually. "The guard, that is. The Baron died in a rather freak accident. The Baroness, a largish sort of woman, sat on his case. Smashed him to splinters, but he went out with a song. As to your guard, he was his usual loutish self when I left him last night. Perhaps he suffocated." Simkin held the orange silk to his nose. "I know he had that effect on me."

"He was poisoned," said Blachloch, ignoring Simkin, his hooded head turned to Joram. His eyes might well have been fingers, probing the young man's brain. "So, you were here all night? What were you doing, playing in the firepit?"

Glancing down at his soot-blackened clothes and skin, Joram shrugged. "I didn't bother to wash when I got home from the forge yesterday."

Without a word, his hands still folded before him, Blachloch turned and walked over to where Mosiah had finally succeeded in rousing the catalyst.

"You were in all night, too, Father?" the warlock said.

"Y-yes." Saryon peered up at the black-robed Enforcer, blinking dazedly. Though half-asleep and completely unable to figure out what was going on, he could feel danger crackling in the air. Trying desperately to shake off his drowsiness, he sat up, rubbing his eyes.

Blachloch reached down and snatched the blanket from Saryon's body. "The hem of your robe is wet, Catalyst. And covered with soot and mud as well."

"The chimney leaks," said Mosiah sullenly.

Blachloch smiled. "Grant me Life, Catalyst," he said softly.

Saryon shuddered. "I cannot," he replied in a low voice, staring at the floor. "I have no energy. I . . . spent a bad night . . ." Realizing the irony of his words, and having the terrible feeling that the warlock was aware of it too, Saryon paled, waiting in uncaring exhaustion for whatever might come next.

Nothing came. Turning away from the catalyst, Blachloch cast a final glance at them all and, without saying another word, vanished.

The four stared at each other in silence for long moments, afraid to talk, afraid even to move.

"He's gone," Saryon said heavily. His muscles ached with weariness. His numb brain, unable to cope with whatever had occurred, kept urging him to ignore everything and go back to sleep. Shaking his head firmly, the catalyst staggered to his feet, crossed the chill floor, and plunged his head and face into a washbowl of icy water.

"How long do you suppose he was here before we knew it?" Mosiah asked in a strained, tense voice.

"What does it matter?" Joram replied with an uncaring shrug. "He knows we're lying."

"Then, why didn't he do something!" Mosiah cried, his taut nerves snapping. "What kind of game is he playing—"

"The kind of game you're losing already if you don't get hold of yourself," Simkin said languidly. "Look at *me!*" He held out his lace-covered hand. "There. Not a flutter. And *I* discovered the body. Speaking of the body, I wonder what jolly thing they plan to do with it. If they dump it in the river, I, for one, am not taking a bath for a year—"

"Body!" Saryon's eyes widened.

"Explain things to Briar Rose, will you, dear boy? I really couldn't go through it again. Quite fatiguing. By the way"— Simkin asked in bored tones, glancing across at Joram— "did everything go well last night?"

Joram did not answer; lapsing into despondency once more, he sank back onto the bed.

"I say, you might at least tell me what you were doing, after all the trouble I went to—"

"Murdering guards!" Mosiah snapped viciously.

"Well, if you want to put it in that crude fashion. Still, I— Almin's blood, you lout!"

This exclamation was occasioned by the door to the prison flying open, nearly knocking Simkin over. Casting a sneering glance at the irate young man, one of Blachloch's henchmen stepped inside as Simkin was trying to go out.

"I say, do move to one side or the other," Simkin said, the silk to his nose. "I can't go through you. Well, I suppose I could, but you wouldn't like it much. . . ."

"You're not going anywhere. Orders. I came to tell you. Not till—"

"Oh, no. Really, this won't do at all," Simkin said. Coolly stepping past the guard, he gave the man a wide berth, his nose wrinkling. "I'm certain you're mistaken. Those orders do not apply to me, now, do they? Only to these three."

"Well, I—" the henchemen stammered, frowning.

"There, there." Simkin patted the man on the shoulder as he walked out the door. "Don't tax your brain so, old chap. You're liable to go into a fit." With a final flourish of orange silk, he glanced back into the prison. "Farewell, dear friends. Delighted to have been able to help. I'm away."

"Help!" Mosiah muttered as the door shut behind the gaudily clad figure, the henchman pacing back and forth outside.

Going over to the window, Mosiah saw the young man make his mincing way across the street to the house where the guard had died. Two of Blachloch's men were removing the body, and Simkin fell into step beside them, holding his orange silk over his nose and mouth. At the same time, several more guards took up positions in the window, keeping their eyes upon the prison. Slamming his hand on the window ledge in disgust, Mosiah turned away. "If it hadn't been for that buffoon and his nightshade, everything would be all right. He might as well have turned us over to Blachloch himself! Maybe you'll believe me about him, Joram. Now that it's too late."

Joram lay back on his bed without answering or even giving any indication he had heard. His hands beneath his head, he stared up at the ceiling.

Wiping the water from his face with the sleeves of his robe, Saryon crossed to the window and looked out to see Simkin marching at the head of what had become an impromptu funeral procession, the guards following behind with their grim burden and grimmer faces. Dabbing at his eyes, Simkin called mournful greetings to the few townspeople who were up and stirring. No one answered; they stared at the body in fearful perplexity, then hurried off, whispering together and shaking their heads.

Stupidity? Saryon's mind went back to the forest outside the village of Walren, the forest where he had first met Simkin.

"It is a deep game we play, brother," the young man had said. *"Deep and dangerous."*

What was Simkin's game?

The news of the guard's murder spread rapidly through the small community. The people flitted from house to house, talking in frightened, subdued voices. Blachloch's henchmen seemed to be everywhere, roaming the streets with grim, eager looks, as if they knew what was going to happen and were looking forward to it. Eventually, the townspeople went to work at their various labors, but nothing much got done. Most people left their jobs early. Even the smithy shut down the forge before nightfall, glad to be going home.

It had been a long day for the smith, long and unsettling. First Blachloch's men had arrived, poking around, overturning this, upsetting that, and asking questions.

"Was someone working last night?"

"Yes."

"Who?"

"I don't know offhand." This with a shrug of massive shoulders. "One er two of the 'prentices, mayhap. They're behind in their work. We're all behind and getting behinder when we're stopped and made to answer stupid questions."

Finally, Blachloch's flunkies left, to be replaced by Blachloch himself. The smith wasn't surprised. A middle-aged man with grown sons, the smith was shrewd and obser-vant, if somewhat hotheaded. He had the reputation of bear-ing no love for the warlock; the raid on the village filled him with grief and anger. He heartily approved of Andon's deter-mination to starve rather than eat bread laced with blood. He advocated taking stronger measures against the warlock, in fact, and would have if the old man, fearing harsh reprisals, had not pleaded with him to remain calm.

The smith had agreed reluctantly, and then only because he was storing up a cache of his own weapons for use when the time came. Just when that time was going to arrive, he wasn't certain, but he had the feeling it wasn't far off, judging from Andon's worried face and certain mysterious occur-rences he'd noticed around the forge.

"Did someone work last night?" Blachloch asked.

"Yes."

"Who?"

"I already said, I don't know," the smith growled.

"Could it have been Joram?"

"Could have. Could have been any of the 'prentices. Ask them."

All these questions and more the smith answered shortly without stopping his work, the ringing blows of his hammer punctuating his words with such force it seemed he might have the warlock stretched out upon his anvil. But he an-swered the questions nonetheless, keeping his eyes averted from the black-robed figure. As much as he hated Blachloch, the smith feared him still more.

Watching him out of the corner of his eye, the smith fol-lowed the warlock's movements through the forge as Blachloch searched the premises. He touched little, just sent his penetrating glance into every shadow, every crevice and corner. Finally, he came to a stop. Using a booted foot, he sorted idly through a pile of refuse in a far corner until, bending down, he picked something up.

"What's this?" he asked, turning the object over in his hand, studying it in a casual manner, his face expressionless as always.

"Crucible," grunted the smith, continuing his hammering.

"What is its use?"

"Melting ore."

"Does that residue look at all odd to you?" Blachloch held the crucible out to the smith, holding it in the light of the glowing forge.

"No," said the smith, glancing at it nonchalantly, then looking back at his work. But his gaze darted to it once again, when he thought the warlock wasn't watching. Catching Blachloch's stare, the smith flushed and fixed his eyes once more upon his work, the force of his hammer blows increasing.

Crucible in hand, the warlock gazed at the smith intently. The eyes within the folds of the black hood gleamed red in the fire of the forge. "No more night work in the forge, Master Smith," he said coolly as he slowly disappeared into the air as effortlessly as the smoke rising up the chimney.

Recalling both the words and the look, the smith shivered again now, just as he had shivered this morning. Possesesed of a certain amount of magic himself, though not as much as others, he was overawed by the power of the warlock and even more by his intelligence. It was a dangerous combination, he thought, and his hidden cache of weapons suddenly appeared to him puny and useless.

"Warlock could turn them to a heap o' molten iron, just as they started out," he was saying to himself gloomily, preparing to leave for the night, when he heard a noise.

"What's that?" he called out hesitantly, thinking that it might be Blachloch returning. "Who's there?"

There came a tremendous crash, followed by an oath. Then a plaintive voice rose up from the depths of the shadows in the back of the cavern. "I say, I'm in rather a fix here. Could you give me a hand? Not literally, mind you," the voice added hastily. "Disgusting trick of the Marquis d'Winter. Same old joke, year after year. Yanks it off at the wrist. I've told the Emperor he'd stop doing it if nobody laughed, but —"

"Simkin?" said the smith in astonishment, hurrying through the forge to the back of the cavern where he found the young man attempting unsuccessfully to extricate himself from beneath a mound of tools and implements. "What are you doing, lad?"

"Shhh," whispered Simkin. "No one's to know I'm here. . . ."

"A bit late for that, ain't it?" asked the smith grimly. "You've just waked up half the town by now—"

"It wasn't my fault," said Simkin peevishly, casting a scathing glance at the pile of tools. "I was— Oh, never mind," He lowered his voice. "Was Blachloch here today?"

"Yes," growled the smith, glancing about nervously.

"Did he find anything, take anything? It's quite urgent that I know." Simkin looked at the smith anxiously.

The smith hesitated, frowning. "Well," he said after a moment, "I suppose it won't hurt to tell you. He didn't keep it a secret. He found a crucible."

"Crucible?" Simkin raised an eyebrow. "That's all? I mean, I suppose you have lots of them, lying about."

"Yeah, we do. That's what 'e found, though, and 'e took it with 'im. Now, you best come out the front with me. How'd you get in, without my seein' you?" the smith asked as an afterthought, staring at Simkin suspiciously.

"Oh, I'm easily overlooked." The young man waved his hand negligently, his bright clothes glistening brilliantly in the light of the banked forge fire. "About this crucible. There wasn't something odd with it, was there?"

The smith's frown deepened. Snapping his lips shut, he marshaled Simkin toward the front of the cavern.

"Some sort of strange something in it, for example," the young man continued nonchalantly, tripping over a mold.

"I wouldn't know," said the smith coldly when they finally reached the front of the cavern. "An' you kin tell whoever's interested that there's to be no more night work. Not for a long time. Maybe never." The smith shook his head gloomily.

"Night work?" repeated Simkin with a shrug and a strange smile. "Ah, I think you're wrong about that. There'll be one more piece of night work—but it needn't concern you," he said reassuringly to the startled smith, who—glancing at him grimly—shut the door to the forge and sealed it with a magical spell.

10

The Fall of the Cards

The Chamber of Discretion was a one-way-only communication device. Bishop Vanya could contact his minions. They could not contact him. Thus the early designers made certain that the minion remained under the power of his master. It did have a drawback, however, and this was that the master could not be contacted on matters of urgency or those that required immediate instruction. This drawback did not bother Vanya overmuch, the Bishop being in such complete control that he deemed it unlikely any such situation should arise.

He was somewhat disagreeably startled, therefore, to enter the Chamber of Discretion on this late fall evening and feel the very darkness around him humming and vibrating with energy. Though minions could not contact him, the Chamber was so sensitive to the minds of those it touched that any of them, concentrating their thoughts upon their master, could make him aware of their need.

Annoyed, Vanya sat in the chair. Closing his eyes, he calmly and deliberately cleansed his mind of any obtrusive or obstructing thoughts, leaving it clear and open to impressions. One formed almost immediately. An ominous feeling of foreboding oppressed the Bishop. He had been expecting — no, dreading — this for some time now, he realized.

"I am here," Vanya said to the impression in his mind. "What do you want? We have not spoken in some time. I assumed everything was going well."

"Everything is *not* going well," the voice replied, responding with such immediacy that Vanya knew it had been waiting for him. "Joram has discovered darkstone."

It was well the minion could not see the change that came over the master at this point, or his confidence might have been shaken. Vanya's heavy-jowled face sagged; the hand that had been crawling spiderlike upon the arm of the chair in irritable restlessness suddenly twitched, the fingers curling in upon themselves, forming a tight ball. How cold this place was. He had never noticed it before. His heavy robes were inadequate. . . .

"Are you there?"

"Yes," Vanya replied, licking his dry lips. "I thought perhaps you had made a mistake in what you said. I was waiting for you to correct yourself."

"If a mistake has been made, I haven't been the one to make it," the voice in the Bishop's head retorted. "I told you the ancient texts existed here."

"Impossible. According to the records, they were all accounted for and destroyed."

"The records are wrong. Not that it matters now. The damage has been done. He knows of the darkstone, and not only that, but with the help of your catalyst, he has learned to forge it!"

Vanya closed his eyes. The darkness whirled around him. For a startling moment, he actually felt his chair begin to slide, tilting him backward. Grasping hold of the armrests in desperation, he forced himself to relax and consider the matter calmly. No good would come of panic. There was no need for panic. This was an unexpected development, but one that could be handled.

"Waiting for me to correct a mistake again?"

"No," said Vanya coldly, "I am merely considering all the ramifications of this terrible occurrence."

"Well, here's one you may not have considered. Now that we have the darkstone, Sharakan and the Technologists could *win* this war. No need to maintain the balance of power. Balance becomes meaningless if we hold the scales in our hands."

"An interesting thought, my friend, and one worthy of you," remarked Vanya dryly, the slow fire of anger burning away his fear. "But I remind you that there are matters working here of which you have no conception. You are just one card in the deck, so to speak. No, this alters our plans, but only slightly. It is imperative, of course, that I have the boy immediately now, *plus* whatever it is he has created out of the darkstone. You must send me that fool catalyst, as well, I suppose. What on earth did you do to the man?" Vanya found vent for his frustration. "He had the spine of a brittle twig when he left here. You were supposed to break him, not strengthen it!"

"Twig! You have mistaken him as you have mistaken other things. As for sending the boy to you, that is risky. Let me kill him and the catalyst—"

"No!" The word exploded from Vanya. His pudgy hands clenched over the armrest, white dents appearing in the region where a thinner man's knuckles might have been. "No," Vanya repeated, swallowing. "The boy must *not* be killed. Is that completely understood? Disobey me in this and you will think mutation a beneficent fate compared to yours!"

"You have to catch me first, Bishop, and I remind you that you are very far away . . ."

Vanya drew a deep, quivering breath. "The boy is the Prince of Merilon," he said through clenched teeth.

There was a moment's silence, then a mental shrug. "All the better. The Prince is supposed to be dead. I will simply correct what I assume was another of your mistakes—"

"Not a mistake," Vanya said, his mouth parched. "I tell you again, the boy *must not die*! If you insist on knowing the reason, I ask you to remember this—the Prophecy."

The silence was longer, more profound this time. Vanya could almost hear its thoughts, whispering about him like the wings of bats.

"Very well," the voice said finally, coldly. "But it will be more difficult and dangerous, especially now that he has darkstone. This was not in our original bargain. My price goes up."

"You will be compensated according to your deserts," Vanya remarked. "Act quickly, before he becomes fully aware how to use the stone. And bring him personally," the Bishop added as an afterthought. "There are certain matters I wish to discuss with you, your reward among them."

"Of course I'll have to bring him personally," the voice returned. "What else am I to do? Rely on your spineless catalyst? I will come through the usual channels. Look for me when you see me."

"It must be *soon!*" Vanya said, endeavoring with all his power to keep his thoughts calm. "I will contact you tomorrow night."

"I may or may not answer," replied the voice. "This matter must be handled delicately."

The communication ended. The Chamber was silent.

A trickle of sweat ran down the Bishop's tonsured head and trickled into the collar of his robe. Pale, quivering with anger and fear, he sat in the Chamber for many hours, staring unseeing into the darkness.

For there will be born to the Royal House one who is dead yet will live, who will die again but live again. And when he returns, he will hold in his hand the destruction of the world. . . .

II

Saryon's Turn

"**L**isten, Saryon," said Joram in low, persuasive tones, "it will be simple." Sitting beside the catalyst, he slid closer still, resting his hand upon his arm. "You go to Blachloch. You tell him that you cannot rest, you cannot sleep. You are so horrified by what I have done and what I made you do that you think you might go mad."

"I am not a good liar," Saryon murmured, shaking his head.

"Would it really be a lie?" Joram asked, a bitter half-smile lighting his dark eyes. "On the contrary, I think you could be quite convincing."

The catalyst did not answer, nor did he raise his gaze from the table where the two of them sat. A fat, almost obscene autumn moon grinned down from the clear black sky. Shining through the window, it sucked all color and life into its bulging cheeks, leaving everything a stark, bloodless gray. Bathed in the moonlight, the two sat close together at the table beneath the window, talking in hushed voices,

Joram's watchful gaze divided between the guards in the house across the street and Mosiah, sleeping restlessly on a cot in a dark corner.

At the sound of voices, Mosiah stirred and muttered in his sleep, causing Joram to grip the catalyst's arm in silent warning. Neither said a word until Mosiah had drifted off again, throwing his arm over his eyes in his sleep as the moonlight crept stealthily across the floor and up the cot to examine and gloat over his pale face.

"And then what must I do?" asked Saryon.

"Tell him you will take him to me. You will help him apprehend me and"—Joram's voice lowered—"the Darksword. You will lead him to the forge, where I will be working, and there, we will have him."

Saryon shut his eyes, a shudder convulsing his body. "What do you mean—have him?"

"What do you think I mean, Catalyst?" Impatiently, Joram withdrew his hand and leaned back in his chair, glancing again at the guards, whose shadows could be seen against the background of a blazing fire in the house opposite. "We have talked about this before. Once he is drained of his magic, he will be helpless. You can open a Corridor and call the *Duuk-tsarith*. No doubt they have been waiting eagerly many years to get their hands on one who is a disgrace to their Order." He shrugged. "You will be a hero, Catalyst."

Saryon sighed and clasped his hands together upon the tabletop, his fingers digging painfully into his flesh. "What about you?" he asked Joram, his gaze going to the young man. The stern face, reflected in the moonlight, looked almost skull-like.

"What *about* me?" Joram asked coolly, staring out the window, the half-smile playing about his lips.

"A Corridor will be open, the *Duuk-tsarith* will be there. I could turn you over to them, as I was instructed to do by my superior."

"But you won't, will you—Saryon?" Joram said without looking at him. In the corner, Mosiah moaned and turned fitfully, trying to wriggle out from beneath the moon's gleeful stare. "You won't. I give you Blachloch and you give me my freedom. You need not fear me, Catalyst. I have no such ambition as Blachloch. I do not intend to use my power to take over the world. I simply want back what is rightfully mine. I will go to Merilon and, with the help of this sword I have forged, I will find it!"

Watching him, Saryon saw the young man's face soften for a moment, becoming as wistful and longing as a child's gazing at some bright, jeweled bauble. Pity surged through the catalyst. He recalled the dark stories he had heard of Joram's youth, of his insane mother. He thought of the hard life the young man had led, the constant struggle for survival, the need to hide the fact that he was truly Dead. Saryon, too, knew what it was like to be weak and helpless in this world of wizards. Memories came back to him — the longing to be able to ride the wings of the wind, to create beauty and wonder with a wave of the hand, to shape stone into towers of grace and usefulness. . . . Now Joram had this power, only it was reversed. He had the power to destroy, not create. And all he wanted to buy with it was a child's dream.

"You will undoubtedly be a hero." Joram's voice came to Saryon as if out of this dream. "You can return to the Font, go back and crawl under your rock again. I trust your failure as far as bringing me to justice will be overlooked. They can always try to apprehend me in Merilon. If they dare. . . ."

Joram was silent a moment, then he returned to reality, the wistful, childlike face hardening, becoming the face of the Sorcerer who had murdered the overseer with a stone. "When the warlock is in the forge, I will attack him with the Darksword and absorb his magic —"

"You hope," Saryon retorted, angry because he was suddenly discovering he was beginning to care for this young man. "You have only the vaguest idea of the sword's power. You know nothing about wielding such a weapon."

"I don't need to be skilled in swordplay," Joram said irritably. "We're not going to kill him, after all. When I attack and the Darksword begins to draw off his magic, you must attack also, and drain him of his Life."

Saryon shook his head. "That's too dangerous. I've never been trained for this . . ."

"You have no choice, Catalyst!" Joram said, his teeth clenching, his hand gripping Saryon's arm again. "Simkin says that Blachloch has found the crucible! If he doesn't already know about the darkstone, he soon will. Do you want to make Darkswords for him?"

The catalyst put his head in his trembling hands. Slowly releasing his arm, Joram sat back in his chair again, nodding to himself in satisfaction.

"How can we get out of here?" Saryon asked, raising a haggard face and glancing around the prison.

"Run to the guards. Tell them you were asleep, and when you woke, you discovered I was gone. Demand that they take you to see Blachloch. In the confusion, I'll slip out."

"But how? They'll be searching for you! It's—"

"— my concern, Catalyst," Joram said coldly. "You worry about your part. Stall Blachloch for as long as you can, to give me time to get there."

"Stall! What should I—"

"Faint! Be sick on him! I don't know! It shouldn't be difficult. You look as though you could do both right now anyway." With a scathing glance at the catalyst, Joram stood up and began pacing restlessly about the room.

"I am not as weak as you consider me, young man," Saryon said softly. "I should never have agreed to assist you in bringing this weapon of darkness into the world. I did, however, and now I must accept responsibility for my actions. I will do what you ask of me this night. I will help bring this evil warlock to justice. But not because I will be a hero, not to enable me to go back." Saryon was silent a moment, then, drawing a deep breath, he continued. "I can never go back. I know that now. There is nothing for me there anymore."

Joram had stopped walking and was regarding Saryon silently, intently. "And you will let me go . . ."

"Yes, but not because I fear you or your sword."

"Then why?" Joram asked, with a slight sneer.

"Exactly," Saryon murmured. "Why? I've asked myself often enough. I could tell you . . . many reasons. That our lives are bound up together in some strange way, that I knew this the first time I saw you, that this goes back to a time in my life before you were even born. I could tell you this." He shook his head. "I could tell you about a druid who counseled me. I could tell you about a baby I held. . . . It all seems tied together somehow, and it doesn't make sense. I can see already you don't believe it."

"Whether I believe you or not doesn't make a damn bit of difference. I really don't care what your reasons are, Catalyst, so long as you do what I ask of you."

"I will, but on one condition."

"Ah, now we come to it," Joram said, scowling. "What is it? That I turn *myself* in? Or maybe remain buried in this godforsaken wilderness —"

"That you take me with you," Saryon said in a low voice.

"What?" Joram stared at the catalyst in astonishment. Then, nodding to himself, he gave a short, ugly laugh. "Of course, I see. Every Dead man needs his own catalyst." Shrugging, he almost smiled. "By all means, come with me to Merilon. We'll have a jolly time together, as our friend Simkin would say. Now, are we ready to get on with this?"

Moving carefully and silently to avoid waking Mosiah, Joram turned his back upon the startled catalyst and walked across the small room. He knelt beside his bed, put his hands beneath the mattress, and, slowly and reverently, drew forth the Darksword.

Saryon watched him in puzzled silence. He had expected rage, refusal. He had expected to have to stand firm on his position, to resist arguments, even threats. This casual, uncaring acceptance was, somehow, worse. Maybe the young man didn't understand. . . .

Joram was carefully wrapping the sword in rags. Coming up behind him, Saryon put his hand on the young man's shoulder. "I'm not going to turn you in. I only want to help you. You see, you can't go back either. Not to Merilon —"

"Look, Catalyst," Joram said, standing up, angrily jerking himself free of the man's touch, "I've already said — I don't care what you do or where you go so long as you help me in this. Understood? Fine." He looked down at the sword he held cradled in his hands. The moonlight reflecting white off the rags made the skeletal-looking metal object lying within seem that much darker by stark contrast. The image of the Dead baby, wrapped in the white cloth of the Royal House, came to Saryon's mind. Shutting his eyes, he turned away.

Seeing the catalyst's reaction, Joram's lip curled. "If the sermon is ended, Father"—the word was uttered with such venom Saryon flinched—"we must go. I want to get this over with."

Thrusting the sword into a leather belt he had fashioned and now wore about his waist—a crude imitation of those he had seen pictured in the texts—Joram threw a long, dark cloak (provided by Simkin) over his shoulders. He walked the length of the prison cell, looking down at himself critically. The sword was hidden. Nodding to himself, he turned to Saryon and gestured peremptorily.

"Go on. I'm ready."

Am I? Saryon asked himself in agony. He wanted to say something, but he could not talk and, coughing, tried to clear his throat. It was useless. He could never swallow fear. Joram's face darkened, scowling at this delay. Saryon could see the muscles stand out rigid and stiff in the young man's firm jawline, a nerve twitched in one eye, and his hands, hanging straight at his sides, clench and unclench nervously. But in the eyes burned a light brighter than the moon's, brighter—and colder.

No, there was nothing to say. Nothing at all.

Reaching out, his own hand trembling, Saryon gently and silently opened the door. Every nerve, every fiber, of his being warned him to turn around, to refuse, to stay within this house. But the momentum of his past life was rising around him like a great wave. Caught in the tide, he could do nothing but ride the foaming waters hurling him forward, even though he could see clearly the jagged stones looming dark before him.

12

King of Swords

Blachloch placed his folded hands upon the desk in front of him. "And so, Father, feeling wretched over committing one immoral act, and terrified that you might be forced to commit another, you saw as your only alternative the commission of a deed so heinous, so black, it was banned by your own Order centuries ago?"

"I have admitted that I was not thinking clearly," Saryon murmured, the warlock's bald statement of the facts unnerving him. "I — I am a scholar. . . . This type of life frightens and . . . and confuses me."

"But you are confused no longer," Blachloch said wryly. "Appalled and horrified, but not confused. You will surrender the Darksword and Joram to me."

"The sword must be destroyed," Saryon interrupted. "Or I will not go through with this."

"Of course," Blachloch replied with a slight shrug of his shoulders, as though this were nothing more than a cracked ale mug they were discussing, not a sword that could conceivably give him power to rule the world. What a fool he must take me for, Saryon thought bitterly. Blachloch clasped his hands before him. "Now, as for the boy . . ."

"He must be turned over to Bishop Vanya," Saryon said, his voice rasping.

"So, Simkin was right," Blachloch remarked. "That is the real reason you were sent to this coven."

"Yes." Saryon swallowed.

"I wish you would have confided in me," the warlock said, his two index fingers coming together to form a small sword, pointed at the catalyst. "Life would have been much simpler for you, Father. Your Bishop Vanya must be an imbecile," he muttered, a tiny line appearing in his forehead, his eyes staring into a shadowy corner, "to think a scholar like you could deal with a murderer like this Joram. . . ."

"You will see that he is taken to the Font?" Saryon pursued, flushing. "I cannot do so myself for . . . for obvious reasons. I presume your contacts in the *Duuk-tsarith* —"

"Yes. That can be arranged," Blachloch cut in. "You say 'for obvious reasons.' I presume you mean that you dare not return to the fold. What of yourself in all this, Father?"

"I should surrender myself to Bishop Vanya," Saryon answered, knowing what was expected of him. He lowered his head, his gaze on his shoes. "I have committed a grievous sin. I deserve my fate."

"The Turning to Stone, Father. A terrible way to . . . live. I know. As I told you, I've seen it done. *That* would be your punishment for helping to create the Darksword, as of course you yourself know. Such a waste," Blachloch said, running his finger over his blond mustache, "such a waste."

Saryon shuddered. Yes, that would be his punishment. Could he face it? To live forever with the knowledge of what he had done? No, if it came to that, there were ways of ending things. Henbane, for example.

"Still, you might be forgiven, considered something of a hero . . ."

Saryon shook his head.

"Ah, this is your second infraction. I had forgotten. So your options are immortality of a most horrible sort or staying here with the coven and reconciling yourself to committing further immoral acts." Blachloch's fingers raised slightly, pointing at Saryon's heart. "There is, of course, another alternative."

Glancing up quickly, Saryon saw Blachloch's meaning plainly expressed on the cold face and in the unblinking eyes. The catalyst swallowed again, a bitter taste filling his mouth. It was uncanny the way the man could see into his head, uncanny and frightening.

"The . . . the last is not an alternative," Saryon said, shifting uncomfortably. "Suicide is an unpardonable sin."

"Whereas assisting me to rape and plunder or assisting Joram to create a weapon that could destroy the world is not," Blachloch said with a sneer. His hands unclasped, spreading out, palms down, upon the desk. "I admire the neat and tidy way you catalysts think. Still, it works out usefully for me, so why should I complain?"

Sweating beneath his robes, Saryon found it safer not to reply. Matters were going well, almost too well. Probably, as Joram had said, because he was not having to lie. Well, not that much. Suicide was an unpardonable sin only if one believed in a god.

"Where is the young man?" Blachloch rose to his feet.

Saryon, too, stood up, thankful for the flowing robes that covered his trembling legs. "In . . . in the forge," he said faintly.

No fire burned in the forge this night. A faint red glow glimmered from the banked coals, but it was the white, cold glimmer of the sinking moon that touched the blade of the sword, it surface pockmarked with hammer blows, its edge sharp, though irregular and uneven.

The sword was the first object Saryon saw as he and Blachloch materialized within the moonlit darkness of the forge. The weapon lay upon the anvil, basking in the moonlight like a perverse snake.

Blachloch saw it too, Saryon knew. Though he could not see the warlock's face, hidden as it was by the shadows of his black hood, he could tell by the sharp intake of breath that even the discipline of the *Duuk-tsarith* could not suppress. The clasped hands quivered, their fingers twitching, longing to touch. But the Enforcer was in command of himself.

Every sense alert, his mind reached into the shadows, seeking his prey.

Saryon himself looked about almost casually for Joram. The catalyst had expected to be paralyzed with fear; his hands had been shaking so when he left Blachloch's dwelling that he had barely been able to open a conduit to the warlock. But now that he was here, his fear had left him, leaving a cold, clear feeling of emptiness inside.

Standing in the forge, looking around for what might be the last minutes of his life, Saryon felt the world rush in to fill the void. It was as if he were living each second separately, moving from one to another with the steady regularity of a heartbeat. Each second absorbed his complete attention; he literally saw everything, heard everything, was aware of everything around him in that one second. Then he moved on to the next. The oddest thing was that none of it had any meaning for him. He was detached, an observer, looking on while his body performed its role in this deadly play. Blachloch could have cut off his hands right now, severed them at the wrist, and Saryon would not have cried out, would not have felt a thing. He could almost envision himself, standing there in the moonlit darkness, staring calmly at the dripping blood.

So this is courage, he thought, watching as a hand, glowing white in the moonlight, reached out from the shadows and silently grasped the hilt of the sword.

There was no sound and only the barest hint of movement. Indeed, if Saryon had not been staring straight at the sword, he would never have noticed; Joram had acted with the skill and deftness of the art his mother had taught him as a child. But the *Duuk-tsarith* are trained to hear night itself creep up behind them.

Blachloch reacted with such speed that Saryon saw only a black wind whirling through the forge, scattering sparks from the coals. With a motion and a word, the warlock cast the spell that would leave his opponent powerless to move or act or even think, the spell that drained magic, drained Life.

Except Joram had no Life.

Saryon almost laughed, so tense was he, as he felt the magic spell hit the young man a blow that should have been shattering. It fluttered down around him like so many rose petals. The white hand continued to lift the sword. The metal did not gleam. It was a streak of darkness slashing through the moonlight, as though Joram held the embodiment of night.

Stepping into the light, Joram lifted the sword before him, his face tense and strained, his eyes darker than the metal. Saryon could sense the young man's fear and uncertainty; despite all his study, Joram had only the vaguest idea of the metal's powers. But the catalyst, every sense alive and attuned for the first time — he might have been newborn in this instant — could also sense Blachloch's uncertainty, astonishment, growing fear.

What did the *Duuk-tsarith* know of the darkstone? Probably not much more than Joram. What thoughts must be rushing through the warlock's mind. Was the sword responsible for blocking his Nullmagic spell? Would it block others? Blachloch must make his decision on his next move instantaneously, split-second. For all he knew, his life might well depend upon it.

Coolly, calmly, the *Duuk-tsarith* chose his spell and cast it. His eyes lit with a green glow and instantly a greenish liquid condensed from the air onto Joram's skin, where it began to bubble and hiss. Green Venom, the spell was called. Recognizing it, Saryon winced, his stomach clenching. The pain was excruciating, so he had heard, as if every nerve ending were on fire. Any magus strong enough to shield himself against the Nullmagic must fall victim to the venom's magical paralysis. He would not be able to protect against both.

And it apparently affected the Dead as well as the Living. Joram's face twisted in agony. He gasped, his body beginning to double over as the liquid spread and the fiery pain burned through his flesh. But it was a spell whose casting drained a magus rapidly.

"Grant me Life, Catalyst!" Blachloch demanded, his eyes glowing a more brilliant green as they stared at the young man.

This is the time, Saryon knew. The time I must decide. I am Joram's only chance. Without me, he must fall. He cannot control the sword, if the darkstone is even working. The catalyst glanced swiftly at the weapon and a shiver of exultation swept over him. Joram's body glowed green, the young man screamed in terrible pain. He was literally crumbling to the floor as the venom surged through his body. But his hands still gripped the sword, the hands themselves were not coated with the deadly liquid, and, even as Saryon watched, the venom began to disappear from Joram's arms and upper body — the Darksword was absorbing the magic.

It was doing so too slowly, however. Joram would be worse than dead within seconds, his body a convulsing, writhing blob upon the sand-covered floor of the forge.

Saryon began to repeat the ancient words, the words he had learned seventeen years ago when he became a Deacon, words he had never spoken, never expected to speak. . . . Words each catalyst prays he will never be forced to speak. . . .

He began to suck out Blachloch's Life.

A highly dangerous maneuver, it is generally practiced only in times of war when a catalyst will attempt to weaken an opponent through this means. Instead of closing off a conduit, which cuts the supply of Life given to a magus, the catalyst leaves the conduit open and simply reverses the flow. The danger lies in the fact that the wizard will instantly feel the Life beginning to seep from him and can, unless distracted, turn upon the catalyst and reduce him to dust.

Saryon knew well the danger he was in and he didn't flinch when Blachloch's cry of outrage split the darkness, the green-glowing eyes moved to turn their venomous pain upon him. His courage held, even as he saw his fingertips began to turn green and felt the first bursts of pain dance up his arms.

"Joram!" he shouted. "Help me!"

The young man was on his knees, sobbing. With Blachloch's attention withdrawn and the sword absorbing the magic, the venom was vanishing from his flesh, though still slowly. At Saryon's cry, Joram lifted his head. Gritting his teeth, he tried to rise. But he was too weak to manage on his own and there was nothing near him he could use to lean upon. Finally, plunging the point of the sword into the dirt floor of the forge, he gripped the handle and dragged himself to his feet.

"Joram!" The venom ate into Saryon's body, and the catalyst cursed himself. With all his logic, he should have foreseen this! He was absorbing Life from the warlock, but there

was nothing he could do with it! In battle, he would have had
a wizard as his ally. He could grant this Life to his partner,
who could then use it to enhance his own strength and fight
off the enemy. But the catalyst could give no Life to Joram,
he could give him no aid.

Then Saryon saw the sword.

It stood in the ground, its arms spread like a man pleading for help. Its black metal reflected no light. It was a creation of darkness, it *was* darkness. Like a man pleading for
help.

A feeling of shock and horror hit Saryon, numbing the
growing pain spreading slowly over his body, slowly because — even still — he was draining the Life from the warlock and he could feel the man weakening.

I can not give Life to Joram, but I can give it to the sword.

Closing his eyes, Saryon blocked out the sight of the
black, hideous parody of a living being that seemed to be
opening its rigid arms to clasp him in its embrace. I can surrender. My torment would end.

Obedire est vivere . . .

He saw before him the flames of the burning village, the
young Deacon falling dead upon the ground, Simkin dealing
a hand from a deck of faceless, colorless cards.

Vivere est obedire. . . .

Opening his eyes, Saryon watched Joram draw the blade
from the ground and raise it above his head. But the young
man appeared in Saryon's mind only as a shadow in the
moonlight. All he truly saw or could focus on was the sword.
Stretching out his hand toward it, the pain making his fingers
twitch involuntarily, Saryon opened a conduit to the cold,
lifeless metal.

The magic surged through him like a blast of wind, its
force so strong that he stumbled backward. The pain ceased
abruptly, the liquid on his skin vanished. The sword glowed a
brilliant white-blue and, with an inarticulate cry, Blachloch
fell to the floor, the combined power of the sword and the
catalyst sucking the magic from his body, leaving him
nothing more than the empty shell of a human.

The sword fell to the ground. Unprepared for the tremendous jolt of power that jarred his very being, Joram had
dropped the weapon and now stood staring at it in amaze-

ment as it lay on the floor, ringing and humming with an eerie, almost human screech of pleasure. Turning, he looked from the sword to the helpless warlock. Snarling in rage, Blachloch fought on, trying to regain the use of his limbs. It was a feeble attempt. Weakened by the full use of his magical power and now completely bereft of Life itself, the warlock flopped about in the dirt like a landed fish.

Appalled and sickened at the sight, Saryon turned away. Leaning against a workbench, he realized, slowly, that it was all over.

"I will open a Corridor," he said, without looking around at Joram. He couldn't face the sight of the warlock lying helpless on the floor, deprived of all his dignity as a human being. It was bad enough hearing his incoherent sounds and pitiful thrashings. "I have enough of his Life force left within me to do so. I will place him inside a Corridor, then close it again before the Enforcers figure out what has happened. I don't think it likely anyone would come back here. They seem intent on avoiding this place and, once they've got Blachloch, I believe they'll let the Technologists live in peace. Still, it would be best for you if you left, just in case—"

A scream interrupted him, a scream of fury and terror. Rising to a shrill shriek of excruciating pain, the scream became a wail, dying horribly in a dreadful, choking gurgle.

His soul riven by the awful sound, Saryon turned around.

Blachloch lay dead, his eyes staring straight up into the night, his mouth open in the scream that echoed still in Saryon's brain. Joram stood above the warlock, his face stark white in the moonlight, his eyes hollows of darkness. In his hands, he held the Darksword, its blade protruding from the warlock's chest. With a jerk, he pulled it free and Saryon saw blood glisten black upon the Darksword.

Saryon could not speak. The man's death cry shrieked in his ears. He could only stare at Joram, trying to stifle the sound of that dreadful scream enough to be able to think.

"Why?" the catalyst whispered finally.

Joram looked over at him, and Saryon saw the half-smile glint in the dark eyes.

"He was going to attack you, Catalyst," the young man answered coolly. "I stopped him."

An image of the helpless, flopping body came vividly to Saryon's mind. A sudden rush of burning liquid rose to his throat. Gagging, he turned quickly from the ghastly sight upon the floor at his feet. "You're lying! That's not possible!" he said through clenched teeth.

"Come now, Catalyst," Joram said sardonically. Stepping over the body, he picked up the rag that lay upon the floor and began to wipe the blood from the blade. "It's ended. You don't need to keep up the game."

Had Saryon heard right? He seemed to hear nothing but that shriek. "Game?" he managed to ask. "What game? I don't understand. . . ."

"Almin's blood! Who do you take me for? Mosiah!" Joram laughed but it came out a snarl — bitter and ugly. "As if I'd tumble for that sanctimonious blabbing." His voice rose to a high, whining mockery of Saryon's. "'I'll open a Corridor. You get away . . .' Ha!" Tossing the blood-stained rag upon the floor, Joram carefully laid the sword down beside it. "Did you think I'd fall for that? I knew your plan. Once you had that Corridor open—"

"No! You're wrong!"

Saryon's impassioned cry caught Joram by surprise. Glancing over his shoulder, he looked intently into the catalyst's face. "Well, of all the — I believe you meant it," he said slowly, staring at Saryon in wonder.

The catalyst could not answer. Sinking down upon the workbench, he closed his eyes and, shivering, hunched deeper into his robes. The dead warlock was having his revenge, it seemed. His scream had drained the life from Saryon as effectively as the catalyst had drained the magic from the magus. Sick, cold, filled with hatred and revulsion for himself as well as for the young man, if Saryon had believed in the Almin enough to ask him for one final favor, it would have been for the blessed oblivion of death.

He heard Joram's footsteps moving across the sand floor and felt the presence of the young man behind him.

"You meant it," Joram repeated.

"Yes," Saryon said tiredly, "I meant it."

"You saved my life," Joram continued, speaking in low tones. "You risked your own to do it. I know. I saw. . . ."

Saryon felt a touch on his shoulder. Startled, he glanced around to see Joram's hand resting there hesitantly, awkwardly. He could see the face in the waning moonlight, dark eyes shadowed by a tangle of thick, black hair. In the eyes, for the briefest second, there was longing, hunger. The catalyst knew the truth now, as he had known it all along.

Years ago, Saryon's mind whispered to him, I held this child in my arms!

Reaching up, he started to grasp Joram's hand with his own. But as soon as he did, the hand on his shoulder jerked away.

"Why?" Joram demanded. "What do you want of me?"

Saryon stared at the young man for a moment, then a slight, tired smile twisted his lips. "I don't want anything of you, Joram."

"Then, what was your reason, Catalyst? And don't give me any of that holy honey you use to keep people like Mosiah sweet. I know you. There has to be a motive."

"I've told you," Saryon said softly, his gaze going to the weapon that lay on the floor like another corpse. "I helped bring this . . . weapon of darkness into the world. It is my responsibility, *partly* my responsibility," he amended as Joram started to speak. Saryon's gaze went from the sword to the warlock. "I have failed. It has drawn blood, it has severed a life —"

"*I* drew the blood! *I* severed the life!" Joram cried, coming to stand before the catalyst. "The Darksword was just a tool in my hands. Quit talking about the damn thing as if it were more alive than I am!"

Saryon did not reply. Staggering with fatigue, he walked haltingly across the sand-strewn floor of the forge and came to kneel beside Blachloch's body. Gritting his teeth to quell a wave of sickness, keeping his gaze averted from the ghastly wound in the chest, he stretched out his hand and closed the eyes that were staring upward in horrified astonishment. He did his best to shut the gaping jaws, composing the face in some semblance of peace. Lifting the cold hands, he started to fold them across the breast, as was traditional, but found he could not as a wave of nausea overcame him. Letting them drop, he turned away hurriedly, slumping against the workbench, shivering in a chill sweat.

"I'll take the body into the woods," Joram said.

Hearing a rustling sound, Saryon glanced back to see the young man tug the warlock's hood over his face and cover the body with the man's cloak. "When they find him, they'll figure centaurs got him."

A *Duuk-tsarith*? Saryon thought, but he didn't say anything. He didn't care anymore, anyway. Looking wistfully outside, he half-expected to see the dawn burning its way along the horizon. But the moon had just set. It was only a little past the deepest flow of night's tide. He wanted his bed. Though it was cold and hard, he wanted to lie down and cast his own cloak over his head and maybe . . . just maybe . . . the sleep that had eluded him for nights would steal upon him and, for a little while, he could forget.

"Listen to me, Catalyst!" Joram's voice was harsh. "The only other person who knows about the Darksword besides you and me is dead —"

"So that was why you killed him."

Joram ignored him. "It must stay that way. While I'm moving the body, you take the sword and go back to the prison."

"Blachloch's guards are all over town, searching for you. . . ." Saryon protested, remembering the hue and cry that had been raised when he reported Joram missing. "How will you —"

"How do you think I got in here? There's a way out, in back of the forge," Joram said impatiently. "The smithy's used it for over a year with his secret stash of weapons."

"Weapons?" Saryon asked, uncomprehending.

"Yes, Catalyst. Blachloch's days were numbered. The Technologists were bound to rebel. We have only hastened what was going to come sooner or later. But never mind that now! Take the sword and go back to the prison. No one will bother you. After all, you were with Blachloch. If they do stop you, tell them the warlock followed my trail into the wilderness. He went in alone after me. That's all you know."

"Yes." Saryon murmured.

Joram stared at him, scowling. "Did you even hear a word I said?"

"I hear!" Saryon said sternly. "And I'll do what you say. I don't want word of this terrible weapon to get out any more than you do." Rising to his feet, he looked directly into the young man's face. "You must destroy it. If you don't, I will."

The two stood, confronting each other in the darkness that was lit now only by the dimly glowing coals. The fire glimmered in Joram's eyes and on the lips that spread in a dark, red-tinged smile. "What if someone offered you the Magic, Catalyst?" he asked softly. "What if someone said to you, 'Here, take this power. You no longer have to walk the ground like an animal. You can fly. You can call up the winds. You can banish the sun and bring down the stars, if you desire.' What would you do? Wouldn't you take it?"

Wouldn't I? Saryon thought, a sudden memory of his father coming to him. He saw a little boy kicking off the hated shoes, drifting over the land in the arms of the wizard.

"This is my magic," said Joram, his gaze going to the sword lying on the floor. "Tomorrow I start for Merilon. You, too, Catalyst, if you insist on coming. Once I am there, in Merilon, in the city that ended my parents' lives and robbed me of my birthright, this sword will bring down the stars and put them in my grasp. No, I won't destroy it." He paused. "And neither will you."

"Why not?" asked Saryon.

"Because you helped create it," Joram said, the forge fire lighting his face. "Because you helped bring it into this world. Because you gave it Life."

"I —" Saryon began, but he could not finish. He was too scared to search inside himself for the truth.

Joram nodded, satisfied. Turning, he walked over to the body, issuing instructions as he went. "Wrap the sword in those rags. If anyone stops you, tell them you are carrying a child. A dead child." Glancing over at the pale, shaken catalyst, he smiled. "Your child, Saryon," he said. "Yours and mine."

Bending down, Joram picked up the body of the warlock in his strong arms. Heaving the corpse over his shoulder, he turned and made his way through the clutter of tools and stacks of wood and coal, heading toward the back of the cavern. The body bounced horribly as the young man walked, the hands dangling limply down behind, brushing against objects as though trying in vain to hold onto the world their spirit had left. Joram finally disappeared into the blackness beyond, leaving Saryon alone in the forge, staring at a splotch of darkness on the floor.

For long moments he stood there, unable to move. Then he had the strangest feeling — as though he were slowly rising up off the floor and, drifting backward, could look down and see himself still standing there. Up and up he floated, watching his body slowly walk over to the sword. Spiraling around, going ever upward, moving further and further away, he saw himself wrap the sword in rags. He saw himself lift it carefully in his arms. Cradling the sword to his bosom, he saw himself walk out of the forge.

The heavy oaken door shut upon the catalyst's shuffling tread and the whisper of his robes. Silence flowed back into the forge like the shadows of night, seeming to quench even the glowing coals with its heaviness. It was shattered suddenly by a clattering bang. A pair of huge tongs slipped from the nail upon which they were hanging and landed in a water bucket with a splash.

"Sink me," muttered the tongs. "Didn't see that damn thing in the dark. And it *would* be full."

The sound of a bucket overturning, followed by water running out onto the floor, was accompanied by a wide and varied assortment of oaths until Simkin stumbled out of the wreckage to stand in the middle of the forge, dressed in his usual, gaudy, if somewhat damp, finery.

"I say," remarked the young man, wiping the water from his beard and glancing about him, "what an extraordinary business. I haven't been so entertained since the old Earl of Mumsburg flew a rebellious serf over his castle. Tied a rope around his ankle and hung him out in a stiff breeze. 'Chap tried to rise above his station,' the old boy said to me as we watched the peasant flapping in the wind. 'Now he knows what it's like.'"

Shaking his head, Simkin walked casually over to stand near the dark splotch of still-wet blood that had soaked into the sand on the floor of the forge. He gestured, and a bit of orange silk materialized at his command. Drifting gently down to the floor, it covered the splotch. With a snap of his fingers, Simkin caused the silk and the blood spot to vanish.

" 'Pon my honor," he murmured with a languid smile, "we should have a jolly time in Merilon."

Then Simkin, too, was gone, drifting away into the air like a wisp of smoke.

The Last Card

There was no dinner party at Bishop Vanya's this night.

"His Holiness is indisposed," was the message the Ariels carried to those who had been invited. This included the Emperor's brother-in-law, whose number of invitations to dine at the Font were increasing proportionately with the declining health of his sister. Everyone had been most gracious and extremely concerned about the Bishop's welfare. The Emperor had even offered his own personal *Theldara* to the Bishop, but this was respectfully refused.

Vanya dined alone, and so preoccupied was the Bishop that he might have been eating sausages along with his Field Catalysts instead of the delicacies of peacock's tongue and lizard's tail which he barely tasted and never noticed were underdone.

Having finished and sent away the tray, he sipped a brandy and composed himself to wait until the tiny moon in the timeglass upon his desk had risen to its zenith. The waiting was difficult, but Vanya's mind was so occupied that he found the time sliding past more rapidly than he had expected. The pudgy fingers crawled ceaselessly along the arms of the chair, touching this strand of mental web and that, seeing if any needed strengthening or repaired, throwing out new filaments where necessary.

The Empress — a fly that would soon be dead.

Her brother — heir to throne. A different type of fly, he demanded special consideration.

The Emperor — his sanity at the best of times precarious, the death of his beloved wife and the loss of his position might well topple a mind weak to begin with.

Sharakan — the other empires in Thimhallan were watching this rebellious state with too much interest. It must be crushed, the people taught a lesson. And with them, the Sorcerers of the Ninth Art wiped out completely. That was shaping up nicely . . . or had been.

Vanya fidgeted uncomfortably and glanced at the timeglass. The tiny moon was just now appearing over the horizon. With a growl, the Bishop poured himself another brandy.

The boy. Damn the boy. And damn that blasted catalyst, too. Darkstone. Vanya closed his eyes, shuddering. He was in peril, deadly peril. If anyone ever discovered the incredible blunder he had made . . .

Vanya saw the greedy eyes watching him, waiting for his downfall. The eyes of the Lord Cardinal of Merilon, who had — so rumor told — already drawn up plans for redecorating the Bishop's chambers in the Font. The eyes of his own Cardinal, a slow-thinking man, to be sure, but one who had risen through the ranks by plodding along slowly and surely, trampling over anything or anyone who got in his way. And there were others. Watching, waiting, hungry . . .

If they got so much as a sniff of his failure, they'd be on him like griffins, rending his flesh with their talons.

But no! Vanya clenched the pudgy hand, then forced himself to relax. All was well. He had planned for every contingency, even the unlikely ones.

With this thought in mind and noticing that the moon was finally nearing the top of the timeglass, the Bishop heaved his bulk out of the chair and made his way, walking at a slow, measured pace, to the Chamber of Discretion.

The darkness was empty and silent. No sign of mental disturbance. Perhaps that was a good sign, Vanya told himself as he sat down in the center of the round room. But a tremor of fear shivered through the web as he sent forth his summons to his minion.

He waited, spider fingers twitching.

The darkness was still, cold, unspeaking.

Vanya called again, the fingers curling in upon themselves.

I may or may not respond, the voice had told him. Yes, that would be like him, the arrogant —

Vanya swore, his hands gripping the chair, sweat pouring down his head. He *had* to know! It was too important! He would —

Yes. . . .

The hands relaxed. Vanya considered, turning the idea over in his mind. He had planned for every contingency, even the unlikely ones. And this one he had planned for without even knowing it. Such are the ways of genius.

Sitting back in the chair, Bishop Vanya's mind touched another strand on the web, sending an urgent summons to one who would, he knew, be little prepared to receive it.

A SELECTION OF SCIENCE FICTION AND FANTASY TITLES AVAILABLE FROM BANTAM BOOKS

THE PRICES SHOWN BELOW WERE CORRECT AT THE TIME OF GOING TO PRESS. HOWEVER TRANSWORLD PUBLISHERS RESERVE THE RIGHT TO SHOW NEW RETAIL PRICES ON COVERS WHICH MAY DIFFER FROM THOSE PREVIOUSLY ADVERTISED IN THE TEXT OR ELSEWHERE.

All Corgi/Bantam Books are available at your bookshop or newsagent, or can be ordered from the following address:
Corgi/Bantam Books,
Cash Sales Department,
P.O. Box 11, Falmouth, Cornwall TR10 9EN

Please send a cheque or postal order (no currency) and allow 80p for postage and packing for the first book plus 20p for each additional book ordered up to a maximum charge of £2.00 in UK.

B.F.P.O. customers please allow 80p for the first book and 20p for each additional book.

Overseas customers, including Eire, please allow £1.50 for postage and packing for the first book, £1.00 for the second book, and 30p for each subsequent title ordered.

NAME (Block Letters) ....

ADDRESS ....

....